AN AMERICAN IN VIENNA

Chip Wagar

iUniverse, Inc.
Bloomington

An American in Vienna

Copyright © 2011 Chip Wagar

All rights reserved. No part of this book may be used or reproduced by any means, graphic, electronic, or mechanical, including photocopying, recording, taping or by any information storage retrieval system without the written permission of the publisher except in the case of brief quotations embodied in critical articles and reviews.

Certain characters in this work are historical figures, and certain events portrayed did take place. However, this is a work of fiction. All of the other characters, names, and events as well as all places, incidents, organizations, and dialogue in this novel are either the products of the author's imagination or are used fictitiously.

iUniverse books may be ordered through booksellers or by contacting:

iUniverse
1663 Liberty Drive
Bloomington, IN 47403
www.iuniverse.com
1-800-Authors (1-800-288-4677)

Because of the dynamic nature of the Internet, any Web addresses or links contained in this book may have changed since publication and may no longer be valid. The views expressed in this work are solely those of the author and do not necessarily reflect the views of the publisher, and the publisher hereby disclaims any responsibility for them.

Cover image of Strauss Denkmal by Franz Bauer (http://www.pbase.com/bauer/vienna_nightshots) and used with his permission.

ISBN: 978-1-4502-6766-3 (pbk)
ISBN: 978-1-4502-6768-7 (cloth)
ISBN: 978-1-4502-6767-0 (ebk)

Printed in the United States of America

iUniverse rev. date: 1/24/11

Preface

VIENNA. 24 November 1916—At precisely ten o'clock this evening, a pair of huge double doors at the top of a marble staircase at the Schönbrunn palace here slowly swung open. On cue, muffled drums from somewhere in the darkness that could not be seen began beating a slow, rolling cadence. Snowflakes, falling gently in the cold night air, melted as they settled on dark, gold-braid uniforms and white gloves while undulating jets of flame shooting out of sconces on the walls of the palace cast an eerie, yellow light on the scene. Tens of thousands of black-clad citizens of this mourning imperial city waited with anticipation for the somber drama that was about to begin. They had quietly filed through the high gates of the palace over the course of the evening and into its spacious grounds to wait patiently for history to unfold before their eyes.

A tall young man stood in the crowd, making penciled notes in English. Andy Bishop, a journalist for the fledgling *New Republic* magazine was, on this solemn occasion, the only American present among the hushed subjects of the late kaiser of Austria and king of Hungary, bearing witness to a ritual dating back to the fourteenth century. He had secured a good vantage point. He had removed his gloves to make notes of what he saw. His fingers were growing numb from the cold as he jotted down every detail that caught his practiced eye for the story he would cable through Zurich to New York the following day. It would be his last dispatch from Vienna.

Nothing about his appearance this evening would have conveyed the slightest hint of his American citizenship after his residence for a year and a half in the Austrian capital. Gone were the telltale signs. The shoes, the hat, his overcoat, and scarf—even the thin mustache on his face he had grown in the past year—marked him as a typical Viennese. Occasional questioning glances directed toward him as he scribbled in his notebook were motivated by wonder at why a man of his young age was not in the army as he bore no outward signs of the disabling war wounds so common among men his age in Vienna these days. Many in the crowd pressed forward, some standing on tiptoe to see, Andy noted. A little boy on his father's shoulders, face impassive as he stared. An old woman, draped in black, her white hand covering her mouth with a handkerchief, eyes shining.

Andy's black bowler hat concealed a full head of straight, black hair combed back, front to rear. Beneath the brim, his brown eyes darted inquisitively between the scene and then back to his notes. Full lips were pursed against the breeze and cold as he made notes and sketches here and there. He was taller than the average Austrian, with a frame constructed in the corn-fed Midwest of the United States, but lately somewhat thinned. Wartime privations of food in Vienna and the harrowing experiences of the past eighteen months had pared him by a good ten pounds, one would think, since his arrival two summers earlier. The tanned complexion of his first summer had long since faded to the pale white of central Europe at war.

Andy had come to Vienna from his home in Columbus, Ohio, after graduating from the University of Notre Dame in early June of 1914. He had come to make contact with distant Austrian relatives with whom his mother's family had lost contact over a century and a half before his birth. He had come to practice his then nascent journalistic skills. He had come to try to find the answer to a family mystery: why his aristocratic ancestor, Matthias zu Windischgrätz, had come to America so long ago. That genealogical quest and all of his original reasons for coming had quickly been swallowed whole by the cataclysm that now grimly held this tottering empire and all of Europe in a death grip.

So much had happened since he had arrived. He was no longer the naïve young man from Columbus, Ohio. The times had changed so much. He had changed too. It was as if he had unknowingly boarded a strange train that had carried him, not to his intended destination, but faster and faster, deeper and deeper, into dark places he had never meant to go and to sights he had never imagined he would see. It was as if he were living an uneasy dream that he had slowly come to realize would end badly but from which he couldn't wake up.

It had started so well, almost like a fairy tale from a children's book. The Vienna of June 1914 was a dazzling city in such contrast to his hometown. Self-confident, new, bustling with capitalistic optimism, Columbus was red brick and smoke, breweries and shops, slaughterhouses and railroad tracks, the soot-covered YMCA on High Street and dime lunches, a metropolitan island surrounded by miles of farms on rolling hills with red barns and dairies.

Vienna was ancient and cynical, neo-Baroque palaces and green parks, cafés and whipped cream, uniforms and ministries, royalty and socialism, art and music with tree-lined boulevards older than America itself. Vienna had been like a beautiful wedding cake with sweet frosting piled layer upon layer, topped with a groom resplendent in a red-trimmed, white uniform and green, feather-plumed hat, waltzing with his dark-haired, beautiful bride, all in white, to the music of Strauss.

As Andy watched and listened, his heightened journalistic senses took in every detail. His writing had changed too. No longer merely a purveyor of facts, he had become known for recreating a feeling of "being there" to his readers back home at their kitchen tables in America. Even now, he searched the faces of the crowd as they quietly waited and watched. Sometimes he scribbled only a couple of words such as "priest fingers rosary" to remind himself of a fleeting image he would incorporate later into his narrative.

> A rumble of wheels and horse hooves suddenly out of the nighttime darkness. An enormous, black wooden hearse slowly approached the torch-lit portico of the palace. Two liveried coachmen wearing ceremonial cocked hats with black fur drove eight black Spanish stallions trimmed with black plumes between their ears. One of the coachmen was seated on a high bench at the front of the hearse. The other rode the back of one of the immense beasts in the second rank. High atop the four corners of the carriage, velvet-draped, carved, double-headed eagles, iconic symbols of the House of Habsburg, glared down as they passed, wings spread and predatory beaks open, in silent challenge to anyone who would disturb the late kaiser's passage.

Andy had arrived from America on June 7, 1914, only three weeks before the assassination of the kaiser's nephew in Sarajevo, the Habsburg Archduke Franz Ferdinand. In those halcyon days, the kaiser's enigmatic gaze from innumerable portraits and sculptures could be seen everywhere, but the ruler himself was almost never seen in public. He was somehow both inaccessible, and ever-present. Ubiquitous, but just out of reach, hovering at the edge of everyone's consciousness, but always there.

> A double line of equerries bearing beautiful antique lanterns slowly filed out of the doors from a darkened, candle-lit hallway above and took their positions on the marble steps, lighting the way. Their heavy, gold-framed glass lanterns were perched atop long

rods they held, painted with black and gold spirals, the colors of the Habsburg dynasty. Glittering in the intermittent, medieval flickering, the gold-ringed spokes of the imperial hearse slowed to a stop as the coachmen drew up to the foot of the staircase and descended, opening glass doors to receive the body of their master.

A contingent of Life Guards of the imperial household, bodyguards of the late emperor, came slowly marching in lockstep from the dark palace grounds behind the hearse to the steady beat of the drums. They split into two lines of two on each side of the hearse until, on command, they came to an abrupt, military halt. The halberdiers with their axe-headed poles were in two parallel lines closest to the hearse with black-plumed helmets. Pikemen arranged in two parallel lines flanked the halberdiers with their white-plumed helmets. Black ceremonial tassels swayed from the tops of the pikes and halberds as the guards stood rigidly silent, at attention. Another contingent of Life Guards took up parallel positions on either side of the staircase to form a path to the hearse.

Prince Montenuovo, the court chamberlain, emerged through the doors alone and walked down the black, carpeted steps to a landing. Gold embroidery covering the chest and the cuffs of his tunic glowed in the flame light. A golden, ceremonial sword hung in a golden scabbard from his waist. White gloves. High black boots. He stopped halfway down the steps and turned around like the conductor of an orchestra to face the doors from which the body of the late emperor would emerge. He stood motionless, his white hair mildly ruffled as a slight breeze passed, but his position and presence signaled his Majesty's final departure from the palace where he had been born eighty-six years earlier in another era.

Austria might have been utterly exhausted by the war, but Montenuovo, the kaiser's closest and most faithful servant, had spared nothing in creating a magical spectacle that not only his master would have expected, but his people lining the streets of Vienna that night demanded. The war would not cheat his subjects of their right to be a part of something larger than themselves, to share this ancient rite not only with the imperial family, but with their own ancestors as well.

> Silently, the black, velvet-draped coffin appeared at the doors at the top of the stairs borne by eight tall guardsmen, their faces composed in masks of utmost severity. Slowly, they carried their master down the stairs, the flames from the gaslights flickering. The muffled drums beat a slow cadence as the legs of the pallbearers moved with military precision to each beat, down each step, until they maneuvered the coffin into the hearse. The coffin was plainly visible to the crowds.
>
> Thousands of silent onlookers made the sign of the cross as the equerries formed up in front of the hearse to light its way to the chapel at the Hofburg, the old imperial palace in the heart of the city. Some of them nodded their heads or bowed at the kaiser's coffin, while others knelt down in the snow.
>
> The guards, in unison, pivoted smartly toward the hearse and, upon shouted commands, presented arms to their late sovereign. The drums abruptly stopped. The silence was broken by another command. The Life Guards pivoted again, facing forward. Slowly, the gilded wheels began to turn again and the hearse began to creep forward. Then the muffled boom of drums again. A sharp clatter of horses came next as a contingent of mounted archers with long cream-colored capes, wearing white-plumed and crested helmets and wielding sabers that flashed in the flickering light formed up behind the hearse. As the cortege proceeded forward, another contingent followed the archers, this time the kaiser's dragoons in field gray uniform to close the procession.

A Habsburg named Rudolf had acquired the Archduchy of Austria in 1276 and made Vienna his capital. Habsburg rulers who followed Rudolf for more than six centuries clung to their traditions and rituals. None was more sacred or time honored than the funeral rites unfolding that night before some two hundred thousand hushed subjects of the late Emperor Franz Josef von Habsburg-Lothringen in his capital city. The black hearse, reserved by Habsburg tradition exclusively for Habsburg sovereigns, had last carried the body of the late kaiser's wife, Empress Elisabeth, to the Habsburg crypt in the Hofburg, the *Kapuzinergruft*, in 1898. There, she and eleven Holy Roman emperors and Austrian kaisers awaited the interment of the latest ruling member of their ancient house.

> It is the end, not only of the life of a man, but of an era. He was the grandfather of this empire of many peoples, holding his sometimes fractious, quarrelsome subjects together for as long as anyone can remember. His people rallied to war around their ancient sovereign, knowing that, whatever happened, he would somehow lead them through it as he had so many times during his long reign. Now he is gone when they needed him the most. Somehow, they will have to go on without him.

Andy tucked his pen and paper into his jacket pocket and donned his gloves. He had promised his friend, Stefan Zweig, that he would meet him afterward for a late dinner. His watchful eye, however, continued to observe the vast crowd heading back to their homes—or from wherever they had come—as the sound of the drums grew fainter.

There was an old woman, her head covered with a black scarf, her face lined with wrinkles and a large crucifix hanging from her neck. An aristocrat in court dress placed his plumed hat on his head that had been bared for the past half hour in respect. A bourgeois gentleman, dressed in top hat and cane, face downcast and pensive, walked past.

Peasants trudged. Railroad workers muttered in low tones. High and low alike made their way quietly to the palace gates as the sound of the drums gradually faded into the distance. The flames were slowly doused, leaving only a few lanterns still lit on the grounds. The double doors were closed. Gloom and darkness closed in from all sides.

1.
Austria, June 1914

Andy swore quietly as he steadied himself before the tiny mirror in the toilet as the train swayed and rocked along toward the Bavarian frontier with Austria. Despite his best efforts to carefully shave, he had still managed to nick himself under his nose and now dabbed at the tiny wound with a towel. As soon as he managed to stop the blood, he eyed himself again in the mirror, located at about chest height, forcing him to stoop to see. He ran a comb through his hair, parting it carefully on one side. His bare chest and arms revealed the tan lines that his baseball uniform had left from playing in the early summer sun. A varsity letterman on Notre Dame's 1914 baseball team, Andy had the muscular chest and arms of a hitter and the long legs of an outfielder.

Andy figured that the train should reach the border at any moment and then it would only be a few hours to the Salzburg station where his relatives would be waiting. Now would be as good a time as any to put on his suit and tie that his mother had bought for the trip at the Lazarus department store on High Street in Columbus. It was the only one he had. The mirror was far too small to properly inspect himself after he had dressed in the cramped little room, but as he re-entered his compartment on the train, he could vaguely see his reflection in the window and decided that he looked presentable.

About fifteen minutes had passed when the train began to slow and then stop, hissing steam. As Andy waited, he could hear doors sliding open and being shut as the Austrian customs guards made their way down the corridor of the car. Then his door was opened and an elderly guard in uniform entered, nodding his head politely. Making firm eye contact, the guard asked for his papers.

Andy's German was pretty good, but the accent in the guard's voice was peculiar. The German he had learned to speak was the "High German" taught at St. Mary's or the "Rhineland" version spoken by many of his friends' parents in the German village, south of downtown Columbus. The village itself was populated by older German immigrants who had come to America just before and after the Civil War, their children, and grandchildren. St. Mary's, founded in the 1850s by Catholic German immigrants, was in the very heart of the village, a few blocks from the trolley line on South High Street. Here the German community lived, worked, brewed beer, held Oktoberfest and often spoke only the language of their forefathers. *Der Westbote*, or the *Western Messenger*, was the newspaper that fathers of many of Andy's friends read, sitting on the stoops of their tenements, smoking their pipes on summer evenings while their mothers put the young ones to bed.

Andy had been able to make polite conversation with a couple of German passengers aboard the *Normandie* on his Atlantic crossing and with a few others on the train that had left Paris the prior evening. With the guard, however, he could barely understand the Alpine accent. If this was how the Austrians spoke, he wondered whether he would be able to understand his relatives when he arrived at the station.

"What is your purpose in Austria-Hungary?" the older

guard inquired through his low gray mustache. He was resplendent in his dark blue uniform and round cap. Gold epaulettes adorned his shoulders and a small, brass double eagle glinted at the top of his hat. *The uniform of a customs officer in this country was more elaborate than an American general's,* Andy thought.

"I'm visiting relatives on holiday in Salzburg and Vienna." This comment seemed to amuse the old guard who nodded politely, but continued his inquiries. Apparently, he could understand Andy's German very well and that was a relief.

"What is the name of your relatives you have come to visit?"

"Windischgrätz." This reply raised two bushy, white eyebrows. The guard looked at Andy's passport for a moment, and then returned his gaze.

"The military family?"

"Yes, I believe so. Have you heard of them?" The older guard smiled faintly and nodded.

"Most people in this country have heard of them. And you are related to this family?"

"Well, yes. A little bit. From a long time ago. My ancestors came to America in the 1700s."

"Have you been here before?"

"No, sir. This is my first time." Again the heavy accent, but the guard's questions were so simple and direct that Andy was still able to understand. He wasn't sure he would if the conversation became much more complicated.

"I see. And what is this?" He pointed toward an Underwood typewriter on one of the empty seats.

"It's a typewriter, sir. I'm a journalist and I brought it with me." Andy was not really a journalist. Not yet. Not like his father. He had majored in journalism at Notre Dame and had written accounts of baseball games when he was home for the summer for his father's newspaper in Columbus, but so far, that was the extent of his journalistic career. Andy had actually brought the typewriter to practice writing stories of his experiences in Austria at his father's suggestion, to get the hang of it, as his father had said. Again, the guard's eyebrows arched, then he nodded, seemingly satisfied.

"Very good," the old guard said as he handed back the passport with a white-gloved hand. "Welcome to Austria, Herr Bishop. Have a pleasant stay." With that, and a final nod, he opened the door and stepped out. Apparently there would be no further questions about his baggage or what he might be bringing into the country. After another half an hour, the train made steam and began moving again into the mountains.

As the train chugged along through the countryside, Andy had time to reflect on the guard's question about his purpose in Austria. It had all started at a family gathering in Pittsburgh when his mother's sister mentioned that the family was related by marriage to Joseph Hooker, a Civil War general. The discussion eventually led to stories of other not-so-famous relatives and to the question of from where the Windischgrätz name and family had come. Nobody really knew. They—whoever "they" were—had come to America a long time ago, that was for sure. Someone had heard that they were from Germany, but that was not hard to guess, given the Teutonic sounding name and the umlaut. Another had heard that "they" came over due to religious persecution of some kind—a typical reason in those days. Finally, a very elderly uncle spoke up to say that he had always been told that "they" had been "driven out of Europe" after being disowned by the family for some forgotten misdeed.

On the train back to Columbus, Andy remembered that his mother, Susan Windischgrätz Bishop, had mentioned her curiosity about the origins of her family to his father, Arthur Bishop.

"We all came to America for some reason, Susan," Andy recalled his father saying. "Religion, war, poverty, who knows? What difference does it make now?"

For some reason that Andy never knew, it did make a difference to Susan. Perhaps it was because her own family was so small that her thoughts turned to endless generations of ancestors. Perhaps it was because she had time on her hands. Perhaps it was because it might mean something—who knew what—that she had set about finding out. The more she searched in the months and years that followed, the more curious she became.

After giving birth to Andy, Susan had suffered a series of miscarriages and never bore another child, to her dismay. Perhaps because of it, Andy thought, they had always had an exceptionally close relationship as he grew up. He knew that his departure for college had left a huge void in his mother's life. Although still in love with his father, Susan had found the empty hours alone a lonely burden. Intelligent, with an inquisitive mind, she read a great deal and volunteered here and there, but it was not until she became intrigued with tracing her own family lineage that her restless energy was absorbed. In researching her own lineage, the trail ran cold with most of Susan's ancestors, but not with her mother's line: the Windischgrätz family.

After a year or so of research on family lines that ran here and there, she began mapping out a family tree that, when spread out, covered the dining room table. The Windischgrätz branch was the most fulsome, occupying about a quarter of the tree and ending at the topmost branch with Matthias zu Windischgrätz who had entered the country in Philadelphia in 1754 with his wife, Sarah, from Trieste. On a map, Andy had found the city and the fact that it was the biggest seaport of the Austrian Empire during the time of the Empress Maria Theresa.

Much of Susan's research had been done with trips to cemeteries and letter inquiries to various churches and government registrars, mainly in Pennsylvania where, it seemed, the family had grown in numbers. The further back in time she went, the more difficult the task became. Sometimes, weeks or months went by before she received replies from parish priests or bureaucrats from distant counties who, after being prompted several times, took the trouble to search their baptismal records or registries for names, dates, children, and so forth.

Who would have believed that his mother's little hobby would have led to his being on this train? Her fitful progress was often discussed on Andy's trips home from college, but for a long time, it seemed to lead to nothing but satisfaction of his mother's curiosity. Andy noticed that his father seemed bored by the whole thing and even Andy found her excited discoveries somewhat tedious, although he had often feigned interest to please her. There was a little gossip here and there to go with an ever-widening list of names and dates on the tree. Yes, it had been something about persecution that had brought "them" to America, but who exactly and why?

The Bishops were Catholic. The Windischgratz family (the umlaut having been dropped in America somewhere along the way) had been Catholic. The German village in Columbus was full of German-speaking Catholics, some of whom had come from Austria as well. Austria was a Catholic country, like Ireland and Italy, Susan had explained to Andy one day, so why would a Catholic ancestor from Austria have been "persecuted" there to the extreme of fleeing the country? It didn't make sense. There must have been another reason.

Shortly after Andy had begun his senior year at Notre Dame, Susan Bishop made contact with an elderly widow in Philadelphia whose maiden name was Windischgrätz and who shared an interest in the family genealogy. It was

An American in Vienna

Gertrude Windischgrätz who had completed the last link to a certain Matthias and Sarah zu Windischgrätz, Susan explained to Andy over his Thanksgiving vacation, but there it stopped. Gertrude did write, however, that family lore vaguely suggested that some scandal had prompted the couple to emigrate, but nobody knew what it was. Furthermore, Matthias seemed to be related to a noble family in one of the provinces of the Austrian Empire known as Styria. It was the first time Andy could remember being interested in his mother's work. He couldn't deny it. It had thrilled him a little bit to think that he might be related, however distantly, to some noble European house.

Andy's interest and Susan's enthusiasm about this news from Philadelphia did not stir similar feelings in Arthur.

"I really don't understand this at all," Arthur said evenly as he lit his pipe on their front porch one evening. The Bishops lived in a modest red brick house on East Mithoft Street on the south side of the village. It was a quiet street just a few blocks from the trolley line on South High Street that Andy had used to ride to school at St. Mary's, the Catholic church and school that was the heart and soul of the German Village. "I wouldn't be so proud to be related to European aristocrats," Arthur said to both of them as they rocked in the chairs on the porch.

"If you look at the history of Europe, you will see that there is not much that the kings and aristocrats should be proud of. People like us have no rights in those countries. The kings and their nobles have kept them down forever, just as King George III tried to do to us and King Louis did to the peasants of France. Here, we're free. No kings or rich, titled families to bow down to. Personally, I'm not very fond of their ways. Democracy. That's how it should be. All men created equal. That's why our ancestors came here—to get away from that sort of thing."

"Not my ancestors," Susan rejoined. "They came in 1754. America was not a democracy then. It didn't even exist. We were colonies. I don't disagree with what you said, Arthur. I'm just curious. This man and his wife, Matthias and Sarah, were aristocrats. So why did they come here? I wonder."

"You'll never find that out now. That was hundreds of years ago," Arthur replied. "If it amuses you, that's fine. As for me, I don't really care."

Arthur Bishop was a news editor and part owner of the *Columbus Tribune*, one of several local papers in the growing and very self-confident modern town that was the capital of Ohio and home of the Ohio State University where Andy had decided not to go, much to the dismay of his father, several years ago. The expense of tuition at Notre Dame appalled him, but in a Catholic family like the Bishops, the prestige of their only son attending one of the most eminent Catholic universities in the United States had proved irresistible. Andy had gotten a partial scholarship, but it had still been a financial strain to send him there. Nevertheless, Arthur was delighted when his son elected to major in journalism with a minor in history. It had been a secret hope that his son would follow in his footsteps, and Arthur had never missed a chance to encourage his son in that direction ever since he was a little boy.

However, it was Andy's interest in history, piqued by the revelation that he might be related, however distantly, to a prominent aristocratic family in Europe that proved a second confluence in the river of life that put him on the train that day. It led him to do some research on his own when he got back to Notre Dame. With the help of the school librarian one cold winter's day, Andy had found a small collection of books in the history section that covered central Europe seemingly hidden away from the vast collections on English and French history. It seemed that the farther one strayed from the European countries that bordered the Atlantic Ocean, the fewer and more obscure the books became, but soon Andy found the Windischgrätz name in one of the indexes of a book about the Revolutions of 1848.

He checked the book out of the library and read it over the next week.

In 1848, revolutions against the monarchies had boiled over in nearly every capital of Europe. In Paris, the last king of France had been overthrown and a republic declared, at least for a few years, until a Bonaparte coup reinstituted monarchy again for a couple more decades. Farther to the east, however, revolutions had blazed into bloody civil wars and rebellions that lasted much longer but, in the end, had been even less successful.

As he read, he felt his heart skip a beat when he came across Alfred zu Windisch-Grätz. Despite the hyphenated spelling in the book, the name was too similar and the location in Austria, where the port of Trieste was located, could not be a coincidence, Andy thought.

As he read on, it turned out that this man had been instrumental in crushing resistance to the Habsburg monarchy in the Austrian Empire that sprawled over a vast area of central and eastern Europe and half of northern Italy. Andy learned that Alfred had fought against Napoleon in 1813 and became a field marshal in 1833. After his wife was killed by a stray bullet fired by a revolutionary mob in Prague in 1848, he had led the imperial military forces that "restored order" there. He had then been called upon to suppress a rebellion in Vienna that had driven into exile the Habsburg emperor, Ferdinand, together with his family. He led a military siege against the Viennese revolutionaries, bombarding the capital with ruthless efficiency until they surrendered and the Habsburgs could return. In his final campaign, he suppressed a full Hungarian uprising in Budapest until he was relieved of his command and retired from public life. For his service to the crown, he was made a prince. His aristocratic descendents remained to this day in Austria. In a letter to his mother, Andy revealed what he had found.

At home for Easter recess, Andy's mother had news for

him. She had learned that the present-day Windischgrätz family was living in Vienna and, on a lark, she had written to an Otto zu Windischgrätz from an address given to her by the Austro-Hungarian consulate in New York City. Much to her surprise and delight, weeks later, she had received a long letter from him, in English, confirming that indeed, according to the family records, Matthias zu Windischgrätz was an uncle to the famous Alfred that Andy had read about and yes, the family had been from Styria in the eighteenth century. He inquired about her research on the family in America and was eager to know more about it. They had been corresponding ever since.

They were definitely related, that was for sure. There it went, down the side of the page on the dining room table: an entire family on the other side of the ocean linked at the very top by the father of Matthias. Even more startling was the revelation that Otto, himself a prince, was married to the granddaughter of the present emperor of Austria-Hungary, Franz-Josef von Habsburg-Lothringen.

Andy had often felt a little twinge of chagrin with his friends and acquaintances at Notre Dame because of his middle-class status. Most came from quite well-to-do families. His friends shrugged off Andy's inferior status, but some of the young men at school were snobs and occasionally had not been shy at exposing Andy's relative inadequacy, much to his embarrassment. Perhaps for this reason, Andy nursed a growing sense of exultation in learning that, in a small, distant way, by marriage to be sure, he was, in fact, connected to—no, actually *related to*—a reigning monarch of a great European empire.

Many scions of the upper classes at Notre Dame sent their sons off on a grand tour of Europe after college before they got married, but again, the Bishops were not in that financial stratum. Andy knew this, but couldn't help but think how fitting it would be if he could go to Europe, just like some of his friends, to meet Otto zu Windischgrätz and about whether, perhaps, a *petit tour* to Europe might possible in his case. Knowing what his father's opinion would likely be, Andy resorted to the time-honored tactic of converting his mother first.

Susan had now sketched into the family tree the "Austrian" side of the family based upon information Otto had given her in one of his letters. It was difficult to say in the spring of 1914 who had been more curious about whom as letters crossed the Atlantic between Susan and Otto, one after another, but eventually Susan mentioned Andy's dream of making a trip to Europe. A fortnight later, an invitation to Andy to visit the Windischgrätz family at their summer home near Salzburg followed. Andy smiled as he remembered how he and his mother had teamed up to wear down Arthur's resistance to this "poppycock" and "tomfoolery" until he finally agreed to help finance Andy's dream summer trip to Europe.

Andy had saved a fair bit of money of his own that he was willing to invest in the trip. He had worked every summer at the newspaper while in college and saved almost all of the money that he made there. At first, he had worked as a laborer in the pressroom, but gradually he began to write articles in the sports section under the watchful eye of his father and the sports editor. Andy would compile the baseball scores that came in over the wire in the evening and summarize them in a paragraph or two on the sports page. He could hardly have imagined a better job. He could follow the exploits of his favorite baseball team, the Pittsburgh Pirates, and their star shortstop, Honus Wagner. Now, to his delight, his savings would be used on the trip of a lifetime.

The train shuddered and throbbed as it raced along the tracks. Wisps of black coal smoke occasionally wafted by his open window, mixing with the cool air of the open pastures and farms they passed. A door opened and closed. The conductor announced the approach of the Salzburg *Bahnhof* in a few minutes as he passed by in the corridor.

Had fate ordained this somehow? Andy mused. Growing up in a German-speaking neighborhood. Going to St. Mary's, a German school. Discovering, with his mother, his fantastic connection with Austrian relatives that had seemingly materialized out of the blue. He felt grateful for the love of his parents who were willing to sacrifice so much to permit him a once-in-a-lifetime trip such as this. He would make the most of it, he thought. He would make every minute count. He would keep track of it all in the "practice articles" he would write to his father, honing his craft, while all the time putting down on paper his thoughts and adventures that he would read back to himself years later.

The train slowed down and people began stirring in the other compartments as luggage bumped the walls and floors. Doors slid open and closed. He heard the whistle blow as his train steamed into the station. He felt a little nervous, looking out the window at the waiting crowd and wondering if he was looking into the face of one of his family members. He gathered his luggage and the typewriter and, looking his Sunday best, set foot for the first time on Austrian soil.

As the Orient Express let off steam, Andy set down his luggage on the platform and looked about the station. A whistle blew somewhere. A number of men he saw had green felt hats with short feathers and leather shorts, talking to porters or family come to bring them home. There were women with long skirts and large summer hats. It was a cool evening and a breeze wafted across the platform, bringing a tingle of what seemed like mountain air. How would he recognize his relatives? He looked down at his department store suit and realized that it was not he that would recognize them, but the other way around.

A young man wearing lederhosen coming toward him

caught his attention. He met his eyes and then the young man called out.

"You there, porter," he said in a loud but friendly way. "You might as well stay with us a little longer and bring those out to my car. You must be Andy?" The young man smiled as he approached and looked expectantly at Andy.

Andy saw a slender and somewhat shorter version of himself with a mustache. He had thought about growing one while he crossed the Atlantic and Europe, but had held back, uncertain. Now he wished that he had. It made the young man who was about his age look so much more sophisticated.

Dressed casually in dark brown leather shorts, alpine walking shoes and high stockings, the young man seemed to bounce along with exuberance and energy. He had dark hair and a fair complexion with large brown eyes, long, almost feminine black eyelashes and he flashed a potent smile with very white teeth. Andy felt a little overdressed in his suit and tie. *A very different German sound to his voice,* Andy thought. *Much easier to understand than the customs officer.* It was probably a Viennese accent, but the offhand elegance of the inflection suggested someone with education and rank. A porter standing nearby in his uniform noticed it too. He straightened up and then bowed to the waved, casual thanks of the young aristocrat.

"Yes, I am," Andy replied to the sudden, breezy greeting.

"Cousin," said the young man softly, wrapping his arms around him in a polite hug and kiss on each cheek. Andy remembered his mother's warning about this very European gesture and not to be surprised or offended. He stepped back smiling and extended his hand.

"Rudolf zu Windischgrätz!" he exclaimed as they shook hands. "But everyone calls me Rudi. Welcome, cousin," he said enthusiastically and gestured sweepingly toward the archway leading outside. Andy's luggage was carefully piled on his trolley by the porter who followed them.

"You'll love the ride. Do you use the motorcar much in America? My father got this roadster a few years ago that I'm going to show you and this is the best time of day to enjoy it."

Rudi continued talking as they ambled toward the car with the porter in tow. While the porter carefully put his luggage in the backseat and compartments of the car, Rudi politely asked Andy all about his trip. Did he have a pleasant trip? How was the weather on the Atlantic? Had he heard about the *Empress of Ireland* sinking in Canada? After the *Titanic*, it was getting a little dangerous, yes? Was he hungry or tired? Not to worry.

Straining at times to understand the rapid flow of words and managing his own replies carefully, Andy replied to these polite inquiries, trying to pronounce each word slowly, with as good an accent as he could manage. Occasionally, he lost a word or phrase, but Rudi seemed to take no notice of it and to understand him perfectly.

As Andy climbed in the car and sank into the black, tufted leather seat he saw that this motorcar was nothing like his father's Tin Lizzie back in Ohio. He saw Rudi say something to the porter and drop a gold Korona into his hand as the porter bowed again. In a moment, they were winding through the cobblestone streets of Salzburg at dusk. The gas streetlamps were being lit, giving the ancient streets a yellow glow intermingled with the waning rays of the sun. He was now deep in Europe.

Andy saw the brass plate on the dashboard, which said, simply, "Graf & Stift." The power and speed of the motorcar amazed Andy. Words could not do it justice. Whistling air poured over the windshield, billowed through his hair, and massaged his face. Rudi's head turned and his eyes made contact with Andy, smiling impishly. He arched his eyebrows comically and then said in English over the noise, "Quite a motorcar, eh?"

Rudi had put the top down as they sped along the paved country road leading to Bad Ischl. The fortress castle on top of the mountain in the middle of Salzburg was soon lost from view. The smell of wet grass, cow dung, and fragrant pine buffeted them after leaving the city behind. Rudi practically shouted conversation over the wind noise.

"My father gave me this for my twenty-first birthday. He bought it a few years ago from Karl Graf himself."

"It's a fantastic car!" Andy replied in English.

Further details of the car were discussed in Rudi's British-accented English. Forty miles per hour, the speedometer said. The pools of light flowing from the huge headlights of the car became more and more intense as the soft pink and red glow of the sun setting behind them faded to black and dark silhouettes of tall pine trees whished by.

After nearly an hour, chatting as the motorcar climbed in altitude and the temperature dropping, Rudi began braking. The soft glow of a roadside inn appeared around a curve. Rudi pulled into the private drive. The sounds of crickets when the motor stopped. Diners sitting at tables under lines of electric lights. A violin. The cool air and smell of the alpine forest around them mingled with smoke from the kitchen of the inn as they walked toward the yellow light at the edge of the restaurant. As Andy's ears adjusted to the quiet, he noticed a low buzz of chatter and a laugh from some part of the restaurant. Some men with dark green felt hats and feathers sat at some tables outside smoking pipes. So this was Austria?

"The turns get a little sharper now as we get close to home," said Rudi smoothly. "I won't drink, but I hope you will." They sat outside at a wooden table covered with a plain tablecloth. Three gypsy musicians played for a table of guests the melody of a waltz of some name that he could not remember, but had heard before. Smoke from cigars at a nearby table drifted through the night air.

Rudi ordered dinner and beer for Andy. They talked for a while about the countryside they had driven through, the food in Austria, and Andy's family. Rudi was very interested in life in America. Where was Ohio? And what was it like there? And what about baseball? How do you play it? After a couple of beers and a hearty meal, Andy held forth on a game he had played against Purdue on the Notre Dame team in which he had had the game-winning hit, much to Rudi's amusement. A congratulatory pat of family pride in Andy's accomplishment came at the end of the story.

"Perhaps we should be going?" Andy asked. "Won't they be waiting for us?"

"Actually, they probably aren't," Rudi replied. "My father is not at home this evening. He and my brother went to Vienna yesterday on some business, but they should be back tomorrow. My mother is having dinner with the kaiser this evening and may not be back when we arrive. You know my mother is the granddaughter of the kaiser?"

Andy already knew this.

"My father married the Archduchess Elisabeth, my mother. She is the only child of the kaiser's only son."

"I am guessing you must have been named after your grandfather," Andy replied.

"Yes. Very good. I see you know something of our family, then. Yes, my grandfather Rudolf. I never knew him, of course. This is something that is not discussed in our family, as you can imagine. My mother was just a little girl when my grandfather ..." Rudi paused. "I hardly know how to say it delicately in English. You must know about the Mayerling incident?"

Andy's mother had discovered and told him a little about the kaiser's heir having committed suicide under mysterious circumstances. The mention of the word Mayerling referred to a hunting lodge where the dramatic event took place and had become synonymous with mystery and intrigue. Andy decided not to admit too much knowledge of the subject and to see what Rudi had to say about it.

"Not very much. What happened?" Andy asked quietly.

"It was a long time ago, but it still affects my mother and her family to this day. It was in January 1889. My grandfather was having an affair with a Viennese baroness much younger than he was. He and my grandmother were living separately by then, although that was not known to the public. My grandfather and his lover were both found dead of gunshot wounds in his hunting lodge in Mayerling. It's not far from Vienna."

"Of course, it was a great shock to the family and all of Europe. He was the crown prince and the heir to the kaiser's throne. The kaiser was nearly sixty and who knew then that he would live to such an old age? But worse than that was the question of how the two deaths had happened. Nobody knows for sure, but it seems that my grandfather may have actually shot the young lady and then killed himself. A double suicide. As a Catholic, you know what that means."

Andy did know what that meant. According to Catholic doctrine, both murder and suicide were mortal sins. Andy began to appreciate the magnitude of the incident now that he was actually in the country where it happened and speaking to one of the dead crown prince's relatives. His cousin looked at him from across the table and lit a cigar. He offered one to Andy. "No, thank you. I don't smoke."

"The kaiser had to petition the pope himself to allow my grandfather to be buried in the Habsburg imperial crypt in Vienna. It was decided by the medical authorities that he was insane at the time and this provided an exception to the rule." Rudolf puffed on his cigar while continuing the story. "I tell you this only because you will meet my mother tomorrow and, as I say, we never speak of this in our family."

"I understand," Andy said. "I won't say a word about it. Thank you for telling me."

"Not at all. It's really not something that we think about very much nowadays. After all, it happened over a quarter century ago. Yet, in some ways, I think it has always hung over our little branch of the family. My grandmother remarried and lives now in Hungary. She never comes to court and my mother sees her only once in a while. My mother is a favorite of the kaiser and they're together often. As I said, she was having dinner with him this evening. I think he looks at her as his last link with his son. It's a little sad, really."

A skeleton in the family closet, thought Andy. *Perhaps there were more.*

"You know, it's interesting what you told me because a long time ago, our ancestor Matthias came to America supposedly because of a family scandal. Nobody knows what it was," Andy said.

"Really? There are not many scandals in the Windischgrätz family," Rudi continued, "unless you count bombarding the city of Vienna." Andy knew that he was alluding to the counter-revolution led by Alfred in 1848 and saw his cousin flash a mischievous smile. "I wonder what it was."

"It's a mystery. I was hoping I might find out the reason while I am here."

"Who knows? It was a long time ago, wasn't it?" Andy realized from this comment that Otto must have mentioned it to Rudi before he arrived.

"Well, I suppose we really must be going. It is getting late," said Rudolf as he looked at his pocket watch. The tables had slowly emptied and many of the waiters now stood around idly chatting. They drove through the darkness again toward Bad Ischl and soon arrived at the Windischgrätz summer home.

Nestled in woods on the outskirts of town, a virtual

palace glowing with lights came into view. The sound of crushed pebbles under the wheels of the car announced their approach to a pillared front door, which swung open to reveal two male servants who quickly came to the car. They bowed and then took Andy's luggage quietly into the house. The brilliant light assaulted his eyes as Andy stepped into a large vestibule with black and white terrazzo floors. A huge crystal chandelier hung over their heads and Andy found himself gawking at it. One of the servants with the luggage mounted a massive staircase that ascended up to a landing where it split into two separate stairs that eventually reached the second level. A gallery of paintings was on the walls between a number of doors that each presumably led to some room.

"May I get you something?" the other servant inquired of both of them.

"No, no. Not for me. Andy?" Andy declined as well, still looking around the spacious room, which echoed their voices. "Come, let me show you around." Rudi walked with Andy from room to room. Priceless furniture and paneled walls. Crystal stemware, mirrors, fireplace mantels, and elaborate clocks. Rudi pointed out this and that, telling little stories about some of the objets d'art or things that had happened in one room or another. Eventually, they completed the circuit of the ground floor.

"You must be tired, cousin," Rudi said at last. "Let me show you to your room." They went up the stairs and down a corridor that had been obscured from the lobby until they came to a door that Rudi ceremoniously opened. Andy could hardly believe his eyes. There was a huge bed with a canopy over it suspended from four posts of carved wood. A fireplace. Huge windows that let out on a wide balcony. A water closet all to himself.

"This is too much," Andy exclaimed. He thought of his own bedroom at home which was only slightly larger than the water closet. He looked at his cousin, who was eagerly searching Andy's face for his reaction.

"Not at all," Rudi said. "I hope you'll like it. I'll be in to see you in the morning. If you need anything at all, just pull this bell cord over here." Rudi showed him a long ribbon of thick fabric that hung in the corner and was connected to something on the other side of a small hole in the ceiling.

"Just pull it and he is one of the servants will be at your door in a minute and get you anything you need," Rudi explained.

"I'm sure I won't need anything. Thank you for everything." In a moment, Rudi was gone and Andy was alone again. He saw that his typewriter had been unpacked and placed on a mahogany desk, ready for his use. His luggage had been opened and his clothes hung in a closet or had been tucked away in a dresser. There was nothing for him to do.

Andy felt tired—but excited—as he undressed and got into bed. The next day, he thought, he would type out his first "dispatch" to his father. It took a little time, but eventually drowsiness settled down on him and then, little by little, he fell into a deep sleep.

The next morning, lying in bed, Andy heard the door open and Rudi come into the room. Out the window, low gray clouds drifted over the massive mountains Andy could see from his bed. The air was cold and scented with the smell of pine. A man was leading a horse and cart toward a path that disappeared from view in the woods in the distance. The view from Andy's balcony was fantastic. He had never seen mountains like these. They disappeared into the clouds. Everything slanted here, either sloping up or down into pasture or open fields. Thick woods covered the mountains over which the fog and mist silently passed.

"It will get better," continued Rudi. "The mist will burn off before noon and then the sun will come out. My mother should be arriving before noon. She and my sister stayed at the *Kaiservilla* last night. My father and my brother Ernst will be coming back from Vienna this afternoon too. How about a ride? Do you ride horses, Andy?"

Andy did not. A middle-class city dweller, Andy had ridden a few times, but had never acquired the equestrian graces of his friends at Notre Dame or the farmers' sons near Columbus whose families could not afford nor have much need for motorcars.

"I'm afraid not," Andy replied, "but I think I could ride a gentle horse if you had one." Rudi smiled.

"Yes, I think I know just the one. Let's go," he exclaimed. Andy observed that, even so early in the morning, Rudi seemed bursting with energy and was ready to satisfy whatever impulse seemed to strike him at any given moment.

With that, Rudi left his room to get one of the grooms to saddle a couple of horses. Andy got dressed and went downstairs, taking in the interior décor of the house in the daylight. The stairway was made of a green marble with portraits of military figures going down the stairs. A drawing room sumptuously furnished. Heavy, dark curtains contrasted with creamy yellow wallpaper. In the breakfast room, where he found Rudi, tea was waiting in a silver pot with exquisite blue and white china teacups laid out on the table by unseen servants along with breakfast bread and rolls with butter.

"Eat up, cousin," Rudi said. He had already begun, Andy could see. Soon they were out in the yard mounting Fritz, a dark foreboding animal that Rudi explained had been his father's favorite until he had gotten so old.

"He should be fine for you," said Rudi. "He was a

cavalry horse in his younger days and heard a few too many cannons, so he's a little deaf. Be firm with him. He'll still obey orders like a good military horse," he said with a smile as he mounted his own much livelier stallion whose frisky personality seemed to match Rudi's. Before long, they were riding out on an alpine trail through the woods.

Andy could not remember any scenery in Ohio or Indiana that could compare with this. Long stretches of forest were punctuated with bursts into open country where the mountains rose abruptly, diagonally, to spectacular heights or gorges that opened below. The sun slanted through the pines in the woods. Then they came to a waterfall.

"This is the Hohenzoller Falls," Rudi said. A sheer drop of water from a gorge in the mountains plunged into a pool of white water. For a while, they both listened to the thundering sound of the water hitting the rocks below. "This is one of my favorite places," Rudi said softly. "My father brought me here when I was a little boy, riding my first horse. It was a spring day—a lot like today. I was about twelve years old. I must have returned here a hundred times and yet I still love it."

Coming down the path from the opposite direction, Andy noticed, were another pair of riders apparently also making for the falls. Rudi caught Andy's gaze and looked up the path as well. They both sat still, watching the riders approach from a distance. Rudi's mouth began to form into a slight smile.

"Well, cousin, it seems as if fate has taken a bit of a hand. Here comes Franz, one of my Habsburg cousins." Did Andy know who he was? No? The kaiser's heir.

"Let me explain a little etiquette before he gets here. You would want me to tell you this, right? Franz Ferdinand does not speak much English, but he will be interested in meeting an American. Just sit on your horse and when I introduce you, simply nod your head. If he extends his hand, then and only then, should you take it. In other words, cousin, the etiquette would be that you should not extend your hand to him until and unless he does so first. If he does so, don't shake his hand like you do in America. Simply grasp his hand for a moment and release it. Royalty, you understand."

Andy did not know any Austrian etiquette for meeting a person of such high rank. He had never thought that he would have the occasion to do so. As the pair came closer, he could see a large man on a rather large horse with a leather hunting jacket and alpine hat with feather. A very large mustache curled up at the ends, which extended beyond the large head. Piercing blue eyes seemed to bulge out of the face. Then the voice.

"Rudolf, is that you?" boomed out the lead rider who now seemed to urge his horse forward faster. Under the curving mustache, Andy now saw large teeth, a wide smile, and a look of genuine pleasure. Franz Ferdinand seemed to be in his fifties, Andy guessed. Another gentleman was riding with him and appeared to be about the same age, but much thinner. Rudi urged his horse forward and waved to the oncoming pair.

"Yes, it's me!" Rudi cried out. Andy turned his horse toward the rendezvous, but at a steady gait. Rudi rode up to the older man who held out his hand. Rudi reined in his horse, took the hand, and bent to kiss it. After a few words between them, he saw the large head turn and catch his eyes with a steady, blue gaze.

"May I present our American cousin, Mr. Andrew Bishop, of Columbus, Ohio," Rudi said, looking toward Andy who was now adjacent to the two of them. "Andy, I have the honor to present to you my cousin, His Imperial and Royal Highness, the archduke Franz Ferdinand and my cousin, the archduke Eugene." Andy nodded his head as he had been advised. The archdukes eased their horses toward him and Archduke Franz held out his hand. Andy grasped a rather large hand in a soft, doeskin leather riding glove and then released it.

"How do you do?" said Archduke Franz Ferdinand, surprisingly, in English. "A pleasure to meet you," said the other archduke who also held out a gloved hand.

"An honor" said Andy in German, trying to remain as calm as he could. Perhaps the correct handshake pleased the archduke, who smiled back at him and then started to dismount his horse, prompting the others to do the same. Andy guessed correctly that it would be a breach of etiquette to remain seated on his horse while His Imperial and Royal Highness stood on the ground. Together, they all walked closer to the waterfall. The archduke reverted to German and started chatting with Rudi about his mother being at dinner the previous evening.

"How long have you been in Austria?" asked Eugene.

"Only a day, Your Highness," said Andy in his best German. "Rudi, uh, Rudolf was just giving me a tour. The scenery is fantastic. I come from Ohio in America where it is very flat. The mountains here are especially beautiful to me."

"Look over there," said Franz in a suddenly hushed voice. "I'll bet you Andy has never seen one of these before! I wish I had my gun." The archduke pointed toward a ledge on the mountain a few hundred yards away. There was a goat-like animal with a white face and two black stripes that went from its nose to its eyes. Little horns bent back from the head. "We call that a *Gämse*, but the English and the French call it a chamois." They all watched as the chamois picked its way along an invisible rocky trail until it went out of sight.

Franz and Rudolf continued to chat while Eugene spoke to Andy about America. He had been to America several years earlier. He had enjoyed Boston very much. He was also impressed with New York. He had met President McKinley at a social function in Baltimore. His favorite part of America was the West, however. He had crossed the country by train to California. The Rocky Mountains were the equal of the Alps, he assured Andy, and the Grand Canyon was among the most astounding sights that he had ever seen.

Andy enjoyed this soft-spoken archduke who by now seemed to have gone beyond just making polite conversation, taking great pleasure to reminisce about his travels in America. After a few minutes, however, Archduke Franz Ferdinand turned to Andy.

"It has been a few years since I was in America," said the archduke. The large blue eyes fixed on him were arresting. Almost unblinking, they had nearly physical force bearing down on him and it was all Andy could do to keep his concentration on what the archduke was saying. "I met your former president, Theodore Roosevelt, four years ago and liked him very much. He was in Europe and visited us in Vienna, you know. Do you know him?"

"I do not, Your Highness. I had no idea ..."

"Walk softly, but carry a big stick," the archduke mused. "Very good advice, I think. And your Mr. Wilson, what do you make of him?"

Andy hardly knew what to say about the present occupant of the White House, President Woodrow Wilson. Andy's father was quite enthusiastic about him, but given the archduke's apparent fondness for Roosevelt, whom Wilson had defeated in the 1912 election, Andy hesitated.

"I suppose it's too early to tell," Andy equivocated. "I agree with you about President Roosevelt though. He was a great president." This seemed to please the archduke and he continued.

"I had no idea that the Windischgrätz family had relatives in America. How interesting." He turned to look at Rudi.

"We didn't know it either until a few months ago," Rudi interjected. He briefly explained the mutual discovery that the two families had made in the past year as the archdukes listened quietly. Rudi finished by mentioning the mystery surrounding the departure of Matthias in 1754.

"Fascinating," the archduke replied at last. "That would have been during the time of my own ancestor, the Empress Maria Theresa. Those were difficult times. Wars with Prussia and all that, but the empire was never stronger. I wonder what it could have been."

With that, the conversation turned to some type of expedition that the archduke was going to take in a few weeks and he drew Rudi aside, leaving Andy with Eugene. After a few more minutes of polite conversation, Archduke Franz began taking his leave of them, mounted his horse, and after an exchange of pleasantries to both of them, the two resumed their ride on the trail in the direction from which Andy and Rudi had come.

"Franz Ferdinand will be the kaiser someday, probably someday soon," Rudi said as they continued down the mountain trail. "He'll be a good one, I'm sure. He has a lot of good ideas that he tells me about sometimes."

"How old is the kaiser?" asked Andy. He remembered a large painting of him in the railway station in Salzburg. Kaiser Franz Josef was bald with short-cropped white hair all the way around the crown of his head, bushy white sideburns, and mustache, but no beard on his chin. Other than the lack of a white beard, he looked like St. Nicholas to Andy's eye, but it was obvious that he was an elderly man.

"Nearly eighty-four," Rudi replied. They rode in silence for a while. The scenery remained beautiful, but Andy noticed that Rudi appeared to be distracted and thoughtful. Then he continued.

"Franz Ferdinand is going to go on some maneuvers in Bosnia in a few weeks. He asked me if I wanted to go with him and his wife. I am not sure whether my parents would allow it."

"Why not?" Andy asked. "I would think your parents would be very pleased he asked you to come." Andy noticed that Rudi was now staring at the ground as their horses continued side by side at a very slow pace. For a long time, he said nothing.

"Andy, I don't know if it is my place to tell you this. I mean, you've only been here less than a day and I hardly think you should be bothering with family … matters," Rudi said slowly. "And yet, perhaps you should know a thing or two about us." Andy said nothing, his curiosity now aroused.

"You see, Franz is something of a black sheep in the Habsburg family, but not to me. It's his wife. According to the law, a Habsburg heir is not supposed to marry anyone who is not also royalty. Even aristocracy is not high enough. The kaiser himself married a Bavarian princess. My grandfather married the princess of Belgium. You see what I mean?"

"Franz scandalized the Habsburg family when he insisted on marrying his wife, Sophie, who was not royalty—and not even what we would call aristocracy of the first rank. She was a mere countess at that time. It became a crisis because Franz Ferdinand was the heir to the throne by that time and …" Rudi's voice trailed off. "This must seem very strange to an American?" A wry smile was on his face.

"It's fascinating," Andy replied. "Please go on."

Rudi pulled a cigarette from his pocket and lit it. "Yes, I thought so," Rudi said. "It's different here, of course. Austria is a very old country and the old ways pass slowly away here. Too slowly, sometimes," he said with a trace of bitterness in his voice.

"The kaiser himself is very old. From a distant time, yes. That has something to do with it, no doubt. But I suppose you should know this anyway because it affects our family. My mother especially, you know. You see, this crisis antagonized the kaiser toward Franz Ferdinand who would not back down. Ever since then, the kaiser and his heir have not been on the best of terms and it divides the family. My mother is very close to the kaiser and so tends to disapprove of Franz Ferdinand and the things he does. Do you see?"

Andy did see. A family rift. Rudi was probably friendlier with Franz than his mother would like or approve. He understood the difficulty in Rudi accepting his imperial cousin's invitation to join him for the military maneuvers. Rudi wanted to go not only for the adventure, but because in the not-too-distant future, Franz Ferdinand would be the ruler of the empire. The future belonged to him, and yet ...

"We should get back. My mother should be home by now and will be anxious to meet you," said Rudi. Urging their horses, Andy and Rudi rode back to the Windischgrätz chalet through the woods and trails as the sun burned off the morning dew in the pastures they passed on the way.

Austrian society was so different, Andy thought. "Their ways are not our ways," his mother had cautioned him. Yes indeed. Kissing gloved hands. Dynastic marriages. Class and rank meant everything here, Andy could see. He thought of his father's admonition at Thanksgiving. "People like us have no rights in those countries ..."

2.
Salzburg Sojourn

During the course of the day, Andy finally met his hosts. First, Archduchess Elisabeth was waiting for Rudi and Andy in the main salon of the chalet. Rudi made the introduction in formal style, but Elisabeth quickly put Andy at ease.

"You are most welcome, Andy," she said with a smile. The same blue Habsburg eyes peered inquisitively at him as she spoke with the assurance of one used to encouraging conversation with people who were initially awestruck by her high station in society. "I'm sorry that I speak very little English, but your German seems very good," she said encouragingly. She seemed genuinely warm, smiling at him frequently and soon Andy felt his initial nervousness fade. Many questions followed about his voyage from America, his family, the horseback ride, and so on. Lunch was served while conversation continued. Andy found himself explaining and speaking about himself and his family at length, but learning little about the woman who would be "looking after him" during his stay. Those details would come later, no doubt, Andy thought.

She was dressed in a summer white dress with pearls at her neck. Her black hair was done up with pins that sparkled and glittered when her head moved, from little gems embedded on them. She was of average height, with a tight corseted waist, long hands, and a firm but soft voice. When she spoke, questions rather than statements were forthcoming with little exclamations of interest or pleasure at his responses. The entire effect was one that gave the simultaneous impression of great interest, but also the vaguely intimidating feeling of somehow being measured.

Otto, Prince zu Windischgrätz, and his son Ernst arrived in the middle of the afternoon to some commotion. The family dogs barked and jumped for joy at their appearance and both father and son knelt down to play with the dogs while the servants brought luggage and some boxes in from the car.

"And this must be Andy?" Otto inquired soon, looking directly into Andy's eyes.

"Yes, father," Rudi replied. The introduction again, not so formal this time. Both Otto and Ernst embraced Andy in enthusiastic hugs as Rudi had done at the station the previous day.

"How delightful," Otto said in English. Like Rudi, Otto's accent had a definite British inflection to it, but it quickly became obvious that he spoke it well. Again, polite inquiries about the family, the trip over, and if he had been made comfortable, to all of which Andy responded as he had before. Conversation continued on the terrace outside with the backdrop of the Alps, which Andy had not been able to see in the early morning mist, now in full view in the summer sun. It was a stunning vista.

Otto was far less reserved than Elisabeth was, often making witty comments with a rueful smile. Andy guessed that he was far more responsible for at least some of Rudi's personality than Elisabeth was. He surmised also, as time went on, that the older son, Ernst, was probably more like his mother. Although cordial and friendly, Ernst participated least in the conversations, seemingly preferring to listen and make his own judgments, revealing little about himself at this first meeting.

Otto was also of average height, slightly shorter than Andy. He had lively, brown eyes with distinct crow's feet at the edges and smile lines that suggested a man of generally jovial disposition. A bushy mustache just beginning to turn gray. A full head of dark brown hair mixed with gray, but with a high forehead caused by a receding hairline. His hands were large and strong and, while well manicured to suit his station, displayed some calluses consistent with horseback riding, shooting, and other similar activities, Andy guessed.

At dinner, conversation turned to Elisabeth's visit the previous evening at her grandfather's chalet, the *Kaiservilla*. She related the discussion between her grandfather and her cousin, the same Archduke Franz Ferdinand that Andy and Rudi had met in the morning. For the first time, Andy noticed some passion in Elisabeth's voice, which became more noticeable by the silence around the table as she went on.

"He'll ride in an open car with Sophie. That's what it's all about. They can be seen in public together. That's why he wants to go down there. It has nothing to do with reconciling the Bosnians to the monarchy. Montenuovo wants to stop it, but the kaiser hasn't the stomach for it anymore. He's worn him down."

Otto contemplated his wife's apparent antagonism toward her cousin Franz Ferdinand as Andy watched. It was the controversy over Franz Ferdinand's marriage as Rudi had forewarned him that seemed to irk Elisabeth and color her view of the trip.

"No one will take any notice of it, Elisabeth. Do you really think anyone cares about whether he and Sophie ride in an open car through the streets of a provincial town in the Balkans? The imperial censors won't allow a word of it or a picture of them together to appear in any newspaper in the empire and it wouldn't occur to the press anywhere else in the world that there was the slightest significance to it. Someone must go. The kaiser can't do it. At his age, with the heat, it's impossible. I really think he must go and if he wants to bring Sophie, what of it?"

Andy could see very well now that Rudi's chances of accompanying Franz Ferdinand on his trip were nil and also the reason why. The subject soon changed to other subjects and the tension quickly evaporated. What should they do the next day with Andy? A hike into the mountains, perhaps? Did he like music? What about Mozart? This is Salzburg, after all.

A few days later, Andy found himself in the Windischgrätz balcony at the concert hall in Salzburg with Otto, Elisabeth, Rudi, and Ernst. Salzburg was the ancestral home of Mozart and the concert this evening would feature two of his masterpieces, *Eine Kleine Nachtmusik* and his 40th Symphony. The balcony offered a perfect view of the orchestra, but Andy soon discovered that for Ernst and Rudi, half the fun of going to a concert was to see who else was there, what they were wearing, and who they were with. Even Otto and Elisabeth peered out into the boxes with their opera glasses. Idle chatter amongst the family. Look, the Baron von Biersdorf. I'm surprised he showed his face. Did you hear about his affair with the wife of that general? What's his name? The glint and sparkle of diamonds from the seats below. The smell of perfume. Look over there. I had no idea *she* was in town. Did Andy go to concerts in Columbus? No? Was there no concert hall there? Austrians love music, you know. An obsession, really.

Andy had watched *Rebecca of Sunnybrook Farms* at the Lyceum Theatre on High Street in Columbus at Christmas with his parents and had always thought it to be opulent. The grandeur of this concert hall was truly something to behold, Andy thought as he surveyed the vast space. The orchestra seats were filling. All around the circumference of the hall were layers of boxes and balcony seats with small electric lights on the front that gave a glow to the red velvet and gold that encased each level like the inside of a jewel box. Huge crystal chandeliers with more electric lights hung from ornate medallions of gold gilding on the ceiling.

The hubbub and buzz of conversation and tinkling laughter below continued with a ripple of applause when the lights were dimmed and the conductor stepped to the box and bowed. Strangely, he continued to stand, facing the audience, looking up toward the back of the hall. What was he doing? Andy followed the gaze of the conductor. In the middle of the back of the hall, there was a large balcony with the black and gold flag of Austria draped in front of it. Curious, the people below also began to turn toward the center balcony to see what was happening. A flash of light pierced the hall as a door opened and the silhouettes of two figures appeared.

The conductor turned to the orchestra, raised his baton, and the orchestra began to play. The audience rose and turned toward the box as an elderly man in a white uniform with a hat plumed with green feathers made his way down the steps to the front of the balcony. He entered the box alone, but was then followed by Archduke Franz Ferdinand and several others wearing white military uniforms and plumed hats. A few voices started singing *"Gott erhalte, Gott beschütze, unser Kaiser, unser Land ..."* It was the national anthem, Andy thought, translating in his mind: "God save, God protect our kaiser, our land ..." More voices joined in, including Otto and his two sons. Rudi glanced at Andy with a smile. "Long live Franz, the kaiser ..." and so it went. As it ended, the audience was singing in full throat as the old man, his white gloved hands on the balcony rail, stood with the archduke beside him.

As the last words were sung to the emperor, the music stopped and the conductor turned and bowed from the waist amidst a roar of applause. Shouts of *"Gott erhalte der Kaiser"* pealed out from the crowd below. The old man slowly waved a gloved hand to the crowd and a new and louder roar of applause and cheering burst like a thunderbolt from the crowd. Ernst gave Andy his glasses and Andy quickly put them to his eyes and focused.

The first thing Andy saw was the large head and dark features of the archduke's head as it turned. His famous upturned mustache over a faint smile. The bulging, hooded eyes narrowed as he turned to look at the kaiser, giving the impression of "Well, we all know who is the surprise here." Andy quickly moved the glasses to get a look at the kaiser.

Thin and frail, he nevertheless stood ramrod-straight with one hand on the railing, perhaps to steady himself, perhaps not. He took no notice of the archduke, but instead, looked down at the cheering throng below. Blue watery eyes seemed to twinkle in the dim light as he searched the crowd. A raised eyebrow of recognition to someone below. Then another slow wave and a nod to someone else. Then Andy went back to the archduke who also nodded and then slowly began to clap his gloved hands.

Wild cheering for the old emperor went on for at least a minute or two, Andy guessed. The kaiser seemed taken aback by the waves of shouts, applause, and genuine affection that rolled up in waves from the crowd. The slightest hint of a smile or nod from the elderly man to the faces in the crowd below him brought a fresh roar of cheering. As Andy watched, fascinated, the kaiser turned his head toward the archduke who bent slightly to hear something that the kaiser said and then nodded, smiling again. Finally, the kaiser slowly sat down, followed by the archduke. Only then did the cheering die down. A low murmur of voices buzzed in the aftermath as the audience began to take their seats.

Otto leaned forward from his seat behind Andy until his mouth was only an inch or two from Andy's ear. In a low voice, he said, "You have seen a rare sight, Andy. The kaiser almost never comes out in public anymore. It was not expected that he would come to a concert like this." The crowd was still buzzing and many craned their heads around in their seats to see the old kaiser and his heir in the box, as if they might never see such a sight again in their lives.

At the intermission, waiters served champagne in the Windischgrätz box. With the house lights up, Andy watched the kaiser and the archduke in the imperial box. They were standing in a little group, also drinking champagne and engaging in conversation with what looked to be several military figures in splendid white summer uniforms.

"Fascinating, isn't it?" said Ernst.

"Yes, I've never seen anything like that."

"Yes, indeed," said Otto, joining in. "Perhaps it was the sight of him with Franz Ferdinand that moved the crowd so much. Perhaps they think things between them are not so bad, despite what one hears." Andy thought of the conversation at dinner a few days ago.

"Austrians are very sentimental people," Otto went on quietly as the lights dimmed completely. "Things that have happened to the Habsburg family are well known to almost everyone. The tragedies, the rifts, the ups and downs. It was seeing the kaiser and Franz Ferdinand together that drew such a reaction tonight, I think." Elisabeth remained quiet throughout the whole spectacle, keeping her thoughts to herself. What they might be, Andy couldn't guess.

At the end of the concert, Andy and the Windischgrätz family filed down the special hall and stairwell reserved for high-ranking aristocracy and out into the crisp night air. They were just in time to see the kaiser and the archduke pass through a double line of brilliantly uniformed, plumed Life Guards, arms presented at rigid attention, and get into a huge Daimler automobile. Considering his age, Franz Josef walked deliberately but firmly, his head turning slightly left and right. Then it happened. Just as he came even with them, he turned and looked in their direction. For just a moment, Andy was sure that he had made eye contact with the old monarch. It was just a second, no more than that, but he felt it. And then he was gone. The doors of his car were closed by the guards and the motorcar swept away with their imperial passengers into the night.

"Come, we're going to Luchow's for supper," Otto said. They all climbed into Otto's new blue Mercedes and off they went through the streets of old Salzburg until they arrived at the restaurant.

Andy found himself seated next to Ernst and, before long, apparently trying to be helpful, the conversation turned to a description of rank and precedence in Austrian society.

"It's somewhat different than in England," he explained. This made little impression on Andy since he was unaware of English protocol, but he nodded in seeming understanding.

"A *Graf* ranks higher than a *Freiherr* or baron who in turn precedes a *Ritter*, or knight. Above a Graf is a *Fürst* or prince, then a *Herzog* or duke topped by a *Grossherzog* or grand duke. There is only one of those and he lives in Italy. At the top, essentially royalty in Austria, were the *Erzherzogin* or archdukes."

"Here in Austria, only the Habsburgs are archdukes. Had Otto not been a Fürst, my mother would not have been allowed to marry him because she is a Habsburg and a direct descendent of the kaiser. Since she is not an heir, however, she was able to marry beneath royalty, thank God," said Ernst with a smile. It was all somewhat complicated, but punctiliously observed on formal occasions, Ernst explained. Everyone knew his or her place. It didn't seem complicated to Ernst, Andy thought.

The maitre d' recognized Otto and Elisabeth immediately and escorted the entire party upstairs into a private reception and dining room that was already quite full of other concertgoers gaily drinking champagne and helping themselves to the food laid out elaborately on tables buffet-style. Someone called to Otto from the other side of the room. He and Elisabeth moved off to the table where a man in a military uniformed, seated with several ladies, rose to greet them.

Andy gazed about the dining room at Luchow's; it was full of the *glitterati* of the empire at leisure. He saw dozens of Austrian officers in white uniforms with red trim. Ladies with long gowns sparkled with diamonds and pearls. Tables laden with food. Champagne and crystal glasses warmed the scene with cheer as the crowd chattered and laughter broke out here and there.

"Andy, come and meet some good friends of ours," said Rudi. Andy saw the crowd close behind Otto and Elisabeth and they went out of sight. Ernst was already talking to other friends nearby as Rudi took his arm and gently led him in another direction. He made for a small table where a young couple were seated. The woman was looking in their direction and, as they approached, she smiled. She was amazingly beautiful. They both were, really. The young man next to her wore a white officer's uniform trimmed in red. A round Austrian officer's cap was on the table in front of him. He rose to greet Rudi first.

After a brief hug and exchange of pleasantries to both of them, Rudi gestured toward Andy, beckoning him to come closer. "Andy, I would like to present Franz Johann

Graf Caboga and his fiancée, Maria von Montfort." "Graf" in German was a title, Andy knew, not a name. It translated best to the title "count" in English, although a Graf in Austria was at the highest end of the lower aristocracy.

"Call me Johann," said the young officer, shaking hands with Andy. "Why don't you sit down?" Johann gestured to two empty chairs at the table, smiling. Dazzling white teeth above a neatly trimmed mustache and a handsome face. Johann and Miss Montfort certainly made a stunning couple.

"Wasn't it a surprise to see the kaiser tonight?" Johann said as Rudi and Andy took the chairs. The young lady said nothing, but smiled at Andy as he sat down. As Rudi and Johann talked, Andy could not help but glance back at Maria von Montfort and think that she might be the most beautiful woman he had ever seen. She had dark hair and dark eyes with the fair complexion that was prized in Austrian polite society. A white evening gown. A diamond necklace with emeralds. Long white gloves. Diamond earrings flashed. But it was the eyes. Almond shaped with long black lashes.

As the conversation turned to society gossip that was largely incomprehensible to Andy, he found it impossible not to furtively glance at Maria and felt flushed with embarrassment, at one point, when she caught him. At last, he was rescued when Johann turned to him with questions about America and Andy's first impressions of Austria.

What did he think so far of their country? Tell me about your family tree. Did he know anything about his ancestor, Matthias? A scandal? There were many scandals in Austrian society, Johann laughed. That was not a reason to leave the country. If everyone in our society left the country for a scandal, there would be nobody left! A laugh all around the table.

Then she spoke to him. In English.

"Perhaps a romantic scandal?"

"Well, perhaps," Andy replied, now having the excuse

to look at her directly, which he found difficult to do while maintaining a semblance of coherent conversation. "I mean, we don't know. He came with his wife. We do know that."

She shrugged. The orchestra struck up a waltz. It was the "Künstlerleben," or "Artist's Life" by Strauss. "Do you dance, Mr. Bishop?"

"Well, yes. Would you like to?"

"Of course, thank you." As she rose from her chair, Andy felt his heart skip a beat. The gown flattered her slender figure. Rudi and Johann rose as well, taken a little off guard. Maria serenely extended her gloved hand, Andy offered his arm, and they were off. Dimly, he heard conversation resume between Johann and Rudi.

"So, are you coming to Sarajevo with us?"

"No, I'm afraid not."

There were a few other dancers who Andy observed out of the corner of his eye, but once she turned to him and placed her hand on his shoulder, they were alone.

"Doesn't our society gossip bore you?" Maria asked. Andy replied politely that he found it very interesting. She smiled, obviously unconvinced.

"All is not high society, Mr. Bishop," she said mysteriously. "You should come to Vienna. There is much more to Austria than this," she said as she turned her head and looked about the room before returning her gaze to his face.

"This?"

"This. I have read a lot about America, Mr. Bishop."

"Please call me Andy, Countess."

"So informal. Yes, thank you. The countess is my mother. Please call me Maria."

"Thank you."

"It's the American way, isn't it?"

"What is?"

"Calling people by their first names so quickly."

"Is it?"

"Oh yes. Very presumptuous here."

"Sorry."

"Don't be. I like it. So personal. I would like to go to America someday. So far away."

"Your English is very good. At home, you would be mistaken for British."

"Really? Not many Americans visit Austria, so I suppose we learn it that way. Your German is very good, may I say?"

"Thank you, but I'm sure I wouldn't be mistaken for an Austrian." She laughed.

"Yes, perhaps from the Rhineland, I think. Perhaps from Bonn, I would guess. Was your teacher from there?"

The orchestra was in full swing now, beating out the rhythm of the Künstlerleben as they swirled around the dance floor. She danced effortlessly, taking his lead, light as a feather. Her perfume, sweet and floral. Then it ended. A shallow curtsy from her, a bow from him, and then back to the table.

"As I say, Austria is not all about aristocracy and privilege," Maria continued as he escorted her to her seat. "Vienna is quite different. Very radical in some respects. Why don't you come and see for yourself?"

"I will."

Andy could not help but notice that, while Ernst and Johann seemed locked in some animated conversation, Rudi watched them dance the entire time, nodding and smiling when Andy caught his eye. Ernst had joined the table and a lively discussion was underway with Johann. Maria ignored the two men and continued questioning Andy about his life in America, his education, his thoughts about politics and history. Andy found himself enthusiastically describing it all to her and then asking her to compare it with life in Austria. Rudi joined in at times, also ignoring the conversation between Ernst and Johann, but there came a point where Andy felt that it would be rude to ignore the others and started paying attention to them.

"They would be crazy to start a war with us," Ernst was saying. "We would crush the Serbs in no time. We were just talking about this yesterday at dinner."

"They were crazy enough to attack the Turkish Empire two years ago and they won that war. They're a tough bunch, aren't they?" Johann rejoined.

"Oh, politics now," said Maria.

"No, please, go on," Andy said. "What are you talking about?"

"We're about to conduct our annual maneuvers next week in Bosnia," Johann replied, lighting a cigarette. "As a matter of fact, I'm leaving for Vienna tomorrow to get my gear and I leave for Sarajevo in a week. The army gathers twice a year for training and maneuvers at some place in the empire. This summer, it was decided to hold the maneuvers in Bosnia. We were talking about the Serbs."

"Johann is being modest," said Ernst. "He's not telling you that he is an aide-de-camp to Franz Ferdinand. There's been so much fighting in the Balkans these past couple of years, Johann. Isn't it a bit provocative to have the army so close to the Balkans and Serbia with what has been going on?" A waiter refilled their glasses with champagne.

"I suppose so," Johann replied, exhaling a cloud of smoke. "You must remember, though, the army must train for a war under the circumstances it might expect to fight one. For us, the Balkans has to be the most likely place so that's probably why the high command selected it this time. The provocations from Serbia never stop. Since they came out on top in the war with Bulgaria last year, they're very cocky and we have to be ready for them."

"Maria and I used to play together when we were in kindergarten, didn't we?" Rudi said, casting a sly smile in Maria's direction and changing the direction of the conversation. She returned it with an affectionate smile and a nod.

"Yes, Rudi used to get me into trouble," Maria said.

"Does that surprise you?" Maria asked Andy in a casually sarcastic voice.

"Not at all," Andy replied, also joining in the smiles. That Rudi's devil-may-care attitude went back to childhood was certainly believable.

"Yes, and he still would if you let him," Ernst pointed out, and then continued, "As I was saying ..."

Andy wondered how he could describe it all to his father in a letter. It was almost impossible. He was contemplating the words he might use when Otto put his hand on Andy's shoulder.

"Are you enjoying yourself?" asked Otto.

"Very much," Andy replied. "I was just getting an education in Austrian politics and international affairs," he said, nodding toward the others at the table who smiled in reply. "I had no idea things were so ... complicated."

"Well, America is very far away, isn't it?" Otto replied gently. "Most Austrians know little about your country except what some of us read in the newspapers. America beckons to many of our poor as a place to go to get rich and where everyone is equal. Millions of our people have gone to the United States to seek their fortunes, but when they get there, it's quite different than what they thought, isn't it?"

"I'm not sure what you mean," said Andy.

"I mean, they're not equal. It's sort of an illusion, isn't it?"

"No, everyone is equal before the law in the United States."

"Are you sure about that?"

"Yes, the Constitution requires it."

"Here too. The Edict of Toleration. Kaiser Josef II signed it in the 1700s, but it's not happened here yet. Anti-Semitism in Vienna, for example. I think our countries are very similar that way."

"When I went to the United States a few years ago, I saw in New York the way that the immigrants were welcomed there. It was very hard for them. It seemed that the Americans did not really want them and were afraid of the immigrants taking over their country. They weren't getting rich and they weren't equal. The Jews from Russia. The black ones that live in the South. The Indians in the West. We both struggle with our different races and nationalities and what to do with them. This century, the different races are either going to massacre each other or learn to live with each other, don't you think?"

The party in the private dining room at Luchow's went on for several hours. Andy danced with Maria again. Strangely, Johann did not.

"You waltz well, Andy."

"Thank you."

"And so how long will you be here—in Salzburg, I mean?"

"Not much longer. I think we are leaving for Vienna in a day or two."

"As am I. I do hope you'll call. Rudi knows where I live. It would be very nice to see you again and learn more about America. I have very definite ideas about your country."

"Really? I wouldn't think …"

"Oh, yes. An egalitarian society, isn't it? No nobility. No royalty. Democratic government for all. It has a great interest for me."

Andy could not quite understand why Maria, an aristocrat herself, would have such enthusiasm for his country and this intrigued him.

"I would be delighted to call and will be sure to ask Rudi about it."

"I'll look forward to it, then."

With that, they whirled about the floor for quite a while. It was not until long after midnight that they parted. Andy had enjoyed himself immensely and thought that he would very much like to call upon Maria when he came to Vienna.

3.

Maria and Johann

Back in Vienna, intrusive thoughts of Andy Bishop and the evening at Luchow's played out in Maria's mind as she walked in the garden of the courtyard of her mother's townhouse on the *Landstrasse-Hauptstrasse*. Thoughts that she shouldn't be having had insistently played on her mind since that night. It wasn't just how handsome Andy was, although he certainly was that. His eyes were beautiful. He danced wonderfully. It wasn't just that he was an American, although that had intrigued her too. She had listened with intense interest to his description of his life in America that confirmed in her mind everything she had ever thought about that country. He had listened to her with what appeared to be rapt attention and seemed just as curious about life in Austria. His interest in the Old World from his American perspective was charming.

But it wasn't those things. It was a combination of things, she thought, that kept her thinking of that night. It was that he seemed to be genuinely interested in what she thought and had to say. Her chance encounter with Andy Bishop aroused once again in her mind the wisdom of having accepted Johann's proposal of marriage.

An American in Vienna

For her mother, it was a match made in heaven, Maria knew. The Caboga family was immensely rich and titled. The von Montforts, also titled, were nearly impoverished. Heavy drinking, gambling, and a series of business reversals from risky investments by her father had reduced their family to a life of camouflage and subterfuge to obscure the fact that the von Montforts were practically bankrupt. Then he had suddenly died.

Social invitations had to be declined because the widowed Countess Julia von Montfort could no longer keep up. She could not afford the cost of the dresses, chauffeured automobiles, and other requirements of Austrian high society. Diamonds and other jewelry had been sold off to pay for basic household expenses. The jewelry Maria had worn the other night had been borrowed from a friend. Servants had been dismissed one by one until they were left with a single housekeeper and a yardman. Their home in Vienna was heavily mortgaged now and eventually the money would run out altogether. When Johann began courting Maria, the Countess von Montfort had sunk to her knees in thanksgiving and her daughter's engagement seemed the answer to her prayers.

Maria felt compelled to accept Johann's advances—and eventually his proposal of marriage—without real love for him. Like Rudi, she had known Johann since childhood, yet Johann knew nothing of her inner thoughts nor had he ever really tried to understand her. Maria was sure that he was marrying her because she was beautiful, of suitable class standing, and because it was the right thing to do for an officer in this stage of life. And then there were the rumors about him.

While Johann had always been correct and a gentleman in courting her, she had come to know that there was another side to him that he was at pains to conceal. The knowing looks she sometimes caught in the eyes of other women at social gatherings. The worried advice of some of her friends who had heard this and that.

Maria knew that she had acquired very radical views of society from her forced immersion into the simmering pot of working-class Vienna that her family's poverty had brought into her consciousness. Her attitudes were nothing short of antithetical to Johann's inbred, aristocratic outlook. Often nowadays, dressed at home in plain middle-class attire, she worked with the servants. She shopped for groceries. She rode the streetcars of Vienna and mixed with the working classes. She read radical socialist newspapers that opened her eyes to the other side of Vienna who lived and toiled beneath the gilded, imperial façade.

Suddenly, Maria realized that her mother had stepped out into the courtyard. As she approached, Maria felt a fleeting guilt that she had been thinking things that would have appalled her mother, had she known. Her mother looked tired, as she so often did these days, even though it was only ten o'clock in the morning.

"Good morning, my sweetheart," Julia von Montfort said, kissing her daughter on her cheek. "Will you be going out today?"

"I think so, Mother. Do we need anything?"

"Not today, I think. It may rain. Be sure to take an umbrella."

"I will. I thought I would take a walk in the *Stadtpark* today. Would you like to come with me?"

"No, thank you, my dear. I'm expecting my friend Erika to come by in a little while. Listen, while you are here, I had an idea about your wedding …"

There followed another discussion of wedding details. As her mother went on, Maria thought again about her situation. Countess von Montfort simply could not afford the kind of social wedding that a marriage such as this would inevitably require. Fortunately, Countess von Caboga was aware of the situation and had discreetly offered to pay for an appropriate wedding.

The families had known one another all their lives. The late Graf von Caboga and the equally late Graf von Montfort had known each other since serving as officers together in the same cavalry regiment. The families had often vacationed together in Italy. When Maria's father had faltered, his old friend had intervened on more than one occasion with loans from his immense fortune. Loans that the Graf von Caboga knew full well could never be repaid. Countess von Caboga had graciously extended the same generosity *in extremis*, if only to ensure that her son was suitably wed.

"The invitations must be engraved, of course ..."

It was dreadful to contemplate, Maria thought, as her mother continued with new details that had occurred to her since their last conversation on the subject. She couldn't bear to disagree with anything that her mother suggested. This would be the last time that her mother would even seemingly be in charge of a major social spectacle in Viennese society. Her last hurrah. It was pathetic.

Julia von Montfort still lived in an unreal world of balls and court functions like those of "her day" when, after Austria's humiliating defeat in the Prussian War of 1866 and the near-collapse of the empire when it had to be divided with the dreadful Hungarians, it was all that Viennese society had to cling to. Despite her husband's debts and premature death, appearances had to be kept up. Her inner struggle between the reality of her declining fortunes and the need to pretend otherwise had worn her down as Maria had watched and grieved for her. Her coming marriage was the only way out.

As a teenager, Maria had quickly grasped the situation after the shock of her father's death had receded into a dull ache. She had come not only to accept the new reality, but also to embrace it. She resented the heavy weight of pretension that burdened her mother and, if only in her mind, threw it away with a vengeance. She couldn't bring herself to openly revolt against what she perceived as the stifling social conventions of society for her mother's sake, though, and this was her own special burden. One that had led to this impending debacle, she thought.

"Oh, the flowers. Yes, I made some inquires about that too. What do you think of …?"

To run away from it all, Maria thought, as she nodded at her mother's newest idea. To run far, far away. America. She had read much about America. Titles of nobility were illegal there. It was in the Constitution. A modern country with modern ideas. Millions and millions of people in Europe had fled the old continent to be a part of it all. Why not?

Was the appearance of Andy Bishop at this moment of her life just a coincidence? When Rudi had told her about the discovery of the lost American "cousins," she had wanted to know all about it. Rudi had promised her that he would introduce her to his cousin and he had kept his word. Rudi knew everything. He had told her not to do it, but what could she do? How many conversations had they had about it? It all came back to the same thing. She had to do it.

There were lots of women who envied her. She knew that. And she didn't dislike Johann. He had some fine qualities. He was very handsome. He was a good soldier, she knew, with a promising career. He was quite a prize, really. She knew that, yes. Perhaps she could grow to love him in time, couldn't she? No. She knew that she never would. But it wouldn't be a bad life. Wealth and prestige. Perhaps her children would be the salvation, but no. They would grow up just like him. *Oh, God, help me,* she thought.

"Well, you had better be going, my dear. Remember to take an umbrella. As I said, I think it's going to rain."

An American in Vienna

In Bad Ischl, Johann's valet had just completed packing his master's baggage in his room. As Johann smoothed his hair with his hands in front of the mirror, his mother knocked on the door and entered the room.

"I see you are about to leave for Vienna," the countess began in a cool tone. Patrician to the core, Margaretha, the countess von Caboga, was a taciturn woman who thought much, but said little. Widowed in the past year, she wore black with black beads and a crucifix, which contrasted with her fair complexion and white hair. Johann knew that she had something on her mind.

"Yes, I'm going on the one o'clock train."

"And when you arrive?"

"I'll be in Vienna for a few days, and then I have to report for duty at Philipovic."

"And while you're in Vienna, what will you do there?"

"I suppose I'll spend some time with my friends before I have to go. Why?" Johann could sense that his mother's probing was leading to something. Something unpleasant. She sat down in a chair as Johann stood before the mirror, flicking off some specks of lint from his uniform, real or imaginary, as he waited for his mother's reply.

"I have heard some things about you. About how you spend your leisure time. About this woman …"

"Oh, is that what this is all about?"

"If I've heard these things, then others have heard them. You have been indiscreet."

"Indiscreet, Mother?"

"Yes, indiscreet. As your mother, I should probably be the last to know of any indiscretions. The fact that I know means to me that others know. It was one thing when you were younger, but you're the head of this house now, an officer in the service of His Imperial and Royal Highness, and you're soon to be married. It can't go on. Whoever it is, you must give her up."

It was rare for the countess to speak to her only son

this way. Johann knew that. The inflection of her voice rose as she finished, and he could see the determination in her clenched teeth and narrowed eyes. It would be pointless to directly contradict her and, in any event, it was true.

"I have no intention of seeing her, Mother. Put it out of your mind. I'm going to meet Rudi and Ernst and their American cousin and show him Vienna for a few days. Put your mind at ease. Nothing is going to happen."

"I didn't mean just today," the countess continued. Johann looked back at her, but did not respond.

His propensity to consort with disreputable women was something the countess knew too much about. She wanted to believe him, but nothing he could say would truly allay her suspicions. Yet what could she do? He was a grown man and an officer. Her husband was not there to put things right and she was just a woman, for all her aristocratic position. She grasped his face in her hands and gave him a kiss.

"You must think more about your position, your honor, our family's honor. Now is not the time to consort with these ... women," she said. "Maria is a beautiful woman who, God willing, will provide you with children and be everything you should ever need. You will soon be married. It was one thing before, but now, it would be disgraceful. You can see that, can't you?"

Johann saw the earnest look in his mother's eyes and, as always, wanted to please her, but could he? This was one task too far that his mother was setting for him. She couldn't know how he felt. Best to temporize and do the best that he could. "I'll be back in three weeks when the maneuvers are over. I'll take a train from Sarajevo directly back here. I'll be back before you know it. Now don't worry."

He gently kissed her on both cheeks and nodded to his valet who picked up his bags and followed him out the door. The driver was waiting with the Daimler at the front door. As soon as the bags were put in the trunk, he got in the car and waved to his mother. She came down the steps to give him a final kiss good-bye.

"Johann, remember what I said. If you fall into sin, you must be discreet. Confess your sins to God and ask his forgiveness and for the strength to resist temptation. He will answer your prayers." The countess had always been faithful, but her need for comfort from the Church since her husband's death had become pious. She could be seen praying at the Church of St. Nicholas in Bad Ischl in the early hours of the morning nearly every day. Johann did not seek comfort from the Church.

An hour later, Johann was aboard the train headed for Vienna. As the train rocked along toward the capital, he felt guilt at lying to his mother about his intentions for the evening. He was such a degenerate. His father would have been appalled. He wouldn't have dared. *It wasn't too late*, he thought. He could still call it all off. Why couldn't he help himself? Well, maybe she wouldn't come and that would be it. She might not be able to get away. They might be seen. What about that? He must be careful. Very careful. So much gossip in Vienna.

The small towns and villages that foretold the approach to the *Westbahnhof* train station in Vienna were soon passing by and he began to go over in his mind the arrangements that he had made with Ivanna by telephone a few days earlier. She was the wife of the Serbian consul general in Vienna. They had met at one of the masked balls in January that populated the social calendar in Vienna after Christmas.

Sparks had flown almost immediately when he met her and when he was introduced to her fat, bald, and much older husband, he could understand her reciprocal interest in him. He had lured her discreetly into his bed at the family residence in Vienna late one night after a covert rendezvous at a *kaffeehaus* near the Hofburg Palace. She devoured him that night and left him burning for more of her. He would meet Ivanna at the Imperial Hotel later that evening for wine and dinner with every hope of continuing his debauchery with her.

When he arrived at the house, the servants were downstairs eating their dinner and surprised at his arrival. He bid them pay him no notice and took his bag upstairs to his room himself. A few minutes later, he was out the door, hailing a cab that took him to the hotel a few minutes early.

He had shed his uniform and changed into the anonymous clothes of a bourgeois gentleman to avoid any undue notice in public. He scanned the lobby and went into the restaurant, not noticing any acquaintances who could cause any awkwardness or difficulties. He had a drink while he waited. Would she still come? Or had she had second thoughts? There she was.

Johann guided her to a table and began with small talk. She was ravishing. The candlelight gave her a particularly soft glow and accentuated her beautiful skin. Her dark hair and eyes shined and as they talked, he took in all of her qualities. Vivacious and frivolous, she chattered and sparkled. The tinkling sound of her laughter amused him and she was easily amused by Johann. If there was a sad story to her marriage, Johann heard little of it. She flattered him and distracted him from his cares.

Dinner followed champagne. Music played softly in the background as their conversation flowed. She made him laugh with little stories of her day and the foibles of some of their mutual acquaintances. He was as charming as his education, wealth, and breeding had taught him to be and, as on previous occasions, she seemed as taken with him as he was with her. Conversation turned to his imminent departure to Sarajevo.

She was impressed with his close connection with Archduke Franz Ferdinand and his responsibility for his security in Sarajevo. And when exactly was he going to Sarajevo? What would the archduke do when he got there?

A procession? How appropriate. What day would that be? Would he ride horseback or in a car? Yes, a car would be so much more fashionable these days. Not a carriage. On open car? Of course, so the people could see him. And his wife too? The people would love it. Yes, that would be the best way to be seen. A procession? Sarajevo was a lovely old town. What route would he take to be seen? Yes, it would be wonderful.

They got into the cab without discussing their destination, but when he told the cabbie to bring them to the Caboga house in the first district, she caught his eye for a moment and then smiled. They both knew what was going to happen. As the cab rolled through the now dark and emptying streets, he leaned toward her and pressed his mouth to hers. Her mouth was soft and warm as their tongues softly touched and he could feel himself becoming aroused. His arms and hands pulled her tightly to him. He could hear her breathing while the cab rolled over the cobblestones.

Once again, Johann spirited Ivanna through one of the side doors to a back staircase of the mansion that led to his room. He knew that by now the servants would all have gone to bed and, in any event, would say nothing to his mother for fear of their jobs. The house was dark. Johann held Ivanna's hand as he guided her to the stairway and up with no sound but the rustling of her dress.

The windows were heavily draped with curtains, but the moonlight and streetlamps glowed dimly into the spacious room, illuminating the various pieces of heavy furniture, including Johann's massive antique bed at the far end of the room. He decided not to turn on the electric light, but lit a single candle on the nightstand next to the bed. Ivanna drifted to one of the large floor-to-ceiling windows that opened out onto a balcony that, in turn, overlooked an interior courtyard.

As he blew out the match, he turned to see her looking out

the window. She turned her head toward him and their eyes met. The quiet and candlelight made it seem as though time had been suspended. They could have been standing in the same room one hundred or even two hundred years earlier and, in that light, little would have appeared differently. She looked even more beautiful than in the restaurant and he had to have her now.

He removed his coat and tie and threw them on a small couch at the foot of the bed as she gazed at him. The room was warm—or was it the hot desire for her now coursing through his body? His heart was pounding as she continued to stand motionless, watching him undress. Slowly he padded toward her, naked. His arms enveloped her. He peeled her clothes from her body, one by one.

After several hours, utterly exhausted, they both fell into a deep sleep until Johann heard servants stirring downstairs and noticed the light coming in through the window. He wondered what time it was and looked over at the sleeping woman next to him. She was breathing deeply. Slowly he rolled himself out of the huge bed and pulled on slacks and a shirt. Tiptoeing out the door, he looked over his shoulder to take a last look at her beautiful body sprawled on the bed. She was still sleeping as he closed the door behind him quietly to prepare for the day ahead.

4.

The City of Dreams

Andy lifted a cup of tea to his mouth and gazed out the window of the train as it rolled through the countryside of *Öberösterreich* or Upper Austria. They had just passed the city of Wels and would soon pull into Linz on the way to Vienna. They had left Bad Ischl on the early train to be able to stop for lunch in Melk and tour its magnificent monastery. The mountains had receded into rolling foothills and pastoral countryside and it was a beautiful, early summer day. They had been talking about their plans to begin seeing the sights of Vienna for twenty minutes when Andy brought up Maria's invitation to call.

"Yes, by all means," Rudi said with some enthusiasm. "We must get Maria involved in your introduction to Vienna. She might show you some things that are a little 'off the beaten path.' Isn't that how you say it in English?" Rudi had persuaded Andy to let him practice his English with him at times and they had been doing so on the train ride.

"Yes, that's how we say it," Andy replied. "But how so? What do you mean?"

"I don't think she would mind my telling you this. Maria is not what you would call a conventional Austrian woman of her class. I'd like to think I'm not either, but with her, it's certain."

"How so?"

"As she told you, we have been friends since we were children," Rudi continued. "I don't agree with all her opinions, but I know how she thinks and it's the same for her with me. You understand?" Andy nodded, anxious for the revelation to come. "She actually has bad feelings for the way things are in the Monarchy. She likes to read. A lot more than most women I know. She's become very interested in Marx, for example. You know Marx?"

Andy knew a little about Marx, the father of socialism whose beliefs were widely discussed back home in the German village. He had often heard his friends' fathers debating his radical ideas. He nodded again.

"And Freud. Another one of her favorites. She thinks people like these have opened the door to the truth of our times and the time to come. Take Freud for example. Sexual hypocrisy in Vienna is about the same as it is everywhere in Europe, I suppose, only with a heavy Catholic tinge. Outwardly, sex before or without marriage is simply not discussed here. A dire sin. And a child out of wedlock is a supreme disgrace. Yet prostitution has been legal in Vienna since 1879. Freud has scandalized our polite society by openly discussing suppressed sexual desire that finds its way out in behavior one way or another. Repressed gratification, illicit sex, guilt, and scandal, that sort of thing. It's as Viennese as strudel." Rudi smiled, taking in his friend's obvious surprise.

"And then there's her taste in art. Everyone sees the Baroque masterpieces in the museums in Vienna, but that's not the sort of thing people are talking about today. Do you know Klimt? Or, even better, Egon Schiele? He's a friend of mine."

"I haven't heard of them," Andy replied.

"No, of course you haven't. You probably wouldn't.

Klimt is famous and has done quite a bit of work in Vienna that you might see, like the murals in the Burgtheater. He got the Golden Order of Merit from the kaiser for that. But much of his work is not seen so much in public because it is so 'sexual.' He got into trouble when he was commissioned to paint the ceiling of the University of Vienna. Too erotic, the people said. There was an outcry and, since then, he has accepted no more commissions. Schiele, now he's taken it even further. Pornographic, they say. Such a pity. Anyway, that's the kind of thing that intrigues Maria. And me too, I should say."

"So what are you saying? You and Maria have a taste for erotic art?"

"Not really. It's not that. It's a distaste for the old ways. It's a conflict, I suppose, between the conventions of the aristocrats and the bourgeoisie, on the one hand, and the artists and the ordinary people on the other. Maria was born into privilege and aristocracy, and so was I. But then again, we use our minds. We're open to the new ideas. They are not. It won't be like this forever, Andy."

Andy thought about what Rudi had revealed, both about himself and Maria. Her remarks while dancing at Luchow's began to make sense to him. Looks could certainly be deceiving. That night, she had looked like a fairy princess to his American eyes. Only the tiara had been missing. This pretty book was not like its cover. Could there be more?

Melk was an unusual city, Andy noticed after they arrived. He and Rudi wandered through the town with the intention of visiting the monastery for which it was famous. It was a river city, nestled on the Danube in *Niederösterreich*, or Lower Austria. Its famous Benedictine abbey, however, was perched on a rocky cliff overlooking the river and the city. Built in the early eighteenth century in the Baroque style, its ornate façade with green bulbous steeples and dome radiated the splendor and wealth of the Catholic Church of that era in Austria, Rudi remarked. The interior of the abbey, its library, and church were beyond description. Gilded gold. Fabulous ceiling paintings. Frescoes. The light pouring through the high dome windows emphasized the enormous space within the Church of the Abbey.

After their tour of the abbey, they had a late lunch at a café by the Danube and the conversation from the train was casually reintroduced by Andy.

"What about Johann and Maria? How did they get together? It seems from what you've told me that they wouldn't be a very likely match. You knew Johann from childhood too, didn't you?"

"Oh, yes," Rudi replied between munches on his bratwurst sandwich and occasional swigs of the local ale. "But not so much as my brother, Ernst. They were more the same age and, as you have seen, much more alike. My brother, well …" Rudi paused, seemed to think better of something, and then continued. "But yes, an unlikely match, Maria and Johann. In some ways, but not in others. Our families have always been close. In Austria, that counts for something. The known. The safe. Especially in high-born families and, there you have it."

"But does she love him?"

Rudi shrugged. "She says she does, but I think, if so, she's kidding herself. I told her that." Rudi gazed at him for a moment, not taking his eyes off Andy as he took another swig of beer.

Andy was surprised. Even in their own generation, time and tradition was felt here. The weight of expectations.

"You don't think so?"

"She likes him. She respects him and understands him. How could she not? Maybe it will work out. One hopes," Rudi finished.

An American in Vienna

Andy was given his own bedroom on the second floor of the Windischgrätz residence in the ancient *Innere Stadt*, or "old city." The Windischgrätz *Residenz* was made of stone and plaster masonry and had stood for centuries. It was a work of art in its own right with stone cornices over the windows and doors and black cast-iron balconies. Floor-to-ceiling windows in casements that opened and closed like doors were often open to the streets in the June weather with servants shaking out mops and carpets as Andy walked by. This was where the Rudi and Ernst had grown up, Andy marveled.

> Dear Mom and Dad,
>
> As you can see, the typewriter made it through the whole ordeal just fine. I have now arrived in Vienna and what a splendid city it is.
> At night, the lamplights make the streets of Vienna seem timeless and eternal, especially when the clip-clop of horses can be heard on the cobblestone streets, pulling a carriage or landau, its riders tipping their hats or nodding to acquaintances they pass. There are far more cars here than horses, however, unlike the small towns of Austria that I have seen so far.
> Evenings are spent by society here in cafés, restaurants, bars, and hotels when they are not attending nightly operas and concerts. The Hotel Sacher is a particular favorite of my hosts. Madame Sacher herself sat at our table once for a few minutes and is known to smoke cigars! I visited the Prater a couple days ago with Rudi, Ernst, and Maria. It is the greatest park in Vienna in size with a giant Ferris wheel built in 1897 for the kaiser's Golden Jubilee.
> The highlight of the trip so far, though, was my private visit to the Hofburg Palace arranged by Elisabeth. This complex of buildings is so enormous and ornate that I cannot do justice to it in this letter, but that was not all. Toward the end of my tour, late in the afternoon, the sound of music from a

military band could be distinctly heard deep inside the palace where we were. Elisabeth knew what it was and asked me to come quickly with her.

We walked down many corridors. Elisabeth, of course, knew her way. I wasn't sure where she was taking me, but at last we reached a corridor with two uniformed guards. They immediately stiffened to attention on seeing her and let us pass. There was another door and more guards to pass. Then we were in an ornate, paneled study. The sound of the drums was now very distinct and coming from doors that opened out onto a balcony. On the balcony, his back to us, was the emperor watching the changing of His Majesty's Hungarian Guard.

There was another man in the room as Elisabeth motioned me to come with her as she walked toward the balcony. He turned out to be Prince Montenuovo, the kaiser's chamberlain, who partially bowed, smiling at the sight of us, and not the least disturbed at our sudden appearance. The kaiser must not have heard the door open and close, or else the noise from the courtyard below distracted him, because he was unaware of our presence until Elisabeth lightly placed her hand on his back in partial embrace.

The emperor was in a military tunic that was surprisingly plain, with his hands resting on the balustrade of the balcony. He turned and smiled as Elisabeth greeted him and he gave her a little, affectionate kiss on her cheek, which she returned. I had waited in the room, unprepared for this moment and feeling a little over my head. Soon, however, after a few words from Elisabeth, I saw the emperor turn away from the courtyard to regard me, about ten feet away.

Momentarily, I did not know what to do. Etiquette is very precise and formal here and I did not want to make a blunder. Elisabeth seemed to sense my hesitation and rescued the situation. We were introduced. Elisabeth told me later that the kaiser does not shake hands and disapproves of the practice, except among his most intimate friends, but he shook mine. I think it was because I was an American and he knows that is our custom. If I had been Austrian, I think I would have been expected to nearly prostrate myself before him, so it was a little unnerving.

The kaiser is an elderly man, to be sure, and he moves slowly, but with great dignity. He remained standing and politely asked how I was enjoying my visit with his dear granddaughter. I made the most fulsome reply I could imagine, to which he patiently listened. His face is heavily lined, showing his great age. His eyes are blue with heavy eyelids, which give him the look of bemused watchfulness.

I must admit, time seemed to stand still for me. It was hard to believe that I, a young man from Ohio, was standing face-to-face with one of the great lords of Europe. I felt anxious that the conversation must end soon, not because I wanted it, but because I felt my presence there must be an imposition. To my surprise, the emperor was quite willing to talk to me and Elisabeth for several minutes until Montenuovo cleared his throat, suggesting, I suppose, that they needed to get back to the papers on the emperor's desk, at which point, he cheerily bade us good-bye and wished me well …

Figlmüller's was a restaurant in the old city, near St. Stephen's cathedral. It was a very busy restaurant and they had been required to wait for a table large enough to seat Rudi, Ernst, Johann, Maria, and Andy. They had walked and walked around the old city and the *Ringstrasse*, the main street of Vienna that enclosed it, shaped like an octagon. It had been a good day and it was a relief to sit down.

Johann and Andy, who had not had much time to talk in Salzburg, had gotten to know one another much better in Vienna. None of Andy's new friends had been to America and their interest in comparing the two countries and societies had occupied a number of late-night sessions at cafés or the drawing rooms of their houses in Vienna. Another one began at their table over dinner.

"Well, it's not a monarchy like Russia. We don't have secret police round every corner, pogroms against Jews, and that sort of thing," said Johann.

"Censorship. We have that," Rudi rejoined. "And if the kaiser wants, he can do almost anything, legally. It's not like England. We have a parliament, but the kaiser can veto anything and, if he declares an emergency, he can do anything the Parliament can do."

"I'm not saying it's like England," Johann replied. "I'm just saying it may be different than what Andy thinks. What do you think, Andy?"

"I thought in a monarchy the king could do whatever he wanted, so I'm not surprised. In America, the people wouldn't accept it. They would ask why a man should be the leader of the country just because of his birth. It goes against our revolution and the reason our country became a republic."

Andy enjoyed these discussions. From them, he learned about the city and the country of his ancestors in a way no tourist could have. The friendships that he had made since Salzburg ripened as the days went by and he learned more about them and the curious society in which they lived.

Ernst was like his mother, conservative in politics and cautious. He was slow to say anything at first in the freewheeling discussions, preferring to listen and weigh in with a few carefully considered words after the conversation was well underway. He was watchful over his younger brother, but exasperated at times with Rudi's impetuous nature. An officer like Johann, Ernst took his military duties seriously and often wore his uniform when others did not. He seemed to find comfort in the military world of black and white and his opinions often were categorical and intransigent. Unfailingly polite to the point of awkward formality at times, he seemed to have inherited the Habsburg penchant for aloofness and was slow to show any emotion or affection.

Rudi was, of course, the gregarious extrovert in Andy's circle. Unconventional, rambunctious, amusing, and even reckless at times, he was the first to bring up a controversial subject, have his say, and then argue his side of it. He enjoyed being provocative and, at times, Andy guessed that his opinions were ventured more to get a reaction than from conviction. The taboo and forbidden in anything exerted a magnetic pull and, not surprisingly, he was often on the receiving end of an icy stare from his mother or "a word" with his father.

Johann was perhaps the most interesting of all, Andy thought as the days went by. Like Ernst, he was the heir to an ancient aristocratic house. Unlike Ernst, he had already come into his inheritance with the death of his father. His witty comments about Austrian politics and society were usually funny, but they also made it difficult to tell what he really thought.

In social matters, he could at times be casually snobbish. Rudi was often the subject of his dry barbs. In politics, Andy had worked out that Johann was a monarchist, but of the Franz Ferdinand variety. Anxious to "get on with it," his impatience with the elderly kaiser's static policies often came out in their conversations. Andy observed real passion one evening when Prince Montenuovo and what Johann regarded as petty court protocol were mentioned. In this, he was iconoclastic, but only because it so often involved the archduke, to whom he was devoted.

In art and music, his tastes were as orthodox as one might expect from a military mind. Debates over Rudi's taste in art, in which Maria came to his defense, had been the subject of a lively verbal brawl on another evening. Biting sarcasm delivered by Johann and Ernst were met with equal measures of ridicule from Rudi and Maria—to Andy's great amusement.

Ernst weighed in. "I don't think parliaments are so great. Look at ours. The more democratic we become, the more the chaos. How many times has the kaiser had to rule by decree when Parliament is hopelessly deadlocked? Parliaments are overrated." Johann agreed.

"I agree, our parliament's been disgraceful when it comes to the bickering with the Czechs and all that, but we've only had universal suffrage for seven years. England and America have had it for a hundred. Give it some time," Rudi countered.

"And then the socialists will take over," Johann replied. Andy looked at Maria and, to his surprise, found her looking back at him with this comment. She was watching his reaction as much as he was watching hers. Neither said anything, leaving it to Rudi to carry on the battle, but she knew, Andy thought. She knew that he knew with that look.

The evening before Johann left for Sarajevo, Andy invited Maria to join him and the Windischgrätz brothers the following day on a tour of the Central Cemetery or *Zentralfriedhof* where Beethoven, Schubert, Brahms, and other famous people were buried. She had declined, but invited him to call at her house in a few days to meet her mother.

A few days later, Andy found himself walking in the seventh district in Vienna, known as Neubau. He had decided to take some time to be by himself in the city and had reached the *Mariahilferstrasse*, a street full of shops and stores. He had been walking for several hours when he spotted an inviting *kaffeehaus* and decided to enter.

As the door closed, Andy smelled the aroma of pipe smoke and coffee. It had become so familiar after only a week in the capital. An elderly man was reading a newspaper that was affixed to a cane that had rested in a rack for this purpose. Conversation at a marble-topped table in the corner. A student hunched over papers scattered about on his table. A waiter in a black vest and bow tie appeared. What would the young man like? A mélange? Certainly. Andy had discovered the mélange since his arrival. It was like a café au lait, only with frothy foam on top. A glass of water came with it, gratis.

Andy gazed out the window of the café. A woman with a large hat holding a young girl's hand passed. A landau with two horses clopped by. Suddenly, a woman caught his eye. It was Maria. He was sure of it. He bolted out of his chair and out the door, calling her name. She turned, surprised, and for a moment, seemed not to recognize him. Then she smiled and came toward him.

"What are you doing here?" she asked, taking his hand. A kiss on both cheeks.

"I'm just walking around on my own today. I had just sat down at this café when I saw you. Why don't you join me?"

She seemed to hesitate at first. "Well, yes. I guess I could. For a few minutes," she said, and followed him into the café. They sat down together. Again the waiter. A *Kapuziner* this time, *bitte*. Andy noticed how plainly dressed she was. She noticed his glance and smoothed out her dress.

"I was doing some shopping," she said matter-of-factly. She didn't seem embarrassed, simply conscious of his awareness. Maria hesitated a moment and then seemed to make a decision.

"Actually, Andy, may I be honest with you? We are friends, aren't we?" she said with a wry smile.

"Of course we are, Maria. I mean, I would like to be your friend. Very much," Andy blurted out.

She told him the truth about her family. He listened as she recounted the financial reversals that her father had sustained and how she and her mother had lived the past few years in the growing fear that they would soon be impoverished, while trying to keep up the appearances of aristocracy.

"It hasn't been all bad for me, Andy. You remember what I said to you in Salzburg? That all is not high society? What I meant was that I've come to know so much more about the way things really are since . . . we had to begin taking care of ourselves."

"What do you mean?"

"You're seeing the tourists' Vienna, Andy. The part that everyone who visits wants to see, of course. When I was a girl, I saw what you see. The palaces. The parks and gardens. I attended the balls. Now I see another side. There's much more here than meets the eye of the tourist or the eyes of high society."

"What other side? I know that there are ordinary people who live here. I can see that. I know that I'm not staying in the working-class part of the city, but every city is like that."

"That's not what I meant."

"What did you mean, then?"

"I meant that there is another society in Vienna. A society that is more interesting than you could imagine," she said with enthusiasm. "I've been learning about it in bits and pieces myself for the last year or so."

"Please, tell me about it." Andy wanted to hear it from her lips.

She had met Viktor Adler. Did he know who he was? The leader of the Austrian Socialist Party. In a café just like this one. She had learned about Karl Marx. She talked about the radical side of Vienna that roiled beneath the veneer of imperial splendor and power that she had discovered at first by chance and then purposefully. The artists and intellectuals who lived in the shadows of the imposing buildings and beyond the view of the barons, archdukes, and their liveried servants in the cars and carriages on the Ringstrasse. A half an hour went by, and then an hour. Andy listened and watched the enthusiasm with which she recounted her little discoveries, one by one. Discoveries about Vienna, to be sure, but discoveries about herself as well.

"Look at the time!" Maria said eventually. "I have to go, Andy. I have an idea. What are you doing tomorrow evening?" Maria asked as she stood to leave.

"Andy, I would like you to meet one of my favorite people, Stefan Zweig," said Maria the moment that they walked into the Café Central the following evening.

Stefan Zweig held out his hand and Andy shook it. His hand was soft as was his voice. He had dark hair, closely cut and parted on the right, dark almost black eyes, and an equally full black mustache. Slight of build, in his early thirties, Andy guessed, with long, almost feminine fingers, Zweig smiled shyly at them both, bowing slightly and gesturing for them to sit.

"Andy Bishop."

"Enchanté," Zweig replied. "Please, sit down, both of you, and join me." Zweig was sitting alone at a table. The café looked much like other *kaffehausen* Andy had seen in Vienna. A piano played softly across the room. The clientele made this one like few others in the city, Maria had said on the way there.

"Stefan is a writer, Andy. A very good one, I might add," Maria said as they sat down.

"Tell me about your writing," Andy inquired.

"Ach, a couple of books. I doubt you have heard of them. *Silver Strings. Burning Secret. The Love of Erika Ewald.* Actually, *Erika Ewald* is just a short story."

Andy had not heard of his books or his writing and had to admit it.

"Of course not," Zweig said, smiling amiably. "Not in America. I wouldn't think so. Do you know Arthur Schnitzler or Peter Altenberg or Felix Salten?"

Relieved, Andy was able to say that he had read Schnitzler's play *Anatol* in one of his German classes at Notre Dame

"He's right over there," Zweig said softly with a nod of his head.

Andy turned to see a middle-aged man in his fifties at a nearby table. He was gesturing with his hand to two others seated at his table.

"That's Peter Altenberg, the poet, and Hugo von Hoffmannsthal, the librettist sitting with him." Maria had evidently caught Altenberg's eye. He rose and ambled over to their table, greeting Zweig and bending to kiss Maria's hand.

"Where's Trotsky?" Altenberg asked Zweig, eyebrows raised in mock earnestness.

"I don't know. He'll probably be here soon. Please meet Maria's friend, Andy Bishop, from America."

Altenberg looked him over and then extended his hand. "What brings you to our little café, Mr. Bishop?"

"The lovely lady, of course," Zweig chimed in, nodding at Maria. Andy smiled.

"No argument can be made against that and we like to argue here, Herr Bishop."

"No, but you can argue with Trotsky. Here he is."

The door was closing on two men who looked very much alike except in height and hair. The shorter one had a head of thick brown hair, pince-nez glasses, a mustache, and small goatee. The tall one was bald.

"More Jews here than a synagogue," Altenberg said and winked conspiratorially.

"Ah, Zweig," said the shorter one as he approached. They shook hands, and then turned expectantly to Andy.

"Sit down," said Zweig. "We have an American guest tonight."

"Slumming, I see."

"Andy, this is Leon Trotsky and this is Adolf Joffre."

"Leon is planning a revolution in Russia," Altenberg said with some amusement.

"Somebody's got to do it," Trotsky replied amiably as the waiter arrived.

"Russian revolutionaries are a dime a dozen in Vienna," Altenberg continued. "They dream of a socialist paradise in our cafés while writing pamphlets they send back home where nobody can read." Trotsky laughed out loud. "Ask him how well they're doing."

"How well are you doing?" Andy asked, joining in.

"The Romanovs must think we're doing pretty well. They've chased me out twice and sent Adolf here to Siberia once. Here in Vienna, nobody takes any notice of me."

"Don't be so sure," said Zweig. "I'll be damned if the police don't have a dossier on you."

"Yes, but they're so polite and inefficient here. That's what we all like about Vienna, don't we? And what about you, Mr. Bishop? What brings you here?"

"Maria. She thought I should see another side of Vienna."

"Ah, yes. Maria," Trotsky said, shifting his gaze to her. "My little red countess. I think I have her nearly converted," he said with a smile.

"So charming, you are," Maria replied, a little flirtatiously. Trotsky was a handsome man and, while his Russian accent was certainly detectable, he spoke German very well.

"Leon and Viktor Adler are my teachers in Marxist theory, Andy."

"Nothing but the best for Maria," Altenberg commented. "Pretty soon they'll have Maria carrying a red flag in the streets and all her aristocratic friends will be up in arms. What about that fiancé of yours? I bet he's all for the dictatorship of the proletariat, eh?"

"I'm not converted yet, sir," Maria replied with mock surprise. "I still have some questions, so I haven't said a word to him about it."

"Such as?"

"Such as how it is that the Romanovs and the Habsburgs are going to hand over their crowns to the proletariat?"

"With their heads still attached, I hope," said Joffe, speaking for the first time while relighting his cigar.

"Come, come now," said Altenberg. "The Romanovs I can understand. Bloody Nicholas and all that. But the kaiser? Never. Leave the old man be. He's not hurting anyone."

"We'll take it with or without their heads," said Trotsky.

"Seriously, Leon, your Reds missed their chance in 1905. I thought you might just do it back then, but you blew it. It's too late now. Adler's got it right. You've got to do it democratically. You've got to elect socialists to the Parliament and hope that someday they'll get a majority and throw the capitalists out."

Trotsky snorted. "In Russia? Never. It's got to be a revolution. Like 1789 in Paris. The Romanovs will never give our pathetic parliament any power."

Andy looked around the café as Trotsky and Altenberg traded barbs with each other. There was a buzz in the room. Schnitzler had left the table where he had seen him before and gone to another table where he appeared deep in conversation with some others. More men walked in and were hailed to one table or another. More conversation here and there. They all seemed to know one another and a burst of laughter erupted now and again from one table or another. A haze of cigar and pipe smoke hung in the air. Maria leaned over to him.

"You see what I mean, Andy?"

"Yes, it's very interesting."

"Exactly. And there are more. There are the artists. Schiele and Gustav Klimt. They come in here sometimes. And the psychoanalysts. Dr. Freud and Carl Jung. And the musicians. Arnold Schoenberg, Anton Webern, Alban Berg. Adolf Loos, the architect. Ludwig Wittgenstein, the philosopher. I've met them all here over the past year or so."

"Johann, does he know about this?"

Maria paused. "No. I haven't told anyone about my other life. And you must keep it secret too, Andy."

"But why?"

"Because it would be a scandal to most of her friends and acquaintances," said Stefan Zweig, turning from Altenberg. "She comes from the upper class. The aristocracy. Don't you see?"

"Johann would be appalled at my evening excursions if he knew," Maria added.

"What will you do when you're married?"

"I don't know. I can't think about that right now."

"Why do all these people come here?"

Trotsky, who had also been listening, now spoke. "We come here to talk and we all believe that things must change one way or another, for the good of the masses. In Russia. In Austria. All over the world. It can't go on like this much longer."

"What can't go on?"

"The few oppressing the many," Trotsky continued. His face became serious and he gestured toward Andy with his hands as he spoke. "The masses live in poverty, hand-to-mouth, while the aristocracy and the rich capitalists own everything. The political systems in Austria and in my own country perpetuate the misery. They must be overthrown. Democratically, if possible, by revolution, if necessary."

"Some people, like Lenin, think only of a violent revolution. That's because it's Russia. Here in Austria, or in Germany perhaps, it's different. It may be possible without revolution. Victor Adler and his Socialist Party won universal suffrage here in 1907, but in Hungary, it's the same as it ever was. The landed gentry rule Hungary and make no apologies about it, except to the emperor. If Austrian politicians can ever get beyond their obsession with nationality questions, the overthrow of the capitalists by peaceful, democratic means may come in time. In Russia, it is not possible."

"In Austria, everything gets caught up in the squabbling among the nationalities," Zweig said. "Ironically, the more democratic we have become, the more the race hatred comes to the surface. The Austro-German capitalists and aristocracy have the upper hand over the Czechs, Poles, Italians, Serbs, and others in this half of the empire. The kaiser gave the Magyars in Hungary their own kingdom and rights, but nobody else, and their gentry and bourgeoisie oppress the Romanians, Croats, Slovaks, and still more. So the Magyar and Austrian capitalist classes rule over all the other nationalities—even though together they make up less than half the population of the empire."

"Kaiser Franz Josef will not solve the nationalities problem by granting each nationality its own state within the empire like Switzerland or ... the United States of America," Trotsky swept his arm toward Andy. "The Magyars and the Germans would revolt. So it stays as it is. The oppressed nationalities agitate for equality in parliament and forget about the class struggle in their agitation. Nothing gets done for the workers and peasants who suffer," Trotsky finished. "That's Austria's problem. We have our own."

Andy looked at Maria. She looked back at him, saying nothing except with her eyes. It couldn't have been put better, more succinctly. In three weeks, Andy had learned much of what made this land tick and never more so than the evening he spent at the Café Central on the *Herrengasse* in Vienna.

It was late when Maria and Andy stepped out into the night air of the Innere Stadt and began walking toward the Ringstrasse where they hoped to find a hansom cab near the Opera or the palace.

"So, are you a revolutionary then?" asked Andy, smiling.

"No. I don't think so." Maria turned to him, serious now. "Andy, I was raised in a world of shooting parties on Bohemian estates, masked balls, liveried servants, and afternoon teas on the lawn, holidays in Italy, and immense wealth and power wielded by a thousand families. Until a few years ago, I knew nothing of what we saw tonight. Now I can see so much more. It is another world I never knew existed. Once something like that has happened to you, Andy, you can never go back."

"Maria, surely you must have known that most people didn't live like your family and friends. I mean, simply walking out your front door would have shown you that. These men tonight, they have radical ideas. I'm not sure what world they're in."

"I'm not saying I agree with everything they say, but it's so interesting to me. I'm drawn to it like a moth to a flame. They talk about things that don't exist now, but may yet come to be. Perhaps their ideas are radical to your ear, but they are talked about everywhere. Everywhere except the ruling classes."

"Revolution? Marxism? Are you attracted to that, Maria?" They had turned the corner on the Ringstrasse, but the dim street was largely empty with no cabs in sight. They continued walking and talking, neither wanting the conversation to end and thinking sooner or later a cab would come along.

"No, but as Trotsky said, things can't go on this way forever with the few oppressing the many. I don't know what the answer is, Andy, but I have a feeling. My feeling is that if we could change things a little, there won't need to be a revolution. A little here and a little more there and gradually things would be made right, keeping the best of the old world and gaining the best of the new."

"Take the United States, for example. I think of it as the land of the common man where everyone is free to marry who they want and live how they want to live. A vast, open country where all the land isn't owned by nobility and rich landowners. Where ideas can be freely expressed and be accepted or rejected on their merits and not dismissed by the prejudices of a ruling class. I would so much like to see your country someday, Andy."

Andy watched Maria intently as they walked and talked. They were far up the *Landstrasse-Hauptstrasse* and there was no point to hailing a cab. She had expressed herself with a great deal of passion, gesturing with her hands as they walked to emphasize her opinions. He had never met a woman like her, he thought, with such deep thoughts and convictions and such a consuming thirst to know more and more. It occurred to him that in this way, she was much like himself. As the days went by, he realized, his own curiosity and fascination grew, not diminished, but paradoxically, what she found distasteful about her own land, he found admirable. The ancient culture and traditions, the Baroque architecture, the dazzling imperial structure of this country. At last, they reached the door to Maria's house.

"Would you like to come in?" Maria asked.

"Thank you, but it is very late and I should get home."

"Johann is leaving tomorrow for Sarajevo, and I will see

him off at the station. After that, I do hope you'll call again. I enjoy our talks very much, Andy." Her words hung in the air for a moment. Andy could not help the fleeting thought that crossed his mind. A thought that wished she was not engaged to an Austrian count.

"I would like that very much. Of course, I will call again. *Auf Wiedersehen*, Maria."

"*Auf Wiedersehen*, Andy." She learned forward and kissed him once on each cheek in the Austrian style, turned, opened the gate into the courtyard with her key, and was gone. Andy hoped that he could find a cab on the way back to the Innere Stadt, but his step was very light and if he had to walk all the way home, the evening had been worth it.

5.

The Attentat

Johann removed his hat for a moment to quell the heat that oppressed him as he sat on his horse, watching Archduke Franz Ferdinand confer with Army Chief of Staff Franz Graf Conrad von Hötzendorf. The heat of Bosnia in late June had made conditions miserable during maneuvers and, on this final day, it seemed as if there was no breeze or relief to be had.

Conrad and the archduke had been constantly riding here and there to observe the maneuvers, either by car or by horse. Often they were together, but sometimes not. Within the confines of the army barracks, on the fields, and in the forests of the simulated military battlefields around Philipovic where the war games were taking place, Johann was responsible for the archduke's security as his aide-de-camp.

Today the coordination of artillery fire with infantry movements had exasperated both the archduke and Conrad. Communications were constantly breaking down, preventing the observers miles away from communicating back to the batteries of artillery. Communications between the army high command and the infantry were also confounded by breakdowns. Poor descriptions of where the infantry was in the forests and fields also led to confusion about where to direct artillery fire.

As the archduke and Conrad discussed the latest problem, Johann thought of his return to Vienna that would take place in a couple of days. His wedding was only a few weeks away, he thought. He would soon be a married man. He would have to give her up, just as his mother had said. He must. Much as he enjoyed Ivanna's company, he was sure that he could do that much. But how would he remain a faithful husband to Maria for the rest of his life? That seemed impossible. He knew how weak he was. Why was he this way?

Johann knew that many of his married colleagues kept mistresses. It was whispered that Conrad himself, a widower, had one: the wife of a wealthy businessman in Vienna. A trickle of perspiration dribbled down his face and again he raised his hat, smoothing his hair and wiping the dampness away as best he could with a handkerchief. No, he had to try. He must try. When he got back to Vienna, he would have to break it off with her and try his best to make himself a good husband.

He would have to try to understand Maria. There was some reluctance in her too. He had sensed it. She seemed to have changed from the beautiful girl he had known most of his life in this past year. He couldn't put his finger on it. She seemed distant at times, more now than ever. What could it be? Had she guessed the truth about him?

Not far from the army camp at Philipovic was a country mansion, a *Herrenhaus*. It belonged to a local aristocrat who had made it available to the archduke while he was here. Johann tried to look forward to this evening when the end of the army's maneuvers would be celebrated with the other generals and field marshals at a dinner reception that the archduke had arranged. Franz Ferdinand had personally invited him to be present, assuring him that as his aide-de-camp and his noble house, his presence would not offend despite his relatively modest military rank.

Security had been fairly easy for Johann to arrange since the entire area for miles around had been temporarily occupied by the army. Guards had been posted at every possible road approach and a perimeter around the archduke was guarded by roving soldiers who constantly kept in sight every conceivable approach to His Imperial and Royal Highness by foot or horse.

The detachment under Johann's personal command included plain-clothed, uniformed, and disguised agents within the immediate presence of the archduke. Two of them were introduced at the Herrenhaus as the archduke's personal valet and cook. They did, in fact, cook and attend to the clothing, bedroom, uniforms, and so forth that came with the archduke on every trip, but they were also security agents who overheard conversations and kept an eye on the house servants, ready to pounce on any sign of an attempt on his life.

Johann ensured that he was within eyesight of the archduke at all times, unless he was specifically excused from the Imperial Presence by the archduke himself. When that happened, Johann loitered just outside the immediate area, keeping any approach or entrance within sight in case somehow an assassin should manage to penetrate so far. Johann carried a pistol and, upon ceremonial occasions, a sword hanging from his waist, which he was quite expert in handling as well. He would gladly have laid down his life for this man he so greatly admired.

Johann loved his life in the army and felt that he had been born to it, his father having attained the rank of colonel in his time. He reveled in the fraternal comradeship with the other officers and men. Service as an officer in the army was expected of young, male aristocrats, but it was more than duty that compelled Johann.

The army was where all the national bickering stopped.

An American in Vienna

All nationalities and races served and united together in the army without question. The officers and men were bound by a sacred oath of loyalty to their kaiser and king—not to any parliament or cause. *Here, the stupidities of politics ended,* Johann thought with satisfaction. There were no majorities to be obtained or political parties to be consulted, just the simple loyalty of a soldier to his Habsburg sovereign, as it had always been for six centuries. So let it always be.

"Johann, come with me," the archduke said as he urged his horse into motion, pulling the reins and guiding it off in the direction of the nearby woods. Whatever had been discussed had been settled. Conrad dismounted his own horse and strode into a nearby tent where telegraph and telephone wires snaked out in various directions and several dozen communications officers stood around reading dispatches or dictating new ones to telegraphers hunched over makeshift desks.

The archduke had many contradictions, thought Johann as they rode together into the woods. Imposing in his physical size, as well as his personality, his piercing blue eyes gazed over the famously styled mustache with great effect. Affable but blunt, always fair to the men, as an officer, Johann admired these qualities. He could be stubborn and harsh at times. He did not suffer fools gladly, valued intelligence greatly, and his temper was legendary.

Yet there was a softer side to this man. He loved roses. His rose gardens at his country home in Konopište were famous throughout Europe. He clearly wanted to exercise his power to benefit all his people, regardless of their race or nationality. And whatever people might say about him, Johann knew that he was a devoted father and husband. He had seen that when he had been invited to shoot with the archduke at Konopište, his magnificent estate in Bohemia, near Prague. The tenderness and love that he openly displayed for his wife, Sophie, in private or at home was remarkable in a man most Austrians regarded as irascible.

No, when he got back to Vienna, he would have to end his affair and settle down. His mother was right. Once he married, it would have to stop. The thought that the archduke might discover his sin was unthinkable. The shame of it would be unbearable. Not after all that Franz Ferdinand had done for him in the year since his father had died. He would not approve of such scandalous behavior and he would soon be the kaiser.

Spacious tents were set up outside the Herrenhaus in the warm summer air where, to mark the end of maneuvers, champagne and dinner were served to the very highest commanders. The discussion at dinner was quite lively. Ideas and opinions were frankly exchanged among the generals and field marshals, encouraged by the archduke. The purely military problems encountered during the day's tactical exercises were also laid bare and discussed. There was some embarrassment to a number of the generals whose units were the worst offenders, but after a while, the archduke spoke up again, firmly but optimistically.

"Gentlemen," he said as he lit a cigar, puffing out the smoke until it was drawing nicely. "This is how we learn. This is how we improve. We have worked hard this past week, as have the officers and men. These maneuvers were not the toy-soldier drill that we have sometimes seen in the past. Conditions were realistic and they have exposed some deficiencies to be sure. We will learn from our mistakes, gentlemen. I have every confidence in you, in Conrad, and in the army." There were nods and murmurs of appreciation and agreement all around the table.

"Your Highness is, as always, gracious. To His Royal and Imperial Highness," Conrad said as he raised his glass in a toast. The generals stood and murmured, "Your Highness." Then Conrad continued.

"We must drill these points home. War could occur at any moment. The viper's nest in Serbia is biding its time." Conrad's face slowly began to betray the passion of his convictions as he spoke.

"It is only a matter of time, I am sure, when we will have to deal with Serbia. Their provocations are a matter of record. Their newspapers scream insults at our monarchy and goad the peaceful Serbs in Bosnia to revolt. Their army may be smaller than ours is, but fresh from victory in the Balkan Wars, they are reckless enough to welcome a war with us to annex the very ground under our feet tonight. A murderous and treacherous people they are, who bide their time, waiting for the best moment to strike. If it were me, I would strike them now, before it's too late. It's only a matter of time before they come for us. Why wait?"

Murmurs around the table as dozens of pairs of eyes shifted back to Franz Ferdinand to see what he might say. Conrad had spoken what was on many of their minds. For a moment, Franz Ferdinand puffed on his cigar, looking thoughtfully around the table, as if to measure the feelings of the generals, but then he leaned forward, putting the cigar in an ashtray.

"No. No, Conrad," Franz started. "There will be no preventative war with Serbia. What about Russia? We want no war with her and if we were to be the aggressors, surely Russia would come to Serbia's aid. A disaster. Let Serbia dare to attack us, and then it's another matter. If that were to happen, Russia would surely stand aside. Serbia hopes to provoke us and we must not fall into their trap. Besides, we have our own house to put in order."

Johann listened to the archduke's succinct argument to his top military leaders. Few things were more sacred in his empire than the army was and in this tent was assembled the very apex of its military power and the man who would be the kaiser very soon, as everyone knew. *It was brilliant*, Johann thought. He saw things clearly and decisively. Johann also knew that the archduke had other uses for the army on his mind that he had revealed to Johann when they had been riding earlier in the day.

"What a mess they have made of it today," the archduke had growled. "These new tactics require practice and more practice. We're not ready." A sound in the sky. They looked up to see one of Conrad's pet innovations, aerial reconnaissance. A lone plane had droned across the sky and then passed out of sight. "A wonderful idea, that," Franz Ferdinand had said as he turned back to Johann. "If we could get a wireless radio in one of those things that could target the artillery, it would be a breakthrough."

"Are we trying to do that?" Johann had asked.

"Among other things. We need innovation. We need reform. In all things. Johann, we are running out of time. The socialists are agitating the working classes against the wealthy. The nationalities fighting in the Parliament bring the government to a standstill. The Hungarian government refuses to grant universal suffrage to its people as Austria did years ago. My uncle has given up reform and hopes only to hold the empire together until his time is up. When my time comes, we are going to have to move quickly or else the whole thing will come apart."

"What will you do?" Johann had asked.

"The Slavs must have equality with the Austrians and the Hungarians. The Czechs and the Austrians fight over Bohemia. The Hungarians fight with the Rumanians over Transylvania. And so forth and so on. The Austrians and the Hungarians must make room."

"Then it may be civil war again, like 1848."

"It must be faced, Johann, and I am going to face it. If the Hungarians revolt again, I will call upon the army. I must have the loyalty of the army. There must be equality among the races for us to survive. My uncle didn't go far enough.

He granted only the Hungarians equality within the empire and now we have inherited a mess. If war comes with Serbia or, God forbid, with Russia, we will not be able to rely on the Slavs within the empire. No, it must be faced."

As they had finished their ride, approaching the Herrenhaus, the archduke's dark features had become passionate when he swore that, above all, it was the Hungarians whose nationalistic chauvinism was the worst of all threats. Their pervasive, systematic oppression of all other nationalities within Hungary's half of the empire, after having revolted against Austrian rule when the same had been done to them, was the height of hypocrisy. They were incorrigible. They could not be trusted. Their nobles were the most treacherous subjects of all and would have to be beaten into submission before they would ever accept the idea of equality and, if that was what it would take, Franz Ferdinand was the man to do it.

As Johann listened to Franz Ferdinand's remarks at dinner about putting "our own house in order," he knew what he meant. The empire was too fragile to sustain any significant military conflict, especially against a Slavic enemy such as Serbia. Not yet. Not until a little housecleaning and the army would be of paramount importance. If there were revolts when the archduke became the kaiser and implemented his plans, they would be put down and, in the case of the Hungarians, put down ruthlessly. The army had never failed the Habsburgs. Johann understood that this was the reason why the archduke carefully cultivated his generals—and he did it masterfully.

At last, Franz Ferdinand stood up with his cigar in hand. The generals all rose to their feet expectantly, but Franz Ferdinand waved them down, biding them continue to enjoy themselves. Casually, he put his hand on Johann's shoulder and then said in a low voice, "Let's get some fresh air, shall we?" Johann would be the archduke's personal bodyguard as he went for a walk.

There was a low stone wall along the private road leading from the mansion. They walked along the road. The night air was sultry, but far more pleasant than in the heat of the day. Fireflies were out and there was a low pink band above the horizon as the sun sank while they walked quietly. Across the road, large open fields must have stretched for at least a kilometer, leading to a farmhouse on the top of a hill. The windows of the stone house were lit and glowed across the fields in the distance.

Franz Ferdinand was not saying a word, preferring to walk in silence with his thoughts along the country road, quietly pulling on his cigar every now and again. Despite his growing closeness to the archduke, one never spoke to a member of the imperial family until one had first been spoken to and, in any event, Johann could see that Franz Ferdinand was lost for a time in his own thoughts.

"Sophie will be arriving by train tomorrow," Franz said, breaking the silence after a while. "I will leave the camp tomorrow and we will visit the city. I would like you to come with us and enjoy the occasion since Oskar Potoirek will take charge of my security."

Potoirek was the governor of Bosnia whose invitation to the archduke to come to Sarajevo for the maneuvers had delighted the archduke.

"Yes, of course. It would be an honor to go with you and the duchess to Sarajevo and I am very grateful to accept," Johann replied, bowing slightly.

Franz Ferdinand put his hand on Johann's shoulder as he spoke. "I am very touched and grateful for the service you have done me here, Johann. You have done an excellent job of protecting me unobtrusively, but effectively."

"The thought of Your Imperial Highness riding in the

An American in Vienna

streets of Sarajevo in an open car does give me concern," said Johann. The archduke turned to look him in the eye when he said this, but not in a stern way. Johann continued, "I know you wish to show yourself to the people, but you know that many Serbs hate what they see as our occupation of their country. This would be a great opportunity to toss a bomb in your car or take a shot at you with a pistol. And as far as I know, only the city police will be guarding your presence, Highness. They are not experienced. I would feel much better if I could bring some of my agents."

"I will only be in Sarajevo for a few hours during the day and then it will be back here by evening. Sarajevo is peaceful and they are planning a luncheon gala in our honor. I think I can rest assured that Potoirek will have everything covered," the archduke replied, dismissing his concerns.

Johann nodded, although his misgivings were not assuaged by Franz Ferdinand's confidence in this provincial governor and his police. *At least he could personally guard the archduke by being present,* he thought, although nowhere near as effectively as he could with his agents. Franz Ferdinand smiled and patted him on the back as he turned back toward the mansion, still puffing on his cigar. The glow of the lights in the mansion and the sound of voices could faintly be heard as they started walking back.

The next day, June 28, Johann stood in the gravel driveway of the Herrenhaus as Franz Ferdinand and Sophie, who had arrived on the morning train, stepped out of the mansion. Police officers assigned to the security detail took the other seats in the imperial car while Johann and still more officers followed in another car right behind.

The road into Sarajevo was well paved. As the cars neared the entrance to the city, Johann could see the green feathered hats being donned by the archduke and his companions. As a noble and aristocrat himself, Johann removed his officer's kepi and donned the green, feather-plumed cap that made up part of the formal attire of a high aristocrat. In military uniform, the cap was the only accessory necessary to designate the nobility of the wearer.

The crowds grew as the entourage motored more slowly but still at deliberate speed through the streets. Most waved and cheered at the imperial couple, but as the cars began to enter the old city, the streets became narrower, the buildings higher, and the crowds thicker. The cars had to slow down to almost walking speed at times to safely navigate through the crowd. The noise of the crowds as they shouted out salutations in their native tongues to the passing cars was very loud. The cars crossed a wide boulevard which allowed them to speed up somewhat until they reached the other side where the crowds thickened again.

Just as they reentered the narrowing street, Johann saw a round black object thrown toward the archduke's car in a high arc. Incredibly, as it came down, the archduke himself actually fended it off and it bounced in the street. As Johann's car approached the bomb, it exploded, rocking the car.

The sound stunned him and, momentarily, he couldn't hear at all. He was sitting in the left rear of the car, farthest away from the bomb blast, and—other than his momentary deafness and a smattering of debris of some sort over his face and uniform—he thought that he was fine. As he became conscious of the scene, however, he saw that the two officers on the right side of the car were bleeding and unconscious. The driver was unconscious and slumped over the steering wheel, although he saw no blood.

Johann jumped out of the car as his hearing slowly began to return. He became conscious of the archduke's car pulling quickly away with horn blaring at the crowd. Franz Ferdinand looked back toward them as his car sped off. A mob was pummeling a man who had attempted to flee and was undoubtedly the assassin. Police were running to rescue him from the crowd. Johann knew that the life of this criminal had to be saved so that he could be questioned and he drew his pistol and began running toward the commotion. When he came near the altercation, he shot the pistol into the air, which immediately commanded everyone's attention. The police swooped in and grabbed the man while the crowd jeered and spit at him.

A car pulled up with more police who hustled the man off. Other police began to push back the crowd to open up the street to more police on horseback now clattering through at a good speed toward city hall. Johann spoke with a police officer who, judging by the gold braid on his uniform, appeared to be in charge.

"These men in the car over there have to be taken to hospital immediately. They were hit by the blast and are seriously wounded," Johann said. The police captain turned, looked at the car, and then summoned two officers to whom he gave orders to remove the wounded from the car and take them to the hospital. Johann thanked the officer and then began to consider how he would get to city hall and the archduke.

His mind raced with dark thoughts. This was his worst nightmare. Franz Ferdinand could not stay here a moment longer. If there was one assassin, there could be others. Suddenly, another police motorcar came up behind him. Johann turned and hailed it down. As soon as he explained who he was, the police made room for him. They were also on their way to city hall and seemed to know what had just happened.

"He was a Serbian, Excellency," said one of the officers. They were dressed in gray with brass buttons and a white diagonal leather strap that went from the top left shoulder to the waist. They wore braid on their uniforms as well and had the round, conical hat that signified their profession as police. Johann soon realized that he was with the chief of police of Sarajevo.

"What precautions have been taken for the imperial couple?" Johann inquired.

"Not enough," said the police chief in a low voice. "We have only about a hundred police for a city this size. Normally it is enough," he said with a Slavic accent. "When we heard the archduke was coming and that we would be responsible for his security, it was only yesterday. We asked the mayor to request the army to help us with manpower at least, but they wouldn't do it. We have all our men on duty, but many people came into the city to see His Imperial Highness and, I'm afraid, not all of them with friendly intentions."

Johann was appalled. Why had nobody conveyed to him the request of the police chief for help? *Whoever was responsible would be dealt with harshly,* Johann thought. He would see to that. Shortly, the car pulled up at city hall. Large crowds milled about outside. The imperial car and several others were pulled up at the foot of the stairs. An officer walked over to Dubcek, the police chief.

"The archduke is inside, Your Honor. He arrived here just a few minutes ago. The mayor was greeting him when the archduke interrupted him. He was practically shouting at him, how 'outrageous' the assassination attempt had been. I thought the mayor was going to faint. Then he seemed to calm down and told the mayor to finish his speech. The mayor said it was a divine sign from God that His Imperial Highness was not hurt and assured him of the overwhelming loyalty of the Bosnians to him and the House of Habsburg," the policeman reported. After that, His Imperial Highness and the Duchess went into city hall with all of the local dignitaries and politicians.

As Johann entered the building, his eyes adjusting from the bright light outside, he saw that it was ornate with high ceilings, dark wood, and heavy curtains on floor-to-ceiling windows. Chandeliers were lit and tables were covered with food, china, and crystal. Servants poured champagne. At a table on a dais sat Franz Ferdinand and Sophie as well as Potoirek, the mayor, and several other dignitaries who Johann did not know. The archduke eventually noticed him and waved him over to his table.

"How are you?" Franz Ferdinand said in a low voice. His eyes calmly gazed at Johann's uniform and then came to rest on his face. "What happened to the others?"

Johann told him what had happened as he had seen it. Franz Ferdinand remained stoic and calm as the details were described. He nodded at the end and then, to Johann's dismay, he said, "We will visit these gentlemen at the hospital in a few minutes. Make sure that the cars are ready."

"But, Your Highness, you must give us time to arrange the security. It's not safe for you to ride in an open car now. You must return directly to Philipovic."

"I will not be afraid to go out among my own people," he replied in a low but commanding voice. A fierce and defiant look from the archduke made it immediately apparent that he would not change his mind.

"A sovereign does not skulk about in his own lands, afraid of death. If it happens, it is God's will," he said and then paused. "Do the best you can, Johann. I have every confidence in you." Then he turned away in dismissal to resume his conversation with the duchess who, having overheard Johann, had a worried look on her face.

Johann felt his heart sink. He slowly walked away and found Dubcek, who shook his head in horror as Johann related the archduke's determination to visit the wounded.

"This cannot be allowed. It is too dangerous. What about the cars? They must be closed now."

"We don't have time. Mass your police here and at the hospital," Johann commanded. Dubcek did not question his authority, but nodded in agreement as he listened. Johann continued. "We will not stop the procession between here and the hospital and we will proceed at top speed. Use your mounted police to patrol the route between here and the hospital as best they can, on the alert for anarchists. At the hospital, nobody may come near the entrance for a distance of a hundred meters."

"Yes, my lord," Dubcek replied and hurried to arrange his men.

Johann's plan was the best he could devise on a moment's notice with only a hundred police and the army security detachment miles away outside the town. The weakness of the plan was the route between the hospital and the city hall, he knew. The mounted police couldn't begin to keep much of the route under surveillance, but if the cars were driven at a good speed, it would be almost impossible to accurately throw a bomb or take a clean shot, he thought. They mustn't stop at any time, he would emphasize to the drivers.

He hurried down the steps where the cars waited and signaled the three military drivers over to him and Dubcek. The lead car would be full of police with weapons drawn, including himself in the front seat, looking ahead for any sign of trouble. The archduke's car would be next and followed by another car, also with police, and Dubcek bringing up the rear.

The archduke's driver, who was from Vienna and unfamiliar with the city, asked for directions to the hospital. Johann did not know them, so one of the other drivers quickly tried to explain the route to him, but at that moment, there was a cry from the crowd and the archduke appeared at the top of the stairs with Sophie. He waved slowly to the crowd and smiled, then took his wife's gloved hand in his own and slowly processed to his car. Johann opened the door to the middle vehicle to signal the archduke where to go. His eyes met Johann's and he silently nodded his thanks as he passed his wife to a footman to help her into the backseat.

Sophie was resplendent in a dazzling white dress and

white-plumed hat. She carried a white parasol as she took her seat next to her husband, now with his green-plumed hat marking him out as high nobility. The famous face beneath the hat was unmistakable. To the crowds they would pass, there would be no doubt that they had seen the heir to the throne go past.

Johann hurried to get into the lead car. Once there, he glanced back to see Graf Harrach, wearing just the kepi of an army officer of the lower aristocracy, had climbed on the running board on Sophie's side of the car. He hadn't thought of that and when he noticed that there was no similar rider on the archduke's side behind the driver, he opened the door to get out and take up a position on the archduke's side, but it was too late. Johann's car had abruptly lurched forward and he nearly toppled back into his seat beside the driver. As he looked back, he saw the archduke's car roar to life and proceed forward in line, then the last car.

The cars proceeded along the thinly populated streets. Their route was not the official parade route, Johann thought with relief, so any people along the way would just happen to be there by chance. They turned right on the quay that ran along the river. As his car turned, Johann stood up in the open car and intently scanned the people on the street who looked surprised to see the entourage and spontaneously cheered and waved as they went by. Johann looked back and saw the archduke's car turning on the quay behind them and then spoke to the driver. "All right, pick up speed now. The quay is broad enough." The driver nodded and Johann could feel the car start to surge as he sat down again. He glanced at the speedometer and nodded approvingly at the driver when he saw the needle pass forty kilometers.

As they sped along the quay, Johann allowed himself a long breath of air and felt some relief, but his anxiety returned less than a minute later when he looked back and to his horror realized that a very large gap had emerged between his car and the archduke's. "Slow down," he hissed at the driver, annoyed that he had allowed this to happen. The driver looked into the mirror and put his foot gently on the brake to let the other cars catch up.

Johann looked back again to ensure that the distance closed. He was incredulous as he watched the archduke's car slow and turn right, off the quay, into one of the narrow side streets. The following car also slowed and looked as if it was going to turn as well.

"What the hell is that idiot doing?" Johann shouted as he stood up in his seat, looking back. "Stop the car!" he said. As the car came to a stop, the police officers in the backseat were also staring back and preparing to leap out of the car. Johann got out of the car first and turned to start running toward the side street where he saw that the archduke's car was starting to back out. Then he heard it.

There were two sharp pops, one after the other. Then Dubcek and several police officers were jumping out of the rear car, chasing a man who was running out of the side street with a pistol in his hand. They caught him, but not before Johann saw him shove something in his mouth. Poison. The police wrestled him to the ground as pedestrians began rushing toward the spot, yelling and screaming.

There was a commotion around the archduke's car as it finished backing out and started to turn toward them. He could see a look of panic and horror on the face of the driver. Graf Harrach had somehow gotten around to the driver's side by the archduke and was dabbing a white handkerchief at the archduke's mouth. He couldn't see the duchess.

"Get them to the hospital!" Johann shouted at the driver who looked at him, momentarily stunned, and then nodded vigorously. The car sped away. Chaos was erupting all around him. A group of men crowded around the assassin and the few police who were holding him. They were going to murder him on the spot, just as they had tried to do earlier in the day to the bomb thrower. The police quickly fought off the angry bystanders, hustled the thin little man into the third car, and roared off.

Dubcek was now at his side. "My God, what have they done?" he cried, his face contorted in horror and fear. His hands were on his head and he had clearly lost his composure.

"Get a hold of yourself, man!" Johann said coarsely to the police chief. "Get me another car! I need to get to the hospital. Get your men to question the crowd! Find out where he came from and who he is if you can."

Johann's sharp orders seemed to bring Dubcek to his senses, giving him some purpose. He turned to his men and began shouting orders to them in some Bosnian tongue Johann could not understand. They began to fan out. More cars came up the street from the direction of city hall loaded with the police who had guarded that area. Johann commandeered one of the cars and commanded the driver to take him to the hospital, known as The Cognacs. Dubcek waved the driver on and in an instant the car was speeding toward the hospital.

The nightmare was now complete. Johann cursed the driver. Why had he turned? When he reached the hospital, he found the driver and could not restrain himself.

"Why did you turn, you idiot?" Johann shouted at the driver while grabbing his collar tightly in his hand.

The driver's lip quivered. His eyes were watery as he regarded Johann with a mixture of fear and sadness. "That's the street the other driver told me to turn into. We thought you had missed it. Then Graf Harrach shouted to me that it was not the right way and to back up immediately. Then that man in the crowd next to the car pulled out a pistol and shot the duchess and the archduke one after the other!"

Johann made his way into the hospital foyer. He could hear a voice speaking. It was Graf Harrach. "... regret to say that His Imperial and Royal Highness, our beloved Archduke Franz Ferdinand, has died of his wounds as has his wife, the Duchess ..." Gasps arose from the crowd and muffled sobs. He could hear many voices begin to murmur in the room.

"I invite you now to pray with me for the safekeeping of the souls of our gracious lord and master, the archduke, and for the duchess." Graf Harrach sank to his knees. In a moment, the crowd in the lobby followed his example. Johann kneeled and bowed his head. Silence filled the room except for an undercurrent of whispers as people said prayers in their own way and language.

After a few moments, Harrach slowly rose, donned his plumed hat, and walked to the door near where Johann was now standing. The crowd parted to let pass this brave man who had risked death standing on one of the running boards of the car, but who, in the end, was unable to save the heir's life. His eyes met Johann's as he strode out of the lobby and he inclined his head, signaling that Johann should follow him outside.

Upon reaching the courtyard of the hospital, Johann noticed that police now ringed the area and had pushed the crowd far back away from the doors and where the cars were parked. Flowers had already been laid at the gates. An old woman in black was lighting votive candles near a low wall. Word had traveled quickly. Harrach lit a cigarette and quietly walked toward the archduke's car to examine it again. Johann followed him in silence. As the two of them looked into the car, they could see blood everywhere.

"Sophie was shot first," Harrach said as he exhaled smoke, his gloved hand shaking now. "She seemed not to know she had been hit and looked at Franz. Then, another pistol shot. He hit Franz in the chest with the bullet. Sophie said, 'My God, what has happened to you?' Then she fainted and slumped down to the floor of the car." *That was why he had not been able to see her*, Johann thought.

"I thought he had missed with the first shot and Sophie had simply fainted, so I ran around to his side of the car, but the archduke somehow knew better. He said 'Sophie, don't die! The children, you must live for the children!' I jumped up on the running board and then I saw a stream of blood come out of the archduke's mouth. I tried to staunch the blood with a handkerchief, but it was obvious he was badly wounded. I asked him if he was in any pain. He looked at me calmly and just said 'It's nothing, it's nothing.' The life just poured out of him. He repeated 'It's nothing' several times, ever more faintly, and then he fainted as well. I don't think either one of them was alive when we got here." Harrach shook his head and pulled on his cigarette again. It was unbelievable.

"Who was he?" Harrach asked Johann. "That little man, I mean? A little weasel of a man with a pistol came out of a café just as calm as you please. While the driver was shifting and the car was stopped, he walked right up to the car and couldn't miss. It couldn't have been any easier."

Dark thoughts began to cross Johann's mind. Impossible to miss? Why had the driver turned mysteriously into the side street? Was he party to a conspiracy to kill the archduke? Was there a conspiracy? It seemed as if the archduke had been driven into a trap. Johann had seen the driver and he seemed genuinely distraught. What if it was an act? He summoned a senior police officer to where they were standing and instructed him to detail one of his men to watch the driver at all times and never let him out of his sight. He would be questioned later.

It was late afternoon. The world as Johann knew it had just snapped apart. The man who was his mentor, his friend, and who soon was to have been the master of the empire was suddenly gone. It was unbelievable. How could this have happened? Johann shuddered and felt the grief start to rise within him. Harrach sauntered off, seemingly in a daze. The implications of what had just happened began to invade his consciousness as the shock receded. Johann lit a cigarette.

It was a Serbian terrorist. It had to be. The one earlier in the day was a Serbian. This one must have been a Serbian too. A little weasel of a man. The two of them must have come here to kill the archduke. Maybe more. *Damn them*, he thought. *Damn them all*. There would be hell to pay. Johann felt a bubbling of hatred for the Serbs that chased his bouts of grief for the death of his friend.

There would be war with Serbia, he thought. Good. He remembered Conrad's words in the tent the night before. He had been right. The war party led by Conrad and the generals would be in full cry to crush Serbia once and for all and, with the archduke dead, there would be no one to stop them this time. *No mercy for the Serbs*, he thought. *No mercy.* Johann crushed the cigarette with the heel of his polished black boot. Suddenly he had an odd thought. With the archduke dead, he had nobody to report to for further orders.

6.

Complications

As June 28, 1914 dawned in Vienna, Andy prepared to call on Maria at her house in the Third District. In the days following their evening at the Café Central, Andy had thought about their conversation. Rudi and Ernst had continued to show him the splendid sights, but now he looked at things differently. He found himself wondering, as he watched the ordinary people on the boulevards and streetcars, what their thoughts might be as they walked by the same palaces and statues.

He had taken the trolley that morning from the Ringstrasse that turned up the Landstrasse-Hauptstrasse and brought him within a couple blocks of the Montfort residence. It was another beautiful summer morning as Andy rang the doorbell and was greeted by Herr Klaus, the very old man-servant of the Montforts. And how was it going with him? It was good to see the Herr Bishop again. Yes, she was expecting him. Please be seated. May he get him anything? No? A moment, then. Impeccably polite, Klaus bowed and left to get Maria.

Johann would be returning to Vienna in a few days and then their wedding would no doubt take up much of her time. He felt a twinge of sadness at this thought. He would probably not be seeing much of her after that. Andy could smell her delicate perfume as she entered the room. Despite their increasingly cordial and frank conversations, the initial sight of her still enthralled him.

"I'm going to miss our little sightseeing trips when Johann gets back."

"So charming you are, Andy. Thank you. I hope you will still come see us while you're here. I know Johann will be anxious to see you again when he returns."

"Have you heard from him?"

"Not very much, but that's to be expected."

A light lunch was served in the dining room as they discussed what they would see that day. They decided to visit the *Kunsthistoriches* museum. Maria explained that it had been completed in 1891 to house in one place the enormous collection of priceless art collected by the Habsburgs over the centuries for the public to see. The Italian neo-Renaissance architecture of the building itself was notable and imposing with an enormous statue of Empress Maria Theresa in front.

They left the Montfort house shortly after noon and passed the afternoon in the vast galleries, looking at paintings and sculpture, but even so, only saw a small part of the museum, so great was the collection. At about four o'clock, Maria suggested that they leave for *Jause*, the Viennese equivalent of English teatime, but in Vienna, with coffee and pastry or chocolate. Fidelio's Café was not a far walk and they decided to go there. As they left the museum, Andy offered his arm and Maria took it, smiling at him and chatting pleasantly as they walked along in the afternoon sun.

As they entered the café, Andy sensed that something was wrong. Many of the patrons were huddled together reading the evening newspapers and talking in low, angry voices. Several of the waiters were also intently looking at a newspaper spread out on one of the tables, one pointing, and another shaking his head. A third waiter looked up as Andy closed the door and glared at them with a hard look as they began to sit down at a table.

He came to take their order with a very grave face. Something was very wrong and Maria must have felt it too.

"What has happened? Is there some news?"

"Madam, have you not heard the news? The archduke has been murdered with his wife." He regarded them with tight, pursed lips. At first, it was hard to comprehend it.

"Which archduke was murdered?" Maria asked.

"Franz Ferdinand, madam. In Sarajevo. Early this afternoon. It was a Serbian who did it. They tried to kill him with a bomb and then they shot him to death with his wife, right in the car. It's terrible. Their children, you know. Just terrible." The waiter stared at them, his lower lip trembling. Was it rage or sorrow?

"Damn the Serbs!" someone spat out in a low, angry tone from a nearby table. A murmur of approval from a number of men at different tables. "Barbarians!" hissed someone else. The faces of the men in the café were unanimously grim. Something would have to be done.

"Johann," Maria exclaimed, looking into Andy's eyes. "He was with the archduke." Then to the waiter: "Was anyone else killed?"

"Just the imperial couple, madam," said the waiter. "They arrested the murderer before he could kill anyone else. The police have him under arrest in Sarajevo. Some officers in another car were wounded earlier in the day when another assassin tried to kill the archduke with a bomb."

"My God," Maria said. "That could be Johann. We must go to his mother's place and see if she has heard anything. This is unbelievable."

Without ordering, Andy and Maria hurried out of the café and back into the street. Everything seemed normal. A woman pushing a stroller with a baby passed them. A streetcar went by filled with passengers, blankly staring out. A breeze rippled, bending the summer flowers in one of the gardens. It was still a beautiful day. The evening would be balmy and perfect for promenading around the Ringstrasse and the boulevards of the city. It couldn't have happened, could it?

They made their way to the Caboga residence, but the countess was not at home. She was still in Salzburg. Yes, the servants had heard the news. Maria knew them all, of course. Karl, the forty-two-year-old butler, was in the *Landstrume*, the Austrian "reserve" forces, and imagined that he would be called up immediately. Madame's housekeeper, Elsa, had already sent the scullery maid and cook to get extra supplies of food, flower, sugar, coffee, and a list of innumerable other items that she had thought of in the short time since she heard the news in case of hoarding and shortages.

Maria thought that she might return to her own house, but Andy thought of Elisabeth's connection to the kaiser. Perhaps they might have more news. Maybe they could find out about Johann if they didn't already know. They decided to go to the Windischgrätz house first and then Maria would return home to her mother.

"It's war for sure," said Rudi as they walked in the door. He was excited. "You know the Serbian government was behind this. They wanted this. They're a savage bunch of criminals, aren't they?" Ernst was sitting in the main salon busily reading a newspaper. He looked up at them, and gravely took Maria's hand, bowing slightly, and then glanced at Andy.

"It was only a matter of time, I'm afraid. Now they've done it," Ernst said quietly.

"What about Johann?" asked Maria. "Have you heard

anything about him?" Just then, Prince Otto walked into the room from the far side.

"I was on the telephone with Johann a while ago," Otto said. "He was slightly injured in the bomb-throwing incident, but nothing serious. He asked me to tell you that he will not be coming home Tuesday. There have been riots in Sarajevo. Many Serbs have been dragged out into the streets and killed by mobs. The police are overwhelmed and the army has had to occupy Sarajevo and several other Bosnian towns to stop the violence. Johann said there are demonstrations and riots all over Bosnia."

"The damn Serbs," said Ernst quietly. "They'll never rest until they bring us down. We have no choice now. Russia or not, we have to defend ourselves. They'll keep doing this, just like they did to the Turks before the Balkan Wars. What do you think will happen next, Father?" asked Ernst. Otto shook his head slowly and then shrugged his shoulders.

"It's hard to say. We must be very careful. This is a terrible calamity for the family, no doubt, but Franz Ferdinand himself said many times it would be pointless to go to war with Serbia. What would be gained? We don't know that their government was involved in this. Not yet."

"Germany will come to our side if Russia tries anything," said Ernst. "The Russians will think twice about taking on both Austria and Germany. Kaiser Wilhelm was a very dear friend to Franz Ferdinand. He'll be angry at what the Serbs have done to us, for sure. Even the tsar would be offended, wouldn't he, Father? Assassinating royalty? His grandfather was assassinated. The tsar wouldn't support the Serbs if they did this, would he?"

"Nobody will be very pleased about this, Ernst," said Otto. "But there have been many assassinations these past few years. None of the royal families will be on the side of the Serbians if they did it."

"What does Russia have to do with it?" Andy asked. He

had gathered that this was an important point, but didn't understand.

"Russia is Serbia's protector and ally," Otto replied. "A war with Serbia would be one thing. A war with Serbia and Russia is another. But then, you see, Germany is our ally and we would have to call for help from her if we were attacked by Russia. You see how it is?"

It was a pile of jackstraws, Andy thought. *One thing led to another.*

The front door to the house opened and closed. Elisabeth and Stephanie walked down the hall and into the room. The face of the archduchess was white and grim as she wordlessly laid her hat on a table and looked across the room at her husband.

"I'm so sorry," Otto said simply as he crossed the room. He embraced his wife for a moment. Stephanie looked at her mother and father without saying anything at all. Andy realized that whatever its international significance, it was also a family tragedy.

"I tried to call the kaiser, but he wasn't able to come to the telephone. You know how he hates to talk on the telephone and there was so much going on," Elisabeth said, her composure intact. Andy wondered what mixed emotions might be passing through her mind about the death of her cousin who had caused such controversy within the family.

"Where is he?" Otto asked.

"He's at Schönbrunn this evening. He had been planning to go back to Bad Ischl tomorrow morning, but arrangements have to be made for the funeral. Montenuovo is arranging to have the bodies brought back to Vienna from Sarajevo by ship, for some reason, and then by rail to here. I went to the Belvedere. It was pitiful. The poor children. Why did they kill Sophie too? I just don't understand it. They have no mother or father now. It's just too horrible."

A sad silence fell on the room momentarily and then the

An American in Vienna

telephone rang again. One of the servants announced that it was Elisabeth's mother, Archduchess Stephanie, calling from Hungary. Maria took Andy aside.

"Will you take me home, Andy? My mother will be distraught. I must go now that I know Johann was not hurt." Andy brought her home in a cab.

"It must be a great relief to know Johann is alive and unhurt," Andy said. Maria looked at him quietly for a moment before answering.

"Yes, it is." Then she fell silent again for a moment. "Of course, this could get very serious for him if war comes. Who knows what will happen," Maria said with what seemed to Andy like resignation. Andy imagined that she was thinking about her wedding plans when Maria spoke again.

"I hope you know how much I have enjoyed our time together, Andy. I suppose neither one of us will ever forget where we were and who we were with. I'm glad I was with you. I hope you will call again soon." She touched him on his hand when she said this. Andy placed his hand over hers.

"I would like that, very much. I'm not sure what I will do now. I'll have to think about this in the next few days, especially if there is going to be a war. I should probably leave if that happens. I won't leave without seeing you once more, though. I promise." She squeezed his hand and, to his surprise, tears welled up in her eyes. She leaned forward, gave him a kiss on the cheek, and then the driver opened the door of the cab and she left him.

Andy noticed on the drive back to the house that the streets of Vienna were devoid of traffic and unnaturally quiet. Andy imagined the Viennese were with their families this evening, discussing the assassination and what might happen next, just as he had been doing. He thought of his mother and father, back in Columbus, so far away. A pang of longing for them in this sad moment. He decided to send a telegraph to them the following morning:

> Austrian Heir murdered here today. Not sure what to do. Family believes war with Serbia possibly imminent. Preparing for state funeral. Great sadness and anger. Believe I should return home after. Will advise more shortly. Andy.

The following morning, a telegraph was delivered to Andy in return.

> Murder of archduke front-page news here. Breaking news from there most urgently required here. No reporters presently in Vienna. Strongly request you stay and report news to us if agreeable with family. Please advise. Here is your chance. Arthur.

Andy felt a thrill as he read his father's words on the telegram. He was right. It was the chance of a lifetime for him. It would take weeks for American reporters or journalists to make their way to Vienna, even from the East Coast. Perhaps, with help from Otto and Elisabeth, he might even be able to get some details about developments that other reporters arriving late would never uncover.

Yet it was awkward to remain as the Windischgrätz family prepared for the worst. Andy decided that he would leave it up to Otto and, that afternoon, finding him in the main salon with a newspaper, Andy sat down to speak with him.

"Something has happened, Uncle Otto," Andy began. It had seemed natural to call Elisabeth and Otto "Aunt" and "Uncle" shortly after he had arrived. Their age difference and noble status made "Cousin," which he used with Rudi and Ernst, too familiar. Otto and Elisabeth seemed to like it as well and soon that was how it was.

"What is it, Andy?" Otto replied, folding the newspaper in his lap. His face looked drawn and weary from reading the news, but his eyes revealed a jovial twinkle as he gazed at Andy, ready to listen. It was apparent to Andy that Otto had become fond of him in his weeks there, and the feeling was mutual. A bond of affection and respect had replaced the initial curiosity each had for the other in those first days. Overnight, however, Otto's usual, jaunty disposition had faded. He had become anxious and pensive as the possibilities of what might happen next intruded on his thoughts.

"Well, I feel that under the circumstances, it might be best for me to go home. You and Aunt Elisabeth have been so wonderful to me, but now, with this tragedy, I feel it would be an imposition for me to stay on. And yet, my father has written to me about staying in Vienna and reporting on the events here for his newspaper back home. It's a wonderful opportunity for me but …" Otto interrupted him.

"My dear Andy, you are most welcome here. There is no reason for you to leave us from our part. I'm sorry if you feel this way. We have not been ourselves since this happened and I'm afraid we have neglected you in our grief and worry …" Now it was Andy who interrupted.

"Not at all, Uncle. You have been the perfect hosts and it's not that at all. I simply would hate to be a burden if things were to, well … deteriorate. And yet, if there is going to be a war, if things do get worse, that would make it an even greater opportunity for me to stay on and report this news. Do you see?" Otto listened carefully and paused before answering. It was clear that something had just occurred to him, and then he nodded in understanding.

"Yes, I see. Indeed. I think this is a wonderful chance for you, Andy, and it would be my pleasure to help you. In fact, I might be able to introduce you to a few sources inside the government who might be willing to give you some information that would be of interest at home, in the United States. Yes, Andy. I think you should stay."

And that was how it was settled. Andy spent the rest of the day reading the Viennese newspapers and walking the streets of Vienna to think, before returning home to prepare his first dispatch to his father.

> VIENNA, June 30—In the two days since news of the assassination of the emperor's nephew and his wife reached the capital, a sadness mixed with anxiety and resentment toward Serbia has settled on the capital. Newspapers here displayed photographs taken of the bodies of the imperial couple lying in state in the town hall in Sarajevo. Another remarkable photograph seen in nearly all newspapers here depicted the Bosnian police wrestling down the assassin, Gavrilo Princip, moments after he had shot the couple.
>
> The initial reaction of shock and sorrow, especially for their three orphaned children and the senseless slaying of the duchess, has been transformed by these photographs to a deep resentment toward the Serbian government and people. Although no evidence of complicity in the crime has been found to date, the general opinion here is that if the Serbian government was not directly involved, it is still responsible due to its constant agitation of the Serbian populace against the monarchy since the annexation of Bosnia seven years ago. In either event, it is commonly assumed here that something must now be done about Serbia ...

Andy showed a draft of the article to Otto who read it carefully. When he was finished, he took off his glasses, and looked at Andy.

"It's very good, I think," he said gravely. "My sense is

that you have conveyed the feelings of the people here to the people in America quite well. Very well done, Andy."

"I tried to imagine myself back home, reading this. I wanted to see if I could write something that would give people an idea of what it's like here. I'm glad you liked it, Uncle."

"I did. By the way, Andy, I meant to tell you something the other day, but all this tragedy has caused me to forget. I have made some inquiries about the mystery of Matthias. I have a cousin in Styria. She is quite old. She is interested in these sorts of things. She has a lot of old documents: family Bibles, old manuscripts, that sort of thing. I wrote to her and I can tell you that this has piqued her curiosity as well. It's exactly the sort of thing she likes. So she is going to see what she can find out and write back to me."

"That's great news. It's so long ago, I wondered if it would even be possible to find out."

"We shall see, Andy. If anyone could find out, she will."

Andy sent the dispatch to his father from the central telegraph service, which was quite expensive. Arthur Bishop advised that the newspaper would wire him an advance to defray the cost of the telegraphs and advised him to open a bank account in Vienna. Andy hoped that his story would be good enough to satisfy his father and the newspaper. Time would tell. In the meantime, Andy started to think about what his next story might be.

Later that day, when Andy reached home, he learned that Ernst had been summoned to his unit, the Tyrolean *Kaiserjäger* Regiment. A telegraph had been delivered that morning while he had been out. Ernst was upstairs packing his kit and Andy went to say good-bye.

"It's serious, isn't it, Ernst?" asked Andy. Ernst was already in uniform and being assisted by one of the valets.

"I'm afraid so. I should think that, before long, we will find ourselves at war with Serbia. I'm sorry about your holiday, Andy, but this won't last long, I wouldn't think. A few weeks. We'll make short work of them." His confidence seemed tinged with resignation, as if a long-postponed task had finally to be faced and finished.

"Where are you going, do you know?"

"Bosnia," Ernst replied, looking up at him, as if surprised that he had to ask.

So there was no doubt, Andy thought. The empire was quietly calling her young men to arms, preparing to avenge the wrong that had been done. Like a cat, slowly and carefully gathering itself to pounce. Andy felt his heart skip a beat as the simple point of Ernst's answer hit home. Blood would be spilled after all. It was only a matter of time. Andy also realized that, alone among American reporters in Vienna, he might know something important that he could use in describing events in the coming days to the readers back home. He began to consider his next dispatch.

7.

A Strange Funeral

From the edge of the deck of the Austrian battleship, *Viribus Unitis*, Johann Graf von Caboga felt the stubble that had grown on his face in the two days since he had last shaved. Having no other orders, he had taken it upon himself to accompany his master back to Vienna until he was ordered to do otherwise.

The enormous dreadnought had been docked at the main pier on the waterfront of Trieste late that morning. It was met by the mayor, dignitaries, and large crowds from this Croatian city, the preeminent seaport of the empire. From his vantage point, Johann watched the flag-draped coffin of Archduke Franz Ferdinand brought slowly down a special wide gangplank by a marine honor guard with great ceremony.

A military band played. A heavy pall of grim anticipation pervaded the silent, watching crowd. Something was going to happen. *They knew it, too,* Johann thought. *This had to be done first, though. Pay respect to our martyred dead. Then we'll turn to the business at hand. Then we'll settle the score with them.*

The swish of swords unsheathed rose in unison. The

casket had reached the rear of the hearse. Royal Marines in blue tunics and white trousers gently placed the casket in the gilded funeral hearse, nestled among heaps of flowers inside that could be seen through polished glass windows. Ceremonial swords were sheathed on signal in scabbards as the doors were closed.

Shouted commands. An honor guard of naval officers from the battleship and her escorts formed on either side of the carriage. They waited, faces grim and anxious, as the coachman mounted the carriage. Drums rolled. The coachman snapped his reins. The horses started forward, slowly, at a walking pace. The crowd around the quay began to disperse as Johann watched from above.

As the procession departed to the mournful roll of the drums, Johann gazed at the scene. Balconies facing the quay were draped in black. Black and gold flags of the Habsburg dynasty fluttered. Silent crowds lined the route to catch a last glimpse of their fallen leader who never was and never would be. The man they had known as "the Heir" for a quarter century had not lived to see the day.

Johann turned to gather his gear from below when movement down the deck caught his eye. The coffin of the duchess was being carried down the deck toward the gangplank, but with no ceremony. Several plainly dressed men, a local undertaker's servants perhaps, bore the archduke's late wife to a second hearse supplied by a local funeral home, apparently. By the time they reached the hearse, the crowd had largely gone. There were no drums, no music, no ceremonies at all. *It was very odd*, Johann thought. *They had botched it. Or had they?*

Johann wondered. It couldn't be, could it? From some invisible place, could some unseen, unknown person have deliberately instructed that it be done this way? So the duchess would be reduced to her proper station? Could the old family wound be reopened one last time?

As the hearse quietly pulled away from the quay, Johann

considered his own place in the world. It was one thing that his patron, mentor, and friend was now dead. For the first time, it occurred to him that the faction at court who had been dreading the day the archduke became emperor might now take this opportunity to ensure that his friends and, perhaps, his aide-de-camp, with all their strange ideas and intentions were buried with him.

If so, Johann's career, bright and shining but a few days ago, was in tatters. Those same unseen, unknown functionaries who had obscured the late duchess would have more work to do to obscure the most sensational assassination the continent of Europe had seen since Caesar, Johann thought. Time would tell soon enough.

Johann arrived at the train station shortly after noon to join the escort to Vienna. He estimated that the train would pull into the *Südbanhof* station in Vienna by late afternoon. It was July 2, 1914. He imagined the scene that should await them when they arrived. The bodies of the couple would be taken to the Royal Chapel at the Hofburg Palace. There would be an enormous procession, no doubt, with the Hungarian guards and cavalry arrayed in the streets. That would be what was expected and due, but further suggestions that someone and something was at work to the detriment of the archduke was not long in coming.

The next sign that something was amiss came shortly after the train left the station and the huge crowds in Trieste. They stopped in a small Croatian town about an hour away that had obviously not expected them. There were no crowds and the train simply waited hour after hour. Nobody seemed to know what was going on. Someone heard that there was some difficulty rerouting other trains to make way. Another said that it was it was something else, but it was well past six o'clock in the evening when the train finally started again. In another hour, it was nearly dark and they stopped again.

Several more hours passed. Many in the honor guard

became angry and indignant, Johann observed. Who was in charge of this? An idiot! *Schlamperei*! How could they let something like this happen? Johann said little as he waited and watched. He felt wretched. First he hoped that it wasn't. Then he was sure that it was. In the pit of his stomach, he knew that his suspicions were being confirmed. After a while, after despair and anger had run their course, he wondered how they would do it. It wasn't only Sophie who was going to be lowered, he realized, but the archduke himself.

Finally, the train was allowed to start up again, but not until it was late and completely dark. The train did not arrive at the Südbanhof until nearly midnight. By then, the bitter wrath of many in the honor guard that afternoon had become a bewildered resentment and incredulity. There would be an explanation, surely. It would turn out all right in the end. It always did. But there were no crowds. There was no explanation. There was nothing.

It might as well have been a freight train that pulled into the station after midnight for all the attention they got. The platform was virtually deserted but for a few porters who stood staring as military officers and nobility began disembarking from the cars with no ceremony or welcome. Little groups began to form. Johann stood by himself and lit a cigarette. Low conversation. Someone went into the station and came out again, shrugging his shoulders. Something was going on. What was it? Something had to happen, now that they were here. The porters began removing baggage from one of the cars and placing it on the platform.

One should never ascribe to malice what can be explained by incompetence, Johann's father had often said. *Perhaps it was incompetence*, Johann thought. Or rather, he still allowed himself to hope. Then something did happen.

It could be heard in the midnight darkness distinctly, but from a distance at first. Then a rising clatter of horses on cobblestone streets. Many of them. Then they were there.

Imperial Life Guards filing out onto the platform through the main double doors. One column to the left, the other to the right. Then Archduke Karl, the new Heir, walked through the doors and out to the middle of the platform. Military officers, dignitaries, nobles, and aristocrats all turned to look at him in expectant silence.

Karl was only a few years older than Johann was. Slender, with jet black hair and a pencil thin mustache, his marriage to the stylish and beautiful Princess Zita of Bourbon-Parma had complied with Habsburg law in every respect and had firmly ensured his place and that of his children in the imperial succession after Franz Ferdinand, who had been nearly twice his age. He was dressed in a military tunic, white gloves, and the ubiquitous green-plumed hat, Johann observed. His dark brown eyes swept the platform as he stood, silently for a moment, taking in the scene. Bows from one and all. There would be no questioning of the new *Thronfolger*. One did not speak until one was spoken to.

"His Majesty has asked me to express his deep appreciation for your sympathy and the faithful discharge of your duties to His Majesty and our late cousin, Franz Ferdinand," the young archduke said in a thin voice. "I know this has been a trying day for all of you. I wish to extend my own thanks to you as well, this evening. Good-night, my Lords. Gentlemen." With that, the archduke turned and walked back through the double doors, out of sight and into the night followed by the Life Guards who retreated in the reverse order they had entered.

The contrast in Vienna with the outpouring of genuine grief and respect that Johann had seen from immense crowds from Sarajevo to Trieste could not be more complete. Baleful glances among the late archduke's entourage left standing on the platform. Low muttering from somewhere. An unintelligible, muffled outburst from someone farther up the platform before he was hushed into silence by someone else. *But what could you do?* Johann thought. They had planned it that way. No questions. No answers. It was out of anyone's hands.

Imperial servants from the Hofburg together with the porters made quick work of transferring the pair of coffins from the train to two waiting hearses as the bewildered, exhausted passengers watched, virtually frozen in place. No priest. No bishop to say a few words. It was like unloading a cargo of potatoes.

Johann spotted the red glow of a cigar and a plume of smoke behind a pillar. From his uniform, Johann guessed that it was the stationmaster. He was standing alone in the shadow of a pillar, discreetly watching the passengers filing out through the double doors. Johann approached him. The stationmaster's eyes looked at him warily as he came near.

"So, my friend, what was the reason for the delays? Why were we stopped so many times for so long?"

Johann used a low voice that would not be overheard. The stationmaster looked around as if weighing whether to respond or not or perhaps checking himself to ensure they were not overheard. Then he drew on his cigar and exhaled slowly.

"Orders. From the palace. Under no circumstances should the train arrive here before midnight. What could we do?"

Montenuovo, Johann thought. At the pinnacle of the empire's political, legal, social, and military pyramid, it was above all a time to put things right. To restore the imperial balance wheels to their rightful places. To bury the iconoclast archduke and his presumptuous wife as quickly and quietly as possible, and forget about them.

The next morning, dressed in his full military regalia, Johann went downstairs to breakfast. His mother was already there, dressed in black. He kissed her cheek as he sat down. Her face was lined and somber as she watched him sit down wordlessly. A newspaper was on the table. A footman poured his coffee and then silently retreated. Breakfast rolls sat uneaten in a silver basket, but Johann had little appetite.

"What's happening?" Johann asked. "What are the newspapers saying?"

"The newspaper says that there will be a public viewing at the Royal Chapel at the Hofburg from 8:00 until noon and then the funeral will follow. How strange. Not nearly enough time for most people to pay their last respects. None of the royal families of Europe have time to come. I don't understand what they are thinking."

"Isn't it obvious?" Johann replied softly. "They don't want the people to come. They don't want royalty to come. They don't want Franz Ferdinand and Sophie to get any more notice than is absolutely required. Why else?" Johann related to her his observations of the day before, the indignities that he had personally observed and the thoughts that had formed in his mind all day and kept him from sleeping well all night. Countess von Caboga listened intently and with growing consternation as Johann spelled it all out, culminating with their arrival in Vienna at midnight. She was clearly appalled.

"This is indecent," said his mother. "This is no time to indulge in the old quarrel. This is not just the imperial family's private affair. We've all suffered this tragedy together. How can they not see this? If we are going to go to war over this, we must first honor our dead. He sacrificed his life for the *Reich*. He deserves the highest honors. It's unforgivable."

"Yes, Mother, and it's not just that," Johann agreed. "If we are going to war with Serbia over this, the bloody mess needed to be seen by all the royal families of Europe. The kaiser of Germany, the kings of England, Belgium, Italy,

Bulgaria. All of them needed to come and feel our grief. They should see the three little children the murderers have now left behind. And they should know that this was done by Serbia. A brutal murder. A blow to our old kaiser who has already suffered so many personal tragedies. Then, when the time comes to strike against Serbia, all Europe will be behind us. But no. To gratify old animosities, we will miss a golden opportunity."

Johann and his mother saw eye to eye on this unfolding tragedy on top of tragedy. The empire was going to be denied its right to grieve to satisfy the resentments of some of the imperial family toward one of its own who had dared to flout their traditions. Antique traditions that meant so little in this day and age.

The countess put her glasses back on and continued reading the newspaper. "Listen to this, Johann," she said. "'The palace advised that due to the kaiser's great age and the strain of the last few days, it was his wish, conveyed to all the royal and imperial families of Europe, that they not attend the funeral ...' Kaiser Wilhelm will be most offended," his mother added. "He and the archduke were very close personal friends."

All the pieces were falling into place. Montenuovo at his guileful best. Johann had to marvel, in spite of himself, how cleverly he had orchestrated it. The delays, the excuses, the discreet announcements. There was nothing anyone could do.

After breakfast, their car was brought around and took them to the Hofburg. Johann and his mother walked arm in into the chapel. They entered through a side door. The interior of the chapel was dark, but after Johann's eyes adjusted for the light, they made their way toward the pair of coffins and the bodies lying in state.

Johann felt a throb of grief and despair as he regarded the archduke. Still and white, the flickering of the candles gave him the appearance of deep sleep. There was no sign of the fatal wound. His gloved hands lay across his stomach, holding a crucifix. The great man, vigorous and radiating the power of centuries of Habsburg might, had been denied passage to old age and looked especially tragic to Johann, cut down in the prime of his life.

Guards flanked the coffins on either side, at ease, faces downcast, rigidly still. A line of mourners passed along the side of the archduke's coffin, then across the foot and then along the side of the duchess's coffin and out of the church. Many made the sign of the cross as they looked in dumb amazement at their fallen leader. Many had tears in their eyes, especially as they gazed at Sophie. Others seemed numb and stared blankly at the incredible sight. Johann noticed that Sophie's coffin was on the left and had been deliberately and noticeably lowered below that of her husband. Another insistent sign by the invisible, malevolent chamberlain that she never was and never would be an equal. Not even in death.

Johann and his mother sat down in one of the nearby pews and watched in silence for a time until it was announced that the viewing was over and they must leave while the chapel was "prepared" for the funeral. Promptly at noon, the doors to the chapel were closed. Thousands of mourners were turned away by the palace guards. Then, inexplicably, for four hours, the bodies remained alone in the chapel while crowds stood outside, confused and waiting to see whether there had been a mistake and the doors would open again.

Johann and the countess retrieved Maria and Countess von Montfort after leaving the chapel. They had arranged to go together to the funeral. After a light lunch at the Montfort residence, they returned to the chapel and took their seats among the mourners. There were many empty seats in the chapel when, at precisely four o'clock, the elderly kaiser himself arrived followed by most of the archdukes of the Habsburg family, but not the children of the dead couple. Johann, Maria, and the two countesses watched in quiet disbelief as Cardinal Piffl conducted a funeral mass in a mere fifteen minutes, at which point the kaiser and the archdukes left the chapel and the bodies were again locked in, alone.

8.

Revenge

VIENNA, July 1—Details of the trial now underway in Sarajevo have so far revealed that there were as many as six conspirators in addition to Gavrilo Princip who were involved in a plan to enter Austria-Hungary from Serbia to murder Archduke Franz Ferdinand. Despite denials that the Serbian government assisted in the planning of the assassination, the conspirators have been unable to account for how they came into possession of pistols and bombs used to attack the imperial entourage as it passed through the city.

In particular, the pistol used by Princip, which is in the hands of the Austrian authorities, is identical to those issued to officers of the Serbian army and virtually unobtainable to impoverished youths such as Princip; a fact repeatedly pointed out by the prosecution. Further, none of the conspirators deny that they were members of a fanatical Serbian organization known as "Young Bosnia" whose mission is to violently overthrow Austrian authority in Bosnia and incorporate the province into a so-called "Greater Serbia." Austrian authorities claim that Young Bosnia is known to include members of the Serbian officer corps and secret service in the Serbian royal government in Belgrade.

As these details emerge, editorials and commentary in the Vienna press are already concluding that such a conspiracy could not possibly have escaped the attention of the Serbian government and that, indeed, the Serbian government itself was likely involved in the conspiracy. The Serbian government denies any involvement whatsoever and that it will arrest anyone who is shown to have been involved. These denials are met with scorn and derision here as the trial continues. Strangely, there has been no comment at all from the Austro-Hungarian government …

Maria examined herself in her bedroom mirror as she waited for Johann to call. He had sent her a note the previous day informing her that he had been attached to a new regiment that was being transferred to Bosnia immediately and would call before he left. Rioting and vengeance against the Serbs by Croats and Muslim Bosnians loyal to the crown in and around Sarajevo required additional military reinforcements be sent there, the newspapers had reported. Maria doubted that it was their real reason for entraining to the province. Additional military units, once there, could easily be turned against the Serbs in Belgrade, just across the River Sava from the border, should war begin. Everyone knew that.

A soft knock at the door by the housekeeper. Johann had arrived. Maria took one last look in the mirror and then went downstairs where Johann was waiting.

"Maria," Johann said upon seeing her. He was in his uniform. "I haven't got long. The train will leave at six o'clock. I wanted to say good-bye. I don't know when I'll be back. I'm sorry, but …" He kissed her once on each cheek.

"Of course," Maria replied. "I understand completely. The wedding ..."

"Yes, I know," Johann said, looking at her intently. "We can plan it for the fall. Perhaps in October or November. The war will be over by then. We'll crush them in a few weeks, you mark my words."

"No, I think we had better wait until you return to decide. Who can say what will happen?" The possibility that Russia might come to Serbia's aid was the unspoken, unthinkable possibility that loomed in the Viennese air, but that wasn't it. No, that wasn't it at all. *It was a sign*, Maria thought. It was a sign to turn back before it was too late. She didn't love him. She cared for him, yes. She hoped to God that he came home safe and sound, but this was not the time to tell him everything. Not when he was getting ready to go to war. But it had come to this and it was a relief. She would tell him when he got back. When things got back to normal.

"Yes, I suppose you're right," Johann replied. "I'm so sorry ..."

"Don't be," Maria said. "Don't think about it at all, Johann. It'll be all right. The most important thing is that you come back safe and sound. Then we'll worry about the wedding."

Johann smiled, seemingly relieved. "Thank you for being so understanding. I know you and our mothers have put so much time into planning this and we were so close, but who could have guessed something like this would happen?"

"Exactly. Would you like something to eat before you go? It will be a long trip, I'm sure, and the food must be dreadful ..."

VIENNA, July 22—Press accounts here of the trial continuing in Sarajevo now confirm that the Sarajevo conspirators were assisted by unknown persons in entering Austrian territory from Serbia weeks prior to the assassination and were hidden in "safe houses" whose locations were pre-arranged until the arrival of the archduke and his wife in Sarajevo were precisely determined. In some manner, the conspirators learned after their arrival in Bosnia—not only the exact date, but the planned procession route of the imperial entourage when it would enter the city—which enabled them to carefully position themselves at various points along the route to carry out their murderous purpose.

These newest revelations continue to confirm the existence of a wider conspiracy, almost certainly including numerous other Serbian individuals in Belgrade with access to such information and having the ability to communicate it to known safe locations within Bosnia where the conspirators lay in wait. Austrian judicial authorities continued to press Princip and the others to reveal the identity of these individuals to no avail, claiming their identities were unknown to them.

There has still been no official comment from the Austrian government on these revelations, but unofficial sources within the imperial government have concluded that high-ranking members of the Serbian secret service must have been involved in planning the attack. Viennese newspapers speculate that in due course, the Austrian government will demand that Serbia permit a further investigation of the conspiracy by Austrian officials in Serbia which would, they have no doubt, expose the fact that high Serbian officials were involved. The Serbian government continues to deny any role in the assassination ...

As Andy sent cable after cable back home, war fever swept the capital. All the newspapers were aflame with demands for military action to be taken at last against Serbia, and yet still there was still a strange silence from the government at the *Ballhausplatz*, where the imperial foreign ministry was located. Motorcars came and went. Diplomats and generals went in and out while growing crowds gathered to watch.

Otto von Windischgrätz had introduced Andy to Ottokar Graf von Czernin in the meantime. A close friend of Otto's, the count was the unofficial source of some of Andy's breaking stories. Tall and erect with a long neck and high collar surmounted by a long, narrow face, the count was from an ancient Bohemian family of impeccable nobility. The count, on Otto's encouragement and apparently seeing some advantage in cultivating world opinion outside Europe, was willing to give Andy some information concerning the government's state of mind, but some of the information was "off the record" and could not be used—at least not yet.

"We are concerned about the attitude of Russia in all of this," Count Czernin stated in a very deep bass voice in his most important interview with Andy and Prince Otto to date. "We are convinced, of course, that a number of Serbian military and government officials were involved, but the Russian ambassador insists that there is no real proof and that Russia will view any use of force against Serbia as inviting the 'gravest consequences.'"

"What does that mean?" Andy asked.

"In diplomatic parlance, the 'gravest consequences' means war."

"So what he is saying, then, is that if Austria were to attack Serbia, Russia would attack Austria?" Andy asked.

"At this point, yes."

"What are we to do?" Otto intervened. "Are we to allow the Serbian authorities to continue to send murderers into our own country with impunity?"

"Exactly," Czernin replied. "That is how we see it. It is difficult to know whether the Russians actually desire the Serbians to provoke us into a war that they will then enter against us, or that we swallow this provocation and are shown to the world to be too weak or timid even to protect our own interests. Either way, this would be quite satisfactory to Russia. They have never forgiven us for annexing Bosnia in 1907, you know. It was Russia who was humiliated then and was shown to be too weak and timid to protect her friends in the Balkans, like Serbia. They have not forgotten that. Not at all. This time, they are turning the tables on us, I'm afraid."

"It's a chess game, then, isn't it?" Andy said after a moment. "Serbia, small as it might be, believes that if Austria attacks, Russia will come to the rescue, they will both defeat Austria, and then Serbia will take Bosnia."

"If that happens, I am afraid the monarchy will collapse," Czernin said. "We all do. We have avoided war for more than forty years. It has been the kaiser's wish. It was the archduke's wish as well. Many counseled otherwise. Conrad for one. He warned it would come to this someday. He wanted to attack the Serbs when they had their backs to the wall in the Balkan wars last year and the year before that. Then we would have had allies. Bulgaria for one. And Turkey. Now Serbia is stronger and they have chosen the time."

"But what about Germany?" asked Otto. "Surely if Russia attacks us, Germany will come to our aid. Germany and Austria could defeat Russia and Serbia."

"We shall see," Czernin replied mysteriously. "We shall see. It's not just the Germans, though, Otto. There's the Hungarians."

"What about the Hungarians?" Andy asked. Hungary was the other half of the empire, he knew. It had not occurred to him that they would have to be consulted.

"Hungary wants no war," Czernin replied. "The Hungarian prime minister, Tisza, is against any military action against Serbia now. He's suspicious that Austria would incorporate Serbia into the empire if we were victorious and that there would be even more treacherous Slavs within the empire to deal with. Unless the Hungarians agree, Austria cannot fight alone. Thus, the complicity of Serbia in the assassination must be very clear. That is why we waited for details from the trial. In the meantime, we are carefully discussing the situation with our friends in Germany and Hungary. We must be very careful indeed."

It was monstrously complicated, Andy thought as he and Otto left the Ballhausplatz. He could not report on the things that he had heard in the dispatch. He would have to content himself with the reaction of the people and the press in Vienna for now.

"As you see, things are happening behind the scenes, Andy," said Otto as they walked. He stared at the ground pensively. "Diplomats and generals all over Europe are checking and re-checking their ground while the people wait. The fate of millions is being decided tonight over polished tables under crystal chandeliers. People are holding their breath and waiting to see and hear what happens next."

"But, Uncle, it seems to me there is a problem that will never be solved. The truth about what happened is in Serbia. Serbia will never admit anything. If they do, perhaps they fear Russia will have to abandon her if they are shown to be the murderers Austria thinks they are. The only way to show the world that the Serbian government is involved is for someone inside Serbia to give up some paper or confess to the crime. If that doesn't happen, what then?"

VIENNA, July 24—The Austrian government has sent an ultimatum to Serbia demanding that within forty-eight hours, the Serbian government permit Austrian officials to enter the country to complete their investigation into the conspiracy to murder Archduke Franz Ferdinand nearly a month ago. The Austrian government has also made a number of other demands on the Serbian government to suppress further provocations and terrorist attacks in Austria-Hungary. Although the Serbian government continues to deny any involvement in the conspiracy, it is generally thought here that further investigation will reveal that this was not and is not the case. Clearly, the Austrian government has placed Serbia in a difficult position.

"The Serbian government is in a vise," Otto said as he read the latest newspaper article at breakfast. "It might work, I must say. It's very clever."

Andy had been telegraphing his father almost daily reports of what had been happening in Vienna. His father had encouraged him to keep reporting everything that he could. His reporting was excellent, he said, and they were using every dispatch he sent. The European crisis, as he called it, was again "front-page news" in America. Everyone at home was holding their breath to see what would happen next as the drama played out. Andy devoured the Viennese newspapers that now turned their gaze to reporting the reaction of the other European capitals.

In Belgrade, some newspapers said, the Russian ambassador was reportedly meeting almost continuously with the Serbian government. In Berlin, according to press accounts there, the German government fully supported Austria and the German press clamored for Serbia to submit to Austria's demands. In London and Paris, the reaction was far more reserved and cautious. The British parliament was due to meet in an emergency session to discuss the crisis and the foreign minister, Grey, had just urged an international conference on the matter, whatever Serbia's reply might be. There was an ominous silence from the Russian capital. It could only mean that Russia was carefully considering its next move on the chessboard, Andy concluded.

The next day, after breakfast with Otto and Rudi, Andy found his thoughts turning to Maria. With Johann gone, Maria was alone again. Alone in her house with her mother. Andy hadn't spoken to her in days. He decided to visit to check on her while he waited for further developments and then another dispatch home. He took the streetcar to her house. At first, Andy began to discuss the latest news, but before long, Maria had a revelation of her own.

"Johann and I have decided to postpone planning our wedding, of course," she started. "In fact, Andy, when Johann returns, I've made up my mind to tell him that I will not marry him."

Andy was dumbfounded. As he started to reply, she continued. "Andy, the truth is I have never loved him. Not as a woman should love a husband. Of course I do care about him. Very much. I'm afraid for him now." Tears began to well up in her eyes. Then she wiped them away, brusquely, trying to regain her composure. He could tell that she was embarrassed. Confused. He reached out and touched her hand. To his surprise, she held it tightly.

"It would have been a disastrous mistake," she continued, slowly. "I'm sure of that now. If I had any doubts before, I'm quite sure that this is the right thing to do."

As Andy listened, Maria explained her situation further. She told him about Johann's many liaisons with other women, even after she had become engaged to him. She knew that he would never be faithful to her. Couldn't be. It wasn't in his nature.

"He's so different, really. You know that, Andy. You can see that too, can't you?" Andy wanted to agree, but found himself fumbling for words and could only nod, vaguely, waiting for her to finish. "I know I want a different life. I wasn't meant to be a countess. I want to live in a different world than he could possibly ever understand. I've gone too far, now, haven't I, Andy?" Her eyes were red as she paused, looking at him.

Andy realized that he still had her hand in his and he gently pulled her to him. For a moment, just a moment, they were face to face. He put his arm around her. He only meant to embrace her, to comfort her, but then as he looked into her tearful eyes, her words hanging in the air, the words finally came.

"Yes, I think you've gone too far. Maybe we both have." With that, he kissed her. It was a soft kiss on soft lips. He felt her arms. Then their lips parted, and then another. Longer. And then another.

There was no sound except the tick-tock of a clock from somewhere in the room. Time seemed to stand still—whatever was happening in the world. He knew he didn't want this time to end but, of course, it did.

At noon the next day, Andy bought several Viennese newspapers. All of them had printed the text of the Austrian foreign minister's telegram to the Serbian government:

> The Royal Serbian Government not having answered in a satisfactory manner the note of July 23, 1914, presented by the Austro-Hungarian minister at Belgrade, the imperial and royal government are themselves compelled to see to the safeguarding of their rights and interests, and, with this object, to have recourse to force of arms. Austria-Hungary consequently considers herself henceforward in a state of war with Serbia.

If Count Czernin had correctly described the situation the other day, Andy thought, the Austrian declaration of war could only mean that the resistance of the Hungarians to war had been overcome and that assurances had been received from Germany that if Russia were to attack Austria, Germany would come to Austria's defense. Now that the monarchy had made its move on the chessboard, it remained to be seen what Russia and the other European powers would do next.

9.

The Bloodletting Begins

"Germany has declared war on Russia," Otto said as Andy sat down to join him for breakfast. It was August 2.

They had known since the day before that this was a possibility. After Austria declared war on Serbia and began bombarding its capital of Belgrade, the tsar of Russia called for the mobilization of the colossal Russian army. Russia did not declare war, but it was obvious that the mobilized millions she would call up would quickly be moved to the long frontier with Austria-Hungary in preparation for an ultimatum of her own or invasion.

A day earlier, Kaiser Wilhelm of Germany had made the next move in the form of an ultimatum to the tsar, demanding an immediate stop to the Russian mobilization against Austria or face war with Germany, much to the relief of the Viennese. For twenty-four hours, there had been hope that Germany's bold move would have the desired result: a minimal, local war between Austria-Hungary and Serbia but, alas, it was not to be.

Russia had not agreed to Germany's terms within the appointed time. Ironically, Austria-Hungary and Russia were still not at war but, at this point, declarations of war between them would be a formality. It did not end there.

Two days later, after France refused to confirm its neutrality to Germany's satisfaction, Germany declared a state of war existed with France as well. Then, on the same day, much to the surprise of the Viennese press, Germany began an invasion of Belgium without a declaration of war. An ultimatum to Germany promptly followed from Great Britain, demanding immediate German withdrawal from Belgium. When this was ignored, Britain declared war on Germany on August 4. In less than a week after Austria's declaration of war against Serbia, what had begun as a punitive war against a rogue Balkan state had blown up into the first, all-out continental war in Europe since the defeat of Napoleon at Waterloo almost exactly one hundred years before.

Yet, after the flurry of diplomatic activity and declarations of war, the early days and weeks of August were eerily quiet. The Windischgrätz house seemed listless and forlorn after both Ernst and Rudi had left home for military service. There had been no triumphant invasion of Serbia as had been initially expected since the Austrians had been required to redirect their forces to face the dangerous threat of Russia to the north and east. Soldiers mobilized and trains ran continuously from the stations in Vienna going east, filled with soldiers, artillery, horses, feed, shells, and every conceivable materiel of war, but there were no major battles yet.

"It's the calm before the storm," Otto said one evening as they drank cognac in the drawing room.

"What do you think is happening?"

"This will be a war of millions. It takes time to organize and transport huge armies on this scale to their positions. You can be sure the Russians are massing their forces just as we are. What is amazing is how fast the Germans seem to be able to move. It's their railways. The best in the world."

"You mean the invasion of Belgium?"

"Yes, it's amazing how fast they are cutting through Belgium while simultaneously holding off the French attacks on the Rhine."

Indeed, while the armies in the east slowly formed up for their showdown, somehow the Germans seemed to be a step ahead of everyone. Like the tide coming in, the Germans had washed over Belgium and were now flooding into northern France, pushing the French and British armies back relentlessly.

"They're amazing. If they defeat the French and knock them out of the war in one stroke, the British will have to retreat across the channel and then Germany will turn her full force on the Russians with us. It just might work."

On August 20, Brussels fell to the Germans. Less than a week later, on August 26, the German army won a crushing victory over the Russians at Tannenberg, utterly annihilating a huge Russian army that had ventured into eastern Prussia. A few days later, on August 29, news came of the first major Austrian battle with the Russians at Krasnik. The Austrian general, Viktor Graf Dankyl, had defeated another Russian army, forcing it to retreat. But then disaster.

With scant acquaintance of the geography of the empire and eastern Europe, Andy attempted to piece together what was happening each day from the Viennese newspapers and what interviews he was able to get from Otto's friends and contacts. Otto helped him in the upstairs study that he and Elisabeth had cleared and reorganized for him to work in. Otto found maps of the areas where reports of battles broke out from day to day and then borrowed or bought more when the ones at hand proved inadequately detailed, but there were many obstacles. Obscure places, not on the maps, suddenly became critically important points in the military struggle. Like Galicia.

"It's Austrian Poland," Elisabeth explained, drawing her finger across a wide, crescent-shaped arc of territory adjacent to the Russian border. "The Poles live there and, in the southern part, Ukrainians too. It's flat with many rivers and towns. Krakow, Lemberg ..."

But there were other problems in getting sufficient information and understanding of the daily military situation for Andy to prepare another dispatch. For one thing, there was the sometimes obvious, sometimes subtle military censorship that obscured the movement of armies within the empire or what happened to them. One day, there were reports of a large offensive and then, maddeningly, nothing for days. One assumed an Austrian defeat when this happened, but one never knew or on what scale.

Then there were the rumors that whipped through the city, perhaps as a consequence of the censorship. People heard this and that. Sometimes it was true, but sometimes it wasn't. There were mistakes in the press. Then there was the problem of getting the news home. Austrian telegraph lines to America were cut in the first days of the war. Now wires and cables had to be sent to a neutral country first, such as Switzerland, Italy, or the Netherlands. Then they had to be re-sent from there to New York and thence to Columbus. It took longer, was more expensive, and made for painstaking work, but it all proved to be worth it.

Arthur Bishop cabled back that Andy's stories were very popular. The first news that Americans got through their daily newspapers came from England, he explained, and passed through British censors. News from Germany came later and in bits and pieces. News from Austria and the eastern front was virtually non-existent due to a lack of reporters and sources of information. Millions of German, Austrian, and Hungarian immigrants in eastern Ohio and western Pennsylvania were starved for information about their countrymen and relatives in central and eastern Europe while news of the fighting and maneuvering on the western front dominated most newspapers.

As the weeks went by, Andy's articles in Arthur's *Tribune*

were being purchased and reprinted far beyond the city limits of Columbus. The *Pittsburgh Press, Cleveland Plain-Dealer,* and other major newspapers in nearby big cities with large eastern European constituencies made deals with the *Tribune* to receive articles from the *Tribune's* correspondent in Vienna. Then the *Baltimore Sun, Cincinnati Post,* and *Chicago Tribune* had come calling. Andy's portraits and landscapes of the view from Vienna were practically the only gallery of images that Americans interested in the eastern European war had to read. Soon, Arthur was able to arrange a very handsome salary and expense account for his son from the lucrative deals the *Tribune* had made with the other papers.

> VIENNA, September 16—The skirmishing of the past few weeks has clearly ended in the past few days and it is now obvious that an enormous struggle is raging in the frontier areas of Austrian Poland known as Galicia. Despite their repulse at Tannenberg by the Germans far to the north in Prussia, it is now abundantly clear that the great weight of the vast Russian army has been arrayed not against Germany, but here in Galicia against the Austro-Hungarians. The flat terrain with few natural obstacles offers a nearly perfect battleground for the warring armies of the two empires.
>
> Long aware of the potential vulnerability of Galicia to invasion, the Austrians had created a chain of fortress cities with large garrisons. In the past few days, however, the fortress bastion at Lemberg, thought to be virtually impregnable, has been captured by an invading Russian army. A second fortress city at Przemyśl is being rapidly approached. It now appears that the Russians had been biding their time in the past month, patiently massing their forces and now the hammer has fallen hard.
>
> Vienna itself is feeling the hard blows raining down on the army. Casualties are streaming into the hospitals from the railway station daily. Black

bunting appears everywhere as deaths of Viennese soldiers have mounted with alarming speed. There have been food shortages. The government declared meatless days of the week to conserve it for the army. The initial euphoria of a quick, punishing war against Serbia has largely evaporated here with anxiety over the fighting in the east. Cynical and pessimistic by nature, the Viennese seem to expect the worst.

As important as his work had become, Andy had to fight off the constant temptation to see Maria. His thoughts drifted to her and of the next time he could contrive to see her. It was their secret and had to remain so since Maria was still outwardly affianced to Johann. She had broken the news of her intentions to her mother, but not of her love for Andy.

Today they had arranged to meet at the botanical gardens of the University of Vienna. The chill of autumn was not yet felt during the day, but it was cool and bright as they strolled through the gardens, arm in arm.

"Andy, what do you suppose I could do in America? I mean, as an occupation? What do young women like me do in Columbus, Ohio?" Maria asked.

"Perhaps you could be a teacher? Perhaps you could teach German to American schoolchildren?" He thought of his German teacher at St. Mary's school in the German village who was now quite old, he imagined. Maria seemed to like the idea.

"Teaching is a noble profession, I think. Being entrusted with so many young minds by their parents. Telling them the truth. Bringing them along into the world of adults. Yes, I think I would like that …"

They talked about what Andy might do after the war was over. He thought that he might like to report from some other European countries, but no, if Maria wanted to see America, that would be fine too. It didn't really matter to Andy where he might be—as long as she was there with him, he thought. He was enthralled with her. She was still, in his eyes, the most beautiful woman in the world and, as time went on and they opened their hearts to each other, he fell deeper and deeper in love with her.

Except for her beauty, Andy slowly came to understand why Maria von Montfort was not meant to be a countess, as she had said that fateful day. She disdained officious formality and the doctrinaire viewpoints typical of her class. She questioned conventional wisdom and, if unconvinced by the defense, would reject it and begin a quest for a new truth to replace it. Her education and intelligence made her a sparkling conversationalist on almost any subject. Her feminine gestures and expressions were arresting and irresistibly charming—not just to Andy, but to any man who met her. The most amazing thing of all though, to Andy, was her seemingly reciprocal attraction to him.

VIENNA, September 23—Grave news of another defeat at Rava Ruska reached the capital today. As a result, the fortified city of Przemyśl, garrisoned by as many as 50,000 soldiers has now fallen behind Russian lines and is besieged. The Imperial High Command has confirmed that the army is in retreat at the moment with resultant loss of extensive territory on the frontiers. Pessimism about the ability of the empire to withstand much more permeates the thoughts of the Viennese as death lists in the papers reflect the enormous casualties being sustained daily on the northeastern front ...

On a late September day, Andy met Maria again at Fidelio's Café on the Ringstrasse. The deteriorating situation with the war could not be ignored.

"The last time I saw him, Johann told me he would be back in a few weeks. My God, that seems like ages ago. I wish the war was over by now. How long can it last, do you think?"

"It's hard to say," Andy replied. "Otto thinks it may not end for a long time."

"Not even with the casualties? I worry about Rudi and Johann. I keep expecting any day to hear that they've been killed. And Ernst too. So many dead. Oh God, I wish it would end."

"I know. Have you heard anything from Johann?"

"No. Nothing. It must be horrible."

"It doesn't look good, Maria," said Andy. "If Przemyśl falls, there will be no telling what happens. It's the last bastion left holding the Russians at bay. The Austrian army is falling back."

"I know. I can't think of anything else. Everyone is preparing for the worst. I pray and pray that Johann, Rudi, and Ernst will be spared, but it seems hopeless. Maybe the Germans will be able to do something."

"I don't think so," said Andy. "It looks as if they have been stopped on the Marne and have their hands full with the French and the British. I don't think they can spare anything to help Austria right now."

"They say there were massive defections and surrenders of the Czech units. Can we survive against the Russians with traitors in our own army?" It did look bleak indeed.

Andy was typing the draft of another dispatch in the study upstairs. As he considered his next lines, he gazed out the window. It was October. The leaves had begun to turn and a light rain was falling. A soft knock at the door. It was one of the maids. She had a silver tray with an envelope for him. He opened the envelope.

> Dearest Andy,
>
> The Countess von Caboga sent word a few minutes ago that Johann was wounded in the fighting at Przemyśl and is in a military hospital in a town called Kosice in grave condition. I must go to him with the countess. She is preparing to leave immediately. Could you come with us? The countess will have her driver, but we are just two women and the country around there may be dangerous ...

Elisabeth entered the room as he finished the note. He looked up and handed it to her. She read it quickly.

"Will you go?"

"Yes, Aunt Elisabeth. I hope I can be of some help."

"I think of this every day. I die every time I hear the doorbell. Some days I think it's only a matter of time. Two sons. So much death. What is the chance that both of them will survive? The poor countess. Such an agony, not knowing. I will have the cook prepare you a basket to bring with you. Please give the countess my love and tell her Otto and I will say a novena for divine mercy for her and for Johann."

"You may need money," said Otto.

"I have some, don't worry."

"Yes, but here, take this with you." Otto handed him a fat wad of bills. "Hide it in your suitcase just in case. In situations like this, a bank note won't do. You may need it. There will be a telegraph office somewhere in Kosice. If you need anything from here, wire us immediately and we will do our best."

"Thank you, Uncle."

"And one more thing, Andy. I've heard from my cousin Sophie about your ancestor, Matthias. She needs a little more time to confirm some things, but now is not the time to discuss this. When you get back, we will talk."

Andy looked at Otto, but he was right. Now was not the time. The car was waiting for him and, without knowing where he was going, exactly, or what he would do when he got there, Andy left for the Russian front.

10.

Kocise

The roads east to Budapest and for a few hours thereafter had been well paved and reasonable, but their quality fell off rapidly after reaching Gödöllő, a small Hungarian town whose claim to fame was that it contained another one of the kaiser's residences. Walther, Countess von Caboga's driver, worked the car forward as, at times, it bogged down in caked mud or nearly slid off the road. Then the road would harden again for a while, which usually meant that they were about to approach another Hungarian village through which they would pass, watched in some wonder by children, old men, and farmers' wives. The countess had also brought several picnic baskets of food and condiments, including silverware. They stopped by the side of a picturesque pasture under a large tree and ate lunch, served by Walther.

"It looks like it may rain again," Maria said as she pointed toward the east and the dark clouds that were building in the sky.

"The roads may get worse as we get into Slovakia," the countess worried. "Walther, what about spare tires? Did you bring some?"

Walther replied that he had. One, that is. After that, they

An American in Vienna

would have to patch the tires if need be or rely on local help which, given the need for tires for the war, was probably wishful thinking.

By late afternoon, after navigating more treacherous roads and bridges, at times in pouring rain, they passed an army encampment. A sentry stopped them briefly, sticking his head into the car and, after observing them for a moment, waved them on without asking any questions. By nightfall, they had reached Mezőkövesd, a medium-sized Hungarian railroad town. There were no hotels except at the rail station and the hotel was dark and dingy, well below the countess's standards, but it would have to do. At dinner, a meager fare from a very limited menu. It was a relief the next day to leave, but soon new problems arose.

It was a gray, overcast day and they had been driving for a couple of hours, approaching Miskolc. It sounded like distant thunder, but quickly they realized the low thud was artillery. Another checkpoint, this time more serious. Questions about who they were, where they were going, and warnings that they may not be able to drive much farther.

The next town had been destroyed. There was no other word for it. Stone and brick houses and buildings smashed to bits with debris everywhere. It had obviously been fought over days or perhaps weeks earlier. There were no active fires or smoldering, but clearly there had been much fighting. Barbed wire in coils, now abandoned. Huge ditches where Andy guessed that artillery shells had landed in the battle. Then there it was again, another barrage of artillery in the distance, louder now. Closer now. A convoy of lorries with mud-caked wheels coming the other way. Walther had to drive off the road to let them pass. One car toward the rear stopped upon seeing them. There were officers in the car. One of them stepped out and crossed the road to speak with them.

"May I ask where you're going?" the officer asked politely, but insistently. He looked into the car. Andy imagined how incongruous they must seem to the officer in the huge Daimler automobile, the countess with her hat, Walther in his chauffer livery, miles from any town on this country road. Walther answered that they were headed for Kocise.

"I'm afraid that's impossible. The road is blocked ahead. This is a war zone. You must turn around and go back." Another series of low thuds in the distance caused the officer to pull back away from the car and look in the direction of the sound. He raised his arm, pointing. "You see?"

Walther began to speak, but the countess opened her door and stepped out of the car. Andy instinctively opened his door as well and stepped out as the countess approached the officer. The other officers, sitting in their open car, had all turned to watch and now began getting out of their car as well.

"Sir, I am Margaretha Grafin von Caboga. My son, Johann Graf von Caboga, is an officer in His Majesty's Army and was severely wounded in action around Przemyśl. We were informed he is in a military hospital in Kocise. We are on our way to see him. Can you please tell us how we can get to him?"

The officer was momentarily flabbergasted, Andy could tell. There was something in the imperious manner of the countess that brooked no opposition, but he quickly regained the high ground.

"I am sorry, Countess," the officer replied, nodding slightly to acknowledge her noble status, "but I cannot let you go forward. You must understand. It is extremely dangerous to go any farther. The villages ahead have been evacuated and we are in action right now against the Russians. I regret, my lady, but it is simply not possible."

The countess was about to reply when another one of the officers, having overheard the last exchange, joined the conversation.

"My dear Countess, may I introduce myself. I am General Stanislaus von Puchalski. The captain here is entirely correct.

May I suggest, however, another route? If your driver would turn back, about three to five kilometers, there is a little town that was fairly badly damaged. You must have passed it. Do you know the one of which I speak?" Walther, Andy, and the countess all nodded while Maria watched from the car.

"If you return there and turn right, there is another road north that will take you into the town of Edelény. If you continue north from there, you will drive several hours until you reach Nad Bodvu and another highway. Take the highway east from there and you will reach Kocise. That should keep you far enough away from the front, but I must warn you, the road is very bad in places. If you must go, however, that is the only way open at this time. Good day, my lady." With that, the general bowed and took his leave. It seemed they had no choice.

It was as the general had said, in every respect. As they proceeded east from Nad Bodvu, more lorries, this time with large red crosses, vied with them for the road, proceeding west. Then lines of refugees by the side of the road. More refugees walking toward them on the road, some pushing carts of belongings, some carrying large bundles on their backs. Distant artillery salvos could again be heard. By dusk, they finally reached Peres and saw from a sign that Kocise was only a few kilometers away. They were in desperate need of petrol by that point and had to stop.

Peres had checkpoints at numerous locations and was guarded by soldiers at nearly every intersection. There was a small inn by a square in the middle of the town. Miraculously, it had rooms.

"I think we should stop here," Andy said. "Who knows what we will find in Kocise. The father east we go, the closer we get to the fighting."

"But Johann," the countess protested. "He may be dying. I must see him and we're so close." She was clearly exhausted by now. The strain of the drive, the worry and events of the day had taken their toll. Andy had an idea.

"Countess, let me and Walther go into the town while you and Maria rest here this evening. I will see if I can find the hospital where he is and if I can find him, I will. I'll meet you and Maria for breakfast tomorrow morning when you have your strength back."

"Andy is right, Margaretha. You should rest. You may need all your strength tomorrow. Let Andy and Walther go and we'll have something to eat."

The countess, whose commanding manner this afternoon had stopped an imperial officer in his tracks, appeared frail and overwhelmed. She considered everything for a moment, and then nodded.

"You're right. I am so very tired." She turned to Andy, eyes now red. "I would be so very grateful if you would do this for us. God be with you, Andy. Walther, take Andy and Godspeed to both of you. Thank you." With that, she took Maria's arm and slowly walked to the door of the inn.

Kosice looked very much like a front-line city at war, Andy thought as Walther maneuvered the car into the city. Bombed out shells of buildings. Soldiers everywhere, warming themselves by makeshift fires or guarding streets, buildings, or who knew what. It was dark and difficult to make out exactly where to go next in the maze of streets that went off in every direction. Occasionally, in the distance, the dull thud of artillery again. They spotted a horse-drawn ambulance going down a side street. Walther nodded at it.

"Let's follow it. It's probably going to the hospital," Walther said. Andy agreed. Walther slipped the car in gear again, slowly turning down the side street.

The headlights illuminated the ambulance as it jiggled and bounced over broken cobblestones and holes. Andy could make out what seemed to be a man sitting in the back of the wagon and the feet of others lying on stretchers. He imagined the horrors those men must be enduring—if they were conscious and alive. For what seemed to be an eternity, the ambulance proceeded gradually through the darkened streets, turning left and right and then on to what seemed like a major boulevard. More bonfires. More idle soldiers. Then, as they seemed to be reaching the outskirts of town, what appeared to be a large country home in a field.

There were other ambulances standing on the road, the horses with their heads down, chewing grass. What must have been medical orderlies seemed to be chatting in small groups, smoking cigarettes, no doubt waiting for their next assignment. They looked up at the Daimler as it passed, saying nothing.

"Let's stop for a minute and ask them if this is the hospital," Andy said. Walther stopped the car, letting it idle, and Andy stepped out. He approached the troop of men near one of the ambulances.

"Excuse me, sir, but is this the military hospital?" One of the men exhaled cigarette smoke and shook his head.

"No speak German," he said and then gestured with his head and pointed at another orderly a little farther down the street. Andy walked over to him.

"Excuse me. Is this the military hospital?"

"Yes. They're just using it as a hospital for now. The army has taken over several buildings. This is the biggest one. There are too many to put in one." The man's German was hard to understand. It was not his first language, Andy could tell, but he could understand him well enough.

"Thank you. We're looking for an officer, Captain Johann Graf von Caboga. Do you know if he's here?" The orderly shrugged.

"Many officers are here. Many. Many men. You'll have to ask up there." He gestured toward the house, if that was what it was.

"Thank you." The orderly nodded in return and Andy went back to the car.

"Walther, stay here and wait for me. I'm going up there to see what I can find out." Walther nodded, turning off the car's engine to save petrol. Andy set off in the dark.

There was a gravel driveway that led to the house. There were lights burning in the windows that dimly illuminated the driveway more and more as he got closer. It was an enormous house—a chateau, perhaps—on the outskirts of town. Soldiers again, clustered just outside the door. They regarded him as he approached.

Then, suddenly, just as Andy neared the door, another ambulance truck rolled up the driveway of the hospital, bearing its bloody cargo for delivery. Andy stopped to watch as the driver and several attendants stepped out of the truck and opened the rear doors, revealing several rows of soldiers on each side, on stretchers that were racked one atop the other. The soldiers, whose stretchers Andy watched being jostled out of the trucks, were in terrible condition. Some moaned as they came out into the light and others shrieked as they awoke to their pain. Andy felt sick as they were carried past him, the smell of urine and disinfectant in their wake.

The soldiers by the door must have been hardened to the pitiful procession. Some of them walked to the ambulance to grab another stretcher out of the truck while others stayed where they were. Andy tried to speak with them, but they shook their heads. They didn't speak German either, so he decided to go into the hospital. It took a moment until he could regain his composure enough to step inside.

There was a small table inside the door. A soldier sat behind it and looked up expectantly, saying something in a language he didn't understand. He asked him about Johann in German. The soldier looked around the room and signaled over another soldier who did speak some broken German. They were Hungarians. Johann von Caboga? They looked in a book with lines of names. Not here. Maybe at another place? The Hungarian sergeant tried to give him directions, and then drew a crude map. And so it went.

It was about midnight as Andy and Walther, both exhausted, found a third hospital. It was a stone building of some sort—perhaps a warehouse in its former life. Ambulances. Soldiers. An archway into a courtyard with many soldiers lying rough on the ground. Some lay under makeshift tarps and tents. Others lay in the open on blankets. Some young women, dressed in simple peasant garb, were taking water around in buckets and ladling it into the soldiers' mouths—at least those who could take it. It was dim with kerosene lamps for light.

Eventually another desk and another soldier with another book. Thankfully, he spoke German. Yes, Johann von Caboga was here. An orderly was eventually summoned to conduct Andy to him. They walked back through the courtyard into another building and down a corridor. A stretcher with a blanket over a body passed them going the other way.

Another enormous room with high ceilings. Lines of cots from one end of the room to the other in multiple rows, all occupied. There must have been two hundred soldiers crammed in the room. A constant murmur of pain, punctuated by random shouts and cries from over here and over there. The smell was nauseating. Andy braced himself for what he might be about to see. Then there he was.

Johann lay mercifully asleep on a cot. A bare sheet covered him and was soaked with blood on one side. Johann's stubbled face was bruised and a bloody bandage was wrapped around his forehead. A chart hung from the end of the bed. The orderly read the chart silently as Andy stared, transfixed at the sight. An image of the dashing officer he had first met in Salzburg only a couple of months earlier flitted through his mind. Then the orderly lifted the stained sheet. The last thing Andy remembered was the sight of a bloody stump where Johann's left leg should have been. The next thing he knew, he was laying on the floor with the orderly propping his head up in his lap and speaking to him.

"Sir, can you hear me? Sir, are you all right?"

Andy knew that he had fainted. He wondered how long he had been out.

"Yes. I can hear you. I think I'm all right."

Andy had been desperate for sleep and oblivion when he and Walther returned from the hospital to the hotel in Peres, but he could not stop his mind from thinking. He tossed and turned until finally he drifted off for a while, waking just after dawn to a ferocious artillery barrage that went on minute after minute. He wondered how far off the fighting could be from the city to be able to hear it from the inn. He swung his feet out of bed. Walther continued sleeping in the bed next to him. Andy tiptoed out of the room and down the hall to the bathroom. He looked in the mirror. He was surprised to see himself looking so well. He felt haggard and the memories of the night before surfaced again.

It had seemed that there was nobody in charge. The orderly knew very little. The leg had been amputated below the knee a few days earlier. They were watching for infection. Yes, the sheets needed to be changed, but there was not enough staff. He went off to look for fresh sheets.

Oh, my God, Andy had thought. What should he do? He felt as if he shouldn't leave Johann alone and yet every impulse in his body urged him to flee. The soldier behind him shouted something to him that made no sense. He turned to look at the wide-eyed young man, delirious from his wounds and what drugs had been given to him. The soldier grabbed his pants with an iron grip. Andy had to pry his fingers off to back away. There was nothing he could do.

He waited for the orderly to come back for what seemed like an hour. When he did, the orderly shrugged. Nothing. He couldn't find anything. Andy told him he would be back in the morning and the orderly nodded. Then he had left.

Walther had been waiting by the car. He had apparently been watching more wounded soldiers continue to come in and his face was drawn and white. Andy described what he had found. Walther, who had known Johann since he was a boy, was visibly upset and immediately volunteered to go back in and wait with Johann, but Andy knew that he could never navigate the car through the city back to the hotel. Aside from the prospect of getting hopelessly lost, his nerves were shot. He just couldn't do it and he needed to talk with someone. Reluctantly, Walther agreed to take him back.

Now the prospect of what to tell the countess and Maria was at hand, Andy thought as he washed his face in the sink and contemplated his razor. It had kept him awake all night. He couldn't let the countess see her son like this. It was too devastating, but what could he say? He drew himself a bath after he shaved, dressed quickly, and went downstairs.

Evidently, the countess and Maria had not been able to sleep well either because they were already eating breakfast as Andy approached their table in the inn's tiny dining room. They brightened as he arrived and Andy tried to compose himself as best he could.

"Did you find him?" Maria asked anxiously.

"Yes. It took a long time. There are several buildings being used as hospitals in Kosice. We went from one to another, but we found him."

"Oh, thank God," the countess exclaimed. "How is he?"

"He was asleep, Countess," Andy replied cautiously. "I didn't speak with him. I didn't want to wake him, but I spoke with an orderly who was taking care of him." That was a bit of an overstatement, he knew, but it would have to do.

"And his wounds? What happened to him?" the countess persisted.

"I'm not entirely sure, but ..." Andy paused. The moment had come. He still could not think of how to get around the truth and supposed it was no use anyway. She would find out sooner or later and perhaps telling her now would help prepare her for the sight of him. Maria and the countess were both looking at him and he knew from their expectant faces that they feared what he would say next.

"Countess, I hate to be the one to tell you this, but it's his leg. Something happened. They had to amputate. He seems to have had some other wounds as well. I'm not entirely sure what they are. Not now, at least. I'm so sorry ..."

Andy realized that he had been standing the whole time and now he felt weak again. He sat down. The countess looked away, stunned, gazing out the little window near the table. Her lip trembled as she gamely tried to keep her composure. Maria covered her face with her hands and quietly began to cry. Walther approached, once again in his uniform, and stood silently by the table. After a long while, the countess spoke.

"He was always a brave boy, my little Johann. He was never afraid of anything," she said to no one in particular. "I remember how he used to dive off the rocks at Lake Como. It used to scare the devil out of me, but his father used to say 'Let him do it, Margaretha' and so we did. He was born to be a soldier. It was fate." She paused and nodded her head, making a decision. "Well, he's alive. That's something. We must go."

"Countess, I have to tell you something else. This place where Johann is. It's no place for a lady like yourself. The conditions there are, well ... dire. There is a lot of suffering with the soldiers. It's a terrible place, really. I think you should stay here and let me and Walther go back. We can find his doctor, I'm sure and ..." The countess cut him off with a wave of her hand.

"Out of the question, my dear boy. I am his mother. I would gladly walk into the pits of hell to him. Not another minute. Walther, get the car." With that, she rose from the table. Walther bowed reflexively and left the room. There was real nobility in her, Andy thought. It wasn't just the title or her family pedigree. She was a mother, above all.

"We must get him out of there," the countess said to Maria and Andy. "We must get him back to Vienna where he can be cared for properly." With that, she turned and walked out of the room.

It was a bright, cool October morning as the foursome arrived at the hospital in Kocise. As they stepped out of the car, the countess donned her hat and pulled on her gloves. It was a large black hat with black ostrich feathers. As they approached the door, the countess appeared every inch the high aristocrat that she was. A woman she might be, Andy thought, but a formidable one.

The orderly was no match for her and, in a minute, was a bowing, scraping servant. She dispatched him to find an appropriate person to conduct her to the person in charge. Immediately. The next to fall was a lieutenant who, upon being introduced by Walther, was immediately also bowing, addressing her as "Illustrious Highness," the formal Austrian salutation for her rank, and inquiring if she would like some tea or refreshment. One look answered the question and then it was up the stairs, past a checkpoint of officers who removed their hats and bowed as she and her entourage swept past them. A hallway of officers and officials of some kind apparently waiting their turn to see the Oberst who loomed behind a closed door were bypassed. It was as if the kaiser himself had appeared out of thin air.

"One moment, Your Highness," the lieutenant said quietly as he rapped on the door, bowed again, and backed his way into the room, closing the door behind him. In less than a minute, the door opened and, with another bow and a wave of his arm, the countess, Andy, and Maria entered the room.

The office—and that was what it appeared to have been at one time—was quite spacious with several windows overlooking the ghastly courtyard. There was a desk piled with papers behind which sat a colonel or *Oberst* who had evidently been in conversation with another man wearing a bloodstained white coat, a doctor no doubt. The *Oberst* rose.

"Your Highness," he said simply, coming around the desk now, his eyes locked on the countess. "Please forgive our mess but ... we were not expecting you," he said with tactful understatement. The countess extended her gloved hand wordlessly. Whether from habit or not knowing what else to do, the colonel gently took her hand, bent deeply at the waist, and kissed it. Andy marveled at the boldness of the countess. The appropriate impact had been achieved.

"Never mind that, Colonel ...?"

"Andrassy, Your Highness. Please, won't you sit down?"

She glanced about the room. The doctor hurried to pick up a chair and carry it to the spot where she was standing. As she slowly sat down, she continued. "I am here to bring my son home with me to Vienna. I understand he is here at your hospital." Andrassy and the doctor exchanged a look.

"Your Highness, I am afraid I was not well acquainted with your son's ... situation until just now. This is *Herr Doktor* Doleschal." Andrassy gestured toward the doctor who clicked his heels and bowed.

"Your Highness." The countess nodded and then turned back to Andrassy, her eyebrows arched expectantly.

Andrassy continued. "I have asked the officer who brought you here to fetch Hauptman von Caboga's chart immediately. May I offer you some tea while we wait?"

The countess relented at this point and agreed to accept the colonel's hospitality. And the colonel was charming. He was Hungarian, from Gödöllō. He had been in His Majesty's service for two decades and appeared to be in his early fifties. Close-cropped, prematurely gray hair with a similar mustache. Quick asides to his aides in the Magyar language seemed curt and even surly, but when addressing his guest, he seemed to ooze unctuous charm.

Shortly, the lieutenant returned with the chart, which Doleschal read quickly. After a few moments, he looked up and turned to the countess.

"Madame, your son is in a coma. The left leg was amputated in Przemyśl a couple of days ago when he was wounded in action," said the doctor. "Since then, he has been unconscious from the head wound he got at the same time. He was in a coma when they brought him here. We may have to remove the other leg as well. It was shredded with multiple shrapnel wounds. Most of the vascular components of his leg were disrupted and there were fractures as well. The medics at Przemyśl reduced the leg fractures as best they could, but the circulation of blood to the right leg is problematic. It was a displaced fracture," Doleschal continued, bluntly. "The bone had been projecting out the skin when they put it back together, so to speak. Then they sewed up the wound made from the bone. This also disrupted the blood vessels and, at this point, we will have to see if he can pull through. If not, gangrene will set in and we will have no choice."

"When will we know?" the countess asked in a faint but firm voice.

"The next twenty-four to forty-eight hours will be critical," replied the doctor. "Then there is the head wound.

It seems when he was wounded, there was some kind of explosion or fall that resulted in a terrible concussion of the brain. We think there is some brain hemorrhage that may go away in a few hours or a few days, but you never know." Andy realized that this was the doctor's gentle way of saying that the brain injury might also be fatal—he might never wake up.

"Viktor Leoni in Vienna is a personal friend," the countess said. Doleschal nodded, apparently recognizing the name. Andy gathered that Leoni must be a famous surgeon for a doctor in this remote area to have heard of him. "I want my son brought to Vienna to see him as soon as possible."

"I understand, Your Highness," Andrassy interrupted, flashing a smile, inappropriately. "I must point out, however, that this could be very dangerous for your son. While conditions here are not, ah ... ideal, transporting him poses its own risks and we could not be, well, responsible. You understand?" Andy thought of the huge makeshift ward where he had found Johann and thought Andrassy the master of understatement now.

"Your Highness," Doleschal now joined in. "If I may speak?" The countess nodded. "I cannot emphasize enough the delicacy of Graf von Caboga's situation. His life is really hanging in the balance. The movement from here to Budapest in the ambulance, on the train ..." He shook his head slowly from side to side as he thought about it. "The blood vessels in the brain and in the leg could rupture and death would follow in a few minutes."

"Herr Doktor," Andy started slowly. "For someone in as delicate a medical situation, as you say, the conditions here last night when I found him were appalling. He was, essentially, on his own last night to live or die. It was not even sanitary." He looked briefly at the countess whose face could not hide her anguish at this revelation. "My friend could die of sepsis in your hospital the way I found him. It would seem there is a risk allowing him to remain here, do you not agree?"

Doleschal nodded gravely. "The conditions are terrible. I hope you can understand that we are doing the best we can. Nobody knows the extent of the casualties we have suffered. We are overwhelmed. But the fact remains, moving him could kill him. Letting him stay here ..." Doleschal shrugged.

"Take us to him," Maria said. She had been silent throughout the conversation and her voice broke the silence that had descended when Doleschal had stopped. The countess, now suddenly weary, rose slowly to her feet.

11.

Budapest, October 1914

On October 11, Andy awoke in his hotel in Kosice. They had decided to wait. A huge battle had been raging around Przemyśl for the past several days as Boroevic's army from Serbia had arrived in force and fallen on the Russian army laying siege to the city under the Russian general, Dimitriev. Boroević was a genius, everyone claimed to immediate enthusiastic agreement and nodding of heads, but a fresh river of casualties once again flowed into the city.

    Johann had finally regained consciousness the day before, but only briefly. The pain of the amputation was so great that morphine had to be administered constantly, which made him delirious or put him back to sleep. He would be transported by train to Budapest this morning, Andy had been told, and it was now a matter of getting themselves to Budapest to join Johann at the Royal Military Infirmary. Walther had somehow provisioned the car with food for the journey, lavishly paying the local Slovak peasants the money that Andy had given him. The car had been placed in a barn to the rear of the hotel in Peres where Walther slept, keeping close watch on it.

    They went to the hospital to make sure that Johann

was actually delivered to the train. Sure enough, orderlies arrived shortly after their arrival and carefully lifted him out of his bed on the bed sheets to a gurney after a nurse administered another dose of morphine to ease the movement. Delirious from the medication, Johann seemed confused about who they were as his mother held his hand. The orderlies wheeled him to the stairs and lifted the gurney down the narrow stairwell to the corridor leading outside to the waiting ambulance. As they came out the door, there was a distant cheer from some other part of the hospital.

The orderlies stopped at the noise, wondering what was going on. They conversed in Slovak that Andy couldn't understand. Then another orderly came through a door with a beaming smile, gesturing wildly. One of the orderlies shouted something to him and an excited conversation followed. The faces of the orderlies lit up with smiles and Andy could not bear it any longer. He asked in German what had happened. The orderly who had just appeared was nearly drowned out by more cheering, but managed to say a few words.

"Great victory. Boroević has routed the Russians around Przemyśl and the city is now free!" he said. "Russians retreating. Austrians pushing them back!"

So, Andy thought, *the Austro-Hungarians were not beaten yet.* There was a garrison of something like fifty thousand imperial troops that were now free to join Boroevic's army from Serbia. He would make notes on the train about the reaction of the hospital staff to the news from the battlefield. He had been taking notes in the days since he had arrived to put into a news article and this would go with the others.

A doctor entered the courtyard and came over to have a look at Johann. He felt his pulse and pulled down the sheet to look at Johann's legs. They were a ghastly sight in the sunlight. Maria grimaced. The countess turned her head, covering her mouth with the back of her hand to hide her grief, but the doctor seemed satisfied and pulled the sheets back up. He turned to them.

"Infection is the main thing now. His wounds are healing, but if he gets an infection, it could be bad. He isn't safe yet. Are you going to stay with him?"

"We're not allowed. There is no room on the train for civilians," Andy replied as the countess composed herself. "We will be meeting the train in Budapest if we can."

"Well, that's good," said the doctor. "They will take care of him well on the train. There are a lot of soldiers like this and they will be watching for infection. When he gets to the hospital in Budapest, they will be in a much better position than we are here to pull him through. God bless him."

Andy thanked the doctor and asked him what he made of the latest turn of events. The doctor raised an eyebrow in skepticism.

"Well, if it's true, then it's a miracle. If the Germans can take Warsaw, then maybe that will take the pressure off us," said the doctor. He was alluding to the arrival of Germany's East Prussian army under von Hindenburg that now threatened Russia's largest imperial city in its western provinces.

Andy followed the gurney out to the ambulance, which had already deposited its cargo of freshly mutilated warriors and awaited the arrival of transfers to take them back to the station. Several wounded soldiers were already in the truck when Johann arrived. Johann had lapsed into unconsciousness again, which was undoubtedly a good thing, Andy thought. The next few hours would certainly be a torture otherwise. The roads were fairly good in the towns, paved with cobblestones or gravel, but as one got away from populated areas, they became rutted dirt roads pitted with holes or caked with mud.

As the ambulance pulled away from the hospital, Andy began to walk back into the town center to the hotel with Maria and the countess. He wondered what people back home were doing. He had received a telegram at the hotel from his father, routed to him by Otto and Elisabeth. The World Series. Philadelphia and Boston. He knew his father would sneak into the sports section of the newspaper where the tickertape came inning by inning. The old Germans in the village smoking their pipes on their stoops. Then he stopped short. Could there be any place on earth at the moment that was not absorbed and engrossed in the monumental struggle taking place on this continent? Could there be a place, so far away, that all this was just a distant thunder? For the first time in a long time, Andy felt a pang of homesickness.

He wanted to get away from this horrendous slaughter. As badly as he had been affected by the gruesome scenes he had witnessed at the hospital, he had thought that he might in time get used to the carnage, at least a little bit. He hadn't. The wounds came in all kinds. Shot-off arms and legs. Terrible chest and abdominal wounds. It was too much to bear and yet these people had to bear it and keep going. War on this scale was a ghastly thing. Andy knew that he had only witnessed a small corner of the struggle. He knew that terrible battles were being fought in Belgium and France as well as in Germany, Russia, and Austria. Millions and millions of men were engaged in this brutal business with no end in sight.

When they reached the hotel, Walther quickly placed their luggage and belongings in the Daimler and they left the town slowly, driving down the narrow streets as the people raised their heads to watch the beautiful car pass by. The countess nodded to some of the Slovaks who nodded to them. Peasant women with no teeth. Bent over old men with berets. Untended dogs roaming, looking for anything to eat that the humans had forgotten. They reached the outskirts of town, farmland, and the bouncing, grinding dirt road leading to Budapest and whatever could come next.

The week in Kocise had brought more than a little

uncertainty into Andy's relationship with Maria. They both pretended not to have any special feelings toward one another when the countess was around, of course, but there was precious little time they were together for long. They had divided the time spent with Johann between the four of them. Andy had come to feel a certain distance opening up between them. As the days went on, dark thoughts began to gnaw at him. What were her feelings toward him in light of the disaster that had befallen Johann?

A day's drive brought the little party to the Hungarian town of Miskolc where they stayed the night in a small country inn. The second day, they reached Hatvan, another dreary Hungarian village town where another night was spent in another inn. The weather was surprisingly warm and clear. At the request of the countess, they had put the top down and enjoyed the fresh air of the rural countryside. Eventually, they came upon a Hungarian farm. By the road was what appeared to be a roadside shrine.

"Stop the car, Walther," the countess said from the backseat. Walther slowed the car and they came to a stop.

"Shall we have lunch here, Your Highness?" Walther inquired.

"Yes, Walther. Why not?" Walther turned off the motor and they were enveloped in silence. After a few moments, their ears adjusted to the quiet. The shrine was in a small area where the grass had been cut. Someone nearby apparently tended to it. The Virgin Mary held the infant Christ child atop a small, square stone column. A vase containing some bright yellow flowers at the base. Small gravestones close by. There were inscriptions on the column, but they were in Magyar. The sound of birds. A vast field adjoined the little grassy area. Grapes. It was a vineyard. Little bushes as far as the eye could see. Off in the distance, they could make out a farmhouse of white stucco with a thatched roof. A barn. There were no people in sight.

"How lovely," Maria said as she opened the car door and

stretched. They all did. The countess walked silently over to the shrine. No hat or gloves now, but still dressed in black, she bent to read the inscription. Walther spread a blanket on the ground and began unpacking a basket of sandwiches, fruit, and wine.

"It's hard to believe that there is a great war going on, isn't it?" Maria said to Andy as they watched the countess who seemed deep in thought.

"Yes. It is." There were no sounds of artillery, no ambulances. Andy thought that it was one of the most serene, beautiful sights he had seen in a long time.

Maria walked over to the shrine next to the countess and gently took her hand. As if awakening from a dream, the countess turned and gave Maria a wan smile. She seemed very frail, Andy thought. The strain was clearly wearing badly on her and it was far from over. She made the sign of the cross and knelt down before the little statue. Maria did the same. They prayed in silence together and then, after a while, arose and came to eat.

Something about the country air made the food taste better than anything Andy had eaten in weeks. It was simple fare. Polish ham and some cheese with mustard. Apples. Walther retreated to the car to let them eat and talk.

"Dear God," the countess said at one point. "I was just a child when we had the last war in 1866. I hardly remember it. It was over in a few weeks. Of course, soldiers lost their lives. I think five or six thousand at Königgrätz. That's nothing in this war. There must have been five thousand wounded soldiers in Kocise alone and who knows how many died. This can't go on. We can't stand much more of this."

"Maybe it will end soon," Maria said. "But then what will happen? Will the Russians come?" The countess shook her head.

"I don't know. I don't know anything anymore. I just know that this is a disaster. It doesn't seem fair. We were attacked."

"The Russians will be taking casualties too, Countess," Andy joined in. "I suppose it's a contest to see who can take the most."

"They can take it more than we can. Russia is enormous. They have so many people. The tsar will force them to take it with the whips on their backs. They won't dare stop. With us, it's different. We've become too soft. We have music and culture. We spend our times in cafés arguing about socialism and the rights of nationalities. They don't. They sow their fields and do as they're told. No, I don't see how we can survive this war. I really don't."

On the third day, they arrived in Budapest in the late afternoon. They found the Hotel Gellert on the banks of the Danube. They had rooms available. The hotel was very new and its extravagant luxury overwhelming, considering the bleak accommodations they had all previously endured.

Budapest was a beautiful city, Andy quickly observed. The city was flat on one side while on the other, there were many hills, one of which was crowned by a beautiful palace named for the late Empress Elisabeth who had been very popular in Hungary during her lifetime. Budapest had many of the same charming aspects of architecture as Vienna, although the Danube played a far more obvious role in its topography. It rolled right through the heart of the city, dividing it in half, as the Seine did in Paris. Magnificent streets and boulevards coursed the two halves of the city.

But signs of war were pervasive here too. Soldiers were everywhere, as if the city were under martial law, although it was extremely difficult to make out exactly what was going on. The Magyar language was incomprehensible to Andy and neither the countess nor Maria spoke more than a few words of it or could read the signs. The hotel, had an ample supply of Viennese newspapers in German, however, which would permit them for the first time in quite a while to read about what was happening in the war.

Andy was anxious to read the newspapers, but volunteered once again to go with Walther to the Royal Infirmary to see if Johann had yet arrived while Maria and the countess unpacked.

The Royal Infirmary was a vast network of buildings in central Budapest and was overwhelmed with casualties of war as much as the military hospital in Kosice had been. Once again, Andy had to work his way through a hospital bureaucracy, attempting to communicate to people with whom he didn't share a common language, to determine if and when Johann had been delivered. He had. He was shown to another huge ward with hundreds of wounded soldiers on cots.

Once again, he found Johann asleep, but this time, the accommodations seemed clean. Dozens of nurses and doctors attended the patients or could be seen walking about. Electric lights. Morphine. A Hungarian nurse approached. She could speak only a few words of German, but in a few minutes, Andy managed to make her understand that he was a friend and would be back. She nodded and smiled and Andy returned with Walther to the Hotel Gellert.

After a light dinner, Andy brought the countess and Maria back to the infirmary. As they approached his bed, they could see that he was awake. He seemed to recognize them for the first time as they arrived at his bedside. The countess bent over and kissed his face as tears flowed down her own. Johann was in obvious pain, but kissed his mother as she stroked his cheek with her hand.

"How did you find me?" Johann croaked, seemingly remembering nothing of his stay in Kosice. As he said these words, to his surprise, he noticed Maria and Andy. Maria kissed him as well and Andy took Johann's hand. They explained what had happened, their trip to Kocise, all of it. Johann, pale and weak, stared off blankly at times as he took it all in.

"I haven't been able to see my legs, or what's left of them," Johann said abruptly. "I can't bear to look and the pain is terrible. They keep giving me morphine, but I can't bear it. I'm ruined. I wish I had died. What am I going to do?" The hopeless look on his face as he said these things stabbed Andy's heart with grief and pity.

"I'm so sorry," Andy said. He didn't know what else to say. "At least you're alive. For a while, we didn't know …"

"Andy has been with us the whole time. He volunteered to come with us," his mother said quietly.

Johann looked at Andy and gently shook his head. "I don't know, my friend. I don't know. All I know now is that my life is over. I'm a cripple. And you, what are you to do?" These last words were said as he looked at Maria. Tears welled up in her eyes and she looked away. "You must not marry me now, Maria," he said. "I'm no good for you now. I'm no good for anyone. I release you here and now from our engagement."

"Stop talking like that," the countess said. There were tears in her eyes as she spoke. She took a deep breath. Her voice was firm. "Let it be. There will be time enough to talk about such things when you're better. You must rest and get well. We will take you to Vienna just as soon as you're able and then we will sort these things out. You're alive. Think about your family and those who love you. We've been with you day and night and we're so thankful you're alive. I won't hear of talk about death …" Her voice trailed off and she put her hand to her mouth. Johann grimaced in pain.

A nurse came by. No more morphine could be given for now. The countess organized the three of them into watches so that someone would always be by Johann's bedside. She would take the first watch until midnight and then Maria would relieve her. Andy would come in the morning. After a little more time, Andy and Maria left the ward with the countess sitting by Johann's bed on a little stool that they had found for her, holding his hand as he tried to sleep.

A couple of days later, Andy found himself sitting at a café on Raday Utca, a pleasant neighborhood not far from the Danube. As in Vienna, newspapers were fastened on wooden poles and set in a rack inside the café for readers to peruse as they sipped their coffee. Most were in Magyar, but there were also a few Austrian and German newspapers that he could read. There had been little time for him to speak to Maria since they had arrived. Instead, he found himself alone, exploring the city and talking to anyone who spoke German or English who would share their thoughts with him in parks, streets, or cafés. He had also found a telegraph office and began contemplating an article home from Budapest.

The Hungarians, he had discovered, were loyal to the old kaiser who was, in their half of the empire, the "King," but this war was not really their war, it was clear. The terrible threat of a Russian invasion and occupation was made all the more dreadful because, other than supporting the Austrian half of the empire, the Hungarians could see nothing to be gained for them in this titanic struggle.

Andy waited for Maria to join him. The countess was sleeping and Walther had volunteered to sit with Johann to give them all a break. It was the first time since they had left Vienna that Andy would have any real time alone with her. Time to discuss what had happened and what it all meant. For them. He needed to know that she felt the same way about him as she had in Vienna. He had been tortured by doubts and desperate for clues, which became more and more difficult as each day went on without any sign. She had shot him some knowing looks and had been tender toward him in fleeting moments over the past couple of weeks, but it wasn't enough.

The day was sunny, but cold. Most of the people inside the café were old men. The young men had volunteered or been conscripted into the Honved, the Magyar name for the Royal Hungarian Army, depopulating the youth of the city. It was quiet as he waited and, to pass the time, he began to read the news, which was, as always, preoccupied with the war.

As he sipped his coffee, he made eye contact with an older man who was smoking a pipe at the table next to him. The other man nodded and said something to him in Magyar that Andy could not understand. Andy replied in German, saying that he could not understand, at which point the man replied to him in German.

"You're a young man. Why are you not in the army?" he asked bluntly.

"I'm American. I was visiting some relatives in Vienna when the war broke out. A friend of mine was wounded badly in the fighting around Przemyśl. I came with some of his family to bring him home," Andy replied.

The man puffed on his pipe. "I see. An American? I have relatives living in America," he said. "They live in Pennsylvania. Around the city of Pittsburgh. Do you know it?"

"Yes, my mother's family is from Pittsburgh. I live in Ohio, not far away. Have you been to America?" Andy asked.

The man shook his head no. "What do you think of this war, American? Do you think the Russians will win? The war is going badly for us, don't you think?"

The war was going badly again for the Austrians. Hindenburg had been defeated by the Russians in the attempt to take Warsaw a couple of weeks earlier. The Austrians remained near Przemyśl, apparently recovering from their recent offensive. The Hungarians were now expecting a major Russian counter-offensive into the kingdom that might result in the fall of Budapest to the "Slavic hordes."

The German offensive in France had also ground to a halt, exhausted, and the British were attacking the Germans on the Somme. The desperate hope of a quick German victory on the western front that would have allowed her to turn to help Austria was now gone. The Austrians were largely on their own against the colossal might of the Russian juggernaut and few thought that the empire could hold out for long.

Andy and the old man discussed all of these events while he waited. The Hungarian was pessimistic and reflected the dread that most Hungarians and Austrians felt about the Russians. As the junior partner in the Austro-Hungarian Empire, many Hungarians felt some resentment toward the Austrian half for centuries of domination, but with the virtual independence of Hungary in 1867, their self-confidence had risen. Whatever old resentments had been felt about the past, the Hungarians realized that, without the partnership with Austria, their country would be weak and vulnerable to enemies on all sides. The Rumanians in particular were a threat, coveting their vast province of Transylvania. Nothing compared, however, to the hatred and fear of Russia who had invaded Hungary in the revolutionary war of 1848. Memories were long in the east, the old man said.

"It's a struggle between the civilized world and the backward Slavs that is really at stake in this war," the old man continued. "Hungary had no choice in this war. If we didn't support the Austrians against Serbia, why should they support us against our enemies in the future? The Russians are a curse to us both. They always support the Slavs to weaken us and push their way into Europe."

"It will be very difficult to defeat the allies," Andy mentioned. "When Germany attacked Belgium and brought the British into the war, I think the scales were tipped. The best thing might be to end the war now for Austria-Hungary. I've been to the east and the casualties are terrible. With the winter approaching, the conditions there will be miserable for the troops, won't they?"

The old man nodded again. "And yet, what will all these young men have died for? We were right. The Serbian terrorists will just keep coming and the Russians will dominate Europe if we stop now. I'm afraid we have no choice but to keep fighting and hope that the Germans can send more help. One thing is for sure, the Serbians must be taught a lesson. Perhaps then we can make peace with the Russians. We could give Serbia back its independence, but under a new king who will stop the terrorists." *It was an interesting idea*, Andy thought.

Maria arrived and sat down with Andy. The old Hungarian man nodded at that point, understanding that with Maria's appearance, their conversation was over. A waiter appeared. Maria ordered a coffee in Magyar and then smiled wanly at Andy as the waiter withdrew.

It had been a difficult several days since they had arrived in Budapest to be reunited with Johann. Johann's condition, both mental and physical, was still too delicate to allow his transport back to Vienna. Since his evacuation from Kosice, the main task had become lifting Johann's broken spirit. Almost against his will, Johann was physically healing from his terrible wounds, but his mind was crippled by his loss. He pulled them deep into his depression as they exhausted their reasons why he should continue to live. They played for time each day hoping that Johann himself would find some reason to go on living.

"Let's go get something to eat," Andy said.

"I don't know if I could eat anything."

"Some wine then. Perhaps we'll get some appetite." Maria agreed and they left the café.

Again Andy noticed the familiar looking architecture of the buildings. But for the signs in Magyar, it looked remarkably similar to Vienna. Soon they came across a small restaurant and ordered a bottle of Hungarian wine. To his surprise, Maria went right to the heart of it.

"I feel like a traitor," Maria said. "I can't bring myself to tell him that I want to break our engagement, but making him think I love him and still want to marry him is a lie. If I tell him now, he'll think it's because of his leg—even though it's not that. You know that's not true, but he'll never believe it. Even if he did, then what? How could I tell him the truth now?"

"I don't think you should tell him anything now. Perhaps it is a lie to make him think everything will be the same if he gets well. The worst seems to be over now. I think he's going to live, but who knows? Now is not the time. When we get back to Vienna, you'll find the right time."

"Oh, Andy, I don't think it's that simple. Each day the lie grows. What if Johann survives and starts to want to live again. We all hope for that, don't we? Will it be a good time to tell him then? You see?"

As she talked, Andy noticed her eyes moistening. Perhaps it was the wine. Perhaps it was the ambience, the glow of her face. The flickering candle at their table reflected off the window that separated them from the dark cobblestone street and cold autumnal air outside. Whatever was taking hold of him, Andy felt it and his last reserve gave way. He reached across the table and took her hand. She closed hers on his and, for a moment, they said nothing.

She was still the most beautiful woman he had ever known. Her dark eyes, brimming with tears, gazed back into his and he knew. He knew everything. He had tried to ignore the treasonous feelings that had grown within him every time he had seen her in Vienna. He had invented excuses time and again when he had contrived to see her as often as he could when Johann had left months earlier. She had been untouchable, unreachable, and he knew he had deluded himself into believing that he could settle for just her friendship, but it was more than that. Much more. Little by little, the lies he told himself to prop up his failing rationalizations had become ludicrous and now they collapsed entirely.

"Maria. It's worse than that . . . I've fallen in love with you. I know it's wrong, believe me. I tried not to. It's a terrible time and, under the circumstances, it's unforgiveable, but still …"

"I know. I've known since that day in Vienna when the war started. And I've fallen in love with you too. If it wasn't for you, I would probably have gone through with it, but you made me realize what I really wanted for my life. I would never have been happy with Johann, but I would have accepted it. It was what was expected of me. When I met you, though … I just couldn't do it."

The elderly waiter appeared with their dinner, gently placing the plates of Főzelék or Hungarian stew on the table. His weathered face smiled at them and he said something in Magyar. Maria replied in Magyar; he bowed and was gone. They ate in silence for a few minutes. Andy felt an enormous sense of relief. The doubts about her, about their future had been replaced with hope. Irrational though it might be, his heart soared.

"I know this doesn't make it any easier," Maria said softly, "but now I don't feel so alone. I think I can bear it better, knowing you're with me." She looked at him as she took another bite. "I think I could bear just about anything if I knew I had you, Andy. Something will happen. Something good must happen."

Maria shivered. A cold breeze wafted over them on a darkened street as they stepped from the restaurant and began walking back to the hotel. She clutched her shawl against the cold. The narrow, gas-lit streets of the old quarter were dark and empty as they walked. As they reached a dark archway, Andy took her hand and pulled her to him. He felt her in his arms for the first time since Vienna. His love for her consumed him and he could think of nothing else but what he wanted in this moment. He searched for her mouth with his own in the darkness. It was soft and moist and he kissed her tenderly at first and then with passion as she draped her arms around his neck. He felt the fingers of her hand stroke the hair on the back of his head as she answered his passion.

How long they remained in the archway, it was hard to say. The constraints that had held them apart for the sake of decency and polite convention were now broken by the flood of their love that poured out, minute after minute. The clip-clopping sound of an approaching horse broke the spell that they could not do themselves. At the hotel, they parted with knowing looks, each to their own room.

In his quiet room, Andy tried to prepare another lengthy telegraph to his father about the events of the war for the past couple of weeks from his perspective in Kocise and Budapest. He had not been able to write to his father while on the rescue mission and there were a lot of things to say. With difficulty, he struggled.

> BUDAPEST, October 21—The Austro-Hungarian army has continued to hold Przemyśl, but seems too exhausted to make any progress in driving the Russians farther back out of Austrian territory. The Hungarians this reporter interviewed here in Budapest were pessimistic about the huge offensive that has erupted around Warsaw as their German allies have hammered away at the Russian army there. The residents of this capital note, however, that the Germans seem to have been stopped short of capturing the city and expect a German pullback for the winter months.
>
> Regard for Germany is very high here. The war in France and Belgium seems far away for most

and the war with Russia very near and dangerous. Austrians and Hungarians seem most optimistic when their ally manages to get in a blow against the common enemy. With Germany almost completely preoccupied with the war in the west, however, these times are rare and one seems now about to end. There is dread here at facing Russia alone and for drawing off substantial Russian manpower to stop the recent German drive to Warsaw, the Hungarians are thankful.

At some later time, this period of the war will probably be seen as a prelude to more bloody campaigns that will follow. Nonetheless, the loyal subjects of the king of Hungary seem relieved that an imminent, mortal danger has passed and that if they are not winning the war, at least it is not yet lost.

Andy leaned back in his chair and stretched. There was a soft knock at his door. He looked at the clock in the room and saw that it was after midnight. He crossed the room and opened the door. It was Maria. He let her into the room.

"I'm feeling so alone in my room. May I just stay with you for a while? Until I can fall asleep?"

"Of course," Andy said in a whisper.

Their mouths softly touched again and again, arousing them both. He kissed her passionately as he lost himself in her. He knew that he could not bear to part from her. Not now. Not ever. They fell on the bed. Her skin was soft. Deeper and deeper, they fell into each other, releasing each other from the pent-up tensions that had arisen since leaving Vienna, but knowing, as so many times since then, that things would never be the same.

12.

Return to Vienna, November 1914

"The countess thinks Johann could be brought back to Vienna tomorrow," Maria said. "The doctor thinks it's safe enough for him to make the trip if the weather is good."

They had been in Budapest for nearly two weeks and their secret love affair had lifted their spirits during the days and nights that Johann continued to convalesce in the hospital. They had been discreet, to be sure, but the thought that their time together was nearing its end was disquieting to Andy. Would Maria really find the right time to tell Johann after he was brought home as he had hopefully suggested to her? Andy had come to appreciate Maria's earlier misgivings. As time went on, the dependence of Johann and his mother on Maria to keep up Johann's spirits and give him the will to live had become ever more obvious. Despite their ongoing affair, doubts crept into his thoughts and, now that the return to Vienna was imminent, these feelings began to ripen to real apprehension.

They had settled into something of a routine. Maria left in the morning to relieve Walther at Johann's bedside. Andy would come in the afternoon and the countess would follow. The late afternoons and evening allowed Maria and Andy to have time together since the countess would be with Johann. Earlier, after Andy returned from the hospital, they had taken a walk along the river.

"What will you do when we get back?" Andy asked.

"I should help his mother take care of Johann, shouldn't I?" she replied. "I can't just abandon him when we all get back, can I?"

"No, of course not. I just wondered ..."

"He's so bitter now. He tells me such terrible things. He says if he can't walk, if his other leg won't support him, he'll kill himself. I've never seen him like this. Something has definitely changed in him. The archduke meant everything to him. Not just his career, but his friendship and where he thought his life was going. When he died, Johann was shattered. I didn't realize it at the time. He wanted vengeance. We all did, of course, but it was personal with him. So he threw himself into the war, he told me. He wanted to personally lead his men in battle against the Serbs, but ended up fighting the Russians instead. He always saw himself as a soldier, ever since I can remember. An officer, serving the crown that would soon have been worn by his friend and his mentor, Franz Ferdinand. First, he lost his connection to the crown. Now his military career is over. He is no soldier anymore and never will be again. He's lost, Andy. I can see it now—how he feels. He's not the daring boy I knew growing up. He's not the fearless man I knew who courted me before you came. He's changed."

"I haven't known him as you have, of course ..."

"No, no, Andy. He thinks the world of you. He was amazed when he realized what you had done. Coming with us and all. He thinks of you as a good friend. You really are, you know."

"Not really. He knows nothing about us, but when he finds out, I'm sure he'll never want to see me again. I'm embarrassed when I'm with him, really. It's difficult for me to sit with him. He talks to me about the war and makes suggestions for my articles. Sometimes I can see, when we talk, that his mind is elsewhere, but he has never shared the thoughts you just described with me."

"I feel guilty too. He has told me several times that he releases me from our engagement—that he knows I couldn't possibly want to marry a cripple. He sees himself now as disfigured and repulsive. Of course, I reassure him that none of it makes any difference to me. He just shakes his head, sadly, and won't look at me. And yet, I know that down deep, he hopes it's true and that's what hurts me deeply."

For the moment, at least, there was no honorable way out. Neither of them could accept the thought of abandoning Johann to be together. Maria looked into his eyes. Whatever happened, he thought, he would never forget looking into her soul-captivating eyes.

"There will come a time when I will leave with you, Andy. I don't know when, but as you said, the right time will surely come. It has to."

Suddenly, there was the sound of music nearby. They had been walking for at least half an hour, Andy realized, and he had not been paying very careful attention to where they were. They reached a major boulevard, looked to their left toward the Danube, and saw a large column of soldiers coming across the Szabadsag Bridge.

"Let's watch," said Maria. In a few minutes, the music could be distinctly heard. It was a regimental band, they guessed. Some young kids ran past them down the street to see the oncoming parade of troops. Other people hurried down the sidewalks toward the source of the sound.

A band had drawn up in the middle of a park-like swath of grass and trees that temporarily separated the wide boulevard. Troops were obviously going to pass on either side of the park. Large crowds quickly swelled the sides of the street. Windows opened on the floors above the buildings facing the boulevard with apartment dwellers leaning out to see the approaching army.

Clearly, the spectacle was meant to cheer the people of Budapest and the parade seemed to be having that effect. A rush of horse cavalry was the first contingent to reach Andy and Maria, who had found some stone steps on which to stand to see over the crowd. The horses were large beasts—clearly bred and trained for war—and their hooves clattered on the cobblestones as they approached.

The cavalrymen sitting on them were led by two very well turned-out officers. They wore fairly plain, dark blue overcoats with very little decoration. A stiff collar extended from a tunic underneath their overcoats from their necks to their chins in the Austrian style with a flash of gold on either side. They wore light gray riding gloves. Long swords dangled from their belts to the bottoms of their shiny black boots, denoting their status as officers.

On the heads of the officers were the distinct hats that both the French and Austrians used. Unlike the Germans with their spiked helmets, Austro-Hungarian officers wore a round, pillbox-style hat or kepi with gold braid around the base and over the brim. They also had a sort of gold ornament at the very top of the cap with a line of vertical gold stitching below it. Officers from the Tyrol often had a sprig of evergreen stuffed in the braid surrounding the base of the cap.

After the cavalry clattered past, there followed some open motorcars with what appeared to be very high-ranking officers sitting in the backseats. As the cars rolled past, the officers waved to the crowds who cheered and shouted encouragements in Magyar that Andy couldn't understand. Artillery rolled along after the cars and, finally, rank upon rank of infantry tramped past to a jaunty marching tune that was played by the band. Flowers were thrown out by the crowd as the young men passed down the street and on to wherever they were going. Several thousand of them had passed when finally another gaggle of cavalry brought up the rear and it was over.

"God bless the Hungarians," Maria sighed. "They looked so cheerful. How do they do it?"

"I don't know. You look at them and think that the Russians are doing the same thing. More and more of them forming up and going off to the war. If they took one look at the hospitals we've seen, I don't think any of them would go."

"Would you do it?"

"I don't know. What choice do they have?"

"What choice did we all have?"

"They think they're defending their country. If they don't go, the Russians will be knocking on their doors—wherever they live." They started walking in the direction of their hotel in silence after the parade had ended. Then Maria spoke again.

"I want to go to America, Andy. I want to get away from this. It's all death and horror here now." Maria said as they turned back to the hotel.

The next day was cold and crisp as the family's Daimler was loaded with their baggage. Johann would require much of the backseat of the car. Nevertheless, there was plenty of room for Maria and the countess to sit in the backseat tending to him on the trip.

Andy sat in the front with the driver as they pulled away from the curb and began the trip back to Vienna. They had brought food and drink along with them for fear that there would be little provision along the way. The hours passed uneventfully as the car proceeded along a well-paved road to Vienna. The internal Austro-Hungarian border was passed and, before long, the villages and towns became more frequent and more populous as they neared Vienna.

"I want you to know, before things get confusing in a little while, how deeply grateful I am for everything you have done," the countess said to Andy. "You have been a true friend to Johann and to me. I don't know how we could have done this without you. All of Johann's friends are fighting at the front and some of them have died. There was nobody who could have helped me as you have done. But now I'm wondering, what will you do now?"

It was an awkward moment. Andy replied that he wasn't sure. He told her that he thought he intended to stay in Vienna a while longer, but that sometimes he wondered if it was an imposition to continue to stay on with his relatives under the circumstances. He would just have to see how things were with the Windischgrätz family when he returned.

"My dear boy. I doubt very much that you are any imposition at all to Otto and Elisabeth, especially since their boys are now gone. Nevertheless, if you should decide to stay on in Vienna, you must know that you are always welcome to stay with us. You have our deepest gratitude and, if I might say so, your presence in our house would surely do Johann good."

Andy thanked her for her generous offer and told her that he would certainly think about it. In any event, he would continue to visit Johann for as long as he was in Vienna. In his heart, though, he felt that he was betraying her and her son. Someday, under the best of circumstances, she would come to know what he had done, what he was doing even now. Someday she might know what he and Maria had done after her son had left Vienna for the war or while he was convalescing in Budapest. Her feelings toward him then would no doubt be much different than they were now, Andy thought.

At dusk, they entered the city and, before long, pulled

up at the Caboga residence. Walther went to the door. In a moment, the servants were pouring out of the house to welcome and assist them.

Johann had slept fitfully during the trip, but was quite awake as he was carried into his house. The pleasure of the servants to have the countess and her son safely back home was quickly replaced by looks of concern and pity at the condition of their master. Johann was carefully carried to his room and laid in bed. The war was barely three months old, but it was over for him already. His mother gently sat down on the bed and took his hand.

"I never thought it would be like this," Johann said softly. He turned his head away from them. He couldn't stifle the sobs that welled up in him from deep inside. The countess covered her mouth with a black handkerchief, too overcome to say anything herself now that he was home. Agonizing minutes passed. Downcast servants quietly retreated from the room. Finally, Maria spoke.

"Johann, there is some reason why God has spared you from death. There has to be some purpose for which you've been left alive." Maria's voice trembled as she slowly got the words out. "I don't know what it is, but you must believe it. You have the love of your friends and your family to help you, but you must discover your purpose now. Whatever it is. We'll all help you, but you must help yourself. You cannot have been spared to live out the rest of your days in this bed."

Silently, Andy left the room and hurried down the stairs to the waiting car that would take him back to the Windischgrätz house. He simply could not bear the pitiful scene any longer. Maria caught up with him by the time he reached the portico of the mansion where the car waited. Since it would have been very dangerous to exchange a kiss or any intimate conversation with the possibility of being seen or overhead, they simply looked at one another.

"Good-bye, Andy," said Maria softly. Andy nodded and

looked at her one last time before turning and getting into the car.

The threat to Warsaw having passed, the Russians returned to Przemyśl in overwhelming numbers. The city was soon besieged again and eventually surrendered with the loss of nearly a hundred thousand prisoners from the garrison who had been trapped and nearly starved to death inside. With their chain of great fortress cities broken, the flat plains of Galicia offered no refuge from the Russian onslaught, compelling Austro-Hungarian forces into headlong retreat to the Carpathian mountains to regroup and dig in. Even then, the Russians set to work forcing the mountain passes that, once breached, would open to the broad, flat Hungarian plains and Budapest.

Humiliatingly, due to its preoccupation with Russia, little Serbia continued to stubbornly defy the small Austrian army that remained there. Tens of thousands of Czechs in the Austro-Hungarian army defected *en masse* to the Russian side, opening gaping holes in the imperial defenses. In the cities of the empire, food shortages led to ugly riots compounded, as winter settled in, with fuel shortages and cold.

Yet, as Christmas and the end of 1914 neared, the empire did not crack as everyone, including its own people, thought it would. Just when it was thought that all was lost, Conrad correctly anticipated the location and timing of the main Russian offensive into the Carpathians around Limanowa and delivered a stunning riposte, first stopping the Russians in their tracks and then routing them completely, ending the threat to Hungary. The war would go on.

Austria-Hungary had already lost nearly a million men, dead and wounded, out of a population of fifty million before the war. By the end of the war, the empire would count over a million dead and nearly four million wounded; nearly one in five males would share Johann's fate—or worse.

Part 2

13.
Vienna, April 1915

After the miracle at Limanowa in December, the Austrians had mounted another major offensive in the southern sector in January, driving the Russians from the southern Carpathians back across the plains of Galicia, culminating on January 23 in the Battle of Kolomea. The Russians were routed in this sector and driven all the way to the border of Russia and Romania.

For their part, in February, the Germans opened up an offensive around the Masurian Lakes in Prussia, driving the Russians out of Germany once and for all. General Bulgakov surrendered the Russian Tenth Army on February 21 after being completely encircled by the Germans. The remaining Russian forces in Germany retreated east, never to set foot on German soil for the rest of the war. After this success, however, the guns fell silent on the German front and news began to become scarce again in the censored Viennese newspapers. This was usually the precursor to a loss of Austrian momentum or another Russian counterattack. Indeed, by early March, the Russian bear seemed to awaken from his winter slumber and was advancing again just when the Viennese had dared hope that they had been decisively beaten.

In the more northern sector of Galicia, around Limanowa, the Russians erupted with particular fury. Much of the ground gained by the Austrians after Limanowa was lost again. Once again, the Russians threatened to break the Carpathian mountain chain and sweep down on Budapest. While censorship sought to obscure the scale of the Austro-Hungarian retreat, this actually contributed to the innate skepticism of the Viennese—and even ignited wild rumors of Cossacks seen in the suburbs of the capital, which had never occurred.

With the coming of early spring, the Austro-Hungarian army hung on for dear life in its Carpathian mountain passes, essentially back in the same dire situation it had faced before Christmas—only far more exhausted and bled by casualties than before. How long this go could on was the question on the Viennese lips. Unaware of Russia's own casualty lists, transportation woes, shortages of ammunition, military incompetence, and corruption, the Viennese imagined their enemy had inexhaustible resources that would inevitably overwhelm them in time.

The kaiser dwelled exclusively in the Schönbrunn palace for security and due to his old age. He was not even driven into the Hofburg, as had been his near-daily custom before the war. He was not seen or heard in public. Parliament had been suspended since the declaration of war. What surprised the Viennese and the world was the incredible hardiness of their multi-national army and its ability, time and time again, to come back from seemingly hopeless defeat.

A new general was once introduced to Napoleon Bonaparte just over a century earlier. After his accomplishments and abilities were duly noted, the greatest military mind of his era had only one question: "Yes, but is he lucky?"

Franz Conrad Graf von Hötzendorf, chief of the general staff of the Habsburg armies and former protégé of the late archduke, was not lucky. He was resilient. And this was the quality that came to define both him and the plucky Austro-Hungarian army when all was said and done.

When everything was equal, Conrad inevitably guessed wrong, but his heart-stopping defeats were invariably followed by stunning victories. In less than a year, he had presided over more reversals of fortune than most commanders did in a lifetime—and was still going. He had already outlasted von Moltke, the supreme German commander at the outbreak of the war. He would outlast them all before it was over; France's Joffre, Britain's French, Italy's Cadorna, and even Tsar Nicholas himself. Conrad would go down in the long and illustrious annuls of Habsburg military lore as one of the most important Austrian captains of war—if not its greatest. Wallenstein, Eugene of Savoy, Radetzky, and von Schwartzenberg had never commanded Habsburg armies a fraction of the size of his own, nor were the fortunes of the empire more at stake than they were under his command.

Conrad's daring offensives almost always ended in defeat, if for no other reason than that the vast reserves of Russian manpower invariably overwhelmed his armies. The size and power of his opponent left no margin for error or chance and, perhaps as the result, defensive warfare and devastating counterstrokes became Conrad's specialty as a succession of wounded Russian armies came to appreciate. He took his defeats with aplomb, never doubting for a moment that any situation could be reprieved. When others lost their heads, Conrad was a rock of pragmatic stoicism.

It is an irony of history that of the Great Powers, nearly all of whom had far greater resources at their disposal in terms of money and manpower, Austria-Hungary was granted the most wily and clever commander of all. Conrad and his generals really ruled the empire with the stolid, silent support of the elderly emperor in his palace, and it was he who, when all seemed lost, produced the miracles that saved the empire and, ironically, prolonged the war.

Colonel Ernst zu Windischgrätz was now the commander of the 1st Tyrolean Imperial Rifle Regiment of the 1st Mountain Brigade of the Fifth Army, which had been in action in Galicia and the Carpathians almost continuously since the beginning of the war. Exhausted and depleted by casualties, the soldiers and officers had been relieved and returned to Vienna to refit and regroup. News of Ernst's return home had been received with relief and delight by Elisabeth and Otto. Elisabeth had mentioned it to her grandfather when visiting him for tea one afternoon and the kaiser had issued an invitation to the regiment to visit him at Schönbrunn.

Andy's status as a syndicated war correspondent writing under his byline "An American in Vienna" was now generally known and appreciated in high Austrian government circles. He was granted interviews nowadays both on and off the record by officers and diplomats. Andy had learned from Elisabeth that the kaiser himself had read some of his articles. To Andy's delight, Otto and Elisabeth had secured an invitation to the palace to watch the review of Ernst's regiment and, from a discreet position on the parade ground, Andy watched the proceedings unfold.

An American in Vienna

A dispatch in a series from our Special Correspondent in Vienna, Andrew M. Bishop

A Rare Appearance by Kaiser Franz Josef

VIENNA, April 12—This morning at three minutes to 8:00 the 1st Tyrolean Imperial Rifle Regiment was on the grounds of Schönbrunn palace at attention, ready for a parade. At exactly 8 o'clock his Majesty, Kaiser Franz Joseph, accompanied by his heir, the archduke Karl, stepped out of the doors of the Schönbrunn palace. Immediately, the regimental band began to play the Austrian national anthem or "Volkshymne," after which the buglers sounded the general march. All eyes turned towards their aged ruler.

Colonel Ernst von Windischgrätz, the commander of the regiment and great-grandson of the kaiser, marched up and saluted smartly, stating to the kaiser that the regiment was ready for review. Kaiser Franz Josef approached the ranks of soldiers with the sprightly step of a man much younger than his eighty-four years. As he slowly walked past the front line, every man of the regiment could look the Emperor in the eyes. He paused before many of them saying a few words, taking his time in doing so.

After his review, the officers and officer cadets were then assembled so that the kaiser could speak to them individually, inquire after fallen comrades, ask questions regarding their decorations, and also to shake each officer's hand. After shaking the hand of the last one, the kaiser asked, "Are these all the captains in my Tyrolean Kaiserjäger Regiment?" The kaiser asked after various officers who he personally knew and the Colonel answered time and again that the particular officer had been killed or wounded at some location or battlefield in Galicia or the Carpathians. His Majesty was clearly moved by the loss of life.

The Emperor then summoned all the holders of the *Ritterkreuze*, Austria's highest military decoration. The regiment has at this time twenty-two holders of this prestigious award, although only six were present today. The others are buried either in Poland or are in hospitals recovering from wounds. The kaiser listened with great interest as each of the six described the actions for which they had been decorated, occasionally interrupting with a question of his own. The kaiser thanked each individually with a handshake and the parting "God be with you."

His Majesty then dismissed the officers and the six decorated veterans, saying, "I leave you to continue your brave work. Your kaiser and the Reich thank you for your devoted service. I march by your side in spirit."

The kaiser then went before the regiment so that every man could clearly hear his words and again spoke to all of them:

"My beloved Tyroleans! We follow your every heroic action with special interest. We marvel at your bravery, contempt of death, and your heroism. With deep sorrow we hear of your great sacrifices and losses. Our prayers to God the Almighty belong to you brave men. You have your kaiser's thanks and greetings from us to the other three regiments. God protect you!"

From the mouths of the entire regiment roared *"Hoch unser Kaiser Franz Josef"* and many threw their caps into the air. Then, with a smile and a wave to the men, he and the archduke Karl turned and took their leave of the regiment at exactly 9:00.

The old kaiser spoke to Ernst after his farewell salute with Andy, his mother and father present at the door of the palace.

"My dear Ernst, we commend you for the exemplary discipline shown by the men this morning despite the terrible losses and strain of nearly a year of war. Convey our greetings to all our Tyrolean riflemen of the other three regiments when you next see them and our regret that they could not also be with us today." Then, in a more soft and intimate voice he added "God bless you, my dear Ernst, and be careful in your duty." Andy noticed, for the first and only time, the piercing blue eyes of the old man watered as he said these last words to his great-grandson before retiring to his apartments within the palace.

An American in Vienna

A few days later, Andy sat at one of the tables outside the door at Fidelio's café on the Ringstrasse, waiting for Maria. It was unseasonably warm this afternoon. After weeks of gray, monotonous rain and blustery winds, a bright sun shone down on the imperial city out of a dark blue, cloudless sky. The balmy weather had culled the Viennese from their apartments and houses to soak up the sun and breathe in the rain-washed, earthy scents of the parks and gardens just beginning to brim with flowers and blossoms.

The clear, buffed plate glass windows of Fidelio's reflected the flow of people and images that passed before its impassive but watchful face on Vienna's most imperial boulevard as it had always done stretching back into the last century. Andy imagined the carriages of Habsburg archdukes pulled by teams of horses clopping past that had slowly disappeared in the long life of this café, replaced now by black and gold chauffeured motorcars. Masses of workers singing the socialist "International" had looked at themselves in Fidelio's mirror as they passed by, now replaced by ranks of uniformed soldiers and their officers marching off to war.

Nobody knew exactly how old Fidelio's was or when it had been established, Andy had found. It had been around as long as any of its regular patrons could remember. Some people said that Beethoven himself had sat in the café composing his one opera for which it was named. This was unlikely, Andy mused, since the Ringstrasse had only come into being in the last decades of the nineteenth century when the city walls had been taken down. Fidelio's location on the far side of the street would have put it practically underneath the city walls before they had been taken down.

A half-dozen tables with chairs were put out on days

like this and in the summer months, continuously. Fidelio's clients read their newspapers, smoked their cigars, drank their coffees, and chatted away the hours, folded in a discreet embrace of urns and flower boxes arranged by the waiters on the broad sidewalk, gently deflecting approaching pedestrians away from the tables.

Once inside the door, one was immediately conscious of the warm aroma of coffee and polished wood. There was an enormous brass espresso machine against the wall, carefully shined to a yellow glow that reflected the waiters making coffee. Above the machine was a reproduction of a familiar painting of the kaiser, often seen in public places, the faintest hint of a smile on his face like the Mona Lisa. Gaslights had been replaced by electric ones years ago, but the location of the lights was still on the walls where the sconces would once have been. A mirror across the back wall gave the impression that the café was larger than it really was.

Andy had just finished a long cable to his father reporting news of the war and the scene in Vienna. He was in a routine now, gathering news over the course of a week and then compiling it in a long dispatch that his father received in Columbus, Ohio, for inclusion in his newspaper. In exchange, his father would cable back news from the United States, which was almost non-existent in Viennese newspapers these days. From his father, Andy was able to get a view of the war from afar that put the events he was witnessing firsthand in some perspective.

Arthur Bishop had written how strongly the people in the United States wanted to stay out of the war. There was a civil war going on in Mexico that absorbed the attention of President Wilson. Arthur also wrote that reports of German atrocities against civilians in Belgium and France had turned public opinion against the Central Powers. Feelings in Columbus were mixed but sometimes passionate. Red paint had been thrown against the statue of Schiller in the park, evidently by sympathizers of England and France. In the German village and the Irish neighborhoods, however, sympathies were strongly with the Central Powers or, in the case of the Irish, against the English. The baseball season was about to begin again. Andy's favorite player, Honus Wagner of the Pittsburgh Pirates, was chasing his three thousandth hit.

The waiter had just brought another mélange when Maria arrived and sat down, giving Andy a discrete kiss on both cheeks. Maria had become more and more distant over the winter months as she helped the countess with Johann's convalescence. Dr. Leoni had performed another surgery on the right leg that had improved Johann's circulation and ensured that he would not lose it to amputation as well. They had begun to discuss the possibility of a prosthetic left leg. Maria had become preoccupied with Johann's recovery, it seemed to Andy, and the day of reckoning between them had never come.

"Johann may be joining us shortly," said Maria. "He's trying to walk more every day now that the weather is improving. When I left him he said he was going to try to meet us here on his own this morning. He didn't want my help. He told me to go on alone and he would catch up."

Andy nodded. "It's you that inspires him to these new heights. He does it for you." There she was, sitting so close to him and yet so unreachable. She was as beautiful as ever, her dark eyes glittering in the afternoon sun.

"Yes, I know. He didn't feel this way toward me before the war. Now he's so helpless in some ways, trying so hard to be a man again that when he does something for the first time he wants me there. He wants to share his struggles and triumphs with me day by day."

"Maria, I know this is a difficult time and I don't mean to press you, but when are you going to tell him ..."

"You know I love you, Andy. I will always love you. I could never have gotten through all this without you." She paused, struggling with her thoughts. "I have to put that aside now, Andy. I would be such a traitor to leave him now. I could never forgive myself."

The waiter appeared, awkwardly. Maria ordered a coffee as Andy looked away blankly at the passing traffic on the Ringstrasse, his mind attempting to sort out the jumble of random thoughts that arose and were then displaced by newer, sadder, and darker ones. He felt sick to his stomach. Finally, after the waiter had brought the coffee and left, he looked at her.

"Perhaps I should leave Vienna," Andy said. "If we can't be together, I don't want to stay any longer. I'm an American. I don't belong here now. I would have stayed and waited for you, Maria, but if you think you can't leave him ..." Andy felt himself choking up now, his throat ablaze. "I just want you to know that I would have waited for you."

"Oh, God, don't leave!" Maria replied. "Your career is going so well. Your reporting. I don't know what to do, Andy. It's just like I told you it would be in Budapest. It's just that Johann and I have spent so much time together. More than we ever did before. He doesn't look past me now. I can see it in his eyes. He still has terrible moods and wishes he had died and then he pulls himself together for a while. He's too weak for me to leave him now. Can you understand?"

"What are you saying? Do you love me, Maria? Will we be together, if not soon, then someday? I have to know that, at least."

"I do love you, Andy. I just don't know what's going to happen."

At that moment, the sun came out from behind a cloud and warmed Andy and Maria sitting in their chairs on the wide sidewalk just outside the café. A streetcar rumbled past, stopped, and opened its doors. A couple of people got off. One of them turned to give a hand to a man in an officer's uniform with crutches who was slowly and painfully coming down the steps to the street. It was Johann. Andy started to rise from the table to go help him, but Maria put her hand on his, silently bidding him stay where he was and let Johann manage on his own.

Johann had lost at least fifteen or twenty kilograms and his uniform hung loosely from his frame. His missing leg was concealed by the folded cloth of his trousers while the other leg maintained his balance as he worked the crutches, moving forward. He saw them sitting at the table. A faint smile crossed his face. Slowly he made his way toward them until he reached their table. Andy stood and turned out a chair for him to sit at the table. Johann slowly lowered himself into the chair with a sigh.

"That was not as easy as it looked," Johann said, smiling at both of them while laying his cap on the table. Andy had come to appreciate the peculiar Viennese talent for wry, ironic understatement. Vienna was a city of inexhaustible complexity, subtlety, and shades of gray. The Viennese could be marked by their deadpan humor and quiet pithy comments that so often flew by the tourist or foreigner unnoticed but were answered by their compatriots with a quiet nod or knowing smile.

The waiter appeared almost immediately and nodded deferentially to the wounded war veteran and aristocrat now seated at the table. He silently took the order and then bowed deeply. The sight of crippled officers and soldiers in the streets of Vienna was common. Maimed and crippled veterans who survived the battlefields and military hospitals now posed a daily reminder to the imperial city of the immense cost of the war in blood. Black crepe around doors and windows, black-veiled women in mourning attire and memorial masses for the dead were daily occurrences.

"You're doing so well, Johann," Andy remarked. "Look how far you have come in just a few months. You're getting stronger every day. It's so great to see you out in the city again."

"Andy's thinking of going home," Maria said bluntly. Johann nodded his head.

"I was wondering about that," Johann replied. "You can't be on holiday forever." There it was again. Johann knew well that Andy's holiday had become something entirely different and his comment conveyed the thought in a sentence. Andy could not help but smile and nod his head.

"Yes, perhaps it's time to go home."

"What would you do when you get home to Ohio?" Johann asked while removing a silver cigarette case from an interior pocket of his officer's tunic. He pulled a rolled cigarette from the case, tapped it on the table, and lit it, inhaling the smoke. He looked at Andy impassively but with curiosity.

"I don't know exactly," Andy replied. "I suppose I'll continue to write about the war for the newspaper and learn to be a real journalist with my father. Return to living a normal life, I guess."

"Ah, yes. A normal life," Johann replied, blowing a thin stream of smoke into the air. "That's what everyone should want … a normal life. I don't blame you, Andy. If you can live a normal life, you should do so. I'd like to go with you." Johann looked at Maria.

Andy shifted uneasily in his chair and glanced at Maria.

"Really, Johann? Wouldn't you want to stay and be with your people in this war?" Andy asked.

"Why? What can I do for them now?" Johann replied bitterly, gesturing to his leg. "The war is over for me. The life I was going to live here with Maria is gone. We can't win this war. The English will starve Germany into submission in time with the blockade. The French and the British will wear Germany down. The Russians will wear us down. And when the war is over, the empire will fall. It's a matter of time, I'm afraid. We'll have our victories but, eventually, the rest of the world will overwhelm us. So why not leave now while we can? Can you tell me I'm wrong?"

Andy was shocked at this bleak assessment although it was not far different from the kind of talk one heard in Viennese cafés these days. Then Maria spoke.

"Johann, you're not well enough to go to America and what about your mother? Would you leave her here? She would never leave Vienna for America or anywhere. You're being crazy. And we're not going to lose the war! Something is going to happen. Europe is going to realize soon the insanity of this war with so much death and destruction and it will end."

"They haven't realized it yet, Maria. Look how much blood has been lost already and they still go on. Look at the empire. We're not asking for the war to stop. We're fighting for victory and we're prepared to go on fighting for God knows how long. Just think what it's like in London or Paris. The Germans aren't stopping. No, this war is going to go on until one side collapses and it's much more likely to be us than them." Just then, Johann had a fit of coughing.

"This damn weather. I think I've caught a cold."

A streetcar rumbled by; a reminder of normal life. Conversation stopped for a moment while everyone pondered Johann's surprising question. Andy found himself envisioning Johann meeting his parents, living in Columbus.

"But what would you do when you got there?" Andy spoke at last.

"Live," Johann replied. "What about you, Maria. What would you like to do? Go or stay?"

"It's a very radical idea, Johann. You know that. I can't answer a question like that without thinking about it," she replied.

"You're thinking of what your life would be like with a husband like me in America, aren't you?" Johann asked softly. "I'm not going to marry you now, Maria. I wouldn't condemn you to a life with a cripple for a husband. Why don't you marry Andy instead?"

"What are you saying?" Maria exclaimed.

"You've talked to me about America so many times these past few months. Life, liberty, and the pursuit of happiness. Isn't that it? Andy would be perfect for you." Johann looked at Andy when he said this.

Andy was shocked and looked away. *Could he know?* Andy wondered. If not, it was eerie how close he was to the truth. Maria stared at him, saying nothing for a moment.

"Johann, you can't be serious?" she asked Johann at last.

"Why not? I just want to get away from here. I don't want to see this world die. I want a new life and I want to start it far away from here. I need you both to help me get started and then I'll be all right. What would be wrong with that?"

Johann turned to Maria now and spoke directly to her. "Your love for me these past months ..." Johann paused, collecting himself. "I'm so grateful to you for everything. I would never have made it without you. But I release you now, Maria. I would never have been a good husband before and you know that now. I would not be a good husband to you now. You must know that too. Let's all be friends and love each other for the rest of our lives, but not out of pity. I ask only that."

"No! Stop talking like this," Maria exclaimed. "You're not the man you were before in any way. I love your courage and your will to keep on living despite your wounds. I didn't want this to happen but it did. I'll be your wife if you still want me." Andy felt his heart skip a beat but before he could say or do anything, Johann spoke again.

"I know you would do that," Johann replied. "I won't let you do it. I won't let you throw your life away when you could have a happy life," Johann continued. He paused.

Then, with a roguish smile, "so it's settled, then. You'll marry Andy and we'll all go to America."

If only it were that simple, Andy thought. But Johann's reckless challenge had uncovered Maria's true feelings. Or was she just playing along? He couldn't tell. *Would he ever know?* he wondered. He felt as if his life, as if all their lives were teetering on the edge of a knife. One false move in any direction could bring them all tumbling down.

"I don't know what to say, Johann. Are you serious?" Andy ventured.

"Why not? Yes, I'm serious. I'm serious about going to America. I'm serious about Maria. As for the rest of it, that's up to you. Both of you, I mean."

There it was. Suspended in thin air, the prospect of everything he wanted, Andy thought frantically.

"Well, if you're serious ..."

"Johann," Maria interrupted. "This is insane. What about your mother? What about my mother? There's the war. How would we get there? You can't make a decision like this right now. You're still recovering. What about your leg?"

"They have doctors in America, right, Andy?"

"Well yes, of course." *Why was she resisting?* Andy wondered. Had she decided to go back to Johann after all? It didn't make sense, except if that was it.

They remained at the café for several hours, talking to and about each other and about going to America together until the sun went down and the cold night air chased them away from Fidelio's. At last, they agreed to think about it some more and that was how it ended. Andy bid Maria and Johann good-bye as they got on the streetcar and began his walk home to the Windischgrätz house. As the tram pulled away he could see them walking to their seats inside.

Maria pulled her scarf over her head and ears. The temperature had dropped as the evening arrived. Johann stepped out of the tram carefully and slowly as she watched. Were there trams like this one in America?

She had thought about America for a long time, and after falling in love with Andy, it had become a sweet preoccupation in her mind. Now, the thought of going there terrified her and she could not think why. Yes she could, she admitted. It was Johann.

Gone was the narcissistic, womanizing officer aristocrat she had dreaded to marry. He had died in Galicia and another personality had taken his place. In their time together, she had rediscovered the young boy who had enthralled her as a child, who had boldly flirted with her when she had become a teenager, to the envy of all her friends. His fearless nature, his sly humor, his penetrating intellect and disarming wit had slowly arisen from his shattered body and mind in these past months, but now, for the first time it was wrapped in a self-deprecating awareness she had never seen before.

The truth, Maria thought. It was time to face the truth. She had denied it. She had suppressed it. Today, it could no longer be avoided. She had fallen in love with the new man she had been nursing back to health. His misery and his failures, his despair and his fears had all been laid bare to her as they had never been before. In truth, since their childhood, he had become someone else. Had the war never happened, Maria had been sure that he was not the man for her. And now?

When Johann and Maria got to his house, Johann was cold and tired. Maria asked one of the servants to draw him a hot bath. After eating a little, Maria walked behind Johann up the stairs, ready to steady him if he stumbled with his crutches.

"I never ..." Maria said as they reached Johann's bedroom.

"It doesn't matter now, Maria. Things have changed, and for the better. We can be honest with each other now."

"I was honest when I said I loved you too, Johann. You're not the same man you were. Are you sure this is what you want?"

"I'm afraid, Maria. Don't think I'm not. I've been afraid since I woke up in Budapest. I was a spoiled boy before the war, wasn't I? The privileges I was given from birth that I took for granted have been revealed to me now. I'm just a man, Maria, like everyone else. Our world will never be the same and I'm tired of being afraid of what's to come. I want to take my life in my own hands before it's taken from me. Don't you want that too, Maria?"

"You talk as if all was lost. You don't know that. Nobody knows what's going to happen to us. Our ancestors must have thought all was lost when Napoleon was marching all over the continent and yet it wasn't. The same thing might happen now. We're not going to lose. We can't lose. I don't believe it."

Johann lay back on his bed and smiled ruefully. "And this from a Red like you," he said softly, taking her hand. *She loved him*, Maria thought. He was so brave and yet so vulnerable. She felt an overwhelming desire to kiss him. She leaned forward slowly and felt his mouth on hers.

"Maria, you shouldn't," Johann said.

"I don't care," she said simply.

As they lay in his huge bed, she felt Johann quiver as he stifled a sob. She said nothing but kissed him and held him. She understood him now, she thought. For so long she had tried to help him in his lonely struggle. Now she felt a warm glow of love and satisfaction. She was doing the right thing this night. She thought of Andy. A pang of guilt and regret. She felt she would think about things again tomorrow. It was just too difficult to make sense of anything tonight.

14.

Farewell to Vienna

"Andy, you had better read this," Otto said as Andy came down the stairs into the breakfast room. He lightly tossed a copy of the *Neue Freie Presse* across the table. Andy picked it up and read the lead article.

Sinking of Cunard Liner Lusitania

Berlin, May 8—The German submarine U-20 torpedoed the Cunard liner RMS *Lusitania* off the coast of Ireland yesterday. It is estimated that over 1,000 passengers lost their lives, including 128 Americans. The German Foreign Minister Gottlieb von Jagow responded today to protests from the government of the United States of America to the sinking yesterday afternoon as follows:

"The imperial government has subjected the statements of the government of the United States to a careful examination and must state the impression that certain important facts most directly connected with the sinking of the *Lusitania* may have escaped the attention of the government of the United States. The government of the United States proceeds on the assumption that the *Lusitania* is to be considered as an ordinary unarmed merchant vessel. The imperial government begs in this connection to point out that the *Lusitania* was one of the largest and fastest English commerce steamers, constructed with government funds as auxiliary cruisers, and is expressly included in the navy list published by the British Admiralty.

The imperial government must specially point out that on her last trip the *Lusitania*, as on earlier occasions, had Canadian troops and munitions on board, including no less than 5,400 cases of ammunition destined for the destruction of brave German soldiers who are fulfilling with self-sacrifice and devotion their duty in the service of the Fatherland.

The German government believes that it acts in just self-defense when it seeks to protect the lives of its soldiers by destroying ammunition destined for the enemy with the means of war at its command. The English steamship company must have been aware of the dangers to which passengers on board the *Lusitania* were exposed under the circumstances.

In taking them on board in spite of this, the company quite deliberately tried to use the lives of American citizens as protection for the ammunition carried, and violated the clear provisions of American laws that expressly prohibit, and provide punishment for, the carrying of passengers on ships that have explosives on board. The company thereby wantonly caused the death of so many passengers.

According to the express report of the submarine commander concerned, which is further confirmed by all other reports, there can be no doubt that the rapid sinking of the *Lusitania* was primarily due to the explosion of the cargo of ammunition caused by the torpedo. Otherwise, in all human probability, the passengers would have been saved.

Lastly, the imperial government would most respectfully point out that care was taken to advertise in over a dozen American newspapers, including the *New York Times*, as early as May 1 as follows: "Travelers intending to embark on the

Atlantic voyage are reminded that a state of war exists between Germany ... and Great Britain ... and that travelers sailing in the war zone on ships of Great Britain or her allies do so at their own risk."

The imperial government holds the facts recited above to be of sufficient importance to recommend them to a careful examination by the American government.

Andy put the paper down on the table. "This is terrible news, Uncle."

"Indeed," replied Otto gravely. "What do you think the reaction of the American government will be? Will they declare war on Germany?"

"I don't know. Perhaps, if the facts in this article are true, it will cause President Wilson to think twice. My father says that the country wants to stay out of the war, but there are many people, including our former president, Theodore Roosevelt, who have already said that we should go to war with Germany."

"And as our ally, then I suppose they would declare war on Austria-Hungary as well?"

"It's possible, yes."

"What will you do, Andy?"

"I don't know. I suppose I will have to leave, won't I?"

"It's all so terrible," Otto said sadly. "We have no quarrel with the United States of America. We have no quarrel with anybody except Serbia. Who would have thought a year ago that we could be at war with America? It's unbelievable."

The following day, a telegram arrived from Arthur Bishop.

```
Dear Andy. Sinking of Lusitania has
changed situation here drastically.
War with Germany and Central Powers
a definite possibility now. Please
consider your safety and return
home immediately through neutral
```

> country before situation becomes dire. Wire reply of your intentions at your earliest convenience.
> Love, Dad.

Andy showed the telegram to Otto and Elisabeth that afternoon.

"It's inconceivable that we could be at war with the United States," Elisabeth exclaimed upon reading the telegram. "Surely the German government will go to any lengths to prevent war."

"I don't know what to say, Aunt Elisabeth," Andy replied. "I must think about leaving though, at least temporarily, and if the crisis passes, I could come back."

"Of course you must," Otto replied gloomily. "We understand. Your parents are worried, as we would be if the situation were reversed. You will have to make a decision and reply to your father."

Andy soon rang Maria on the telephone only to find that she was out. He guessed that she would probably be with Johann and rang his house. He arranged to meet them later at Johann's house. As he considered everything, he found himself wondering whether his leaving might finally break the impasse that had developed between him and Maria. He wondered if leaving the country might not just be the thing to complete the final break between Maria and Johann. If he were to leave the country, Maria would have to choose whether to stay or to go with him to the new life she had always talked about in America. Johann would not stand in their way, he was sure. He had said as much, hadn't he?

As the afternoon went on, the decision to leave Vienna seemed more and more the right thing to do. Yes, it would mean giving up his privileged perch in Vienna to report on the war, but he could resume his journalistic career somehow when he got back home, he was sure. It would please his father and mother. It was probably the sensible thing to do under the circumstances. And surely, Maria would decide to fulfill the destiny she had sought practically since the day he had met her.

These past few weeks had been an agony for him. Her distance and ambiguous feelings for him had fired his desire for her all the more and yet, as always, she was just outside his reach. He thought of her constantly. The dreams they had shared before Johann was wounded and the ecstatic feelings of those days came back to him over and over again. He wanted those days—and those feelings—again. He wanted her back.

Andy arrived at the Caboga residence in the evening. Andy's confidence in his reasoning of earlier in the day had begun to waver as he left the Windischgrätz house and, by the time he arrived, he was a bundle of nerves. What had seemed so obvious and clever now seemed questionable and dubious, but as he rang the doorbell, he decided to follow through with his plan and hope for the best. He was quickly escorted into the drawing room by one of the Caboga footmen who answered the door.

"Ah, Andy. So good to see you," exclaimed Johann cordially as he rose from the chair to shake hands. Maria kissed him on each cheek before sitting down next to Johann. For a few minutes, they spoke of Johann's continuing recovery. He had been fitted with a light metal prosthesis with which he struggled, still using the crutches, but things were certainly improving, as was Johann's overall mood, it seemed. Soon the discussion turned to the war and the diplomatic storm over the *Lusitania*.

"My parents are very concerned that there may be war and the best thing for me to do at the moment seems to be to leave Vienna," Andy began, watching Maria and Johann for their reaction. It occurred to him that they were essentially sitting together, across the room from him, and he found himself addressing both of them, together. Johann's face immediately became serious as he heard Andy out. Maria initially turned away at Andy's announcement and then she seemed lost in her own thoughts.

"Where will you go? I mean, what country will you leave from?" Johann inquired.

"I've thought about that," said Andy. "I thought about the Netherlands, but I would have to cross Germany to get there and, since war might break out any day, that seemed a little dangerous. So I think I'll go to Italy. It's closer and neutral. I can book a ship home from Italy that will not go through the war zone around Britain. It seems like the logical choice."

"I see," Johann replied. "When will you leave?"

"In a couple of days, I think. Every day that goes on, the risk of war breaking out seems worse."

"I suppose," Johann said. "Personally, I don't think there will be war. Germany will do anything to avoid war with the United States and, unless I miss my guess, after a little while, there will be no enthusiasm in America to get into a war in Europe. I think it will all blow over, but still, as an American, I suppose you can't take any chances."

Maria had said nothing, but then Andy had not expected her to openly discuss her intentions. He guessed that it would come later, privately, but it was not to be. Once again, Johann raised the subject.

"Well, Andy, I've given it a lot of thought and if you're still willing, I would like to go with you."

This was not what Andy had wanted to hear, but he could hardly stop him. Now Maria finally spoke.

"Have you thought about the possibility that if there is war between Austria and the United States, we could be barred from entering the country as enemy aliens? Or worse, after arriving, we could be forced to return."

"That's true," replied Johann, "But if it's going to happen,

Andy's right. It will happen in the next few days. We wouldn't even be in Italy yet—or perhaps we would—and we could always stop there and come back. I doubt it would happen, though."

"And what about your mother and mine?"

"We can invite them to come too. They'll decline, of course. The decision will be theirs." Suddenly, Johann had another fit of coughing. "I just can't seem to get rid of this cold," he said when he finally was able to stop.

They discussed the pros and cons for several hours. Still, there was no hint from Maria about what her real feelings were for Andy and a future life together. Johann had mentioned nothing further about his own relationship with Maria either, as he had when they had first discussed the subject at Fidelio's. Eventually, Andy rose to leave.

"Well, I suppose you'll have to discuss it with your families. As I said, I'll be making plans to leave in a couple of days, so let me know what you decide to do." He bid them good-night and began walking back to the Windischgrätz house, as confused and forlorn as ever. Would Maria call? He had to know. He couldn't go on like this.

The next day, Maria did call. She asked to meet him in the Stadtpark, near the statue of Josef Strauss. It was about halfway between their respective houses, the largest of the parks along the Ringstrasse and one of the prettiest. As he arrived at the golden statue, he saw Maria waiting for him. She was in a plain gray dress, her head down, apparently lost in thought. Thoughts of him and what she was going to say, Andy imagined. His heart hammered in his breast as he approached and she looked up to see him. A wan smile. A soft embrace. He took her arm and they began walking toward the *Kursalon*, a neo-Baroque building resembling the façade of a palace in *kaisergelb*, the "imperial yellow" color so common in Habsburg public buildings. A few words about the pretty day and then it came.

"I've made my plans, Maria. I'll be leaving in two days. I want you to come with me, but I just don't know how you feel about me anymore. These past few weeks ... no, actually, ever since we came back from Budapest, things haven't been the same. I think back on the things you told me before. Before then, I mean. I was so happy. I was in love with you, Maria. I still am. I want you to come with me. To live with me. I want to marry you, Maria ..." She walked beside him, saying nothing, listening. When Andy had finished, she took a deep breath and sighed. Andy looked at her face. Her eyes were red and watering. Her sigh was a stifled sob. She fumbled in her purse and took out a handkerchief, dabbing her eye.

"I'm so sorry, Andy," she began, struggling for her composure. "I've done you a great wrong. I want you to know that whatever I said to you—everything—I felt in my heart. I would never have hurt you, Andy. You must believe that. But now, things are different. I'm different. Johann is different. The war changed everything. I can't abandon him, Andy. I can't. He must never know about us. I beg you now ..."

She went on talking about how her feelings for Johann had changed and how impossible it was for her to leave him, how she had discovered that she did love him. Her words got lost in the jumble of despair and sickening defeat that welled up inside him and jangled through his brain. Andy caught a little here and there, but it didn't matter. He had lost her. It was over. He said nothing as she continued, but there was more and he gradually became aware of a new issue.

"I can't talk him out of it, Andy. He has it fixed in his mind. He wants to leave and go to America. At least for a while. He wants me to go with him, Andy."

Andy was horrified. Not only had he lost her—not only

were his dreams all shattered beyond recall—but he would also have to endure them together. And he could neither say nor act any differently so that Johann would never know. He would have to suffer in silence.

"Maria, I can't ... I don't know how I could do that. I mean, I just couldn't."

"I know, Andy. I'm so sorry for everything. I've tried to talk him out of going, but he won't hear of it. The countess too. She won't go, of course. He won't talk about anything else. And he has such affection for you, Andy. He's so grateful that you're willing to do this for him. To take him away from here. To start a new life. He's so excited. He's been walking with his prosthesis without his crutches. If he knew about us, or if he couldn't go to America, he would be crushed. I don't know what would happen to him. He wants you to come over this evening. He wants to know your final plans."

As they walked and talked, Andy's gloom and despair deepened, but, in the end, it was too late. He couldn't say no. He couldn't refuse Johann this request without throwing away their friendship and, even then, how could he stop Johann from leaving for America if he really wanted to go? He was trapped, and so, that evening, the three of them made plans to leave for Italy and from there, to America.

On May 15, 1915, Andy took leave of the Windischgrätz family for the last time. Over nearly a year's time together, as the drama of this European war unfolded, the theoretical kinship discovered by his mother in what seemed like another lifetime had become a real and living thing. Otto and Elisabeth had become to Andy the aunt and uncle he had never known in his former life back in Columbus. Perhaps it was because Andy was roughly the same age as

An American in Vienna

their own boys or perhaps because of what they had all been through together, but Andy felt that he had become like a third son in the family and parting with them was keenly felt. As rare French burgundy flowed at dinner their last evening together, so had some tears.

Andy had bought a trunk to send the things that he had accumulated ahead to America. Two leather suitcases would have to hold all of the clothes that he would need in the weeks he would be traveling in Italy and then home. He carefully wrapped the typewriter that he had kept on the mahogany desk in the upstairs study that overlooked the house's inner courtyard. As he wrapped it, he looked out the window from which he had gazed so many times. A wave of melancholy washed over him as he wondered how long it would be before he saw this view again, if ever.

When Otto had first found out that Andy intended to supply his father and his American newspaper with weekly accounts of the war and life in Vienna, he insisted on providing Andy the study and provisioning it with everything necessary for his comfort and convenience. Many afternoons and evenings as the footman brought him cognac or coffee, Otto would join Andy with a cigar and they would talk about what he was writing, events of the day, and philosophy. Andy had treasured those conversations that sometimes stretched on for hours, through dinner and on into the evening.

Andy had learned much from Otto about European history and philosophy, art and politics. Otto's fund of knowledge was immense and his insight into current events as a retired officer was frequently profound. Andy's acquired understanding played out across the keyboard of the typewriter and seasoned his articles, deftly guiding his American readers through current events with context not seen from other writers. Now, Andy gently laid the typewriter in the trunk, cushioned in wrap for the long voyage. One of the footmen would pack the trunk with dry hay to cushion it further.

As he finished packing, Andy sighed and looked around his bedroom for the last time. It was as spacious as the parlor in his parents' house in Columbus. Large windows looked out over the cobbled streets of the *Innere Stadt* that had always been Vienna. Its pale green plaster walls had seen celebrities doze, dress, cavort, and contemplate. Who knew how many Metternichs, Radetzkys, Esterházys, and Schwartzenbergs had gazed up at its creamy white ceiling and plaster medallions spouting Bohemian crystal chandeliers? Dukes of Windsor, York, and Edinburgh, crown princes of Prussia, and countless other aristocratic *glitterati* of a now fading, brilliant past had enjoyed the pleasures of its adjoining water closet. Yet none of these guests, Otto had assured him, had left such a mark on the life of the venerable mansion as Andy had done.

The only servants left in the household were women or old men. The young grooms and under-servants had gone to war like Otto and Elisabeth's own sons and were facing death or worse every day. Their absence and often-unknown fate had left a melancholy behind that could not be dispelled as long as the war would last.

Andy walked down the wide spiral stairs with a heavy heart and, on reaching the bottom, nodded to the footman that he could finish packing the trunk and ready it for the car. Andy instinctively turned to his right and walked through the archway into the vast salon where receptions were held for friends and family. Otto was sitting by the cold fireplace, smoking his pipe with a newspaper spread in his lap. He looked up as Andy appeared in the archway and a smile crossed his face.

"Come here and sit for a minute," Otto beckoned with his hand, gesturing toward a chair. Andy smiled and walked the considerable distance across the room. This room also had large windows that were draped with heavy curtains.

Several magnificent Persian carpets covered the wood floor, giving it a warmth and beauty that seemed especially vivid at that moment.

"It's very hard to leave you and Elisabeth, but what makes it worse is not knowing if I will ever see you again," Andy started. Otto removed his reading glasses and folded the newspaper, placing it quietly on the adjoining table.

"Elisabeth will be here in a moment. She has arranged a basket of food for you to take on your trip. Yes, Andy, it is very hard for us to imagine this house without you after all this time. It will be very empty for us now. We will miss you as much as we miss our own sons and we pray for your safe return to America, but we understand you must go. You know you are always welcome here. I hope when the war is over that we might be able to visit you and our American cousins, but who can say?

"Vienna has survived for centuries and it will survive in one form or another after this war. You have helped us in your own way, sending news of our side of the war to your homeland. This war was not our doing. We were attacked and we had to defend ourselves. The fact that the war spread to all of Europe can't obscure that truth, can it? We are not a perfect country and we have made mistakes, to be sure, but we are not an enemy to America. Perhaps in some way, you can get this across to your people."

"Yes, I will," Andy replied, "But perhaps you overestimate me. My little contribution to understanding this war makes very little impression on President Wilson, I can confidently say. It seems to be Germany, France, and England that get his attention. Austria and Russia get very little notice in the news." Elisabeth entered the room with a brown wicker basket. Andy stood as she came to him and they hugged. She kissed him on each cheek.

"I hope this keeps you well fed until you get to Italy," she said. "I also want to give you something else." The archduchess reached into a pocket in the folds of her dress and pulled out a small velvet box. She handed it to him. Andy opened the box. It was a pocket watch made of gold. His heart skipped a beat as he gently pulled the watch and chain from the box and held it in his hand. The cover of the watch was engraved with a double-headed eagle.

"This was made by Abraham Louis Breguet about one hundred years ago. My father acquired it in Switzerland on his travels. I want you to have it and to think of us when you look at it. Why don't you open it?"

Andy found the catch and the cover popped open. It was magnificent. Its shimmering pearl-white face was engraved with black roman numerals, but then he noticed the engraving on the inside of the cover. *"Um unseren amerikanischen Cousin Andy ... Denke oft an deine Zeit bei uns ..."* (To our American cousin Andy ... Think often of your time with us.) It was a fabulously expensive gift, but even more, the engraving touched his heart.

He looked into Elisabeth's face and saw the familiar cool composure of a Habsburg gazing back at him with her faint smile so ubiquitous in the imperial family. He had come to know her well in his time here, but it had been a sometimes-daunting challenge to penetrate her outward reserve.

Born to unimaginable privilege, Andy had come to know that Elisabeth's early life had been defined by the deterioration of her parents' marriage within the gilded halls of palaces or the confines of coaches pulled by teams of white horses. Although she rarely spoke about him, as a child she had dearly loved her father who, in turn and whatever his failings as a husband, had evidently shown a doting affection for his little daughter. His suicide, the scandal that followed, and the taboo of ever discussing it had left her adrift with her bitter mother who coped with the spectacular demise of her husband by fleeing as far away as possible from her Habsburg in-laws.

Strangely, it was the old kaiser who became the mainstay of her life as she came into adolescence and adulthood.

Cool and distant to most of the world, her grandfather was warm and intimate with his own daughters—and with his granddaughter Elisabeth most of all. Within eleven years of the Mayerling affair, the kaiser was a widower after the murder of his wife, Empress Elisabeth, while she was in Switzerland. In his final decades, the kaiser had become the kindly, loving man that he could only be while in the presence of his daughters and granddaughters.

It was Franz Josef who had come to her rescue, Elisabeth had told him, as she tried to understand who she really was and what she was meant to do in her life. Over teas and cakes at Schönbrunn or on long alpine walks from the *Kaiservilla* in Bad Ischl, they had talked and listened to each other. His grandfatherly love for her was requited. She loved the old man as few in the world did in those times. She understood him.

"I don't know what to say. This is overwhelming. It's a precious thing that I will always keep with me, but not as precious as the memories I will always have of my time with you and Otto. I will never forget you. I miss you both already." Elisabeth smiled and kissed him again on both cheeks.

Karl appeared in the archway. The car was ready to take Andy to the station. Otto stood up and the three of them embraced together for a long time. Missing from the farewell were their sons and their absence was keenly felt by Andy in these final moments. A last look and last kisses good-bye passed all too quickly and, before long, Andy found himself at the Südbahnhof rail station, watching the Windischgrätz motorcar disappear into the streets of Vienna. A porter helped him with his luggage and the wicker basket into the terminal where he scanned the lobby for Johann and Maria.

15.

Italy

Soldiers were very conspicuous in the station at the Südbahnhof. It was unusual to see such large groups of them apparently heading in the direction of Trieste, Austria's main seaport and the last major city before the Italian border. Large groups of them with their packs sat on benches or slept on the floors while military police kept watch. Soldiers had first priority on trains leaving for the front with their units, but it was curious to see so many at this station going west and not east toward the Russian front.

Andy was going to be taking the train for Milan, which would be leaving shortly after noon. It would pass through Trieste. The cavernous hall of the lobby had a number of cafés and restaurants around the perimeter. After Andy and the porter had made sure his luggage was properly loaded on the train, he returned to the lobby to wait for his friends at one of the cafés and bought a newspaper.

It was strange. In the days since the sinking of the *Lusitania*, the scare of war with the United States had slowly receded. The articles in the paper reported more diplomatic notes between the German and American governments while the British made the most of the sinking for propaganda purposes. It was becoming apparent that neither Germany nor the United States desired a war and both sides seemed to be groping for a climb down in the tension between them. The reason for his hasty departure from Vienna was evaporating day by day, it seemed, and Andy wished that he had never decided to go.

Johann and Maria arrived a few minutes after Andy sat down at the café. Two footmen from the Caboga household wheeled the bags to the outbound train platform and ensured they were loaded aboard the train while Johann and Maria sat down with Andy. The details of the trip had been worked out. They would arrive in Milan on May 12 and spend a few days seeing the sights, including Lake Como. Then they would go on to Rome where they would stay until May 27. They had booked passage to America from Genoa aboard the Italian liner *Ancona*, bound for New York.

The soldiers on the platform were patiently boarding the train for Trieste by the time the three of them got downstairs. Johann was doing surprisingly well with his artificial leg, although he still used one crutch sometimes. They had purchased first-class tickets, which was a good thing because the regular second-class coaches were bulging with soldiers, many of whom were standing in the cars. After a while, the three of them found a compartment in the first-class coach and, a few minutes later, the train made steam and lumbered out of the station.

The train moved very slowly west as the hours went by. The countryside just south and west of Vienna was mainly farmland and seemed clean and well tended. After a couple of hours, Andy opened up his wicker basket and the three of them ate the ample fare that Elisabeth had provided for them. There was even a bottle of wine in the basket that they promptly uncorked with pleasure and drank as the afternoon wore on. Johann was excited and chattered away while Maria and Andy listened.

Johann and Maria had been to Lake Como many times

in their youth and described the area to Andy. It was not far from Milan and was definitely worth a visit, Johann assured him.

"The lake is crystal clear and deep, like so many of our alpine lakes. The thing I remember was the little town of Bellagio on the tip of the mountainous peninsula that divides the lake. Then again, all along the shoreline there are beautiful *palazzi*, one after another in beautiful colors. A boat ride on Lake Como is something we must do." Johann reminded Maria of a particular palazzo where they had played as children, recounting several stories and names of friends that they had made in those days, wondering what had happened to this one or that.

Before long, night had fallen and they had all dozed off. The train had stopped in Trieste before they knew it and the lights of the platform shined through the window, awakening Andy. Several hours must have passed. Out on the platform, a group of officers were speaking with what looked like an official from the railway system. Andy noticed more officers drifting over until there were more than a dozen of them. He felt uneasy and sat up. Maria and Johann were still sleeping across from him; Maria had her head on Johann's shoulder. Then he noticed many of the soldiers getting off the train. He watched as they lit cigarettes and began to mill about. Andy decided to stretch his legs and see what was going on.

Quietly, Andy pulled open the sliding door to their compartment and began to walk down the narrow corridor to the door. In a minute, he was on the platform and he moved in the direction of the clutch of officers to see if he could overhear anything. Other passengers in the first-class coach seemed to have had the same idea and were stepping off the train. What was happening? Before long, the officers began walking down the platform, shouting to the soldiers on the train to get off. Within minutes, the platform was full of soldiers responding to the shouts.

Andy walked to one of the officers now and asked him directly what was happening.

"There was a rumor that the border with Italy was sealed, but it's not. We just got new orders to remain here tonight," the officer said.

In a few minutes, Andy was back on the train. He carefully pulled open the door so not to wake Maria and Johann. A few minutes later, he heard the locomotive making steam and sure enough, it started rolling forward. The last Austrian town would be Montefalcone and then they would cross the frontier into Italy.

An hour went by as the train chugged north along the coastline in the dark. It was unnerving not to be able to see anything out the window and Andy couldn't sleep. Why would the border with Italy be sealed? The sealing of the border was usually a precaution taken by European countries when war was imminent. It was meant to screen nationals of the bordering country from seeing military movements near the border. And why were there so many soldiers on the train moving toward the Italian border anyway?

At last, the train slowed down and pulled into the station at Montefalcone. It was past midnight. A few passengers got off and, in a minute, the train started up again, hissing and grinding out of the station as if protesting against its intended mission. Begliano would be the first Italian city across the border.

Maria stirred now and stared at him for a moment. "Where are we?" she asked. Andy told her and Johann awoke too. He related to them his conversation with the Austrian officer at the Trieste station. The lighthearted optimism of the afternoon was now gone in the little cabin as the train steamed forward through the night. The conversation lapsed as all of them peered out the window, but there was nothing but blackness and pinpoints of distant light every now and then.

Within twenty minutes, the train started slowing

down again and then it crept into the lights of the station at Begliano. As the train eased to a stop, Andy noticed a number of what appeared to be carabinieri on the platform. These were the national police of the Kingdom of Italy. They boarded the train. They could hear them as they opened the doors of the adjoining compartments and spoke to the passengers within. Then their door opened. Two tall carabinieri entered.

"*Passaporti!*" said one of them, obviously unaware of what nationality they were. Andy was first and handed over his passport.

"*Ah, Americani,*" the border guard said with a smile. "*Benvenuti in Italia! Di dove è?*"

Andy did not speak any Italian but he guessed that the guard was asking him where he was from. "I don't speak Italian, signore," he said, but then added "Columbus, Ohio."

"*Ah, Columbus ... Si, un Italiano?*" The carabinieri grinned, appreciating his own humor that this American came from a city named after the Italian explorer.

"*Si. Un Italiano!*" Andy replied, smiling back as best he could. The guard turned to Maria and Johann, but the moment he saw their passports with the Austrian double eagle on the cover, the smile faded.

"*Austriaci?*" he asked them both. They nodded. The guard carefully flipped through the passports, studying them carefully. All business, now. The second guard looked over the first guard's shoulder. The first guard eyed them slowly.

"*Amici?*" the first guard said to Andy, questioning him again and inclining his head in the direction of Maria and Johann. Andy knew this meant to ask him if they were his friends.

"*Si, amici,*" Andy replied quietly. There was a long pause as the guard continued to look at the passports and then at Maria and Johann. Then he said "*Tempo di austriaci a lasciare, di non venire"* to the two Austrians, handed them their passports, and left.

"What did he say?" asked Maria to Johann after they left and the door to the compartment slammed shut behind them.

"He said, 'It's time for Austrians to leave, not to come.'" Johann spoke decent, schoolboy Italian he had learned in his younger days on holiday.

"Not a very warm welcome," Andy observed. Minutes went by very slowly as doors opened and slammed down the corridor, and then all was quiet. After what seemed like an hour, the train began to make steam again and crept forward slowly, out of the station.

Somehow they managed to sleep fitfully as the train shuddered along the rails toward Milan. The tracks in Italy seemed much rougher than in Austria, causing the car to lurch suddenly at times, waking them up. Eventually, after another lurch and another train-induced shudder, Andy woke up and realized it was light. He looked out the window and saw the Italian countryside passing by in the same apparent peacefulness as he had seen in Austria.

Vitenza and then Verona passed and, by noon, they arrived in Bergamo where they stepped out of the train to get some lunch at the station. In the late afternoon, they pulled into the station in Milan. The scene there was not reassuring. Hundreds of Italian soldiers were in the station, obviously catching the eastbound trains to the border with Austria. The three of them gathered their baggage with the help of two porters and quietly made their way through the station toward the cabs outside. The porters arranged the bags in the cab and soon they were off through the congested streets of Milan for the hotel.

Upon their arrival, bellmen came out to get their bags and carried them into the hotel, nodding and bowing to them, but the scene at the front desk was similar to the treatment at the border. Smiles and welcome to Andy.

Frowns and caution when it came to Maria and Johann. The concierge took their passports for "safekeeping." In heavily accented German, he advised them that their arrival would be registered with the Milanese police, shrugging as if making an apology.

After depositing their bags at the hotel and freshening up, Johann, Maria, and Andy decided to consider everything that had happened at a nearby café.

"What do you make of all this?" Andy asked Johann.

"It seems as if the Italians are getting ready to go to war. The troops on both sides of the border, the train stopping in Trieste, the comments by the Carabinieri—all seem like the country is preparing to go to war with us," Johann replied.

"What should we do?" exclaimed Maria. "Maybe we should get out of Italy as soon as we can. If war does break out, we're on the wrong side of the border."

"It's unbelievable," Johann continued. "Why now? There's no reason for them to go to war with us unless it's just to plunder while we're fighting for our lives. They must be thinking that they can invade us and take territory cheap with no real fighting."

Andy wondered how Austria could possibly cope with this if an Italian invasion turned out to be true. Hard pressed as she was in the Russian war, an attack by Italy would certainly be the straw that broke Austria's back. With the Reich's forces already engaged hundreds of miles away in a death struggle with Russia and what few could be spared fighting the Serbians, Andy couldn't imagine how the Austrian army could even find the troops to man the border with Italy.

The next morning, the threesome began their tour of Milan and tried to put thoughts of war out of their minds. Johann continued to improve his gait with the prosthetic leg, but after an hour or so, he had to sit down. Maria suggested that he buy a cane in one of the shops and he did, but it wasn't just that. He felt pain in his chest after he had been walking for any length of time and was breathing deeply. It was that damn cold. He just couldn't shake it.

As they toured the magnificent Gothic *Duomo di Milano*, the *Teatro alla Scalla* opera house, the *Castello* of the ancient Sforza family and then wandered around the *Brera*, a beautiful neighborhood of shops and restaurants, Andy found himself often walking alone while Maria and Johann reminisced about the past. Johann's enthusiasm in pointing out the sights to Andy did little to ease his feelings of rejection and he found it difficult to make light conversation as they went from place to place.

It took nearly a day by train and by horse to reach the tiny village of Bellagio on Lake Como, perched at the apex of the triangle of land that separated the two lower reaches of the lake. On a map, Lake Como looked like an upside-down "Y" with Bellagio looking north at the tip of the peninsula. Ancient streets, narrow and crooked, wound up and down the side of the mountain on which the little town lay. The weather was cool and clear as they relaxed in the cafés and took boat rides up and down the lake like tourists on holiday, which, to some extent, they were. The war seemed far away and Johann's spirits soared as each day separated them further from the gloom and tension of Vienna.

On May 21, now isolated from and oblivious to the outside world, the three tourists boarded a train for Rome. The trip took most of the day. When they arrived in Rome, hundreds of soldiers were milling around in the train station waiting to board northbound trains.

"Look at them all," Maria said. "It's obvious. They're going to attack us for sure," she whispered. "Look at the newspaper!" Maria was pointing to a pile of newspapers being sold by some street vendors near the door. Johann gave a boy a coin and took one of them to read. As they settled in the cab for their hotel, Johann quietly began to read it. "*Mobilitazione!*" screamed the headlines. He translated the words as best he could.

"It says that the Italian prime minister, Salada, in a speech in the Italian parliament the previous day says that the nation can no longer bear the cries of their *'compatrioti'* suffering under the kaiser's rule. It says that the Italian cabinet is expected to meet today to decide whether to go to war with us or not." Johann silently read some more, but the expression on his face left little doubt that they had arrived in a capital being exhorted to war by its government.

"Amazing," Johann said as he put the paper down. "They have sat out the war all this time and now, suddenly, they make it seem like it's a crisis ... an emergency. They're mobilizing the Italian army as if we were about to attack them! What imbeciles. They think they're going to walk right into Trieste or Trentino without a fight and just take it? Haven't they seen the butchery in France and Belgium? Or on the Russian front?"

"But what about us?" Maria wondered aloud. "What are we going to do now?"

It was the evening of May 23, 1915. The following day, Italy declared war on the Austro-Hungarian Empire. On the morning of May 24, the Roman police visited their hotel room at the *Hotel di San Floriano* and politely informed Johann and Maria that they had twenty-four hours to leave the country. A train would be leaving Rome with Austrian citizens the following day at two o'clock and they must be on it. Otherwise, they would be arrested. Andy was, as an American, free to stay as long as he liked. Maria and Johann's passports were confiscated, but would be returned to them at the train station the following day, a means of checking to ensure their expulsion from the country.

Maria had felt a growing pain in her abdomen for days. It had started shortly after they had arrived in Bellagio, coming and going since then, but growing ever more insistent and painful as the hours and days passed. She had said nothing to Andy or Johann about it, believing it to be something trivial or embarrassing at first, but she could not get comfortable. By the evening of the twenty-fourth, it could no longer be ignored. By dinner that evening, the pain had become a searing, stabbing pain that doubled her over in her chair.

"What is it?" cried Andy.

"I don't know. It's a pain in my abdomen. I can't stand it anymore." Her face was white. Maria started to stand up from the table, but fainted, falling to the floor. There was a gasp from other diners as Andy leaped up and then knelt at her side. Johann had also risen and called for the waiter to get help. Soon the maitre d' was on the floor with a cold towel and smelling salts.

"*Dottore* ..." Andy said to the maitre d' who nodded. He called another waiter over and evidently dispatched him to get a doctor. Maria came to consciousness, but was again overcome by the pain, grimacing. Andy held her hand and kneeled by her head, soothing her. Johann sat awkwardly in a chair next to him, unable to get to the floor with his false leg.

Soon some waiters came with a long tablecloth that they spread on the floor next to Maria. They gently lifted her onto the tablecloth to carry her out of the dining room and into a bedroom on the ground floor. When they arrived, the waiters positioned her on the bed. The maitre d' returned with a glass of brandy to dull the pain and Maria drank a little of it. Then the concierge arrived and quietly advised them that the hotel doctor would be there as quickly as he could. There was nothing else to do but wait.

Dr. Luigi Olivio was in his fifties with a thick black mane of hair flecked with splotches of silver. His large, hooded brown eyes protruded ever so slightly more than they should from his face, giving his medical gaze an added intensity. His moustache was, like his hair, mainly black and ended in needlelike wax points at each side. Thin but tall, dark, and handsome, he projected an almost theatrical appearance as he entered the sick room with his black leather bag of instruments. A frown crossed his face at the number of people in the room and, with a wave of his hand and a few murmured words in Italian, the hotel staff quickly evacuated, leaving Johann and Andy behind. Arched eyebrows on Olivio's face questioned why they too had not left the room.

Johann explained in his meager Italian that he and Andy were close friends of the patient. This drew an even more penetrating and quizzical gaze from the doctor. No, Johann had to explain, neither he nor Andy were her husband. Then they would have to leave the room, the doctor said. Johann mentioned that Maria spoke no Italian, only German and English. Olivio turned to Maria.

"You understand my English, madam?" Maria nodded. The doctor looked at Johann and Andy, shrugged his shoulders, and said, "You may leave us now." Andy and Johann each gave Maria a discreet kiss on the cheek and left the room to the doctor. In a minute, they were back in the lobby of the hotel. Johann lit a cigarette after sitting down in one of the chairs arranged around a low coffee table.

"Give me one of those," Andy said. Although he was not a smoker, he had an overwhelming desire to do so now to relieve the anxiety of waiting for the doctor. Johann nodded, opening up his silver case and offering it to Andy. Andy picked out a cigarette and lit it, exhaling a plume of smoke. Patrons of the restaurant walked out into the lobby and looked in their direction, recognizing them as having been with the woman who fainted earlier. Soon the maitre d' appeared again with two glasses of brandy. He sat down in the chair and began speaking German with only a slight accent.

"Massimo Allegra is my name, gentlemen. I am so sorry

about your situation especially …" he hesitated, "under the circumstances. You gentlemen are from Vienna, are you?" The cordiality of the maitre d' was in such marked contrast to that of the concierge, the police, or virtually any of the Italians in Rome with whom they had come in contact in the past couple of days that he surprised Andy and Johann.

"No, I am an American, signor," replied Andy. "Thank you for your concern. We appreciate your getting the doctor for us so quickly." Johann nodded his thanks as well.

"It was nothing, *signore*. He will take good care of your young lady. Is the lady your wife or sister?" he inquired. Andy and Johann looked at one another, but then Johann replied.

"Neither, signor. We were all traveling to Italy from Vienna for a little holiday before continuing to America where he lives," Johann said. "Unfortunately, we seem to have arrived at a bad time."

"*Si*, a very bad time, signore. This has taken everyone by surprise." The maitre d' lowered his voice now. "This is a terrible thing that has happened. Few people in the south want to go to war with Austria again. Although the newspapers don't publish it, I know that in other parts of the country, there have been revolts at the conscription. Myself, I am against the war, but I have special circumstances. My father and mother were groundskeepers for the Duke of Parma. I grew up as a boy on his estate. That's why I speak German. All the servants did or had to learn."

"Who is the Duke of Parma?" Andy asked, confused.

"Who was the Duke of Parma, one should say," Allegra replied. "You see, Parma was one of the northern Italian duchies that for more than a century before 1866 had been ruled by one of the lesser branches of the Habsburg family. Unfortunately, after having lost the battle of Königgrätz to Prussia, Austria was forced to hand over Parma to the new Kingdom of Italy. So, you see, I am Italian by birth, but I was raised as a child of Austria in the old duke's service."

"It's a ridiculous war," Johann said. "Look at me," Johann said, raising his trouser leg to show the prosthesis. "This is how young Italian men will look if they are lucky. This is not a war like the last one where it's all over in a few weeks. This is going to be a long war in which millions will die. Italy could have prospered in peace and quiet while Austria, France, and Germany bled to death. Now it will be Italy's turn to bleed. You'll see. There are funerals every day in Vienna."

The maitre d' nodded solemnly. "I know. That's what many of us are thinking. The government thinks they can take Trieste and Trentino quickly with little fighting, but everyone knows better. The peasants hate the government and so make very bad soldiers. They have no wish to die for more territory that won't benefit anyone but the rich landlords and aristocrats, as they see it. It will be a disaster for both countries. In any event, if there is anything I can do for you, signore, please let me know. I have contacts in Rome who are ... ah, friends of Austria."

At that moment, Olivio appeared in the lobby, his eyes searching the area and then settling on the three of them. His expression was serious and Andy's heart sank in apprehension about what he might say. A mere look at the maitre d' sent him bowing into retreat, leaving the two men with the doctor.

Olivio looked back and forth at each of them in the eyes, saying nothing for a moment. Then in English, "She has appendicitis." Before the thunderbolt could be absorbed there was another one. "It is serious. We must attempt a surgery. She cannot travel. She has asked me to tell both of you this news. Now I must make arrangements for her to be brought to the hospital. She wants to see you. I have made her comfortable with a little laudanum. I will be back in an hour and we will take her to the hospital."

"Hospital?" said Andy.

"Yes, this must be done, I'm afraid. Now I must be going, gentlemen."

The doctor picked up his bag and left. Andy and Johann quickly made their way back to the bedroom and found Maria on the bed. She watched them as they made their way over to her. Johann stroked her hair.

"I'm feeling better now, but the doctor told you what was happening?" Maria asked in a feeble voice.

"Yes," Johann replied. "He just left. You've picked a bad time for a medical emergency," he said softly.

"I know," she said, smiling bravely.

"We have to think fast," Andy said. "The doctor will be back before you know it and we have a problem now, don't we? We're supposed to be on a train back to Vienna tomorrow and you can't go. Our ship doesn't leave Genoa for another week." There was silence in the room for a minute while all of them tried to think through the problem.

"Let's face it, they will either arrest me or deport me tomorrow," said Johann. "Either we take Maria as she is or …"

"I can stay," said Andy. "They won't deport me. I'll stay with Maria. You have to go back. You're right. They'll come for you if you're not at the station to pick up your passport and leave. I'll go with Maria to the hospital and stay until she can leave and go back. We'll have to go to Switzerland or something, but I'll bring her back." It seemed the only logical thing to do and, of course, Andy would be alone with Maria. A thought that did not escape him, even now. Perhaps another chance?

"But my passport … what about that?" asked Maria. Andy hadn't thought of that. Maria wouldn't even be allowed into Switzerland without a passport. No doubt the Austrian embassy was closing its doors for the duration of the war. None of them could think of a way to get her passport unless Andy were to go to the train station right at the time Maria would probably be having her surgery.

That was the way things were when Dr. Olivio returned with two orderlies from the hospital. In a few minutes, they had Maria bundled on a stretcher and were carrying her out the door to a waiting ambulance. Andy turned to Johann at the door. His face was ashen with worry and confusion.

"Don't worry," Andy said as soothingly as he could. "I'll watch her and be with her just like we were with you in Kosice. You were in worse shape than she is, believe me. We'll be back in Vienna in a few days. You take care of yourself and get on that train. We'll see you in a few days." Andy wasn't sure whether he believed his own words and Johann seemed sad and dubious. "Good-bye for now, Johann. Courage."

Johann's composure began to fail him. "You had better be back soon. If anything should happen to either of you …" Johann's voice cracked. Andy knew that Johann's dream of escaping to America had now vanished in a matter of hours—and he couldn't help but feel sorry for him.

"Don't worry, Johann. We'll get to America. Just not now. It's fate." Andy tried to make his voice sound reassuring even though he really didn't believe that the three of them would ever get to America. Johann nodded, sadly, not very reassured. As he turned to go back into the Hotel di San Floriano, Andy noticed Allegra standing quietly in the shadow by the door."

"Signor, please, come with me. Perhaps I can help," Andy heard him say to Johann. He placed his hand on Johann's shoulder and gently turned him into the hotel lobby.

There was no more time. The ambulance was getting ready to leave. Relieved that someone would look after Johann, Andy clambered into the ambulance. The horse-drawn rig slowly ambled into the dark street. The pool of light at the entrance to the hotel shrank. They passed latter-day Roman pedestrians on the streets, hurrying home or somewhere else. There was no evidence of any war fever.

16.

Roman Ruins

Andy walked the now-familiar route from the hospital where Maria had been recuperating from the surgery to the hotel. It was a warm, hazy afternoon in June as he made his way, alternating between wide boulevards and small, crooked streets. Rome's sprawling topography had no apparent rhyme or reason to it. The network of streets and piazzas were like a spider's web that had been spun over two millennia by the denizens of the Eternal City and defied any logic.

Maria's surgery had been difficult to endure for Andy. He had paced the halls like an expectant father. When Olivio had finally arrived to deliver the news that the operation had been a success, it came as an enormous relief. She would have to stay a few days, of course. There was a danger of infection, but she was young and so far, so good. He had seen her a few hours later. She was drugged and pale, but she had made it. He visited her twice each day. She had made an excellent recovery, which gladdened him as he walked. She should be able to leave the hospital the next day. The situation with Johann had turned out very differently than he had expected.

Johann had not left Rome. Instead, he had obtained two forged Swiss passports with the help of Allegra, the mysterious maitre d' at the restaurant of the Hotel di San Floriano. They were of passable quality as far as the Roman police were concerned, Allegra had assured them. As German-speaking tourists, a passport from Switzerland would lend credibility to their false identity since half the population of that country spoke an Alpine version of German that only the most linguistically accomplished Italians would distinguish from the Austrian variety. For now, between the laxity of the Roman police and the fair quality of the false papers, Johann and Maria were safe from suspicion.

On the other hand, if they tried to return to Austria via Switzerland, the Swiss police might not only detect the Viennese accent, but perhaps also the forgeries. Switzerland was now a neutral island between France and Italy on one side and Germany and Austria-Hungary on the other. Passports and papers for anyone entering Switzerland would be scrupulously inspected for the possibility of fraud or forgery. The same would be true on the Austrian frontier. Entry into the empire from Switzerland would be a daunting process due to the possibility of saboteurs or spies from the Allied powers. Entry into the United States could pose even greater risk. Two Austrians attempting to enter New York with false Swiss passports would no doubt be suspected as spies and deported immediately.

Johann had changed hotels and registered under his new alias, Johann von Weissgäber from Bern. Andy had remained at the Hotel di San Floriano to avoid suspicion, at Allegra's suggestion. As the days went by, Allegra raised the possibility of obtaining Maria and Johann's Austrian passports from the police. When Andy wondered aloud how that could possibly be done, Allegra shrugged and replied that in Rome "miracles happen every day." It was very queer, Andy had thought. Not only what the maitre d' seemed able to accomplish, but why he had seemingly befriended them to the point of taking such risks for them. When Andy walked into the Hotel di San Floriano from the hospital, Allegra quietly intercepted him in the lobby.

"Signor Bishop," he murmured quietly in greeting. "The two items we discussed previously may be acquired from their owner, it seems. I must tell you, however, that the owner is quite attached to them and will only sell them for a fairly dear price. Perhaps if you and your partner are still interested, I can meet you at the *Ristorante dei Dodici Apostoli* later this evening."

Andy was at first taken aback, then amazed.

"Yes, I'm sure my partner and I would be very anxious to discuss this with you. Where is the restaurant you mentioned?"

Allegra nodded in reply and then said, "It is in the *Piazza Navona*. Do you know it?"

Andy had heard of the square, but had not yet visited it. "It's a little to the west of the Pantheon, isn't it?"

"Exactly. If you want, I will have the concierge draw you a little map and you can easily find it. Shall I meet you and your partner there at 10:30? The *Ristorante dei Dodici Apostoli* is exactly opposite the main church in the piazza, Sant'Agnese in Agone."

"*Grazie mille, signor.* We will be there," Andy said as he made his way to the stairs to his room.

Andy and Johann arrived at the Piazza Navona about an hour early. The square was enormous. Notwithstanding the war, Andy reckoned that there were hundreds of people walking about. Andy had read about the piazza that evening from a tourist guidebook in his room. It was originally a massive stadium built by the Roman Emperor Domitian in AD 86, which accounted for its size and basically oval shape. The piazza was also famous for its three fountains, illuminated this evening by the streetlights and the lights from the many restaurants and hotels around its circumference.

The middle fountain was the largest and known as the *Fontana dei Quattro Fiumi* or Fountain of the Four Rivers, designed by Bernini. It was flanked by the Fountain of Neptune and the Fountain of the Moors. The beautiful church of *Sant'Agnese* was also prominently situated in the middle of the eastern side of the square. Scattered about the square were collections of street entertainers. Little booths and tables sold trinkets and souvenirs. There were street musicians, jugglers, mimes, and fortunetellers who plied their trades to the crowds that loitered in the *piazza* every night. Johann and Andy passed the time before their appointment by perusing the nocturnal amusements before they eventually arrived at the restaurant. They asked the maitre d' for a table outside and sat down.

"If we get our own passports back, we'll use the Swiss ones with the Italians at the border and then put them away. When the Swiss board the train, we'll use our Austrian passports," said Johann.

"Won't the Swiss find it a little curious that two Austrians are crossing into their country from Italy? Whatever you tell them, won't they search your bags, find the Swiss passports, and then what? They'll think you're Austrian spies leaving Italy or Italian spies going to Austria," Andy answered.

"Speaking of spies, I think I see our man," Johann said quietly. Andy looked out into the square. At first he didn't see Allegra, but then following Johann's gaze, he spotted him approaching the middle fountain.

He was still dressed in a tuxedo from the restaurant, but he didn't look out of place with so many restaurants and hotels about. Soon Allegra had reached the station of the maitre d' at the Ristorante dei Dodici Apostoli. Andy and Johann watched as the two of them conversed for a minute. At one point, Allegra laughed out loud and put his hand on his counterpart, apparently sharing a good joke. Then Allegra nodded toward Andy and Johann, at which point he was ushered to their table. A waiter appeared immediately.

"Do you have a good cognac?" Allegra asked the waiter. After discussing the various brands available, Allegra chose an Armagnac instead.

"Gentlemen," Allegra began in greeting. "I see you found the place. It's one of my favorites. I come here every now and then. It's particularly pleasant this time of year."

"Yes, it is," replied Johann. The night was balmy. A light breeze ruffled the white tablecloth and the candle on their table fluttered. "We can't thank you enough for the trouble you have gone to on our account," he continued. "However, before we go any further, I have to inquire a little about the lengths you have gone to on our behalf. Why are you doing this, Massimo? How do we know you are not an agent provocateur? What has happened until now might be explained to the police as bad luck, with Maria falling ill at an inconvenient time. Bribing the Roman police is another matter altogether."

Allegra sank back in his chair. A pained look crossed his face. "But signor, I thought I had already explained why my sympathies ran counter to those of my fellow citizens and the government. Do you not recall our conversation?"

"I do recall it, signor," Johann replied. "Your circumstances certainly explain your sympathies, but your actions since then have gone far beyond any reasonable expectations that any two subjects of the kaiser caught in Italy at the outbreak of a war might have. I ask you now, before we go any further, signor, please explain more deeply. Speak plainly to us."

The waiter now arrived with a goblet of Armagnac, set it down on the table, and withdrew. "Yes, I see your concern. I think you are right to be careful in your circumstances. I must be careful in mine as well. You spoke just now of the kaiser. He has many servants in Rome and throughout Italy. Your situation, shall we say, has reached his attention. In fact, it was his wish that we should assist you in returning home."

Johann looked at Andy and then back at Allegra. "We?" Johann asked.

"Yes, we. You remember, don't you, when I told you there were many friends of Austria in Italy? I cannot make myself more plain than that," the maitre d' returned. He took a sip of the Armagnac as Johann considered his reply.

"You say it was the wish of the kaiser that we should be assisted in returning to our homeland?" Johann continued. "I am at pains to understand how our situation came to his attention. Perhaps you could explain. We did not consult the kaiser about coming here. I would not expect our situation to even attract his notice."

"Signor, in this, I cannot be of much help. All I know is that it has. Do you not have some acquaintance with His Majesty that could explain it?"

"No," Johann replied. "I was in service to the late archduke, the heir to the throne, and in this capacity, I have met him on a few occasions, but I would hardly consider myself an acquaintance of such significance that His Majesty would involve himself in our plight. In fact, to be perfectly frank, having been close to the late archduke is not something that would commend me to His Majesty very much at all, I would think."

"Johann," interrupted Andy. "It's Elisabeth. She may have prevailed upon the kaiser to help us." Andy could imagine the worry that the outbreak of war with Italy might have had in the Windischgrätz household. Then it struck Andy. His father may have passed along word to Elisabeth and Otto about what had happened to Maria and how they were all stuck behind enemy lines.

"Signor, your speculation is probably better than mine. All I know is that the word has been passed to us to help you get out. All of you. If you will allow us."

A minute passed in silence. Then Johann spoke again. "Signor Allegra, we will certainly allow you. I must beg your pardon for ever doubting you, but I hope you can understand my concern. Now, just out of curiosity, I am wondering how many of you there are."

"Well, Signor von Caboga, as I am sure you can understand, I am not at liberty to disclose this to you, even if I knew the answer, which I don't. There are quite a few friends of Austria in Rome, however. Take our hotel, for example. Why did you come to this hotel instead of another? It is quite well known in Vienna, is it not?" Johann nodded in agreement. "It's a favorite of the Austrians for a generation. Many diplomats and officials of the royal and imperial government have stayed with us over the years when visiting Rome." Allegra raised his eyebrows suggestively at this last statement. Andy imagined the hotel swarming with Austrian spies.

"But now that the war has begun, how do you communicate with the government in Vienna?" Andy asked.

"There are ways. The Vatican is not fond of the republic, you know." Again, the raised eyebrows.

"No, I don't know. I would have assumed, since the Vatican is located here in Rome, that the relationship between the pope and the Italian government would be quite good. The pope is Italian." Johann leaned forward, seemingly to explain, but Allegra spoke first.

"It's our history, you see. As an American, of course, what I can tell you would normally be of little interest. But here in Italy, at this moment, I think it would be of great interest."

"The Kingdom of Italy confiscated the papal lands that the Habsburgs had defended for centuries in the aftermath of the war of 1866. The relationship between the Habsburgs and the popes, on the other hand, has always been a warm one.

"You must realize that for nearly four hundred years, there was a nearly unbroken succession of Habsburgs as Holy Roman Emperors. Think about that. In the wars of the Reformation and Counter-Reformation, it was the Habsburgs who took on nearly all of Europe, including Catholic France, to maintain the supremacy of the Church in Germany. The Habsburg dynasty was the 'sword' of the Roman Catholic Church in European affairs. The Kingdom of Italy is regarded by the Vatican as a greedy usurper of its rights. To this day, the Vatican has no diplomatic relations with the Kingdom. The Church can be, at times, the eyes and the ears of the Habsburgs in Italy. You see?"

Andy did see.

"That is all I can tell you, except that we have found the custodian of your passports and, for 10,000 krone, you can obtain them," said Allegra.

This was quite a lot of money. Andy did the calculation in his mind and it came to nearly $1,500 American dollars—a very steep bribe indeed. Andy looked at Johann. "How will we be able to get this much money?"

"My mother could wire it to our bank in Switzerland. They could issue a letter of credit to a bank here. It could be done," Johann replied.

"I will leave you two gentlemen to consider your plans, but I am at your service," said Allegra, swallowing the last finger of Armagnac and rising from the table. "You know where to find me," he said with a wry smile. He bowed slightly and, in a moment, was walking back across the piazza.

"What do you think?" Andy asked.

"I think he is telling the truth, if that's what you mean. Think about it. A hotel would be a perfect front for spies. What surprised me was that the kaiser has involved himself in our little situation."

"Yes, it sent a little chill up my spine when he said that," Andy said. "On the other hand, there are few people in the world who could get his attention and his help as easily as his granddaughter. That has to be the explanation."

Andy imagined Elisabeth visiting the old man once she became aware of their predicament. In his mind's eye, he envisioned the kaiser listening intently to her request in one of his private rooms in the Schönbrunn, nodding his head in agreement that something be done to help them. It would not have required more than a few words for the kaiser to have instructed his chamberlain to do what was necessary to convey his wishes in this regard. The secret service would have had few requests such as this from the All-Highest and would have scrambled to see that his will was carried out immediately.

The night air in the piazza wafted the smell of fine food and murmurs of conversation from countless tables nearby as the two friends sat in silence for a while taking in all that had transpired this day. Andy considered what his next move would be after the Austrian passports had been secured from the unknown Roman policeman who held them. He considered whether he should make new arrangements to return to America or accompany his friends back to Vienna.

Assuming that Maria was able to travel by train, there was no real reason why he needed to go with them back to Vienna. He could see them off at the train station in Rome and then take passage back to New York after they left. The only nagging detail in his mind was what might happen to them if, for any reason, they were discovered to be in possession of forged passports and were arrested either in Italy or Switzerland. If that should happen, if he were present, he would be the only person who might be able to help them.

"Johann, before Allegra arrived, I had asked you what the Swiss might think of two Austrian subjects entering their country from Italy. You might be arrested. On the other hand, if you used the Swiss passports, they might realize that they were forgeries and arrest you both on the spot. It seems a little dangerous, still. Have you thought about that?"

"Yes, I have. Of course. I've been thinking about more than that. Why should we go back to Vienna now?" asked Johann. "It seems to me that to go the United States with our Austrian passports, once we get them back, would be less risky. If it's risky either way—why not just continue our original plan? Even if war breaks out by the time we get to New York, what's the worst thing that could happen to us? Wouldn't they just deport us back to Austria?"

Andy thought about it. Clearly Elisabeth and the kaiser had thought that they would return to Vienna. Had arrangements been made with the Swiss authorities to discreetly pass them through? No similar arrangements would be needed with the American authorities in New York. Perhaps it would be better to return to Austria after all. If only they could know for sure, Andy thought. He shared his reasoning with Johann.

"Perhaps, but I don't want to return to Vienna now, Andy. I would rather take our chances," Johann said after considering Andy's concerns. "There is no risk to you at all, Andy. The risk would be to us and I am willing to take it. Are you?"

"Perhaps we should discuss it with Maria," Andy demurred.

"Yes, of course," Johann said dismissively. "Let's talk to her about it, but if she is willing, would you do it?"

Andy thought about it in silence for a few minutes. "All right. If Maria is still willing to do it, then we'll go. If not, then you must promise me that you'll both return to Vienna. Is it a deal?"

Now it was Johann's turn to think. The restaurant patrons had thinned out and the piazza was largely emptied of people. Johann nodded to the waiter and asked him to bring the bill. In a minute, the waiter returned and Johann paid him, still not saying a word. They got up to leave and slowly walked into the square.

"All right, Andy. It's a deal. We'll let Maria decide," Johann said.

As they made their way across the square, Johann and Andy agreed to visit the hospital the next day and lay out the competing plans to Maria. As they walked, they came upon a group of gypsies clustered around a table near one of the fountains. Earlier in the evening, the piazza had been full of little vendors plying their wares as they did every night. As they neared the gypsies, one of them called out to Johann and Andy.

"Signor, have your fortune told. The *signora* is never wrong. Please, signor. You will be glad you did." The gypsy speaking to them had on clothing that fit him poorly. The clothing, by its cut and style, seemed to be out of the last century, as if the clothes had been handed down for a couple of generations. His face was dark and his eyes were even darker. He had a curious hat—a bowler—that he removed from his head and swept before him in a deep bow. Johann was amused and looked at Andy.

"Why not? Andy, see what the future holds for you," Johann said with a wry smile. Andy was a little bit annoyed at this, but the gypsy, quickly realizing that they were speaking German, changed to this tongue and anxiously bid Andy sit down. With a sigh, Andy reluctantly agreed.

He found himself seated across a flimsy table with a woman who looked to be at least a hundred years old. Her head was covered with a bandana. Her face had deep wrinkles that furrowed her brow and caused her cheeks to sag. Like the man, her skin was dark and her eyes completely black. She mumbled something in Italian and he saw that she had almost no teeth. The gypsy translated.

"She says that you must give her your hand; the hand you write with," the gypsy man said. Andy complied, holding out his right hand. Immediately, the woman grasped his hand and spread his fingers wide. Her hands were bony, with long clear nails and long fingers. She peered at his hand, drawing two candles closer to it so that she could see the lines crossing his palm. She said nothing for a minute, then pulled up from her lap a pair of glasses that she carefully put on, apparently to scrutinize Andy's hand even more carefully. She turned his hand over to look at the back of it and then slowly turned it back, palm up, examining every surface of it. Then her fingers began tracing the deeper lines within Andy's palm. He noticed that she was mumbling something as she continued her searching.

"You must pay first," said the gypsy man. Johann asked how much it would be and then peeled off some lira that he handed to the man. The gypsy counted it and then nodded to the woman. It was enough. The man said something to the woman in a language that Andy did not know. The woman nodded and then looked at Andy in the eye for longer than was polite. She seemed to be searching his eyes for something. At one moment, Andy thought that she might say something, but she didn't. As he looked into her eyes, he realized that he could not look away. The more he looked at her, the more transfixed he became with her face and, as he did, the noise and activity in the piazza faded. It was as if he were starting to dream with his eyes still open.

From some distance, it seemed, he heard Johann say something to the man in Italian, but he didn't know what it was. The woman's face in the candlelight conveyed a feeling of sadness that pulled at him. As she gazed into his eyes, her expression never changed, but his mind began to see visions of her that he could not possibly know. He envisioned her sitting on a makeshift wagon being pulled by horses on some distant country road. There was a caravan of wagons behind her and other gypsies walking on foot. He knew somehow that she had come here from some distant place.

She was old, impossibly old. Andy realized that he had lost track of time and did not know how long he had been at the table. Murmurs of conversation floated around him that he could not understand. At last, the woman spoke to the gypsy man in her strange language without taking her eyes off him, holding his hand in hers. He could feel her bony thumb still tracing the lines in the palm of his hand.

"She says that you will live a long time," the gypsy began softly, in German. More words from the woman followed. "She says that she sees vast waters. She believes you have come here from far away, over the oceans. You have a mother and father who want you to come home, but the waters are dangerous. You have friends. They are in great danger."

Andy felt a chill rustle through him with these words. The gypsy woman said more and the man translated. "She says you speak words to many people far away who know you, but you don't know them. Many famous people know who you are, but you don't know them. They listen to what you say." The man paused as he listened to more of what the gypsy woman said.

"She asks if you want to hear more, but she wants me to warn you that you may not want to hear it. Do you want to know more?" Andy shuddered, but could not help himself.

"Yes, tell her to go on," Andy said. More words poured from the ancient, toothless mouth.

"There is a woman that you will love," the man continued. "She will not be from your land, but from the land of your ancestors. She will cause you great pain. You will return to your home someday, but you will never live there again. You search for a dark secret. It is about your family. You will find the secret for which you search if you are patient. It will change your life."

At this point, the old woman gripped his hand with surprising strength. "She says you are a good man and that you will save the lives of many people with your words. You will be a friend to our people, the Romani people." Her voice trailed off and she shook her head. For a few moments, she said nothing. The gypsy man looked at her and then at Andy and Johann.

"She is never wrong," the gypsy man said quietly to them both. Johann had evidently lit a cigarette at some point and quietly blew the smoke out into the night air. Then the woman spoke again.

She looked into Andy's eyes again. She nodded to him and released his hand, sinking back into the little chair in which she was sitting. A rueful smile crossed her face. She seemed suddenly tired after conveying this information and gestured that she was now finished.

"Thank her for me," was all Andy could say as he arose from the table. The gypsy man nodded and translated. The woman nodded to him and silently made the sign of the cross to him in the air. Andy nodded to her in thanks, but nothing further was said. The dreamlike state that Andy had felt quickly dissipated as he and Johann resumed their walk across the square, leaving the gypsies behind.

"That was strange," Johann said as he threw the stub of his cigarette into the gutter. "What do you think?"

Andy knew that he had been shaken to his core. Perhaps what she had said about him was all guesswork and conjecture, but deep in his heart, he knew her words had unnerved him. The thought of returning to America with Johann and Maria now filled him with dread. He tried to reason with himself that he didn't believe in this kind of thing, but try as he might, for some inexplicable reason, he just knew she was telling the truth.

"I don't know what to think, Johann. I don't know how she could possibly know some of the things about me, like the fact that I came here from America or that I have friends who are in danger, or about my mother and father and returning home. If she could somehow see these things, then it makes me wonder whether the predictions she made might come true."

As Andy made his way through the morning streets to the *Ospedale*, he couldn't get his mind off the weird feelings that he had experienced the night before and the illogical certainty that continuing their trip to America presented hidden dangers to all of them. His mind argued with his heart as he walked. On the one hand, his mind and all logic told him that soothsayers and fortunetellers were all charlatans who by trick or pure luck could persuade people that they were able to divine the future. On the other hand, his heart pulsed with feelings that somehow the old gypsy woman had an inexplicable gift and all she said was true.

The *Ospedale di Spirito Sanctus* was one of the oldest hospitals in Rome, Andy had discovered, and since the first day he had set foot in it, Andy had no difficulty believing it. The hallways that led to the huge ward where dozens of beds lined the walls were dark and dingy. A low hum of groans and moans emanating from the patients gave those who were better off no peace. Nuns in white habits quietly attended the patients, but in Andy's mind, the place was clearly understaffed. The air reeked of a unique combination of stale cheese and antiseptic that would make a healthy man sick, he thought. Family members were the saving grace to those patients who had them, ministering to their loved ones as best they could.

Dr. Olivio had not done the surgery, but had assisted a surgeon on staff at the hospital. He had told Andy that Maria would be in a lot of pain for a few days, but the most important thing was to guard against sepsis or infection.

The worst was probably over, unless she got an infection. Olivio thought that she would have to remain in the hospital for a week at minimum, even if all went well.

A week in this hospital had been daunting, but it was almost over. Maria had gained strength each day, slowly at first, but then by leaps and bounds. As he walked down the center aisle of the ward, he noticed that Johann had already arrived and was sitting by Maria's bedside. *Her special beauty could not be hidden even in sickness,* Andy thought as he approached.

Maria's head and shoulders were propped up on several pillows. She looked alert and was listening intently to Johann when they both noticed him arrive. He bent to kiss her on the cheek and then sat down on the bed. Her black hair had been combed out by one of the nuns and lay loosely in big curls on her chest. Color had returned to her previously pale face. She smiled softly at Andy as he took one of her hands in his own. My God, he thought, what had she been through so far from home.

It soon became apparent that Johann had already explained the choice that the two of them had struggled with the previous night. As they began to discuss the pros and cons of their collective decision, Andy could not help but think about the words of the old gypsy woman. *"She will cause you great pain."* Who else could it be than Maria? He could still feel a burning desire for her stirring inside him, even as he tried to keep up with the conversation between them. Finally, after the better part of an hour, Maria made up her mind.

"I think we should go to America, Andy. Why turn back now? What would we do when we got back to Vienna?"

Andy was surprised at her answer, but he had made a deal with Johann the previous night and he had had his say this morning. There was no danger for him that he could rationally think of—only for his two friends. Then his unease returned. *"The waters are dangerous."* It was ridiculous, he reasoned. He didn't believe in that kind of thing, he repeated to himself. Yet it was so apt, what she had said. How could she know that he must not try to return home? What terrible thing could happen to them?

"Johann, did you tell her about my little session with the gypsy lady?" he asked. Johann looked at Andy and then back to Maria. With a little reluctance, Johann related the predictions the gypsy woman had made to Maria. She listened intently.

"It's amazing," Maria said quietly when Johann had finished. "Perhaps we should reconsider, Johann. Do you think it could be true?"

With a pained expression on his face, Johann quickly dismissed the prophecies. He clearly had his heart set on going to America. "It's irrational to make a decision like this influenced by a chance encounter with a gypsy woman," he exclaimed. Johann's logic was unassailable although Andy could not dismiss the phenomenon so easily and secretly worried that some sinister destiny hovered before them. In the end, though, it was decided. They would take passage once again to New York.

A couple of days later, passports in hand, they sat in the shade of an awning at the *Trattoria da Luigi* not far from their hotel. The *Ancona* was leaving for New York from Naples on June 10, stopping at Messina in Sicily and then at Cadiz in Spain. It would arrive in New York after four days. It was perfect. The stop in Spain would provide a pretext if one were needed for the Austrian passports. Spain was also a neutral country where Austrian aristocrats could conceivably be found even in wartime.

Maria's appetite had returned and Andy watched appreciatively as she ate a plate of spaghetti *margherita* with a glass of red wine. The food in even modest Italian restaurants was truly delectable. Johann was reading articles in *Corriere Della Sera*, one of the main Roman newspapers, as they passed the time. Italy was bracing itself for a major offensive against the Austrians in the Isonzo Valley under the command of Count Luigi Cadorna, Johann read. Heavy fighting was reported along the San River in Russia between Russian and Austro-Hungarian forces and, according to one reporter, the kaiser would not be able to deploy much of a military force to defeat the Italian hammer blow that was about to fall.

Johann snickered as he read the last lines of the news article. "I would love to know what kind of welcome Conrad is preparing for the Italians. They have taken a month to get their forces together in one place and the High Command will have our forces dug into the mountains with the best artillery in Europe at their back. Cadorna has no idea what real war is like nowadays. These toy soldiers are in for a rude awakening, I tell you."

"Keep your voice down," Maria whispered in a low voice. Indeed, the sound of German always brought stares from Italians nearby who had to wonder whether they were German or Austrian spies. Although there were no customers near their table, one never knew how far their voices would carry. Johann's Italian had gotten much better over the weeks that they had spent in Italy and from time to time he had felt it necessary to explain to the quizzical glances of waiters or taxi drivers that they were Swiss, which seemed to relieve their hosts.

Andy parted company with his friends after their late lunch to go to the steamship line to get their tickets. While there, he noticed a telegraph office across the street and decided to wire his father about their plans. In the wire, he asked that his father forward a message to Otto and Elisabeth. The Italian operators would not attempt to send a wire into the empire. After the war had begun, civilian communication to Vienna had been cut.

> *Dear Otto and Elisabeth. We have decided to continue our trip to New York in a few days departing Naples aboard Ancona. Thanks for any assistance that may have been rendered to us during our stay here and Maria's unfortunate illness. She is well now and we are all anxious to leave this country as soon as possible. Expect no difficulties now. Will wire again in a few weeks from home. Hope all is well with you and the family. With Love, Andy*

17.

Death on the Isonzo

Colonel Ernst zu Windischgrätz took off his hat and placed it on the polished mahogany table of the drawing room of the chalet in Gorizia where the officers and high command of the Imperial Fifth Army of the Tyrol had gathered to discuss strategy for the oncoming campaign against Italy. A briefing had been held the previous day to discuss the general situation, which was, on paper at least, rather sobering.

Ernst and his regiment had deployed in Austrian Slovenia on the far left or southern flank of the Fifth Army to face the burgeoning Italian army forming up on the frontier. The Fifth was the Reich in miniature, commanded by the now legendary Field Marshal Svetozar Boroević. Boroević was of Serbian descent, but had grown up in Croatia and spoke it as his first language. The commander of the 1st Mountain Brigade was Major General Geza Lukachich von Somorja, a Hungarian. Eight divisions, eighty-four battalions, thirteen cavalry squadrons, and 356 guns consisting of some 115,000 men were arrayed along the most southwestern portion of the Italian frontier. Among them were an imperial mix of

Austrians, Slovenians, Croats, and Hungarians representing the western nationalities facing Italy.

Against them were eighteen divisions, 252 battalions, 111 cavalry squadrons, 700 guns, and 225,000 men of the Kingdom of Italy led by its supreme commander, General Count Luigi Cadorna.

Uncharacteristically, Conrad had initially recommended to the emperor a retreat away from the Slovenian frontier into the depths of the Alps rather than expending the blood and treasury of the empire in the defense of the relatively low-lying territory of the Carso Plateau adjacent to Italy and across the Isonzo River. Italian success in this area, however, would mean the eventual fall of Austria's greatest seaport, Trieste, to the south. Boroević had opposed Conrad's plan for this very reason and, in a conference with the kaiser at Bad Ischl, the ruler had sided with Boroević. Conrad had accepted the decision graciously and then set about logistically moving Habsburg military chess pieces around the map to support the steely *Feldmarschal*.

While Conrad flashed passion and élan, Boroević was cool, taciturn, and aloof. Also stoic to a fault like his commander, Boroević added a measure of Slavic ruthlessness to the task and a stubborn, determined streak that at times made him seem indifferent to loss of life when the objective required it, in his opinion. He believed that the Croats and Slovenes under his command, on their home soil, would fight viciously against the invaders with the same Slavic ruthlessness and tenacity that he himself brought to bear. The Austrians and Hungarians needed no further encouragement against the Italians. The Russians were respected as worthy opponents. The Italians were regarded with contempt and hate as backstabbing traitors and opportunists.

On June 22, 1915, a week after the kaiser's review, Ernst listened to an Austrian intelligence officer complete his briefing to Boroević and Lukachich and the assembled generals and commanders. Austrian spy networks honeycombed northern Italy. The closer to the Alps, the more pervasive they became. Austrian sympathizers in Italy watched everything. Daily, detailed reports of exact troop movements flowed into the marshal's hands along with intercepted radio transmissions that the Italians were too lazy to encode. Austrian agents bribed, spied, and reported in Italy more than in any other front in the war.

It was now known that the storm clouds would break the following day with an Italian artillery barrage of their positions followed by an infantry attack. Ernst sat with two dozen other corps, division, and battalion commanders at Boroević's table in an ornate drawing room of the mansion in Gorizia as the briefing came to an end.

"Gentlemen," Boroević began. "Make your final dispositions this evening. Make sure the men are protected from artillery fire. Communications are vital. We must be quick and we must strike hard when the opportunity presents itself. Give ground when you must, but exact the maximum cost from the enemy as you go. In my army, obedience is required. I give few orders, gentlemen, but I expect them to be obeyed instantly and without further discussion. Remember, you can't see the whole front, as we can from headquarters. A meaningless victory in your sector may result in disaster if somewhere else the entire army is forced to retreat.

"When the moment comes to strike, strike hard. Not with your fingers. Hit with a fist. Dribbling offensives of inadequate mass that fizzle out demoralize our forces and emboldens theirs. Are there any questions?"

One of the other brigade generals spoke. "Excellency, are we expecting any reinforcements? If there is a breakthrough, are there sufficient reserves?"

Ernst watched as Boroević's dark brown eyes locked on him and his face composed itself into mild contempt. "There will be no need for reinforcements," he replied archly. "We have more than enough to defend ourselves. Our own reserves are ready and sufficient. We have faced much worse than this in the east. Trust me. We will defeat them."

His icy confidence was contagious. Even at odds of two to one, the cream of imperial officers in the ornate study believed it inconceivable that any Italian army could march through theirs in battle. There was a low murmur of approval from the other officers, some of whom nodded their heads. Ernst felt a surge of grim pride as he watched the generals rise from the table and break up into smaller groups for discussion. Geza Lukachich ambled toward him and struck up a conversation about artillery support for his mountain brigade from the XVI corps, to which Ernst half listened.

There was no reason for Ernst not to like the amiable *Generalmajor*, but he didn't. He couldn't help himself. Lukachich was deadly boring in conversation and Ernst always had the feeling that the general was determined to ingratiate himself to him. Although he outranked him and was far older, Generalmajor Lukachich had evidently marked Ernst out as a likely rising star to which he wished to hitch his fortunes. Although a good soldier, Lukachich was the type of ambitious, career-oriented Hungarian that Ernst loathed. It was obvious to the other officers in the battalion that he favored Ernst, which then created tensions that Ernst labored to avoid with them. As a great-grandson of the kaiser, he appreciated loyal Hungarians, but didn't entirely trust them either.

The next morning dawned with a humid mist that obscured his men's positions in the low hills facing the Isonzo River. Ernst had found a "captain's hill" that gave him an elevated view of the entire sector that he was expected to defend. He waited and watched. Ahead of him, due west, was a wide bending curve of the river. On the far side, dense forest came nearly to the water's edge, obscuring the approach of enemy infantry. On the near side of the river, 150 meters in front of him was a wide, crescent-shaped beach of sand nestled in the crux of the bend of the river. Ernst had deliberately chosen to station himself here because it was the most likely place the Italians would ford the river, he thought. The sand was hard packed and would provide good footing for advancing infantry, but a clean field of fire for his men as well.

To his right and left were hilly woods that mostly concealed hundreds of his own men from the eyes of the enemy who had been scouting them, no doubt, for the past couple of days. A road ran north and south behind them, which would allow quick movement of troops from one sector to another. To the east and behind the road were farms where artillery had been positioned. Telegraph wires ran to them from observer posts atop some of the hills to help direct fire.

Minutes ticked by as the sun rose higher in the sky. Had it been a clear morning, the brightness of the sun in his face would have been irritating, but as it was, the sun was a dull yellow bulb rising over the flatlands and forest behind the river. Then there was a thud, followed by a whizzing sound of a projectile cutting the air, and then a blast as a shell exploded on the face of one of the hills to his left.

Within minutes, a deafening cannonade broke on his front. Shells exploded in rapid succession all across the front and Ernst was obliged to retreat from his observation post to a dug-out bomb shelter. For more than an hour, the shelling continued, sometimes reaching a crescendo of cracks and explosions, then dying down as the artillery was serviced for another round. In these momentary pauses, Ernst scrambled out to survey the damage, much to the consternation of his officers. A telegraph message arrived from Lukachich informing him that an offensive had begun across the entire front and inquiring of his situation.

"Tell him we are holding up well and our line is firm. We are ready for an infantry attack that we expect will follow shortly," Ernst dictated to his aide. Another hour of shelling went by that suddenly became sporadic. On his feet again, Ernst rushed up to the top of the hill to look out over the scene. His men had been dug in and positioned on the near side of the hills to brace for the artillery. Blackened areas in and around some of the hills showed that in the avalanche of shelling, damage had been done. Fires raged in clumps of trees, sending up smoke.

To the west, pontoons were being thrown out across the river and flat boats of Italian soldiers began crossing over to their side. In less than an hour, the area below them on the sandy beach would be swarming with Italian infantry. Ernst could see movement on the opposite shoreline where Italian solders waited to cross the pontoons or clamber into the boats. He swung his binoculars to the south and noted with satisfaction that his men were setting machine guns in position now on the top of the hills. He knew that his own artillery, although much inferior in number to the Italians, would have a devastating impact at the close quarters he envisioned would develop in the next couple of hours. He waited.

The Italians evidently had noticed the regiment's machine gun emplacements on the hills and began peppering them with mortar and artillery fire as the ranks of Italian soldiers continued to swell on the sandy beach by the river. Italian officers began directing their men forward to take up positions nearer to the hills to make the last rush to the tops of the hills as short a trip as possible. They were still out of rifle range of the Tyrolean Jägers who made up his regiment. The far bank was thick with tens of thousands of Italian soldiers waiting to cross the river. Ernst decided at 10:15 that the moment had come to strike.

"Begin the artillery bombardment precisely at 10:30," Ernst told his telegrapher. "Tell them to direct all fire to the area between our positions and the river, but particularly along the near shore of the river." Ernst calculated that the Italians in forward positions would be demoralized at seeing their line of retreat under heavy fire. All up and down the line, Austria's famous Skoda artillery was being primed and calibrated for range and location. The barrage that erupted from behind the hills at the appointed hour impressed even Ernst. The ground below churned with the detonation of dozens of shells. Italian soldiers ran for cover when the last shell in the round pounded out a huge crater near one of the cluster of boats discharging its military cargo.

The first salvo was followed in rapid succession by more as the split of land between the river and the hills became a hellish shooting gallery. Within minutes, however, Italian artillery opened up again, this time probing the areas behind the hills, with counter-battery fire to knock out their artillery. Moments later, the Italians surged forward into the hills, probably on the assumption that it was at least as dangerous to hang back on the flat beach as to advance. As the artillery salvos continued, Ernst instructed the telegrapher to order counter-battery fire of their own into the Italian positions in the woods on the far side of the river. In the meantime, the dry rat-a-tat of machine gun fire began to filter across to his position.

With the cessation of shelling on the soldiers below, the Italians frantically pushed more and more men across the river in an effort to bolster the weak advances by small clusters of Italian troops in the hills. On the run, thousands of Italians were making their way forward—only to run into withering machine gun and rifle fire from the Jägers once they got in range. By the time the Italians managed to get to the tops of some of the hills, their ranks had been thinned out and they were easily thrown back. Feeble attack followed feeble attack and Italian dead littered the beach and slopes below the hills.

It was all going rather well, Ernst thought. He expected

the Italians to withdraw to the far bank since it was obvious that they could not break through today, but instead, more Italians swarmed out of the woods to the river.

Ernst decided to move north across his sector to see the situation at close range for himself and what casualties his own forces were taking. He also knew that to show himself to his subordinate commanders in the heat of the battle would stiffen their resolve. He called for his horse and, with a few subordinates, set off at a gallop for the most intense area of fighting to the north. Before leaving, Ernst instructed the telegrapher to signal one of the reserve battalions to move to support some of his beleaguered men to the north and to concentrate artillery fire at their front before the advancing Italian reinforcements.

Through the woods and to the dirt road, Ernst rode to the rear of his troops. The rumble of artillery fire coming from the Austrian batteries up the road and to his right was a comforting sound to his ears. He knew that as long as they kept up their deadly drumbeat, the enemy could not succeed. He spurred his horse up the road with his aides behind him. Half a kilometer up the road, he saw a hospital tent pitched in front of a brick farmhouse. The wounded already overflowed the tent and more were being carried in by the minute. Ernst wished that he could stop, but knew he had to press on.

Another two hundred meters up the road, the forest thinned out and the north end of the sandy beach could be seen through the trees with the river beyond. The ground was high over the river and rocky, but it was the weakest point of the Austrian line. Their field of fire was cramped here. The Italians were massing in the forest that crowded the edge of the river, ready to cross where they were only twenty meters of beach sand away from a string of barbed wire that marked the outermost point of the Austrian defense. Ernst noticed the muzzles of several light field artillery being set on the opposite bank to blast the wire away and open a hole through the line to the road behind. From there, the Italians would be able to fan out north and south, enveloping the Jägers in the wooded hills between the road and the river on either side of the breach.

Captain Damir Martinović was relieved to see Ernst dismounting his horse.

"How goes it here, Hauptman?" Ernst asked simply.

"Getting warmer by the minute, my lord," replied the Captain. "We've been stormed a half-dozen times, but now they're moving up their guns as you can see."

Ernst removed his binoculars from the saddle and peered through the thin line of trees to the opposite bank. Many smaller caliber cannons were being feverishly brought up to the edge of the tree line on the opposite bank and a fearful volley would no doubt start in a few minutes at short range. The Italians had stopped trying to cross the river for the moment, evidently gathering strength to follow their artillery barrage after it had pounded the Croatians who had been tormenting them for the past hour and a half. Ernst turned to one of his aides.

"Ride back to the nearest battery and tell them to direct all fire to the tree line of the opposite bank and to keep firing until I tell them to stop. Go!" To a second aide, he said, "Where's that reserve battalion? Go find out where they are and get them down here. Tell them to hurry, for God's sake."

The lieutenants ran to their horses and in a moment were off. There would be a race now between the Italian and Austrian artillery to see who could find their targets first. The Italians could see exactly where they wanted to fire. For once, it was they who had a clear field. The Austrians, on the other hand, would have to fire blind from the rear, over the heads of their own troops, and depend on observers to calibrate their fire to the Italian artillery. It seemed an uneven match that might depend upon the arrival of the reserves to stem the Italian tide that would come running into their position.

The Croats could see the artillery being mounted and set about five hundred meters away on the other side of the river and knew what was coming. "Pull the men back behind the road, Hauptman," Ernst commanded. "Tell them to get down in the ditches beside the road. Set up the machine guns on the opposite side of the road, behind the men. Space them well. Help is on the way, *Hauptman*. I'll wait right here with you."

Captain Martinović shouted out to his men to evacuate in Croatian. The men obeyed without hesitation, grateful to move away from the coming onslaught. They gathered their weapons and kits and slipped away as quietly as they could. Soon the area between Ernst and Martinović was largely deserted and then the pounding began.

Rocks shattered and pinged about like shrapnel. Ernst realized that he needed to move back and waved to Martinović to follow. They scampered together over the rocks to their horses. A third aide was holding Ernst's horse by the reins as another crash of artillery was heard from the other side. Ernst grabbed the pommel and put his left foot into the stirrup to swing himself up when he felt a hot, burning pain in his back.

The pain was so hot that he involuntarily arched his back and fell on the rocks behind, knocking the wind out of him. Martinović had already mounted his horse and looked down at him in surprise. The lieutenant jumped down from his horse and knelt down beside Ernst. "Are you all right, sir?" he asked. Ernst couldn't breathe. He could catch tiny little breaths and heard himself panting like a dog, but he couldn't help it. He couldn't speak because he couldn't get enough air in his lungs. A bullet or, more likely, a piece of rock had penetrated one of his lungs, he thought, but there was nothing he could do about it.

As he gasped for air, he felt himself being lifted up

by the shoulders and the legs and then carried out to the road where two soldiers came running to help. Blood was pouring from the wound in his back and Ernst began to feel very sleepy. "Stay with us, sir," said Martinović. They had laid him in a grassy field next to the road.

Ernst looked up at the blue sky and the puffy white clouds that were slowly passing overhead. Some black birds were circling above him, he noticed, and he felt the sun warming his face, becoming sleepier even as he tried to breathe more deeply. "Turn him over," someone said. As they gently reached under his shoulders again, Ernst felt pins and needles all over his face. It was strange. There were more and more black birds, he thought, and they kept getting larger and larger. He stared at the black birds that filled the sky until the sky was completely black.

The emperor heard the news from Elisabeth in his study at Schönbrunn two days later. He had outlived his younger brother, executed in Mexico. He had outlived his son, who had committed suicide decades earlier. He had outlived his wife, stabbed to death by an Italian anarchist seventeen years before. His nephew had been assassinated at Sarajevo. Yet the death of his great-grandchild pained him as much as any of them. "Nothing has been spared us," he said to Elisabeth, sadly shaking his head. "Nothing ... has been spared."

18.

The Ancona

Andy awoke in his room on Wednesday, June 23, at the hotel in Naples, in a sweat. The windows of his room had been left open, but the heat was uncomfortable, especially at night. He had not slept well. They had left Rome the day before and arrived in Naples in the late afternoon. After a light supper, they had all retired to their rooms. Andy had written out a telegram to his mother and father that he would post from the hotel before they boarded the ship.

> ```
> Dear Mom and Dad. We leave today
> from Naples for New York aboard the
> Ancona. I expect I will be seeing
> you in little more than a week's
> time. I will wire you from New York
> on our arrival. My friends, Maria
> and Johann, are coming too. Please
> wire Elisabeth and Otto regarding
> our plans. Love, Andy.
> ```

As he stepped out on the balcony of his room, Andy saw a misty fog in the bay of Naples. Their ship, the *Ancona*, was docked at a long pier that he could see from his balcony.

Hundreds of passengers with their baggage had swarmed onto the pier. Porters wheeled crates and bags up the gangways and into the hold of the ship while long lines waited patiently as Italian customs officials checked papers and documents. The passengers boarding *Ancona* were largely peasants and poor working people, Andy noticed.

It had been a jumble since leaving Vienna, he thought. Nothing seemed to work out as they had planned and yet, here they were, about to embark for home after all. What his life would be like when he returned, he couldn't say. He knew his series of reports from Vienna had been very popular, syndicated to dozens of newspapers, particularly in the Midwest and on the East Coast. His career seemed bright and that was one thing, but the loss of Maria still wounded him. Perhaps seeing her every day with Johann reminded him of their once-promising romance. He couldn't help but wonder if Maria's claims of a new love for Johann weren't just rationalizations of her need to do the honorable thing and that, down deep, perhaps she still loved him. He would never know, he supposed. With a sigh, he returned to his room and began packing again to leave.

The second- and first-class passengers were boarding at a more distant gangway farther down the pier, Andy noticed as the three of them arrived in a taxi. Since they had purchased first-class tickets, they were able to avoid the long lines and waiting that was the fate of the rest of the crowd.

In due course, they all came to the Italian customs officers who glanced at their passports and waved them aboard. *So far, so good*, thought Andy. Once aboard the ship, they were lost for a while trying to figure out the poor instructions on the signs, but eventually they found their staterooms. As the day passed, while the rest of the passengers boarded and their luggage was brought to them, Andy stepped out on the deck to survey the ship that would be their home for the next week and a day.

The *Ancona* was not an old ship at all, but neither was it the *Normandie* aboard which he had crossed the Atlantic the first time. A single yellow funnel projected skyward from the top deck of the vessel. The green, white, and red Italian flag fluttered from the stern. The white paint on the bulwarks and walls was dull in the morning mist. He wandered into the first-class dining room, which was spacious but modest in décor compared to the French liner. A blast from the ship's horn announced their imminent departure.

The passengers crowded the decks to wave good-bye to their friends and loved ones and then the tugs began pushing the massive ship away from the pier and out into the bay. Black smoke from the coal-fired boilers billowed out of the funnel and Andy could feel the shudder of the engines far below coming to life. Slowly the ship turned out to sea and began gathering speed. The late afternoon sun was warm as it radiated off the white walls and wood deck, but the breeze from the moving ship blowing past him made it comfortable.

Johann and Maria joined Andy on the stern of the ship and together they watched the shoreline of Naples become ever more distant. Soon they could barely make out the coastline of Italy off the port side as the *Ancona* steamed south toward Sicily. They peered over the railing and bulwark of the stern and saw the churning white foam from the propellers while occasional wafts of smoke descended on them from above and behind.

Johann was especially excited to be underway and, indeed, it felt to all of them as if a great weight had been lifted. It would be a long voyage, but in a little more than a week, they would be in New York. It seemed to Andy that he had been away from home for a long time indeed. So much had happened in the year that he had been in Europe.

That evening, they ate dinner in the dining room where the food was quite good, but the service slow and inconsistent. They retired to a lounge that was restricted to first-class passengers. Johann quickly became engrossed in reading one of the newspapers from Naples while Maria struck up a conversation with a Canadian couple in English. The Canadians were from Kingston, Ontario, and Maria was practicing her English. She waved Andy over, to the amusement of the Canadian couple.

The conversation was a bit dull with the usual inquiries about where they were from, where they were going, and so forth. Maria was doing quite well in English, Andy thought. Bored, Andy's mind wandered. He noticed for the first time a young woman sitting nearby. She was quite pretty with blonde hair and blue eyes—not at all Italian looking, Andy thought. He caught her eye. She had evidently been listening to the conversation and, embarrassed, quickly resumed reading the book in her lap. Andy excused himself to go to the bar and ordered a cognac. He noticed a chair next to the young woman and decided to sit down next to her. She was reading *Swiss Family Robinson*.

"Is anyone sitting here?"

"No," she responded in English. "I don't think so." Andy detected an Italian accent.

"May I?"

"Of course."

"A very good book, that one," Andy ventured.

"Ah, yes. You have read it?"

"Yes, in college a couple of years ago. I liked it very much."

"My English is not so good," the young woman replied. "I am reading it to improve for when I get to New York." *The accent was definitely Italian*, Andy thought. He asked where she was from.

In a short while, he learned that Katarina von Dürnstein was Italian, but her family was of Austrian descent, which explained the accent and the name. Since the outbreak of the war, having a German-sounding name and being of Austrian lineage had become a liability in the small town near Milan where she had grown up. There were many like her family, she said, who had remained behind in Italy in the middle of the last century when the Habsburg tide had run out in Italy. Her father had decided that she and her younger brother should wait out the war in America with relatives in New York, given the likelihood of fighting in the north of Italy.

"And you are from America, Andy?"

"Yes. I've been in Austria for a year. I'm on my way home with some friends." Andy nodded toward Maria and Johann. He told her where he was from and a little bit of the circumstances of his visit to meet his own distant relatives, how he had gotten caught up in the outbreak of the war, his writing of articles about the war for his father's newspaper, and his decision to return to America. She listened, occasionally asking a question or nodding in understanding.

"May I get you something from the bar?" Andy's cognac had run out.

"No, thank you. I should be going to bed. I am wondering where my brother is," she said. "I hope you will help me with practicing my English on the trip."

She rose to make her way out of the salon. Andy noticed that she was tall for a woman. She was wearing a white blouse that modestly came all the way to her neck with a ruffle and a black skirt. A silver brooch of some kind was fastened to her blouse around her neck. It was a very tasteful outfit, but it did not conceal from Andy her very fine, slender figure.

Andy rose as she did and impulsively reached for her hand, which she extended in return. He took it gently.

"It would be my pleasure, Katarina. Until tomorrow, then." She smiled and nodded.

"Yes, tomorrow. It was a pleasure to meet you, Andy." With that, she glided out of the lounge, looking back at him once as she reached the door, and smiled. He was already looking forward to what the next day would bring.

"Who was she?" Maria asked after a few minutes had passed. The question was posed in a neutral tone, but Andy could not repress a twinge of embarrassment—or was it guilty pleasure? Maria, dark and lovely as ever, gazed back at him waiting for his reply.

"Katarina von Dürnstein is her name. Italian. She's on her way to New York to stay with relatives there." It was a matter-of-fact summary of the conversation and the woman. Maria nodded.

"She's lovely."

"Yes. Lovely. I think I'll go to bed now," Andy said. Maria nodded and watched as he went to bid Johann goodnight. The warm night air greeted him as he closed the door to the lounge behind him. He could hear the splashing of the water below as the ship effortlessly made way through the sea toward Sicily.

The weather was calm during the first night with very little motion of the ship. Andy slept soundly and awoke the next morning to find that the *Ancona* had actually docked in Messina early in the morning. He watched the scene below over the railing, which was a miniature version of what he had witnessed in Naples as another couple of hundred passengers came aboard.

By noon, the horn gave another low blast and the early afternoon saw the *Ancona* once again underway, bound for Cadiz. They headed due west. Andy had seen on a map that they would pass between the southern coast of Sardinia and the northern coast of Tunis, then through the western Mediterranean Sea until they reached Cadiz, only slightly north and east of the British stronghold of Gibraltar.

Another day was passed at sea. During the day, Andy sat in a deck chair, watching the blue water of the Mediterranean wash past while reading Franz Kafka's *The Metamorphosis*, a horrifying story of a man who awoke one day to find himself transformed into an insect. He had heard of the book while in Vienna and, when he found it in the ship's library, was eager to read it. The strange plot of the book transfixed him as he read it in the bright sunshine while Maria and Johann read books of their own. Maria was practicing her English by reading *A Far Country* by Winston Churchill about a man who journeyed to America. He had written the book before the outbreak of the war, but it had just been published by Macmillan. Johann contented himself reading a shipboard newspaper from cover to cover, alternating between rage and hysterical laughter at the Italian coverage of the war.

Andy encountered Katarina again while walking the deck. She was dressed all in white, befitting the summer weather, and wearing a clever straw hat to keep the sun off her face. They were soon in conversation, sitting on some deck chairs, watching the blue waters of the Tyrrhenian Sea go by. At lunch, they determined that they were now passing south of Sardinia. Off the port bow was the French colony of Tunis. At times, as they walked the deck, they thought that they could make out the shoreline of Africa.

"I would like to go there someday," Katrina said. "So exotic, don't you think?"

"Yes, I'm sure," Andy replied. "I've heard the people there are very poor and primitive, though."

"Like the south of Italy," said Katrina. "Did you see the peasants who boarded in Sicily? It's very different than the north where I live. We say that Africa begins south of Rome," she said with a smile.

"I see," said Andy. "Have you traveled much in the south?"

"Not much. I went to Pompeii once on an expedition when I was in school, but not to Sicily. We went on holidays in the Alps and I have been to Paris. I love Paris. And Rome."

"What about Austria?"

"Yes, Austria also. We have relatives who still live there. I have been to Vienna too. It's lovely. Different than Paris, though. Paris is so, well … gay and energetic. Vienna always seemed different to me. A little sad, really. Like something bad was going to happen. Now it has, I suppose."

"Why do you think so?"

"I suppose it was my relatives. Always complaining about something. The Jews. The people from the east taking over their country. The Czechs. It always seemed like something was going wrong. Like their country was changing and they didn't like it. The way they talked, it was always as if the country was about to fall apart unless someone did something, but they never did."

After lunch, Katarina excused herself again to check on her brother whom he had yet to meet. Andy found Johann and Maria in the lounge again.

The heat of the sun had persuaded them to go inside. A card game of whist was underway. Johann had been persuaded to join the game and was engrossed in it while Maria read at a table near one of the windows, which was open to allow the balmy sea air into the cabin.

Suddenly, there was a loud explosion. It sounded like it came from the stern of the ship. Conversation and cards came to a stop as everyone looked up. Then there was another loud explosion, this time from the bow. Andy rushed out the door to the deck, followed by many of the other passengers from the lounge. At first, nothing seemed amiss except that the ship seemed to be turning hard to port. Black smoke from the funnel spewed down as the speed of the ship seemed to be increasing. Several members of the crew and some of the passengers were running toward the bow and Andy decided to follow them.

When he reached the deck on the bow, he looked to the starboard and saw a low, dark ship perhaps a kilometer away, quite small compared to their own. It was a submarine.

There was a gun crew on the deck. From the conning tower and mast in the middle of the boat, he could make out the black and gold flag of Austria-Hungary and what looked to be an officer with binoculars watching them.

Then he realized that there was a second submarine closing on them from a little father ahead of the first one, but also off the starboard bow. The ship was turning away from them and making speed toward the coastline of Tunisia. There was a flash of red and yellow from the gun and in a few seconds, another loud explosion accompanied by a geyser of water just head of their ship. The commander of the nearest submarine was demonstrating that the *Ancona* was within his gun range. Johann and Maria were soon by Andy's side.

"My God," Maria exclaimed. "They're going to sink us! Our own countrymen!"

"Can you believe it?" Johann exclaimed. "A passenger ship like this? Surely not?"

Andy had a hard time believing it as well. After the *Lusitania*, Andy had come to the belief that Germany would never again allow its submarines to sink a passenger ship. It had never occurred to him that Austria would do so. In fact, Andy had never even realized that the Austrian navy in the Mediterranean had submarines. It was unforgivable, he thought.

The decks had now swelled with passengers, all babbling in Italian and other languages. Andy looked up from the deck to the bridge of the vessel and noticed the ship's officers looking out the windows with their binoculars at the submarines. The most distant one had now moved directly ahead of them and had aimed its deck gun at them. Anxiously, everyone waited for another gunshot, but it didn't come. Instead, the *Ancona* began to slow down. It was obvious that the ship could not outrun the two submarines that had ambushed them and the crew had decided to give up on any plan to do so. Slowly the ship came to a stop and now the two submarines closed to within five hundred meters.

The passengers on the bow deck anxiously watched and waited to see what was going to happen next. Pursers appeared and shouted to the passengers in Italian. Gasps and shouts could be heard from many of the passengers. Suddenly, Andy thought of the gypsy woman's warning that "the waters are dangerous." She had been right again.

"What is he saying?" Maria asked.

"He says that the submarines have given everyone forty-five minutes to get off the ship. Then it is going to be torpedoed," Johann said flatly, as if he couldn't believe it was really happening. "They say that women and children will be taken off first and should come to the deck below. They say no baggage can be brought—there isn't enough room." Already the crowd had begun to surge toward the stairwells. There was no point in going to their stateroom, so the three friends began to follow the crowd below.

"What about you?" Maria exclaimed. "With your one leg, you can't swim or survive in the water if anything else should happen. You must talk to them and make them let you get into one of the boats with me. Andy, oh my God, what about you?"

Minutes were passing and, given the number of passengers, Andy doubted that even half of them could be put in the lifeboats in the short time they had. The crowd wasn't moving. The stairs were clogged with passengers waiting for those ahead of them on the next deck to get into the lifeboats hanging on the davits that the crew was frantically uncovering and making ready to lower into the sea. Andy looked at the watch that Elisabeth had given him. It was 4:10 in the afternoon. He estimated that at least ten minutes had passed and they were nowhere near the stairs. More shouts could be heard ahead of them and then he could make out some pushing and shoving among the passengers as panic began to set in.

"We're never going to get down these stairs in time," Johann said calmly. "Let's try to move around to the other side. Maybe the line is shorter there, or maybe we can get to the stairs at the stern or even one of the interior stairwells."

"No!" Maria exclaimed. "We've been waiting here for fifteen minutes already and, if we go, we'll give up our place in line. It could be worse over there." Johann said nothing and Andy didn't know what to do. After a few minutes, they were able to take a few steps forward. They could see the entrance to the stairwell. There was a line of passengers on the opposite side of the stairwell, also trying to get down. That was where the pushing and shoving had taken place a few minutes ago as the competing lines tried to get into the stairwell. Andy looked at his watch again. It was 4:30. They only had fifteen more minutes. Then he had an idea.

"Johann, I'm going to try and get around to the other side and see how things are there. You and Maria stay here. They may let you into the boat with Maria because of your leg, but they're not going to let me into it anyway. If there's a faster way down, I'll come back and shout for you," Andy said.

"And if not?" Maria's eyes were wide with terror at the fate she imagined was waiting for him. Suddenly, a pistol shot rang out from somewhere below and the sounds of a commotion could be heard coming up the stairwell. Then another shot. Screams and cries came from below. All the passengers around them began shouting and talking to each other, but Andy couldn't understand any of it.

"If not, I'll just have to figure out something else," Andy said. He was lying. There was nothing else to do. He couldn't stand the look on Maria's face and Johann was just staring at him. He made up his mind.

"God bless you both and good luck," Andy said as he grabbed Maria's head in both his hands and gave her a kiss.

She grabbed his arms tightly, sobbing. He turned to Johann and hugged him too, giving him a kiss on both cheeks.

"Take care of her, Johann. We'll meet again someday soon."

Johann's eyes reddened and he pressed his mouth to Andy's ear. "It's all my fault. We should have gone back to Vienna. It's all my fault. Please forgive me."

"We all decided. It's not your fault. Don't worry about me. Get yourself in Maria's lifeboat whatever you do. Goodbye!" With that, Andy pulled himself free of Maria and pushed his way through the crowd behind them until he was in the clear. He could hear Maria's cries of anguish fade over the bedlam of the crowd, but he pushed on. In a minute, he was on the deck of the bow again, free of the crowd.

It was strange. It was a beautiful day. The sun was shining and the blue water looked beautiful. The sunlight reflecting off the water was almost blinding. Andy made his way around to the other side, but the crowd around the port stairwell was just as jammed as the other one. There was no way out. He was amazed at how calm he was. Slowly, he walked toward the rail at the very point of the bow to look out at the scene.

There was the first submarine, riding on the slowly rolling waves. The deck of the submarine was crowded with more than a dozen sailors and officers who were calmly watching from safety. Suddenly, far below, he caught sight of a lifeboat being rowed by a couple of sailors from the ship along the starboard side, clearly making for the opposite side of the boat for some reason. Andy looked up and thought that he could see the faint, low form of the coastline of Africa far in the distance. Someone must have told the crew to make for Tunisia as the closest place to land. He looked back at the submarine and noticed that, for some reason, the officer in the conning tower and the crew were no longer looking at the ship, but off to the north, toward Sardinia, which would be over the horizon. Some of the submarine's crew were pointing. Andy followed their gaze.

Off in the distance, just on the horizon was another ship. It was just a speck of black, really, but it was definitely a ship. It was hard to tell how far away it was or in what direction it was moving, but after a few minutes, Andy realized that it must be coming toward them because otherwise, he would see the silhouette of its broadside. He looked at his watch. It was now 4:38. Only seven minutes left.

Andy couldn't see the other submarine. He was too far up on the bow. He looked back at the submarine ahead of them and saw—much to his dismay—that the crew was now climbing up the conning tower and returning inside the hold of their ship. The officer was watching the approaching ship through his binoculars. Andy reasoned that the approaching ship must be an Allied naval vessel of some kind that may have heard a distress signal from the crew of the *Ancona*. The submarine began to turn away from the ship, crossing to the port side where several lifeboats could now be seen moving away from the ship. He watched as the submarine came about and faced the port broadside of *Ancona*, which was dead in the water.

Two thin white lines came from the submarine and moved inexorably toward the ship. Andy knew that these would be torpedoes and quickly realized that they would hit right below him by the bow, just below the waterline. He ran to the opposite side. The crowd going down the stairwell was now much smaller, but he couldn't see Maria or Johann. *Perhaps they had gotten down the stairwell and were at the lifeboats*, he thought. Then the torpedoes struck.

There were two enormous concussions. The deck rocked as the detonation blew a mass of water and flame into the air. Smoke blew across the deck, stinging his eyes, and he fell to the hard wooden deck from the force of the blast. He was not hurt, but cries of panic could be heard from below and down the top deck. He got up, but as soon as he got to his feet, he could feel the ship slowly starting to keel over ever so slightly to port. He imagined the water gushing into the hold of the ship, weighing it down more and more as the water rushed in. He remembered that this was how the *Titanic* had sunk after striking an iceberg in the North Atlantic only three years earlier.

Andy staggered over to the port railing of the bow and definitely noticed that he was walking downhill. When he reached the railing, he peered over to see the damage, but the curvature of the hull was too great to visualize. He looked up and saw the U-boat turning away from the ship, its work complete. The stern came into view and he could see the wash from its propellers pushing it at an ever-increasing speed to the south. It made no attempt to molest the lifeboats as it pulled away. The passengers and crew in what he counted were nine lifeboats all looked back at the stricken ship in horror, helpless.

As he turned his head to the left, Andy could see more lifeboats hitting the water. The listing of the ship swung them out away from the hull. They were dropping quite quickly now, but Andy noticed that many of them were filled with white uniformed crewmembers instead of passengers. Once in the water, the crews frantically pulled away from the ship. Andy remembered someone once telling him that when a ship of this size sank, it created an enormous suction that would pull anything and anyone near the sinking ship down into the depths with it.

He realized that the portside stairwell seemed to be clear and he limped over to it. The first flight of stairs was empty and he scampered down to the landing. At the foot of the stairwell, a mob pushed and fought their way toward the stern. Andy imagined that the lifeboats toward the bow had already been lowered and the passengers must be frantic to get into the remaining ones toward the stern. Once again, there seemed to be no hope for him. He wondered if Maria and Johann had managed to get off the ship.

An American in Vienna

Andy walked back up the stairs and down the now-deserted first-class deck to the lounge where, an hour earlier, everyone had been peacefully enjoying themselves. It was deserted too. He went back out on the deck and found the stairs to the bridge. The list of the ship was now decidedly to port and forward, which made climbing the ladder-like stairs somewhat difficult, but he made it to the bridge. It was deserted. He looked out the huge plate glass windows toward the bow and saw that in a few minutes the bow would be under water. He looked at the gold watch again. It was 5:17. Judging by the time it had taken for the bow to sink to the waterline, Andy estimated that the ship would sink below the surface in something like twenty minutes. The flow of water into the ship would accelerate as it filled ever more rapidly, the weight pulling the vessel down deeper and deeper into the sea.

It was then that he noticed the life jackets secured to the ceiling inside the bridge. He pulled one off and put it on. *The water should not be cold*, he thought. Perhaps the naval vessel he had seen would be able to rescue him and some of the other passengers who were not so fortunate. He considered for the first time that he had not seen any life jackets below and wondered if the hundreds of passengers who would soon be in the water might need one. He pulled a few more off the ceiling and then tried to reach the starboard side door of the bridge, which was now something of an uphill climb. He couldn't make it. For the first time, he began to consider the possibility that the ship might capsize. He decided that the time had come to take his chances in the water.

The next few minutes were a blur. Andy somehow made it back down to the bow. Waves were now cresting halfway up the bow to the forward bulkhead of the ship. He kicked off his shoes and waded into the water. It wasn't cold, but it wasn't terribly warm either. He looked out over the water, to the south and now saw a dozen—perhaps two dozen—lifeboats making their way toward Tunisia.

The water quickly came up to his chest and he realized that the ship was sinking fast and actually moving forward and down into the sea. He began to swim away from the ship. He saw a deck chair floating in the water ahead of him and made for it. By the time he got to it and looked back, he watched in horror as the ship moved down into the water. The yellow funnel went under the water and amazingly, in only a minute or two, the huge ship disappeared and was gone.

Andy turned around in the water and saw the retreating, white specks of lifeboats far away. There was no way he could possibly swim to shore. His only hope would be another passing ship. He turned to the north where the approaching ship had been and could see far in the distance that it was a warship. His heart pounding, he allowed himself to consider the possibility that he might actually be saved. He managed to turn the deck chair right side up and sat in it while the minutes went by. He looked at the watch again and saw that it was still keeping time. It was 5:48. An hour went by as the cruiser continued toward the scene of the attack. Black plumes of smoke were billowing out of her funnels high into the air, he noticed. The sky was still blue, but it occurred to Andy that night might come before he could be found and the ship might miss him. At that moment, he noticed the ship start to turn, revealing its broadside to him.

The ship's stern came into view and Andy peered out to see the flag. It was so small against the ship and was fluttering, but then it became clear. It was the red, white, and blue tricolor of the French fleet. The ship had clearly slowed to almost a standstill and was picking up other passengers still floating in the water. Andy watched its slow progress. Lifeboats were lowered over the sides and began to fan out over the area, stopping now and again to haul someone up over the side and into the boats. He waved again and again at the boats, but nobody seemed to notice him.

It was dusk and, in a few more minutes, the sun would

slip down below the horizon. *So this was how it would be,* Andy thought. *So close.* A cold breeze rushed over the surface of the sea now, a harbinger of a drop in the temperature. Andy looked at the French ship, now much farther away and pointing away from him. He could not make out the flag any longer. It seemed that for some reason, he had ended up away from other passengers who had managed to survive on the surface of the water. The lifeboats were mere specks, slowly making their way around the wreckage, still picking up survivors, no doubt. The nearest boat he could make out was perhaps a kilometer from him to the west, where the sun was setting.

He took out his watch. It was now nearly 8:00. Once again, he read the inscription on the inside of the gold cover and felt a lump in his throat as he recalled his parting from Otto and Elisabeth in the salon of their residence in Vienna. *"... Denke oft an deine Zeit bei uns ... Think often of your time with us."* He held the watch in his hand, resting on the arm of the deck chair, looking at it. The sun's rays blazed off the gold watch into his eyes. Then an idea came to Andy. He held the watch up with the cover facing toward the sun and the lone lifeboat to the west. He wiggled it this way and that, shining the rays of the sun back toward the boat.

For a while, it seemed that nothing changed, but Andy had nothing else to do but keep trying. The sun was right at the horizon now, a red ball about to plunge into the sea. As the red ball sank beneath the waves, Andy's heart sank with it. In the fading twilight, he realized that he was drifting farther and farther away from the others. Then darkness.

It was terrifying as he bobbed on the water. He imagined huge sharks in the black water beneath him that would soon find him and attack. He was exhausted and thirsty. He could make out thin white lines in the far distance that he imagined were ships still searching the water. Occasionally, a bright light would sparkle from the distant ships that he imagined were searchlights. Hours went by. Several times he caught himself nodding off. He tried to stay awake for fear he might miss a passing boat, but it was hopeless. He awoke time and again in the night to immediate panic and terror, in the blackness, realizing that it was not a nightmare, but was really happening to him.

In one of these intervals, he shouted out in the darkness—hoping to be heard—but it was no use. He no longer could see the lights of any ships at all. He cried out of fear. He cried out of sadness that he would never see his mother and father again. He imagined them hearing the news of his death at sea and he cried again. He cursed the heartless submarines that had done this to him. Then he fell asleep again.

The next time he awoke, the sun was rising in the east. He could feel the warm rays on his face and shuddered, shaking himself awake. He used his arms to paddle and turned around in the waterlogged deck chair. To his surprise and shock, not far away, there was a lifeboat. They were still searching. He screamed, but only a croaking sound came from his dry mouth. His lips were cracked. Then he saw the lifeboat turn toward him.

He sat up in the chair, holding his arms as high above him as he could, waving toward the boat. He could see the oars of the boat as they rhythmically stroked the water. Then an answering wave from the bow of the boat confirmed at last that the crew had seen him. Within about a half hour, Lifeboat 3 pulled alongside. Andy pushed off the deck chair to which he felt an irrational gratitude and swam to the side. Two burly French sailors pulled him over the side and he flopped down on the deck of the boat.

"*Stai bene?*" asked one of the sailors. They were asking in Italian if he was all right, Andy surmised. He responded in English.

"Thank you so much. I'm an American. I'm sorry, I don't speak Italian," he said.

"Ah, *un Americain? Parlez-vous français, monsieur?*" the sailor asked.

"Non, je suis désolé, mais je ne parle pas français non plus," Andy replied in one of the few phrases he had learned to say in French on the transatlantic voyage a year earlier. Apparently none of the other passengers or crew spoke English and, under the circumstances, Andy thought it best not to try his German.

The sailors nodded and pointed to the east, toward another cruiser that must have arrived during the night. They were going to return to her, Andy guessed by this gesture. The other sailors began to row again. A few more survivors, apparently Italian, nodded at him as he shivered in the morning air. One of them wordlessly tossed him a blanket. Another one in the bow cried out to any survivors who might be in the area, but there were no responses. This continued for over an hour, until the lifeboat finally reached the ship. Hooks and cables from the davits overhead were fastened to the boat and slowly they were cranked up to the deck.

As the lifeboat reached its secured position in the davit, there were several sailors and officers waiting for them. All looked at the wretched survivors with grim pity. The sailors extended their hands to lift or guide the passengers out of the boat. Several of the female survivors were sobbing as they put their feet at last on the solid deck of the cruiser. One of the officers said, *"Bienvenue à bord du navire militaire français Montcalm."* A sailor standing by the officer translated this and more the officer said into Italian, none of which Andy could understand. At the end of it, the officer led the little group down the deck to a room where there were dry clothes and the galley staff had prepared a meal for them. Andy realized that he was famished. He changed into the clothes in a little area cordoned off for the men and made his way back to the table. The language barrier between the French crew and Italian passengers made conversation between them scarce, but among the Italians, animated conversation flowed.

Since Andy could not understand anything that was being said by anyone, he was left alone with his thoughts. Two huge possibilities loomed in his mind. Both Maria and Johann were dead or they had made it to Tunisia in one of the lifeboats. In either event, he simply would not know for some time. Then it occurred to him that they would be thinking the same thing about him, wondering if he were dead or alive. His parents in America would hear about the sinking of the ship and so would Otto and Elisabeth. At that moment, the captain arrived in the galley.

The captain was in his full white uniform with gold braid. He was tall and had a crew cut of gray hair and a black and gray mustache with dark Gallic eyes. Then, to Andy's delight, the captain said, in English "Which one of you is the American?"

"I am, sir," Andy replied, now standing up.

"Sit down, monsieur, please," the captain said. "I am Capitaine René Leveque." He extended his hand, which Andy shook warmly.

"Very grateful to you, sir. You and your men saved my life. Thank you so very much," Andy said.

"Such a disaster," the captain replied. "It was brutal what they did. We are so sorry we couldn't reach your ship in time. So many dead. What is your name, American?"

"Sorry, I completely forgot. I'm Andy Bishop. I left Italy a couple of days ago …"

"Yes, yes … I know," the captain replied. "Bound for New York, of course."

"Yes, sir," Andy replied. He wanted to ask about Johann and Maria, but then thought better of it. If he gave their names, it would be suspicious. Then he remembered Johann and Maria's Swiss alias names. "I was with some Swiss companions, Johann and Maria von Weissgäber, from Bern. Do you know if they survived?"

"No. I regret I do not. We are getting the names of all the survivors we picked up in the water, but many were in lifeboats that have reached the shore in Tunisia. The colonial authorities there will take care of them and soon we will know. We have asked the customs authorities in Naples and Messina to send us the names of all the passengers who boarded to compare with our lists. It will be several days, I'm sure. Let's hope for the best, monsieur," the captain replied.

"What will happen next, Captain? Where are we going?"

"This ship is bound for our home port of Toulon. We were on our way there when we received the distress call. We have stayed as long as we are able. We have several frigates and destroyers searching the waters for any more survivors. We will stay until morning or the afternoon, until we are sure that there are no more. Then we will return to port in Toulon where the passengers can disembark and go back to Italy or, perhaps, in your case, continue to New York on another liner. That is the plan for now. Please finish your dinner and then you will be shown to a place where you can sleep. I'm afraid the accommodations here will not be what they were on your ship, but you will be safe with us. If you need anything, let one of the sailors know. We have a few who speak some English. I will see that they check on you. Good luck."

Andy thanked the captain again, and he was gone. After a while, lonely and depressed, he lay on a hammock below the top deck somewhere in the belly of this mighty warship as it gently rocked in the Mediterranean Sea. Other passengers slept all around him on hammocks that must have normally been used by the sailors who were off watch. Dark thoughts gave way to darkness altogether as, bone tired, Andy sank into a deep sleep.

19.

North Africa

Tunisia was the heir of ancient Carthage and, indeed, the ruins of that empire were all around the city. It was a cosmopolitan mix of Arabs, French, and Turks predominantly, but a huge colony of over 100,000 Italians lived in and around the city with other Europeans in one of the largest and oldest cities in North Africa.

Ahmed II, ben Ali Pasha Bey was the nominal "Protector" of Tunisia, but the country was really a French "protectorate," occupied by the republic's army and fleet. As such, it was an Allied base, but with an otherwise aloof, uninvolved, and unexcited population with respect to the war in Europe. A few Berbers had volunteered for service with the French army in Europe, but most of the Arab population saw the war as none of their affair.

The French, who had completely rebuilt the infrastructure of Tunis since its occupation in 1881, were tolerated since they seemed to be investing far more in the city than they could possibly be taking out. Their colonial architecture, the wide leafy boulevards they had built, and the relative efficiency in the city's administration had transformed the city and blended well with the prevailing and underlying Moorish architecture and culture. A "live-and-let-live" relationship prevailed between the Arabs and their French overlords.

Like the Europeans, the Berbers, and then the Ottoman Turks, had built and maintained walls around the old city, a maze of tiny cobblestone streets and alleys surrounding beautiful plazas, fountains, and ancient buildings, including, invariably, a citadel or Kasbah. In many old North African cities, the old quarter was itself called "the Kasbah," but Tunis was special in this respect. Their old quarter was called "the Medina."

The heat was oppressive during the middle of the day and virtually everything came to a stop. In the evening, the Medina really came to life. Arab vendors set up their stalls in the market while hundreds of customers milled about, both Arab and European. Europeans were prime targets and were accosted immediately in the market by the peddlers of trinkets, jewelry, leather, and other local goods. The most unctuous, persistent tactics were employed by the native vendors to lure the Europeans into purchases that they never came intending to make.

Johann and Maria's lifeboat, along with all the others from the *Ancona*, had been met by a French military patrol at a beach not far from the city shortly after they reached the largely deserted shoreline of Tunisia. They had been directed there specifically to rescue the passengers at the behest of the French naval vessels that had belatedly arrived to rescue the other passengers in the water. It had taken a few days before Maria and Johann were released by the French authorities to return home—to Switzerland. Nobody had passports in the lifeboats, which had made the absence of their own unremarkable to the French authorities. The couple seemed innocuous enough and the officer who had briefly interrogated them basically took their word for their nationality.

Upon their release, the stranded pair had tried to find news of the *Ancona* disaster—and, more particularly, Andy

Bishop. An Italian newspaper published in Tunis turned out to be the best source of this news, since neither Maria nor Johann spoke much French. However, their frantic scanning of the newspapers, when they were printed, had revealed nothing as far as the fate of their friend was concerned.

It was reported in the Tunis press on June 27, 1915, that twenty-seven Americans aboard the ship had died, provoking a new protest from Washington—this time to the Austrian government.

An Arab waiter in a spotless white tunic with a red fez served Maria and Johann from what appeared to be an ancient silver tray at their table under a large awning. Maria took off her bonnet and smoothed her hair back from her face as Johann scanned the latest newspaper article on the *Ancona* incident.

"It says here that several survivors were later picked up by other French naval ships from a squadron en route to Toulon and have been brought there for repatriation to Italy. Maybe he was picked up by them. Maybe he's on his way to France."

Johann had been racked with guilt and grief since the sinking. He had made a terrible scene about getting into the lifeboats, screaming that he would rather stay with the ship until Maria refused to get into a lifeboat without him. A sailor had eventually shoved him into the boat just before it was lowered into the sea. Johann had sat down with his head in his hands as the boat pulled away, shaking his head and sobbing, all the while repeating, "It's all my fault. It's all my fault."

Maria had also been heartsick at the fate Andy would face on the doomed liner as it receded from view and finally sank. Yet she hadn't fully understood Johann's remorse.

The grim look on his face returned each time he read a newspaper or spoke about it—and it was no different this evening.

"How long can our money last at this rate?" Maria had asked. The French authorities had provided a little money to the refugees to hold them over until they could board the first boat back to Italy. Johann and Maria had not taken that ship, however, until they had carefully considered their options. Time was running out. The thought of being in Tunisia with no money was frightening. Johann had no way to send a telegram to his mother in Vienna to even inform her of their rescue, let alone that money be sent.

"A week at most, I think," Johann replied. "After that, I don't know what we can do. Maybe I can find work here—at what, I don't know." They were staying in rooms that they had rented from a Tunisian family, to whom they had been helpfully directed by the French authorities, to conserve costs. The family owned a small leather goods shop not far from the old city, and demanded payment in advance. Maria had pawned some jewelry that she was wearing.

"I never thought it would turn out like this. Never." He was becoming agitated again.

"Of course you didn't, Johann," Maria said, trying to sooth him. "I don't know why you seem to think this is somehow your fault."

"Because it is my fault, Maria," Johann replied with some vehemence. Maria was startled.

"Why? How can you say that?"

"We should have gone back to Vienna, but I knew that you would never get to America if we had. Don't you see, Maria? It's Andy you should marry. He loves you. You know this. And I know it. I've known it for a long time. And I know you loved him too. I knew you wouldn't leave me in Vienna to go to America with him. So I decided to go with you and Andy. I wanted you to have your dream, Maria. Don't you see? You love Andy and you were meant to be with him in

America. That was why I kept pressing to continue our trip. Now do you understand? I won't marry you, Maria. Not like this. I'll never marry you. I won't let you marry me."

Maria was speechless. She fell back into the chair as she tried to comprehend what he had said. She thought she would go mad. But Johann wasn't finished.

"There's something else I have to tell you. Something I haven't told anyone. A few days before I left for Sarajevo, I met a woman. I was having an affair with her, Maria. Yes, an affair. During our engagement. She was the wife of the Serbian ambassador. I had been seeing her for a couple of months. Just before I left, I was with her. We talked about the archduke's trip. I must have had too much to drink. I don't know. But I talked to her a lot about it. Exactly when he would be in Sarajevo. The route he would take. How he would ride in an open car with his wife.

"It didn't mean anything to me at the time. But afterward, I started to think about it. Maria, I'm sure she was a spy. I'm sure she told all those details to her husband, or to the Serbian secret service. Do you see? I may have been responsible for the assassination! Me! The man who did so much for me—the man who I loved and was like a father to me—died because of me. Because of my weakness and lust."

"Now you know everything, Maria. You couldn't possibly want to marry a wretch like me. A philandering traitor. That's who I really am, Maria. So you see, I thought the one last thing I could do that would be decent, would be to get you out of Austria before the end came, to America, with Andy. Then I want to die. I wanted to die when the *Ancona* was going down. Now, I'm here with you and all is lost. Unless Andy is still alive. That's the only thing that matters now."

Maria couldn't believe it. It was too much. She stared at him for a long time as her mind went round and round it all. There was the philandering. This was no surprise, although she had not known of this particular liaison. Yet it aroused dormant feelings about Johann and the way that he used to be that she had forgotten since he was wounded in Galicia. He had to be telling the truth. What motive would he have now to lie? His treason? That was another matter. Could it be true? Even so, he had never intended to betray the country. It was his weakness, just as he had said, but still ... It was plausible. She was a Serbian. Then there was her own affair with Andy. How could he have known?

"Walther," Johann replied when she asked. "He saw you, by chance, in Budapest. Both of you. He was discreet. And he told me one day in Vienna when I was better. He's loyal to me. I've known him since I was a boy. He felt it was his duty. It made sense, though. In the end, it made no difference. I understood. I understand it all very well. We were never meant to be, Maria."

"I have to go," Maria said, rising. "I have to be alone. I have to think. I'll see you back at our rooms. I just have to think." She turned to leave.

"Maria!" Johann exclaimed. "I'm sorry. I tried to tell you. I really did. I can't marry you. Not like this. I won't let you marry me." Maria nodded, and then walked away into the Medina.

The strange Arabic music, the smell of cooked lamb and spices, the vendors, and odd twists and turns of the ancient streets lent a surreal quality to Maria's wanderings as she tried to come to grips with Johann's stunning revelations. She might have well smoked a pipe of opium, Maria thought. Thoughts and emotions confused and bewildered her despite her efforts to make sense of it all. One moment, she was furious with Johann and the next, full of grief for him. She thought of Andy and how she had rejected him, breaking his heart and her own. Had she really fallen in love with Johann? Or had she fooled herself into believing it out of pity and a sense of honor? Or was she simply fickle?

She tried to concentrate on what to do next, but inevitably her thoughts returned to Johann and what he meant to her now. Did he really love her, beneath all the self-loathing? And what if he did? Could she ever marry him? And even if she wanted to, even if he did love her, would he allow it? And if not, could she ever regain Andy's love—if he was alive? And what should they do now, here in Tunis, of all places? Should they return to Vienna? Could they?

They must return to Vienna, she thought. Whatever happened, they must return home to sort it all out. If Andy were alive, he would soon be back in America and perhaps someday she would see him again. If not? Well, she couldn't think about that, but in any event, Johann needed to be home. She needed to take him there. She would have to sort things out there when they got back. That was all she could decide for now. They must get back to Vienna somehow, and soon, before the money ran out.

"We can always go back to Italy and then to Switzerland," Johann thought out loud, "but then we have no papers again."

"But if we can get back to Italy, perhaps the maitre d' at the hotel in Rome could help us again," Maria suggested. "Maybe he could get us another set of false passports like he did before. And your mother could wire funds through Switzerland to us again." They had been through this before and it always seemed to come back to this basic plan, Maria thought. Today, it seemed, Johann finally accepted the idea for lack of a better one.

"Let's see when the next ship leaves for Italy and whether

we can get on it," Johann ventured as they walked in the increasingly narrow streets toward the *Porte de France*, the massive gate that led to the *Ville Nouvelle* or "New City" which contained the commercial hub of the capital.

The city streets became wider and more organized and the European presence predominated. Johann was dressed in a shabby European-style white suit that really didn't fit him and a white hat. As Maria looked at him, the shadows from the palms and other trees played over him. After a few inquiries, they located the office of the *Society di Navigazione a Vaporetti Italia*, the Italian shipping line, where they discovered a ship left nearly every day for Naples, but cost far more than they could manage. They were trapped.

For an hour, they discussed ways out of their peculiar circumstances. The letters of credit and bank notes that Johann had brought with him on the ship could have been deposited in a French bank, but they had been lost aboard the *Ancona*, of course. In normal times, money could have been wired from his bank in Vienna, but these were not normal times. Their enemy citizenship complicated things further. They decided to take a chance and wire Allegra in Rome. He seemed to be their only hope and a slender thread at that, but what else could they do?

The next day, Johann sent a telegram to the maitre d' of the Hotel di San Floriano in Rome:

```
Dear Uncle,

As you know, we decided to continue
to America since the last time we
saw you, but we had the misfortune
of taking passage aboard the
Ancona, which was attacked and sunk
a week ago. As you can see, we have
survived, thanks be to God. Maria
and I are now in Tunis without
means of securing passage from
```

here back to Rome. Please convey to the family our situation and, if possible, that they should transmit funds to enable us to return to Rome as soon as possible.

Many thanks for your help in this difficult time, Uncle. Please reply to this telegraph office where we will check for your reply.

Your nephew,
Johann von Weissgäber

For two days, Maria and Johann checked at the telegraph office and found no reply. They wondered if Allegra had received their telegram or, if he had, whether he had thought it too dangerous to reply. Then, on the third day, it came.

My dear Johann,

The family and I are overjoyed to hear that you survived the terrible ordeal of the *Ancona* disaster. We had all feared you and Maria were dead. God be praised for your deliverance. What of your American friend? I have passed along news of your situation to the family at home who began immediately to take measures for your passage back here. In this regard, please visit the office of Monsignor Alfredo Lovecchio of the Cathédrale de Saint-Vincent de Paul in a few days. He will assist you in returning to us. Please post us regarding your specific plans so that we will

```
be  ready  to  celebrate  your  safe
return.

Your uncle,
Massimo Allegra
```

The Roman Catholic *Cathédrale de Saint-Vincent de Paul* was located in the new city, dominating a major *Place* with a mixture of Moorish, Byzantine, and Gothic styles reflecting the long history of the Mediterranean colony. Maria and Johann sat in one of the pews in the front several days later, looking at the ornate altar.

A door opened and closed somewhere in the vast expanse of the interior of the church. The gloom was punctuated by bright sunlight that came through the stained glass windows so that their eyes could never really adjust to the ambient darkness that pervaded where the light did not touch. A perpetual flame in a brass and glass sconce hung over the steps up to the altar, suspended on a brass chain that descended from some point in the ceiling so high above that they could not see. A priest in black appeared from behind one of the side altars, no doubt from some door or passageway that they could not see. He noticed them and nodded. Maria and Johann nodded back to him.

"Johann," said Maria. "I'm going to pray now." With that, she slipped to her knees. Johann silently did the same. For a few minutes, Maria was alone with her thoughts in the quiet church. She prayed that Andy had been spared. She prayed that if he hadn't been spared, that God take care of him in heaven. She prayed that she and Johann would make it back to Vienna without further incident.

Johann started coughing again. After a moment, he stood up and shuffled his way out of the pew. He drew a handkerchief from his pocket and held it to his mouth to stifle the coughs in the silent church. Maria crossed herself and stood up. She saw him take the handkerchief from his mouth. There was blood. Johann looked back at her.

"Don't worry. It's happened before. It's nothing. I just can't get rid of this cough."

"My God, Johann! Why didn't you tell me? Something is wrong. You must see a doctor."

"Not here, Maria. I'll see one when I get back to Vienna. It's nothing, I'm sure." Maria was not reassured, but it was another reason to hurry home.

Johann walked slowly around to the aisle on the side of the church where they had seen the priest. He lit one of the many flickering votive candles before a statue of the Virgin Mary. Maria arose and walked to where he stood as Johann blew out the taper.

"For Andy?" she asked.

"For my father," he replied. "It has been too long since I lit a candle for him. I miss him at times like this. When I feel lost and helpless."

"I remember him," Maria said. "He was a great man. So strong and confident. So generous."

Johann turned to her and nodded, his eyes a little glassy now.

"You light one for Andy." Maria hesitated and then nodded. She found the collection box and put in a coin. Then she lit a candle for Andy and placed it on the stand with all the others. For a moment, they both looked at the two candles, side by side. Johann took Maria's hand and slowly they walked toward the doors. When they reached the front of the church, the same priest they had seen earlier was there and greeted them.

"Welcome to our church and blessings to you in the name of our Lord," he said, making the sign of the cross over them.

Johann responded in Italian. "Thank you, Father, you are most kind. We were marveling at your beautiful church and wondered when Mass is said."

"Vespers is celebrated at seven o'clock in the evening, my son. Please come and join us. Are you visiting Tunis?"

Johann explained that they had been aboard the *Ancona* and then about their predicament. The priest listened carefully.

"My sympathies to you both," he said, bowing slightly. "The Holy Father calls this war the suicide of civilized Europe, you know." Benedict XV had been elected pope on September 3, 1914, upon the death of the late pope, Pius X. The war had preoccupied his papacy.

"Where are you from, my son?"

Johann paused, and then said, "We are from Switzerland, father. We were visiting our uncle in Rome and then took passage from Naples to America. We're looking for a Monsignor Alfredo Lovecchio. Do you know him?"

"I am Lovecchio. I have been expecting you. Come with me."

Johann whispered in German to Maria, telling her what had transpired. They followed the monsignor out the door into the blinding sunlight to another building nearby, which was the office of the Archbishop of Tunis, Barthélemy Clément Combes. The priest brought them to his own study on the second floor.

"Here, my son. I have something to give you." There was a large envelope on his desk. He picked it up and handed it to Johann with a nod, then stood behind the desk with his hands folded over his waist, watching them. Lovecchio was probably in his early sixties, Johann guessed. He had steel-gray hair and blue eyes.

"Where are you from, Father?" Johann queried.

"From *Milano*, my son. I was asked by the Holy Father to come here several years ago to help minister to the Italian flock, so to speak." He smiled. "I was a chaplain to his Holiness before his recent death." He paused and looked at the envelope in Johann's hands. "You should open it, my son."

Johann had hesitated to open the envelope in view of the monsignor. He wondered how much this priest knew of their real circumstances. Nothing about the priest gave him any clue one way or the other. It had become awkward to stand in the room without opening the package, so Johann gave in to his curiosity.

Out of the envelope slid two Italian passports and a thick wad of Italian lira. There was no note or letter. There didn't need to be. He counted the lira as the priest watched, saying nothing. There was plenty—more than enough to sustain them for another month, buy two first-class tickets to Naples, and buy clothing. He looked at the passports. They were excellent forgeries again. Johann put the passports in his coat pocket, split the money with Maria, and put half in his trousers pocket.

"Thank you, Father, for what you have done. My family will be so very grateful to you for helping us in this way. I don't know what else I can say."

The priest nodded. "May the Lord watch over you and bless you, my son. Come see me again if you should need our help. God bless you both on your voyage home." With that, the visit was over and they returned to the street with newfound relief.

It was just after sunset when they reached the Medina. The setting sun bathed the sand-colored buildings of the ancient subtropical quarter in a blaze of orange and purple shades and shadows. A cooling breeze blew in from the desert and the smell of cooked lamb drifted in the air from dozens of braziers seen and unseen as they walked the streets. From a nearby mosque's minarets, there arose a long, wailing chant that was the call to prayer. In the glow of the early twilight, the sound was like nothing heard in Europe and they stopped to listen and watch.

Men rolled prayer carpets out on the floors of their shops, while others simply knelt, facing east toward Mecca. Through habit or little visual cues on ceilings and streets, the direction was known or discerned and with an almost magical uniformity, life came to a standstill as the chant dominated the relatively quiet streets. The Muslims touched their foreheads to the ground in submission to Allah several times. Silent prayers were said by one and all, oblivious for a couple of minutes to anything and anyone around them. Then, in a few minutes, it was over and life returned quickly to normal.

"That was beautiful," said Maria. "The devotion of the people is really amazing to watch, isn't it?"

"It is amazing," Johann replied.

They were in a different world, she thought. It was hard to believe, walking through the Souk, that a war consuming millions of souls was raging at this moment somewhere across the Mediterranean Sea, particularly here in the old city among the Arabs. Whatever was happening on the other side of the Mediterranean was just another war in the vast ocean of time that this ancient city had existed.

Soon their walking brought them to a little café that looked inviting and they sat down at a small table. Instantly a waiter appeared to take their order. Johann spoke to him in Italian to which the waiter responded. The facility of the Arabs with European languages when it came to the purchase of anything was remarkable. Seated at another table, almost uncomfortably close, was an old man occasionally drawing smoke from a hookah located next to his table. He was dressed in a flowing white robe in the Arab Berber style with a red fez and tassel on his head. He was reading an Arab newspaper. He had looked up at them as they sat down, saying nothing, but now greeted them in Italian. Johann replied and for a while they engaged in conversation that Maria could not understand. Her thoughts drifted while they talked.

Now they would return to Italy and then home, she thought. God protect them. God forbid that something should go wrong. So many things had gone wrong. So many things. She watched as the Arab man got up and left, nodding to them, and then they were alone.

"Johann, what will you do when we get back to Vienna?" This thought had been suspended in air between them ever since they were rescued, unspoken but never entirely absent since their conversation a few days earlier.

"It's a depressing thought," Johann replied after a while. "I don't know. What will you do, Maria?"

"I don't know either," she replied.

"If Andy is still alive, if he is in America, I want you to promise me you will go to him. Go to America."

"I can't promise that, Johann. Even if he is alive, why would he want me to go to him? I told him I loved you and would marry you. Can you imagine what he must have felt?"

"I will write to him. I'll explain everything."

"Oh, Johann. I think it's too late for that now. Let's not think about that now. There will be plenty of time to think about that when we get home."

They booked passage on an Italian liner bound for Naples the next day and then wandered the streets and parks, toured the mosques and churches, killing time. They watched a colorful parade of the small French colonial army marching down the main boulevard of Tunis that evening, reviewed by the governor and Ahmed Bey. Johann sent a telegram to Allegra earlier in the day, informing him of their arrival in Naples in two days' time.

When they arrived at the pier the next morning with their baggage, Maria and Johann queued in line to pass French customs. The French customs office at the pier was in a plain white building. The French tricolor flew from a flagstaff over an arch that framed a wide double door that was open to allow a line into the lobby where there were tables set up to handle the passengers. At each table, on one side, sat a French customs agent in a dark blue uniform with the round, white kepi that French colonial and military officials wore. Another uniformed customs agent directed the next in line to a newly available empty table as the process continued.

Johann and Maria reached the head of the line and were brusquely waved to a table off to the left in the lobby. Maria could see which table it was. Her heart sank as they approached.

One of the officers from the rescue patrol was standing behind the customs agent. Johann had spoken to this man several times when they had been taken from the beach into Tunis. As they sat down, the officer was engaged in conversation with another officer and hadn't noticed them. Maria prayed that the process here would be as quick and cursory as the Italians had been when they left Naples.

"Bonjour, madame et monsieur," the customs agent said pleasantly. *"Vos passeports s'il vous plaît."*

Johann took out their Italian passports and handed them to the agent. The agent looked at the first one, which was hers, Maria guessed, because he looked at her almost immediately after looking at the picture. He started to thumb through the passport. Then he frowned.

"Vous avez été en Allemagne en Juin, 1914? Quelle a été votre entreprise là-bas?"

Before she could answer, Johann said something in Italian that Maria could not understand. She sensed that something important was being discussed. The customs guard now replied in Italian and Johann again replied.

The guard's eyes had narrowed. Maria noticed now that he had the hard face of a bureaucrat who momentarily had complete control of anyone who came to his table and their fate. His brown eyes were set in a bronzed, tan face. Jet-black hair, including a jet-black mustache, accentuated his Latin heritage. Again, he said something to Johann in Italian, then looked to Maria, and then asked a question in Italian.

Something was clearly wrong. She looked at Johann and could tell he was becoming very anxious. Again, more conversation in Italian between Johann and the guard, ending with a very brusque comment from the guard. Again, he turned to her and spoke to her now in German.

"Madame, this is very important. Listen to what I ask you very carefully. If you do not tell me the truth, you and your husband can be arrested. Do you understand me?"

Maria felt her heart pounding in her chest. "Yes, of course. I understand you. What is it you want to know?"

"Have you ever been to Germany?"

"No, never," she replied.

"Madame," the officer said in a sharp voice now. "Answer this question. If your husband says a word, you will both be arrested. Has your husband ever visited Germany in the last two years?" The officer now turned and glared at Johann, silencing him.

Maria felt a rising terror. What had he seen in the passport? And what had he said to Johann? Why was he asking these questions about a trip to Germany? Perhaps it was just a precaution, since France was at war with Germany, but something told her otherwise. Something told her that her answer to this question might make the difference between getting on the ship and being arrested.

"I don't know," Maria said quietly.

"There is a visa mark here for a visit you made to Germany. Did you go alone, Madame? I see no visa mark for your husband in his passport," the agent said, flipping the pages of Johann's passport and then turning the passport toward Maria, as if to invite her to show him the mark he had missed. Maria took the passport dumbly and fingered through it herself, saying nothing. "And yet, Madame, your passport indicates you were in Germany in June of last year. Just before the war. Had you forgotten?"

"No, I was not in Germany," Maria said, her voice quavering now, completely unconvincing.

"You speak German, Madame. But no Italian? And yet you have an Italian passport and are supposed to be an Italian citizen?"

Then the officer behind the customs agent spoke in broken Italian.

"You ... from *Ancona*, yes?" he asked.

Johann looked up at him. "Yes, we were. We were on our way to America."

The agent stood up and spoke to the officer in French that neither Maria nor Johann could understand. Several times during the conversation, one or both of them looked at Johann and Maria, sometimes pointing at them. It was maddening not to know what they were saying. Then the officer nodded and walked away.

"Please take a seat in those chairs over there," the agent said. "We will have to investigate this further." He pointed to some hard wooden chairs against the blank wall opposite the tables. The wall had nothing on it but a clock. It was 11:15 in the morning, Maria noticed.

"What just happened?" Maria asked frantically.

"The damn passport had a visa stamp from Germany. Your passport indicates that you were in Germany in June 1914. He wanted to know why. When he asked you in Italian, I said you didn't speak it. Naturally, he was suspicious."

"What did you tell him?"

"I said you were Swiss and were just learning Italian. It was all I could think of to say."

"And then?"

"He asked what language you did speak. I told him you spoke German and English and that's when he asked you about being in Germany."

"Did you tell him I was Austrian?"

"No. But then he noticed my passport had no visa from Germany. I had told him you were there with me but, of course, my passport doesn't show that."

"We're doomed," Maria said, putting her face in her hands.

"I'm afraid so."

A few moments after they sat down, the officer from the beach returned with two armed guards. He motioned to them to stand up and then swept his arm toward the door, indicating they should walk out, behind him. The two guards would follow. Their passports had evidently been confiscated by the customs agent. Maria looked at Johann. There was no panic on his face now, only sadness. *The game was finally up*, she thought. She reached out her hand to him and he took it.

A French military police car was waiting for them and took them away, into the winding streets that led to the pier and then into the Ville Nouvelle where the colonial military and civilian government buildings were. They kept holding hands in the backseat of the car with the guards in a third seat behind them, rifle butts on the floor but at the ready. There was no thought of escape.

All too soon, the police car pulled up at a building marked "Police Militaire." They were ushered into the building, down some corridors, and into another hallway that led to another hallway lined with cells. Johann was motioned to enter one of the cells and then the door clanged shut on him and was locked. Maria was then taken to her own cell, far away.

A matron took charge of her and put her into a cell and locked the door. She sat down on the bed and looked around. There was a hole in the floor, apparently for the purpose of relieving herself when the time came. A metal cot with a mattress that swung down from the wall suspended by two chains. There was nothing else. The cell was painted green and the light came from the hallway. Sounds echoed off the walls from other rooms.

They would interrogate her now, she thought. Johann would never know what she told them when they came to interrogate him. They would bluff him into giving them more evidence and then use that against her to get more. The process would continue, she knew, perhaps for days, weeks, or months until they were satisfied. They were in no hurry. She felt sick. She lay down on the cot and faced the wall. She wanted to sleep. Perhaps it was a nightmare. If she could just go to sleep, she might wake up and everything would be all right.

20.

Toulon

The French battle cruiser *Montcalm* entered the harbor at Toulon on Tuesday, June 29, 1915, with thirty-eight survivors from the torpedoed *Ancona*. Andy Bishop and most of the other passengers were topside watching the warship carefully navigate the harbor, coming alongside Pier 4. A number of the Italian passengers had family gathered on the pier below, who waved up at them. Several passengers on the deck shouted down to them and waved back enthusiastically. There was no family waiting for Andy as he descended the gangway to the pier. He watched as the Italians on the pier hugged and cried when their relative or friend finally made it off the ship.

Andy slung a small duffel bag that he had been given by one of the sailors over his back, making his way through the crowd toward the shoreline. It was the first time that his feet had been on dry land in nearly a week. A small military band assembled by the local authorities for the occasion struck up *"La Marseillaise"* as Andy walked by. A breeze of moist summer air portended a steamy, subtropical afternoon in this ancient port city that for hundreds of years had been home to the largest French naval base in the Mediterranean.

The pier was quite long to accommodate ships of this size, but at a distance, Andy noticed a man coming toward him. He was about his age and dressed in a light blue pin-cord suit with a straw hat. He carried a soft, tan briefcase. As the man approached, he seemed to be searching Andy's face with his eyes and meant to speak with him.

"Hello, sir. Are you Andy Bishop, the journalist?" the man asked. "*You speak words to many people far away who know you, but you don't know them ... they listen to what you say.*" The man was an American. His accent betrayed him as a New Yorker.

"Yes, I'm Andy Bishop. Who are you and how did you know me?"

The American smiled at having correctly guessed Andy's identity. He extended his hand. "I'm David Bernstein with *The New Republic*. I've been waiting for your arrival for the past couple of days. News that you had survived the sinking reached our office in Paris yesterday and I came down to meet you. I wonder if you could spare a few minutes to talk with me."

"I've just got off this ship as you can see," Andy replied. "I have no clothes, no money, no place to go, and no papers. There are a lot of things I need to do so perhaps we could talk some other time."

"I understand, sir," said Bernstein. "I thought that might be the situation and I'd like to help you. Let me come straight to the point. My magazine, *The New Republic*, would be willing to pay you three hundred dollars for the exclusive rights to your account of the sinking of the *Ancona*. We would like to do an article in our next publication on the submarine war. If you could spare the time, sir, I think it would be worth your while."

"I'm not familiar with *The New Republic*. What is it?"

"It's a bi-monthly magazine, sir," Bernstein replied.

"We've only been in circulation for two years. Have you heard of Walter Lippmann?" Andy replied that he had not as they reached the gate and the waterfront of Toulon. Bernstein seemed surprised.

"He's the author of *Drift and Mastery* which was published last year and he is one of the founders of our magazine. I know his book hasn't been published in Europe yet because it came out right before the war, but back home, it received great critical review. He knows President Wilson who consults him regularly, even though Mr. Lippmann lives in New York."

It all sounded vaguely interesting to Andy, but of more importance at the moment was the offer of money Bernstein had mentioned.

"Look, Mr. Bernstein, I would like to discuss writing an article for you, but as you can see, I'm a little hard-pressed right now. I ..."

"Please, let me help you," Bernstein interrupted. "I'm staying at the Grand Hotel Dauphiné in town. Won't you come with me and let me buy you lunch? And please, call me David."

The thought of food appealed to Andy. He had been eating military cuisine since his rescue. David seemed genuinely to want to help him and, more than that, anxious to get to know him. Why not? Andy accepted his invitation. In a few minutes, Andy and David arrived by taxi at the hotel.

The *New Republic* correspondent let Andy into his room, which had a private water closet, and invited Andy to bathe and join him downstairs in the dining room where he would wait for him. The bath was like heaven and refreshed Andy enormously. Unfortunately, he had to pull some grimy clothes out of his duffel bag to wear because he had nothing else, but all in all, he felt much better when he joined David in the dining room. Bernstein had been reading a copy of *Le Monde* that he lay on the table when Andy arrived. After both of them had ordered from the menu, conversation resumed between them.

"The issue of submarine warfare is huge in the States right now," David began. "There were a lot of people who thought we should declare war on Germany after the sinking of the *Lusitania*."

"What do you think about it?" asked Andy as the first course arrived at their table.

"I can see the problem from both sides," said David. "The British and the French are starving the Central Powers with their blockade. It's only natural that the Germans would want to strike back and do the same to them, but the only way to do it is with their submarines. If I were them, I wouldn't torpedo passenger ships, though. There are some people who would use the submarine issue as a pretext to get us involved in the war. Most Americans watch the slaughter here and want to stay out, but the sinkings play right into the hands of the war party."

Andy realized that this was the first time in a year that he had been in the company of one of his own countrymen. His long absence from home had given him a perspective that was probably very different from mainstream American opinion on the war. If he had never come to Europe, they were views that he would probably have shared, he realized.

As Bernstein continued, Andy noticed that not a word was said about the war in eastern Europe or the issues raised by the conflict there. It was all about the war in western Europe and Germany. "... and that's why we're so interested in your account of the sinking of the *Ancona*," Bernstein finished.

"How soon do you need it?" Andy asked.

"As soon as you can write it. Just a couple thousand

words. There's a lot happening in the war right now, but the story about the *Ancona* is still in the headlines. I don't know how much you have seen, but diplomatic notes are being exchanged between the United States and Austria-Hungary over the incident."

"I could write it this afternoon," Andy said, "but I need a place to stay and some necessities."

"I've been authorized to advance you half the money right now. We can go to my bank after lunch. I'll cash a check for you. Will that be sufficient?" *It would be more than sufficient*, Andy thought. The advance alone would pay for a room in this first-class hotel for two weeks.

"Thank you. That would be fine. I'll have the story to you tomorrow morning to proofread."

"Excellent. I've read quite a bit of your work, you know." Andy was a little surprised to hear this.

"Have you?"

"Oh yes. For news on the war in Eastern Europe, you're the best source in America right now, I'd say. You should think about your career now that you've left Vienna, Mr. Bishop."

"Call me Andy, please." Andy found himself liking this young man from *The New Republic*.

"Sure, Andy. Thanks. As I was saying, you should think about writing for one of the New York papers now. I'm sure you could make quite a lot more money than that paper in Columbus is paying you now and I'm sure one of the New York papers would pick up your column in a second. If you'd like, I'll be happy to ask Mr. Lippmann for you. He'd be interested, too, I'd think. What are your plans now, Andy? I know you were headed back to the States, but really, your reporting from here would be picked up by someone for sure."

"What about you, David? How did you get into journalism and what are you doing over here?"

"Me? Well, I grew up in a Jewish neighborhood in

Brooklyn. My parents were immigrants from Russia who came over on the boat in the eighties. They put me through New York University. When I graduated, I tried to sign up with one of the major New York papers, but they weren't hiring. Then, through family connections, I got an interview with Walter Lippmann. He had just started *The New Republic*. I couldn't believe it. Before long, I was living in Manhattan. Me! A poor Jewish boy from Brooklyn who used to deliver telegrams on my bicycle for Western Union! Before long, they sent me over here because I can speak French."

"Paris is fantastic," Bernstein continued, almost with a sigh. "Even in wartime. I admit it was a little hairy there at first when it looked like the Germans might take it last September. I had just arrived from New York to cover the war and things looked pretty grim, but the French stopped them at the Marne. The soldiers get leave once a month from the trenches and many of them spend it in Paris so the nightlife is still quite lively despite the war. Will you be coming to Paris now?"

"I don't know. Perhaps. I need to get word to my parents and relatives that I survived. And I need to find out about some friends of mine who were on the *Ancona*. I don't know if they made it or not. I haven't even begun to think what I'm going to do next. I really appreciate your advice on writing for one of the New York papers and I might just take you up on your offer on Mr. Lippmann. Right now, though, would you mind if we got that advance?"

"Of course, Andy. Let's go right now." After leaving the hotel by taxi, they visited Bernstein's bank where 750 francs were counted out and placed in Andy's hands.

"I'd like to go to the telegraph office and send off a few cables and then buy some clothes," Andy said. "Could you get me a room at your hotel in the meantime and I'll call you later when I've finished the article. Do you have a typewriter that could be put in my room?"

"Sure, Andy. I'll drop you off at the telegraph office in

the *Ville Centrale* where you'll find some clothiers nearby. There will be a typewriter in your room when you get back." In a few minutes, Andy was in front of a French post office that displayed a little symbol of a telegraph and bid David Bernstein a good afternoon.

The first telegraph he sent was to his father. He found a clerk who spoke English. He confirmed that he was alive and asked for money and news of Maria and Johann. He asked his father to wire Otto and Elisabeth to see if they had heard anything of them. He was silent about his plans to return home because, in truth, he needed some time to rethink his whole situation. He asked his father to reply to his hotel and that he send whatever money he might be due for his last articles. He spent nearly 250 francs on two suits, shirts, slacks, underwear, shoes, and some basic toiletries to tide him over until he got to Paris. By late afternoon, Andy was back at the Grand Hotel Dauphiné. He wasted no time pounding out the article that *The New Republic* so desired.

The next morning, Andy had breakfast in the hotel dining room, waiting for David Bernstein. He found in the lobby the previous day's edition of the London *Times*, evidently for the hotel's English guests. He read the news at his table.

On the western front, there didn't seem to be much activity, but in Italy, the paper reported a raging battle. The Italian ministry of war was reporting "excellent progress" against the Austro-Hungarian forces although "temporary logistical difficulties" had so far delayed the Italian armies from exploiting their "victories" over the retreating imperial forces.

Another article described heavy fighting in the east and was not particularly cheery or optimistic. There was no way to conceal the fact that a vast retreat by the Russian army had been underway for weeks. German claims of over one million Russian casualties and nearly three quarters of a million Russian prisoners taken were denied, according to the *Times*, by the Russian Foreign Ministry. Nevertheless, the war did not seem to be going well in the east for the Allies, Andy noted.

Andy realized that in his heart he was not and could not be neutral in this war, at least not the war in the east. Here, in France, he would have to watch himself. The conversations Andy had with the captain and some of the English-speaking crew of the *Montcalm* had awakened Andy to the hatred for Germany—at least among the French—and the determination that once and for all, Germany's power in Europe had to be broken, whatever the cost. The humiliating defeat of France in 1870 and the loss of her provinces in Alsace and Lorraine to the new German Reich in the aftermath of that war had guaranteed perpetual animosity between the two countries until this defeat was avenged.

Russia was France's ally against Germany and that was all that counted in this part of the world, he had come to realize. But Germany's military assistance to Austria-Hungary at the outset of the war had been crucial. Without an ally of Germany's caliber, it was clear to Andy that the empire could not have withstood Russia's immense power alone. The alliance with Germany brought with it a great liability, however. The undoubted benefit of Germany's military prowess was counterbalanced by the cost of her bringing Britain and France into the war against the Central Powers.

The waiter arrived at Andy's table with a telegram on a silver plate that he extended with a slight bow. He opened it.

```
Your mother and I are ecstatic
to receive your telegram. Wild
celebration here at word of your
miraculous rescue. Vive la France!
Sent word to Otto and Elisabeth
of your happy fate with inquires
about Johann and Maria. What are
```

```
your plans now? Please send word.
Love. Mom & Dad
```

Andy pondered his situation. From his conversations with David, he had come to realize that he had a large audience in America. It would be squandered if he returned home now and, since Maria had decided to stay with Johann, he had regretted his decision to return home. His article on the *Ancona* sinking would reach millions of readers in the next week or so, boosting his stock still further, but if he stayed in France, he would have to compete every day with all of the other writers there. He had no contacts in France or in England. Vienna and the war in the east was a niche he had all to himself, he thought. As David Bernstein approached his table, Andy thought that he should discuss David's proposition.

Andy handed David Bernstein his article. Wordlessly, David read it as the waiter brought them coffee and croissants. Eventually, he laid it on the table and looked at Andy.

"Brilliant. Absolutely brilliant. It's exactly what we wanted. I'm going to cable this to New York this morning. I doubt they'll edit a word of it. In a week, ten million Americans will know this story."

"David, I've been thinking about what you said about writing for the New York papers."

"After this," David said, gesturing to the pages on the table, "you'll be the talk of the town." He meant New York, of course. "The papers will be lining up to get your byline, if that's what you want."

"What would *The New Republic* be prepared to offer?"

The remark brought a smile to David's face. It was clear that this suggestion was one that he had already considered. "I'm quite sure Mr. Lippmann would be very interested. He's already said as much. What did you have in mind?"

"Five hundred a month plus travel and living expenses when outside of Vienna. I want to return to Vienna and continue reporting on the war in the east from there. If my articles are syndicated, my father's newspaper gets them free. I don't know if I'm out of line here as far as salary goes, but it seemed fair."

"It's more than we pay any of our other writers, but let me ask Mr. Lippmann. You're not just any writer anymore, Andy. I'm sure Mr. Lippmann will want a contract—say three years with one article every two weeks, delivered one week before our deadline. The lawyers in New York would prepare it, of course. All copyrights assigned to us during the contract. That sort of thing." Andy nodded. "You could probably do better with the *New York Times* or the *World*, but the pace would be much more frequent and more hard news rather than the essays you do so well."

"If you can do that deal, David, I'd consider it. If not, then I would appreciate any help you could give me with the New York papers. I'd rather write for you guys, though."

David smiled again. He stuck out his hand. "That's great, Andy. Let me see what I can do. Now, is there anything I can do for you right now? If not, I need to get this to New York."

"How soon will you know? I'd like to make plans for returning to Vienna soon. I still don't know if my friends survived. I'll have to discuss this with my father."

"A day or so, I would think," David replied. "Like I said, Mr. Lippmann had already raised the subject." With that, David walked toward the lobby, leaving Andy with his thoughts.

Andy was pleased with his own boldness. If *The New Republic* agreed, his annual salary would exceed the price of his parent's house in Columbus, he thought. Reimbursement of his travel expenses would mean he could travel virtually anywhere in Europe to cover the war.

In the afternoon, David returned with a check for the rest of his advance and reassured him that he should hear back from *The New Republic* the following day or the day after—at the latest. In the meantime, he suggested that Andy visit the American consulate in Marseilles to get a new passport. This Andy accomplished the next day. The consul wanted to meet Andy to express his personal regards for this minor celebrity and rushed through the paperwork for him. A passport was granted and prepared for him on the spot. Upon his return from Marseilles to the hotel that evening, another telegram awaited him.

> Otto and Elisabeth say Johann and Maria survived shipwreck and are in Tunis. Efforts being made to return them to Vienna, but contact difficult due to the war. Nothing heard from them in days. Will you stay in France? Mother and I fear another sinking in Atlantic should you try to return now. Please let us know your plans. Love, Dad

Andy thought back to the last time he had seen Maria and Johann in the chaos aboard the *Ancona* and how he had watched the little white lifeboats making their way to the shoreline, hoping they were aboard one of them and felt weak. He had to sit down and then, to his own surprise, began to sob quietly in relief. They were alive! The concierge noticed and quietly came to him.

"Monsieur, is there something we can do for you? Are you all right?"

Andy nodded his head. "Friends ... just heard ... survived the sinking of the *Ancona* ... in Tunis," he croaked. The concierge smiled and placed his hand on Andy's shoulder.

"*Mais, monsieur,* this is wonderful news. Let me bring you something." In a minute, he was back at Andy's side with a small glass of cognac. "Please, monsieur. With our compliments." He handed over the glass and Andy drank it down in a couple of gulps. The liqueur coursed its way down his throat to his stomach and warmed him. He thanked the concierge, who patted him on the shoulder and then quietly returned to his desk where he began spreading the news to some of the other hotel staff.

In a few minutes, a small crowd of bellboys, valets, and waiters had gathered around the concierge to hear the news. As each new staff member arrived, another one pointed in Andy's direction to the smiles and nods of the others. David Bernstein came down the stairs into the lobby. The concierge intercepted him. He pointed across the lobby at Andy as he told him the news. David approached with a wide smile.

"Andy! Great news! I'm so happy for you. Let's have a drink!" At that, there was a rush from the staff who gathered around the two of them, each extending his hand, and congratulating Andy, who had regained his composure. Smiling now, Andy thanked them, touched by the show of support. He had seen this before. The French always assumed that, while America was neutral, the sympathies of Americans were with them, their oldest ally. The French never tired of pointing this out. Now, the French spontaneously wanted to show where their sympathies lay.

Andy and David Bernstein entered the dining room and sat down to discuss the day's events. David ordered a bottle of champagne.

"New York is very receptive about your proposal. As you know, we have no correspondents in Vienna at the moment. It would fill a gap for us, they think. They loved your story. It's all going swell, Andy. What are your plans for tomorrow?"

"I don't know. I was thinking about that earlier. I was thinking that I could check the schedule of trains leaving for Switzerland tomorrow and begin planning my return to Vienna. I suppose that's the best way to get back, under the circumstances. I was just thinking it might be possible to get a telegram to my friends in Tunis tomorrow, but I don't know where they are, exactly, or how to get word to them."

"I'm sure we could get some help from the French authorities here. They might have information where the survivors are staying."

"Yes, I thought of that too, but it's a little delicate." Andy briefly explained the awkward situation Maria and Johann had been forced to deal with in Italy after the declaration of war. David listened intently.

"I see what you mean," David said quietly after Andy had explained the problem. "It's a very difficult situation, obviously. I wish I had a suggestion for you, but nothing is coming to mind."

"I know. I wonder how they're managing right now."

"Well, they can't sail to Switzerland from Tunis, so they must be thinking of finding some other way back home. The countries to which they could sail from Tunis would not be very friendly. The countries that would receive them from Tunis would likely be hostile."

"I need to get to Vienna as soon as possible. I don't know what else to do."

The more Andy thought about Maria and Johann, the more uneasy he became. His earlier elation had now been superseded by a growing anxiety about their safety in Tunis. The more he thought about it, the more Andy realized just how precarious their position was.

Andy awoke early and, after a brief breakfast, he walked to the *Gare de Toulon*. After some investigation, he determined that there was a train that left for Geneva every morning at 10:15. There was no information available regarding Swiss trains leaving for Austria, of course. He would just have to figure out how to get to Vienna after he got to Geneva. Once he heard from David regarding whether his proposal was accepted, Andy would make definite plans.

As he walked across the street from the train station, Andy noticed a little café. A few tables were outside. There, seated at a table was a woman reading a newspaper who caught his eye. It was Katarina von Dürnstein. As he approached her table, she seemed to sense his presence and looked up. Her shock and surprise at seeing him was complete. She stood up, awkwardly and then extended her hand.

"My God, Andy. You survived! I had no idea."

"And you, Katarina ..." Andy took her hand in both of his. It seemed vaguely inadequate to convey his surprise and happiness at seeing a familiar face in Toulon. "I've been wondering what happened to you ... and your brother."

At the mention of her brother, Katarina's slowly shook her head. "We think he must be dead. We were separated at the boats, you know ..." The Italian accent, now suddenly sad. "Please, sit down. Won't you join me? I want to know what has happened to you since, you know ..." Andy sat down and for the next hour they exchanged their stories. Katarina was clearly moved by Andy's harrowing tale, her eyes widening as he told her about his last moments on the *Ancona* and stifling a cry with the back of her hand when he described the night he had spent in the water.

"If only we had known," Katarina said as he finished. Katarina had been taken aboard one of the lifeboats he had seen while sitting in the water that night. Hers had almost no passengers and she was, at least at first, the only woman.

"It was shameful, really. The crew thought only of their own safety and wouldn't wait for passengers. One of them grabbed me, I suppose, because I was a young woman and then they lowered the boat. I think they rowed a different way than the others because of how they acted. Anyway, we were out there all night. It was dreadful. You could hear voices crying for help, but they had no light. We went to the sounds they made and sometimes we found one or two. I suppose they made up for what they had done a little bit that way.

"In the morning, we saw one of the French ships. The *Jeanne d'Arc* picked up our boat and brought us to Toulon. We were told eventually that some of the other passengers had been rescued at sea by the navy and some went to Tunis and some came here. I just came yesterday. The French told us that there was no information about my brother, but they found your name. I was so happy, Andy. I asked where you were, but they didn't know where you had gone."

"What are your plans now?" Andy inquired.

"My father insists that I return to Milan."

It occurred to Andy for the first time what an unusual woman Katarina must be. She was quite independent, now that he thought of it. Andy had never seen her brother aboard the ship, yet she had not hesitated to converse with and spend time with Andy, a stranger. Here she was again, making her arrangements independently, without any man to guide her or take care of her. *A modern woman*, he thought. He liked her.

"And you, Andy? What are your plans now?"

He told her about the developments of the past few days and his decision to return to Vienna. Her face displayed an intense interest, her cool blue gaze never wavering as she listened and nodded occasionally.

"When are you leaving for Milan?" Andy asked.

"Friday. At 10:25." The idea came to both of them at that moment, but it was Andy who spoke first, knowing intuitively her answer to his question.

"Would you care for me to join you as far as Milan? Then you wouldn't have to travel alone. I could leave for Switzerland from there, and then to Vienna."

She hesitated. "Oh, I couldn't ask you to do that. It would be out of your way," she replied unconvincingly. A sweet smile crossed her face.

"Not at all, Katarina. It would be my pleasure. I would appreciate the company, actually. It would be far more bearable to be with a companion than to go on my own. You would be doing me a favor."

"Well, since you put it that way, it would be rude of me to say no. Thank you, Andy."

She insisted that he stay with her family for a day or two when he arrived in Milan and before he resumed his journey to Vienna, which Andy accepted. He walked her to her hotel and then made his own way back to the Grand Hotel Dauphiné where he rang David's room.

"It's a deal, Andy," said David Bernstein over dinner. "Since your story will run in our next publication, it will give you two weeks before the next deadline." They discussed how he would cable his articles from Vienna to David in Paris. Over coffee, they discussed the war and *The New Republic's* editorial policies.

"The war is not going well for the Allies at the moment, Andy. The stalemate is continuing in the west, although the British are now building up a huge army in northern France, probably for an offensive soon. It's obvious now that the Italians have been defeated along the Isonzo with heavy losses and the Russians are retreating also. It seems that the Germans have managed to concentrate a much larger part of their army against the Russians than was thought possible. The Austro-Hungarian forces to the south and the Turkish invasion from Armenia are giving the Russians all they can handle and more," David related.

"I must tell you, Andy, that Mr. Lippmann supported a declaration of war against Germany after the *Lusitania* was sunk. Initially he was for neutrality, but the submarine war has tipped the balance at home against the Central Powers.

There's no hostility toward Austria-Hungary in America. Even some sympathy because of what happened in Sarajevo. Maybe your articles have something to do with that, Andy. But Austria-Hungary is Germany's ally and Mr. Lippmann thinks that we will eventually go to war with Germany. I just want you to know that."

"I understand," Andy replied. "What if Germany and Austria stop the submarine war—at least against passenger ships? Would that change Mr. Lippmann's mind?"

"Perhaps, but that hasn't happened yet. And a lot of American businessmen and bankers are making a lot of money trading with Britain and France, let's face it. Sinking cargo ships, even, ruins their profits. They have a lot of influence in Congress, Andy. There's a lot of American money invested in the Allies now. Then there's the issue of democracy. France, Britain, Belgium, and Italy are democratic countries like us. The Central Powers are monarchies."

"What about Russia? That's the most despotic country on earth," Andy exclaimed. "Germany and Austria have parliaments. They may not be like us, but they're not like the tsar."

"No, they're not, but I'm just saying. There are a lot of powerful people in America who are looking for an excuse to get us into the war. Theodore Roosevelt openly ridicules Wilson as a coward. So far, the president has resisted them, but if the war goes on much longer, who knows?"

Andy found himself appalled at the thought of his own country entering the war. It was complicated, he conceded, but the possibility of a Russian victory in the east seemed in his mind at least as dangerous as a German victory in the west. In Andy's mind, the United States should stay neutral and hope that—before much longer—some kind of peace would be negotiated where both possibilities were precluded.

After taking leave of David Bernstein that evening, Andy found it difficult to sleep. Perhaps his taking this position had been too hasty. Yet he needed the money, the connections, and the backing of this emerging, popular magazine to support his own desire to remain in Europe and see the war through. And then, the decision he had made and regretted to leave Vienna had been rectified. He would get another chance and he had taken it. *"You will return to your home, but you will never live there again."*

The next day was the Fourth of July. It was also his last day in Toulon and he awoke late in the morning after a fitful sleep. He wrote out a long telegraph to his father, explaining his plans and the deal he had made with *The New Republic*. He felt a twinge of guilt at having made this career choice alone, without consulting his father, but he hoped his father would understand his decision. He spent the afternoon shopping for more clothes and luggage. At dinner, he explained to David Bernstein his plans to accompany Katarina to Milan before returning to Vienna.

"I almost forgot, Andy. Here are your press credentials and some cards I had made. Just don't forget the deadlines, Andy. This business lives on deadlines. And remember to cable me where you will be staying in Vienna when you get there. I'll be back in Paris by the time you get to Vienna. Here's my card. It has my address on it. I've put the cabling instructions on the back."

David had become a friend and Andy felt grateful to him for everything he had done since meeting him on the pier at Toulon. His fortunes had changed dramatically since that forlorn day and most of it was due to David Bernstein.

"I can't thank you enough for everything you've done, David. I hope you may come and visit me in Vienna soon and see how things are there for yourself."

"Don't mention it. Come back to France anytime you get the chance. You know where to find me. This is a great opportunity for both of us. *Au revoir,* my friend, *et bonne chance!"*

21.

Diversions—Italy

The von Dürnstein's mansion on Lake Como could fairly be called a palazzo, Andy reckoned. As he sipped from a glass of cool Italian white wine on the wide, semi-circular terrace that jutted out over the surface of the lake some five meters below, he thought that the sunset he was witnessing might be the most beautiful one he had seen in a long, long time.

Golden rays played on the forest that cloaked the mountainous hillsides on the opposite shoreline, perhaps three or four kilometers away. The façade of the Venetian-style, stone and plaster house was in the shade that cast itself halfway across the terrace. Pillowed chairs were arrayed in both the shade and the sun so one could choose the warmth or the cool evening air that breezed off the lake. Andy watched a passenger boat passing by on its way from Como to Bellagio through the dark blue waters of the lake.

Andy and Katarina had explored the ancient village of Bellagio earlier in the day together and Andy had been fascinated again by its almost medieval architecture. It seemed hard to believe that he, Maria, and Johann had visited this same place just a few weeks earlier. So much had happened since then. The von Dürnstein's property was within a short boat ride of Bellagio. The war raging in the Alps a few hundred kilometers away might as well have been on the moon for all the impact it made in this idyllic setting.

Katarina had intrigued Andy too. An initial reserve on the train ride from Toulon had soon given way to mild flirtation after they reached Milan and her family. It turned out that her late brother was, well, not actually her brother, but a business associate of her father who had been sent to "escort" her to New York. That part, which came in a little confession, was a bit vague. Nonetheless, Katarina's charms had gradually eroded his own reserve. The initial plan of merely stopping along on his way to Vienna to hand Katrina off to her family had evolved into something else. He had now been with her nearly a week and his intention to resume his trip to Vienna had been postponed twice. He felt relaxed in this beautiful setting and Katarina's vivacious personality awoke in him a spark of romantic interest that had died by Maria's hand in the Stadtpark of Vienna months earlier. He couldn't deny that it made him feel good to be so looked after by such a pretty woman whose destiny had crossed his own in the most bizarre way.

Katarina—the youngest of the von Dürnstein family—had an older sister and two brothers, but she was clearly the most spirited of them all. At the train station, Katarina's mother cried with relief as she hugged her smiling daughter tightly. Her father, Frederico, was able to maintain his composure, but quietly hugged her to him before turning to Andy. Katarina had seemed mildly embarrassed by the overwhelming display of relief and affection, discreetly rolling her eyes at Andy at one point.

"This is Andy Bishop, Papa, an American," Katarina said in English. Apparently her father understood it, but initially he said nothing, just looking at Andy with some surprise. "He was on the *Ancona,* too, and we met again in Toulon. He volunteered to escort me home on his way to Vienna. Wasn't that nice of him?"

Andy's luggage was next to where he stood on the platform, making it awkwardly obvious that Katarina had invited him to stay, but Katrina had forgotten to mention it in her introduction. Frederico extended his hand and in slow, heavily accented English, thanked Andy for his gallantry, as he put it, with the cordial but wary look of a father taking the measure of possible suitor. An invitation to stay at their summer home was graciously extended by her father as Katarina and her mother, speaking rapid-fire Italian, bustled toward their car.

"Vienna?" politely inquired von Dürnstein as they settled in the car.

"Yes, Papa, he's a reporter for a magazine in America," Katarina said, turning around from the middle seats with a happy look on her face. Her father cast a reproving but indulgent look.

"I'm sure he could have told me that himself, my dear."

"Yes, signor," Andy replied. "Vienna. I have relatives there and I'm taking up a new post to report on the war."

There was no apparent reaction from Frederico von Dürnstein's face when Andy mentioned his unusual assignment. Unusual considering that Italy was now at war with Austria-Hungary and Andy was in the process of going from one to the other.

"Ah, yes. I see. I have relatives in Austria too. As Katarina might have told you, our family came here from Dürnstein in Austria several generations ago. The war is a tragedy for us, as you can imagine. My two sons are in the navy."

"Yes indeed. If you had seen what I have seen of it already, it's a tragedy for everyone."

"Of course. Do you speak Italian?"

"Only a few words, signor. I speak only English and German."

"Ah, you speak German?" von Dürnstein replied, and

then continued in German. "I don't get a chance to speak much these days, but I imagine your German must be better than my English." The accent was largely gone now and his grammar was excellent.

Andy regarded the older man carefully. He had a full head of largely gray hair streaked with black, but his eyebrows and mustache were almost completely black. Slender and aristocratic in build and posture, he lounged comfortably in the plush seat of the car. Long, fine hands with manicured fingernails were folded casually in his lap as he gazed back at Andy. Frederico von Dürnstein's most prominent features, however, were his large, almost protuberant brown eyes that completed the transformation of his Austrian heritage with a mainly Latin appearance. Only his last name suggested his non-Italian heritage.

Angela, his wife, seemed of different stock. She was tall for a woman, with blonde hair and a fair complexion. She had obviously been a beauty in her day and was still a handsome woman. Although undoubtedly wearing a corset, her figure even now was quite good. Her blue eyes were soft, but the lines of her face betrayed the effects of the Italian sun and her age. It seemed that Frederico and Angela had a good marriage from the little touches, kisses, and affections that unabashedly occurred from time to time in his presence.

"My father is a businessman in Milan," Katarina confided to him. "He owns a company there that manufactures leather goods sold in Italy and all over Europe and even the United States. His company was given a big contract from the government to make leather boots for the army, but Papa still thinks that the war is a big mistake."

"It's a disaster, as I knew it would be," Frederico explained in another conversation a couple of days after Andy arrived. "The peasants of this country will never fight for the king and the rich. They're all socialists or anarchists. They don't care if we capture Trieste or take Dalmatia or the Tirol from the Austrians. That's what it's all about. We cry when the

Austrians supposedly oppress our countrymen in the Tirol, but think nothing of subjecting the Austrians to us. An Italian will fight hard for his homeland if it's invaded, but not to support rich, capitalist politicians' dreams of conquest."

Worse than that, the war had started going badly for Italy. To the amazement of the world and the chagrin of the Italians, the Austrians and their smaller, multinational army had repulsed assault after bloody assault, giving almost no ground and inflicting terrible casualties. The Austro-Hungarian Empire did not collapse, as the Italian newspapers had gleefully predicted when war had been declared. The rocky terrain of the Alpine region was especially cruel to Italian soldiers as Austrian artillery shells shattered rocks into showers of deadly shrapnel, maiming and crippling those who were not killed outright. Hospitals in Milan and all across northern Italy were filling up with soldiers with hideous wounds. It was all so familiar. *It was all so depressing*, Andy thought.

This evening, Angela and Frederico had left to have dinner with friends near Como. Katarina's bookish older sister, Constanza, had remained behind as a discreet chaperone. Katarina had gone to her room to "freshen up" for dinner, which would be served on the terrace. She now reappeared, dressed in summer white, with a glass of wine in her hand. She glided over to the stone railing and looked out at the passing boat.

"It's really beautiful, isn't it?"

"Yes, stunning." Her blonde hair was swept up and glinted in the evening sun. The reflected rays off the water played on her white dress and face as she stood quietly, perhaps taking in her effect on him as much as the view. She seemed to become more beautiful every day as he got to know her better, Andy thought, and she was clearly interested in him, he had concluded that afternoon. He moved toward her and clinked his glass to hers.

"Cheers, Katarina, to the *Ancona*. I would never have

dreamed while I was sliding into the water that a few weeks later I would be sipping wine with a beautiful woman in such an amazing place. I'm so glad we're alive, aren't you?"

"I never thought I would die until long after," Katarina said as she sipped her wine, acknowledging the compliment with a smile. "It's ridiculous now, but I just naturally assumed that somehow I would survive—and I did. Now when I think about it, I shudder. I know we could both be dead. Do you think it's for some purpose, Andy, or just random chance?" Her blue eyes looked earnestly into his, blinking as she said it.

"I don't think God gets involved in our fate, if that's what you mean. I don't think God spared our lives for some purpose to be fulfilled. If God got involved in human affairs, he'd stop this war, wouldn't he? He gave us free will to do what we want. That's what I believe."

"But God may have some plan for us that we don't know. Maybe it was meant to be." Her ambiguous statement hung in the air for a moment. The servants had finished making up the table and were lighting candles with some difficulty due to the breeze off the lake.

Constanza joined them and listened with her sister as Andy related a few of his experiences of the past year. Constanza was amazed that Andy had met Archduke Franz Ferdinand only weeks before his assassination and listened with rapt attention to his encounter with the murdered heir at the Hohenzoller Falls.

"Why did they shoot his wife?" asked Constanza. "That's what I could never understand. She was an innocent. Only a savage man would do such a thing. It was like when the kaiser's wife was murdered in Geneva by an Italian. Luigi Lucheni. I'll never forget it. How could he murder an innocent woman? I remember what Lucheni said. 'I wanted to murder a royal. It didn't matter which one.' He didn't even know her. It was the principle of it. Anarchism. I suppose it was the same with Princip. He didn't even know them. He wanted to kill a Habsburg. It didn't matter which one."

"People say it was just a murder," Andy said. "They happen all the time, people say. He was a crazy man, like Lucheni, people say. But it wasn't just a murder. Princip had nothing against the archduke personally, let alone the duchess. He wanted to provoke a war. He was the tool of people in the Serbian government who wanted a war and then pretended to be the victim when the war came."

"Well, then, he succeeded, didn't he?" Katarina said.

After dinner, the night air became chilly and they moved inside. The windows were left open. A cool breeze occasionally wafted into the room. Conversation shifted amiably to Andy's youth in America and the places in America that Constanza and Katarina wanted to see someday. After a while, Constanza announced that she was going to retire for the evening. Andy stood up and bid her good-night.

"I should go to bed too, Andy," Katarina said. Constanza looked over at Katarina, nodding in agreement. They both knew that it would not be proper for Katarina to remain alone with Andy at this time of the evening. Andy took Katarina's hand and bid her good-night as well. The sisters left the room together. Katarina looked back as she was about to go through the door with a mysterious smile and then she was gone.

In his room, in bed in the dark, Andy found it hard to get to sleep. He thought about Katarina and what she would be like to hold in bed. He wanted her. He knew that he shouldn't, but he did. And he thought she wanted him too. Fantasies entered his head of situations that might arise the next day or the day after that alternately shamed and aroused him.

Sometime after midnight, Andy realized that his mind was not going to allow sleep to come. Annoyed, he threw aside the bedcovers and dressed in slacks and a shirt. The house was quiet. In bare feet, he opened the door and quietly closed it behind him. Dim light from a window at the end of the hall illuminated shapes and shadows as he reached the stairs and began his descent into the huge atrium where he, Katarina, and Constanza had sat a few hours earlier. Nervously, carefully, Andy opened one of the doors to the terrace and stepped out into the moonlight.

The lake was black and calm and the image of the moon hanging above the mountains on the opposite shore reflected in the water like a long line of chalk, smeared in a thick milky line across the surface. It was chilly and Andy wished that he had brought a blanket. The cold slate of the terrace tortured his feet and, in a few minutes, Andy retreated back inside. He had not been in the house for more than a few seconds when he heard a door close. He froze. He imagined the embarrassment of explaining to Frederico what he was doing in the middle of the night walking alone around his house. Then out of the corner of his eye, he saw a shape at the top of the stairs, silently gliding down to him.

The figure said nothing and, in the dim gloom of the room, Andy could not tell at first whether whoever was coming down the stairs had even noticed his motionless form. He felt his heart beating as the figure reached the bottom of the stairs and began advancing toward him. It was Katarina.

"I couldn't sleep," she said in a whisper.

"I couldn't either."

Then she was in his arms. They kissed, but then she pulled away.

"Come, let's sit down," she said breathlessly. She led him

by the hand to a large couch in the middle of the room under a darkened chandelier.

"My father. He mustn't know. Not yet."

"Of course."

"He's very suspicious. Very protective, Father is," she said. "It's too much to explain right now, Andy, but he mustn't know."

"Know what, Katrina?" Andy whispered.

"How we feel about each other," Katrina said, pulling away from him gently. "You do like me, don't you, Andy?"

Her blunt question surprised him. He had only a few seconds to think and reply. She was looking at him expectantly.

"Yes, Katarina. Of course I do." She bent forward and kissed him on the mouth.

"Good. Now I can sleep," Katarina said rising.

"What are you going to do?"

"I'll see you tomorrow morning, Andy."

Confused, Andy watched her figure recede into the darkness and up the stairs until she vanished from sight. It was like a weird dream and for several minutes, as he sat alone again in the hushed darkness, Andy found himself wondering if it had really happened. Gradually, he began to climb the stairs and return to his room, hoping to sleep and trying to imagine what was going to happen next with this tantalizing woman.

The next morning, Andy sat down to breakfast and was soon joined by Katarina and Constanza. Idle conversation eventually turned to what they might do that day. Katarina suggested that they should go horseback riding and take a picnic with them. Constanza hated riding and immediately turned it down—to Andy's silent relief—and as Katarina no doubt knew she would. A compromise was reached. Constanza agreed to take the boat to Bellagio while Katarina and Andy would proceed along some mountain trails beside the lake on horseback. They would all meet in Bellagio for a late lunch, rather than the picnic Katarina had originally proposed.

Andy took little part in the discussion, amiably agreeing to virtually any suggestion either sister made, but at the end of the discussion when the plan had been agreed, Katarina shot Andy a sly smile. Andy's heart leaped. He smiled back and nodded discreetly. They would be together. Alone. They both knew it. Andy thought of the sensual kissing of the night before.

Katarina met Andy at the stables half an hour later in an English-style riding habit. The jacket fit her form perfectly, Andy noticed. Her long legs were accentuated by high black riding boots. Her hair was captured under the black velvet cap, all of which gave her an almost boyish appearance. She refused to ride in womanly fashion, dismissing it as old fashioned, and Andy could tell by the way she swung herself into the saddle that she was quite experienced. Her horse was spirited, yet she seemed completely unconcerned and mastered the beast easily. Delighted, Andy nudged his own horse after hers toward the trailhead.

The paths through the mountainous forest were sometimes narrow and at other times quite wide. Panoramic views of the lake through the tall, alpine trees punctuated their ride and a number of times they stopped to take in the view. The path was deserted. Perhaps if the war had not taken so many men into the cavalry, they might have met others on the trail, but it seemed as if they were alone on their morning canter.

After about an hour and several such stops, Andy dismounted at another beautiful spot. They were in the midst of the forest and they had reached a little mountain stream that rushed by them over rocks and fallen trees.

"There's a waterfall over there," Katarina said. "Would you like to see it?"

"Yes, I'd love to." Andy couldn't take his eyes off her ahead of him as she walked casually along the path. *Her figure was perfect*, he thought. She didn't look back at him.

It wasn't long before Andy could hear the sound of falling water and then they came to a small pool where a waterfall plunged from a height of perhaps twenty meters. White water churned near the middle of the pool at the bottom of the cascade, the source of the sound he had been hearing. They silently tied their horses to a tree. For a few minutes, they watched the water in silence.

Andy took her hand quietly. She turned to look at him, but made no move to take her hand back and instead gazed at him expectantly.

"Were you really with me last night, Katarina?" She put a finger to his lips as if to quiet him. A most beguiling smile came across her face. Slowly, softly, she ran her finger over his lips. He let her do it, bewitched by her seductive power. He pulled her toward him. Her eyes never left his, but gently closed as Andy's mouth pressed on hers. He could feel her respond as he pulled her ever more tightly to him and he kissed her again and again. After a few minutes, she pulled away gently.

"If there is to be something between us, I'd like to know, Andy," she said seriously. "I am very attracted to you. I suppose you know that by now."

"I was hoping ..."

"Yes, I was hoping too. It started on the ship. I liked you right away, but it was nothing, was it? We were going different places, weren't we? But now ..."

"I don't know where I'm going, Katarina, except to Vienna. Eventually. I didn't expect this to happen."

"No, nor did I. And yet there you were, at the train station. In Toulon. And I thought, perhaps God had plans for me. It was quite a coincidence, no?"

"Quite. I must admit. I suppose what I call random chance, you give credit to God. You know I don't believe that, Katarina. And my life in this past year has convinced me more and more that the plans we make and the intentions we have are nothing. My intentions and plans have all been ignored by the Almighty or overtaken by random chance. I came to Austria for a holiday and became a journalist. I wanted to discover the reason why my ancestors came to America. I still have no answer. I fell in love with a woman, Katarina. I might as well tell you. I thought she loved me and would come to America with me, but she didn't. I thought I would return to America and then the *Ancona* was sunk beneath my feet. Nothing has turned out as I planned or expected. I have few plans now and no expectations. I'm sorry, Katarina. Perhaps it was a coincidence we met again, perhaps random chance. What difference does it make? Whatever I might say about you or me would be just words. Anything can happen, Katarina. Anything."

Katarina had listened intently to him and, when he was finished, she paused and then spoke.

"You're right, Andy. It doesn't make much difference, does it? Here we are, though, and what I feel is what I feel. Here is the question I have. It has been barely a week. We have gotten to know each other a little. The time is coming when you will have to leave, I know. Will that be all, then? Shall we part as friends? Or is there something more in you for me? You kissed me just now. That is not a great thing, but it is not nothing."

"No, it was not nothing, Katarina." He kissed her again. In truth, he couldn't answer her question. He knew that he was still raw and hurt by his affair with Maria, but he needed to move on. Everything he had seen of Katarina had delighted him and there was no reason that he could think of not to continue, but instinctively he held back. It would be difficult to come back here from Vienna and, as an Italian, she could certainly not visit him—even if she would.

Objectively, there was a lot against it. And he didn't want to hurt her. He didn't want her to hold out for him when he had, he thought, so little to offer.

"Here is my answer, Katarina. I can't promise anything but that I will come back to see you again as soon as I can. I do like you. Very much. We haven't had much time and precious little is left. Too little to say more than that and be honest. I want to be honest with you. If anything is to come of this, let's be honest and realistic from the start, shall we?

"Yes. Of course," Katarina replied. "But you must promise me that you will write and tell me what is happening to you in Vienna. And what your true feelings are. If you decide it's not to be, then you must tell me. And I will wait for you, Andy. Because, whatever you say, I believe there was a reason we were spared. I believe there was a reason we met again."

"All right, then, Katrina. You have my promise."

Soon they remounted and continued on the mountain trail on horseback. Andy watched her body undulating with the slow rhythm of the horse's strides. Was it lust or love? He must be careful. Occasionally, Katarina looked over to him, smiling, but saying little, pointing out a pretty sight now and again, but otherwise saying little. There was nothing else of consequence to say—or was there?

Katarina was not like Maria. Andy had always been racked by uncertainty with Maria. He had never known exactly where he stood. Her flashes of affection or passion seemed inevitably followed by withdrawal to cool reserve. The ecstasy of those few intimate moments floated in an ocean of hopeful anticipation and angst that had eventually carried him to the shipwreck of their parting.

Katarina was not like that. She minced few words. She was direct and sincere, as far as Andy could tell in the short time that he had gotten to know her. Where Maria was intellectual, Katarina, while not unintelligent, was sensual.

Where Maria seemed on a journey to find her true self, to unlock the paradox of her aristocratic birth with her attraction to Marxism, for example, Katarina seemed content and secure with who and what she was. While Maria had veered here and there as far as her life path, probing and searching, Katarina appeared to have a firm idea of what she wanted and, for the moment, Andy felt flattered that it was him.

The appearance of a small cottage as they came out of a bend in the trail foretold the approach of the village of Bellagio. As they continued, the path became cobbled with brick and their horses' hooves clattered methodically as they eased into ever narrowing streets.

"What took you so long?" Constanza asked as they arrived at the tavern where they had agreed to meet.

"I took Andy to see that lovely waterfall along the way and it seems we lost track of time," Katarina said breezily. Constanza regarded her sister with a mild, questioning glance, but did not press her further. Lunch was pleasant as was another walk through the quaint town at the foot of the mountains, jutting out into the lake. Eventually, Katarina and Andy saw Constanza off at the pier and then made their way back to their horses.

"We need to hurry. It will be dark in a couple of hours," Katarina said as she swung up into the saddle of her horse.

So much of what he had seen in his time in Europe had turned out to be deceptive and inexplicably complex, Andy thought as they rode back to the villa. The frank conversation with Katarina that afternoon contrasted with the conception of Europeans Andy had imagined before his journey began and even the impressions he had been led to believe were real when he had first arrived.

The outward façade of old Europe was breaking apart with the war, Andy realized. Perhaps it was because of the war, or perhaps it was the other way around. Perhaps it was the immense strain of maintaining the outward appearances of old Europe's institutions and conventions that, in a way, was a cause of the war itself.

The old boundaries of class and civilized behavior that Americans saw from a distance covered deep, conflicting undercurrents that Andy had now seen from close proximity. Perhaps the blood and energy devoted to the titanic struggle had sapped the strength of European society to suppress them any longer. Whatever the outcome of the war, Andy thought, the societies that emerged hereafter would be quite different from what he had observed when he had arrived in Europe, a naïve boy from Ohio.

In a couple of hours, Andy found himself at dinner with Katarina's family. He watched and listened as conversation at the table flowed back and forth largely in Italian with occasional polite breaks in English for Andy's sake. The food was delicious. Andy watched absentmindedly for the most part as Katarina spoke to her parents and her sister, pondering the events of the day. Finally, Andy announced to his hosts that he would be leaving the next day, thanking them for their hospitality.

The next morning, at the train station in Como, Andy boarded a train for St. Moritz in Switzerland and began his journey back to Vienna through the Alps. Alone with his thoughts, he gazed at the scenery that passed by his window as the train climbed higher and higher into the mountains, snowy and icy even in July. He wondered when he would be able to see Katarina again and under what circumstances. He wondered what lay ahead when he returned to Vienna.

He was looking forward to seeing Elisabeth and Otto again, and wondered about Maria and Johann. He realized that he hadn't thought about them in many days. He worried about them, but what could he do? *Somehow they would return to Vienna*, he thought. He realized that meeting Katarina had dulled the pain of his disappointment in losing Maria, but it was still there. Imagining Maria with Johann still pained him, but he must get on with his life and it wasn't so bad, was it?

On July 15, the train passed through Swiss customs far more easily than he had thought it would. There were not a lot of passengers on the train by the time it reached the border so the customs officials came through the cars fairly quickly. He was alone in his compartment when the door slid open and he presented his American passport. In German, the Swiss guard asked him a few questions about his purpose for visiting Switzerland. He seemed unconcerned that an American would be passing through his country into the Austro-Hungarian Empire and in a few moments was gone.

The train was soon rolling through the Alps and Andy found his mind wandering. He found himself thinking about what had been on his mind a year ago at this time. His thoughts turned again to why his ancestor, Matthias von Windischgrätz, had left the empire back in the eighteenth century, as the train passed through several tunnels in the mountains. Had Matthias von Windischgrätz never left for the New World over 150 years ago, Andy knew that he wouldn't exist. He thought about the gypsy in Rome for the first time in a while. *"You will discover a dark secret that has been kept for more than a century. It is about your ancestors and your family. You will find why they left their land long ago and this knowledge will change your life."*

What was it that had made him leave their homeland? He decided to renew his personal quest when he got back to Vienna to see if he could finally solve this mystery that the gypsy had predicted would change his life. What could it be?

The train pulled into St. Moritz in the early afternoon. It was a small train station and, after consulting the timetables, he found that it would be several hours before the train for Salzburg and then Vienna would depart. It was quiet, with few passengers sitting or walking around the lobby. He purchased a Swiss newspaper and, for the first time in quite a while, he caught up on the news of the war.

The news regarding the Italian war would not be censored, Andy guessed. The neutral position of Switzerland, precariously situated between the two warring alliances, would make accurate and timely reporting of the war of crucial interest to the people here. Initial worry that, like Belgium, they might be used by one power to pass through and outflank another had caused a precautionary mobilization of the Swiss army in 1914, Andy remembered, but now the Swiss would have settled into their position as spectators of the massive struggle going on beyond their borders.

The Battle of the Isonzo River, as the Swiss press called it, had ground to a halt. The collapse of the offensive was being noted with satisfaction in Vienna by the minister of war, Alexander von Krobatin. Andy had met the minister months earlier when he had been reporting from Vienna. There was even some talk of an all-out invasion of Italy to come, but this was unlikely, according to the newspaper. The Austro-German offensive in Russia was still gathering momentum, and it was doubtful that Austria could spare the troops for the Italian front.

Vast chunks of Russian territory were being gained by the Central Powers and the military editor thought that before much longer, Warsaw would finally fall. On the western front, the stalemate had continued since the Second Battle of Artois had fizzled out in late May. All in all, Andy concluded, the war was going surprisingly well for the Central Powers—and amazingly well for the Austro-Hungarian Empire after its initial disasters.

The train to Salzburg was even emptier than the train to St. Moritz had been. Snowflakes in July fluttered down as the train headed east, high into more mountain passes. The train reached the tiny border town of Martina at about 7:00, discharging passengers for the last time in Switzerland and then heading across the bridge over the River En into the Monarchy. The train chugged to a halt in Nauders where it was boarded by imperial customs officers in dark blue uniforms. They were quite old, Andy noticed, much older than the Swiss. *The young men were off to war*, Andy thought.

Once again, Andy presented his American passport. The exit stamp from Italy, freshly printed from earlier in the day, drew some questions from the guards. Andy explained that he was a reporter from an American magazine—bound for Vienna—and showed his press credentials. His luggage was opened and searched, but after a short time, the officer handed Andy back his passport and wished him well, closing the door behind him. Soon, the train gathered steam again and slowly started its night passage into the Reich and back to Vienna.

22.

Trials and Tribulations

Maria watched from her prison bed in Paris as a large black spider delicately traversed its silken web to capture a fly that had strayed into its lair. The fly struggled to free itself from the sticky trap, but as it struggled to escape, it became even more entangled in the sticky twines of the net. Patiently, the spider waited and watched as its victim quickly tired and the fly's twitching and thrashing became more and more feeble. Then, as the fly paused to regain its strength, the spider attacked, biting and paralyzing the fly, whose fate was now sealed in a gauzy bundling that the spider employed to preserve it for an eventual meal.

Maria had learned that *La Prison de Saint Lazare* had held its victims fast in its dark, cold embrace since the Revolution of 1789, including the doomed French queen, Marie Antoinette, herself an Austrian and a Habsburg. Its gloomy stone corridors and cells had seen little improvement in the 127 years of intervening time. Maria's cell had only a single caged window that looked out into the courtyard of the prison and only briefly, in the late afternoon, did the rays of the sun shine into it. A cot and a two bowls were the only things in the room. One bowl contained water. The other functioned as a chamber pot. There was no provision for her to bathe except once each week an extra bowl and sponge were delivered to her cell for this purpose. Nights were cold and days were hot and the ever-present smell of mold and wet stone permeated everywhere.

The door to Maria's cell also contained a small barred window through which the sun never shone. The sounds of the prison echoed down the corridor into her room. Doors opened and closed. The ravings of other female inmates and their pitiful sobs punctuated the silence from time to time. Her own sobs had filled the room and corridors in the early weeks that she had been imprisoned, but lately she cried very little. It did no good, and the spontaneous, unbidden episodes of grief and panic had subsided, enveloped in a never-ending, mind-numbing boredom. She had prayed many times and felt, in her lonely isolation, a closeness to God that she had never felt before. It had become her only comfort.

From her bed, she heard the footsteps of a guard approaching the door and then the sound of the key in the lock. Maria was surprised because it was not yet time for the delivery of her meager breakfast of bread and coffee and she swung her bare legs from the cot to the floor. Her feet felt the coldness of the stone. A matron of the prison was behind the door that swung open. Another male guard stood in the corridor outside.

"*Mademoiselle,*" the matron said, holding a dress in her hand that she flung at her from the middle of the room. She turned and walked to the door, retrieving a bowl of water, a sponge, and a cake of soap, which she set down on the floor. "*Vite, Mademoiselle. Je reviendrai. Dix minutes.*" The matron held up all ten fingers. Maria understood enough to know that she was supposed to bathe, dress herself, and be prepared in ten minutes—but for what?

As she lathered the sponge with the soap, she examined her naked body. She had lost a lot of weight, she knew. Her skin had lost the light tan color from Tunis and was now a milky white. There was no towel to dry herself so she used the clothes she had slept in the night before and then put on the dress that had been given to her. True to her word, the matron was back in ten minutes. She placed handcuffs on Maria's wrists behind her back, pocketed the key, and nudged Maria toward the door.

It took several minutes for Maria and the two guards to make their way down the corridor, down the stairs, and out into the courtyard. It was an overcast day as they walked across the cobblestones, Maria noticed. Then into another corridor, up another flight of stairs, another long corridor, and finally they arrived at another room where Maria was escorted to a chair and made to sit down. The male guard left the room. The matron sat down in another chair, waiting. After a few minutes, an older man, perhaps in his sixties, entered the room through a door opened for him by the male guard.

The man was dressed in civilian clothing: a dark suit and tie. As he put his black bowler hat down on the table, Maria noticed thinning gray hair, a gray mustache and goatee with pince-nez glasses over dark, brown eyes. He carried a briefcase, which he laid on the table with his hat, and then he sat down across the table from Maria where he regarded her for a few moments before saying something to the guard in French. She nodded, moved to Maria's back, removed the handcuffs, and then left the room.

"Fraulein," the man said gravely in French-accented German. "My name is Gerard Villiers. I'm a lawyer and I have been appointed to represent you at your trial. I understand you have been a prisoner here for some two weeks. You are charged with espionage for the Central Powers. I suppose you know that in wartime this is a crime punishable by death. They say you were arrested with a former officer in the Austro-Hungarian army attempting to use a forged passport to embark from Tunis to Italy. Beyond that, I know nothing."

Maria regarded the old man warily. His brown eyes were magnified in his glasses as they gazed steadily back at her. Had he said "death"? It surprised her how little fear or emotion she felt as she contemplated his words and her situation. So she was facing a death sentence?

It was all so unreal. So ludicrous, in a way. How could things have gone so far? She looked away at the large window with vertical bars on the outside. She could see a large courtyard leading to a gate. Outside the gate, she could see cars and horses passing in the street. She listened and could faintly hear the normal, everyday sounds of a city for the first time in weeks. A woman with a baby carriage caught her eye. The woman pushed it across the breadth of the gate without looking at the prison. She looked back at Monsieur Villiers, saying nothing.

"Fraulein, I am here to help you if I can. Anything you tell me will remain here in this room. I know that this is all very strange to you, but in order for me to help you, you must trust me."

Trust him? She thought about that. He looked like a lawyer, but he was a French lawyer. He was a lawyer for an enemy country with whom her own was at war. What could she really expect? The weeks of confinement had dulled her thought process, she knew. Try as she might, she just couldn't make herself think clearly. It was like a dream. A nightmare. Why had they not returned to Austria when they had had the chance?

"Mademoiselle. Will you let me help you?"

It took so much energy to answer him. So much energy. There would be so much to tell and she was so tired. She tried to think. It really didn't matter anymore whether she trusted him or not. He was the only hope she had. If he was a spy, then she was doomed anyway. If he was a real lawyer, perhaps there was some hope.

"Monsieur. I am innocent. I am not a spy."

The lawyer blinked at her first words to him, then leaned back in the chair.

"Then, my dear, why don't you tell me what happened."

For the next hour or so, Maria told Villiers her story. The circumstances of the trip to Italy. The sudden declaration of war and her attack of appendicitis. Her stay in the hospital. The aborted trip to America and the sinking of the *Ancona* at sea. The rescue. The stay in Tunis and her capture with Johann as they were attempting to leave and return to Austria.

The lawyer made notes as she spoke, interrupting every so often with a question or two to clarify one point or another, but mainly letting her get it all out. At last, she came to the end of it and stopped. Villiers put down his pen, removed the pince-nez, and rubbed his eyes with his fingers.

"My dear, I have much work to do on your case, but I don't think it is hopeless. I must tell you, however, that we must gather some corroborating evidence and you must be prepared to tell the truth to the court. The judges will be very interested in the contacts you and your friends had with the Austrian agent in Rome while you were there and again in Tunis."

"I don't know much about him. Most of the time, it was Andy or Johann who spoke with him."

"Yes, but you must understand that the authorities here will want to identify this man and his network of spies in Italy and, unless you are prepared to give complete details of who he is and what he did, they will view you as an accomplice and …"

"And I will be found guilty."

"Undoubtedly. And possibly executed. Let's leave this detail for a moment. I have some more questions about some of the other matters you mentioned."

Another hour or so went by as the lawyer pressed her for

details and still more details, checking his notes and writing still more as she answered his questions as best she could. Finally, Villiers put down his pen again.

"This is enough for today. Your trial is scheduled to begin in a week's time. There is much I need to do to prepare. Is there anyone you know here in France who could vouch for you? Someone who knows you who could testify at the court that you are not a spy. Someone who could verify or corroborate any of the information you told me just now?"

Maria could think of nobody. She had never been to France before, so of course, she had no friends here. Then she thought of Johann.

"What has happened to Johann? Of course, he could verify everything."

"I know nothing of his case. I don't know if he was brought to France or not. If he is here, I will try to find him. What about your American friend? It's likely that his testimony would find more favor with the judges than that of an—"

"Another Austrian. Yes, of course," Maria replied. "I don't know if he's alive. If he's alive, I don't know where he is. Yes, of course, he could verify everything too. Can you find him?"

"Perhaps, Fraulein, but it will take time and we really don't have much time. I will take my leave of you now, my dear, but I will be back. We will meet again before the trial. Let me see what I can find out in the meantime." He gathered his notes and carefully placed them inside his valise. Then the old man walked over to her and took her hand. He placed it in the palm of one hand and put his other hand over hers.

"Courage, my dear. Courage. This has been a terrible mistake. You are a beautiful young woman. The court will hesitate to convict you if they believe you are telling the truth. I will bring you some new clothes when I come again that you can wear in court. Say nothing to anyone else about your case unless I am there. Nothing. This is France. We have a republic and we have laws and rights. Don't give up, my dear."

With that, the old man let go of her hand, picked up his leather case, and knocked on the door. The guard appeared in a moment and let him out. In a few minutes, the matron returned and took Maria to her cell.

Villiers adjusted the bowler on his head as he walked slowly out the gate into the tenth arrondissement and the *Rue de Paradis* and then to the metro station at the *Gare de Nord* railway station. It was a difficult but compelling case, he thought to himself. Only a week. It was so unfair. They could have given him the case weeks earlier when she was first brought to Paris, he thought. Perhaps it was a sign of weakness. Perhaps they knew that, with time, they could be defeated. Yes, that was it. They had a weakness. What was it?

He arrived at his little office on the *Boulevard Raspail* on the Left Bank at noon and quickly summoned his secretary, Valerie, and his grandson, Emile, who had followed him into the law just a year earlier.

"Listen to this," Villiers said to them as they sat down. He explained the case to them in detail, referring to his notes as they listened in silence. After he finished, he looked up at them.

"We have much work to do and little time. I need you to drop everything you are doing. Valerie, I need you to ring the hospital in Rome. See what you can find out. Get some documents that show she was a patient there. Then the hotel. Ask for the maitre d' there. Allegra. Documents. That's what we need. Anything to prove that she was there and that she had appendicitis."

"Emile, I want you to find out about the other prisoner. What's his name? Yes, Johann von Caboga. See where he is now. If he is in Paris, prepare an application to summon him to the court on Monday. The same for the American, Andy Bishop. See if he survived. Contact the Italian shipping lines. Find him. Quickly now, we have no time to lose."

"Grandfather," said Emile slowly. "Why did you take this case? There is no money in this. They're Austrians. We're at war with Austria-Hungary. Why are we doing this?"

Gerard Villiers sank back in his chair for a moment. Again the pince-nez came off and he rubbed his eyes.

"Emile. This is the French Republic. Do we have justice in this country or not? Are we barbarians? Do you want to see this young woman executed by a firing squad if she is innocent?"

"If ..." Emile replied. "If. How do we know she's innocent? What about the passports? They were obviously in contact with enemy agents in Italy. What about that? They lied about their citizenship. Why were they coming back into Italy?"

"Yes, yes, I know. I know. I haven't got all the answers right now, but she's innocent, I tell you. I know it. She's no spy. For now, just do as I tell you. We'll talk about it more later. Now go!"

As Emile and Valerie hustled out of the room, Gerard Villiers gathered his favorite beret and a walking stick. This was not a case that was going to be quietly tried in the bowels of the *Palais de Justice* if he could help it. *It would be easy for the government to convict on marginal evidence if there was no publicity*, he thought, *but not so easy if the world was watching*. The world. Yes, that was it. *Le Monde*. The London *Times*. The *New York Times*. A survivor of the *Ancona*. A beautiful young woman. On trial for her life. *There would be some interest in that*, he thought. He would make the rounds this afternoon, then back to work on the pleadings and the case.

Chip Wagar

Two days later, Gerard Villiers called upon the prosecutor, André Mornet, a lieutenant in the French army, at his office near the *Ecole Militaire* on the *Champs de Mars*. Like the Villiers, the Mornets were a family of lawyers spanning several generations. Villiers had known Mornet's father professionally for years before his untimely death. André had been wounded in the Battle of the Marne in 1914, losing his left arm above the elbow. Unfit for active military service so, due to his legal background, the army had transferred him to the military bureau of prosecutions. At thirty-two, Mornet was a "youngster" in Villiers' eyes, but the aging "Lion of Raspail" had long ago learned to take every opponent seriously.

"You are looking well, Monsieur Mornet," Villiers began amiably. "How are you managing?" He meant the arm, without saying it.

"It's difficult sometimes. I won't deny it. What can you do?" Mornet picked up a pack of cigarettes on the table and shook out several with his right hand, offering one to Villiers. The old lawyer took one. With the fingers on his right hand, he pinched one of the cigarettes while holding the pack, letting the others slide back inside and then laying it on the desk. He picked up a matchbox and held it out to the older lawyer.

"I still have trouble with these. Would you mind?"

Villiers took the matchbox, slid it open, and took out a match. He struck it on the side of the box and held the flame to Mornet's cigarette, lighting it and then lighting his own. The two men smoked for a moment, contemplating one another across the desk.

"Would you like some coffee?"

"Yes, thank you."

Mornet rang a little bell on his desk and, in a moment, an orderly appeared.

"Would you fetch Monsieur Villiers and me a *café au lait*, please?" The orderly nodded and left.

"Interesting case, this Montfort woman," Villiers began.

"Really? How so?"

"Well, there's really nothing to it, is there? I wonder why the government even bothers."

"Espionage is a serious matter, Monsieur."

"Indeed. Have you wondered why the Austrians would put two of their own spies aboard a ship they intended to torpedo? A ship bound for America?"

"Perhaps the sinking of the *Ancona* wasn't planned, Monsieur. Perhaps it was just random chance that two Austrian submarines happened to cross the path of the ship when they did, not knowing that two of their agents were aboard."

"And what state secrets does the government contend they passed on to the enemy? That's what spies do, don't they?"

"I'm not at liberty to say," Mornet replied coolly. "After all, if that were disclosed, it would no longer be a secret, would it?"

"But if they're spies, then the enemy already knows the information. What is the point of keeping it secret now? Are you saying you're going to prosecute my clients without proving any act of espionage on their part? That's tantamount to prosecuting them merely for their citizenship and that's beyond the pale, André. May I call you André?"

"Why yes, of course," Mornet replied warmly. For a moment, he forgot about the war and remembered only the eminent advocate from his days as a fledgling lawyer. His father had known Gerard Villiers. Everyone in the legal community of Paris knew Gerard Villiers. The Lion of Raspail. Then a thought crossed his mind. How had this

Austrian woman gotten so lucky to have such a powerful representative in court?

"May I be candid with you … Gerard?"

"Please do."

"It's not her we're after. We're interested in her fiancé and the American she was with in Italy. We're interested in the spy network operating in Milan and Rome. We're interested in any involvement the Vatican may have had in facilitating activities in Italy and Tunis. I admit, she is not of major importance to us. The information she has is of significant importance to the republic and she must be prosecuted as an accomplice if she will not cooperate with us."

"I see," said Villiers. His mind raced with possibilities and cards yet to be played. "So if my client were to give you this information, then what of the prosecution?" Gerard was, after all, a lawyer. Specifics. That was what he now sought from Mornet.

"A passport infraction. In Italy. A fine. Sent home."

"What makes you think my client knows all this information?"

"She knows. We've interrogated Monsieur von Caboga. We have pieces of it already. We need more. We know she knows."

"I would like an opportunity to question Monsieur Caboga myself, André. Will you allow it?"

Mornet shrugged in the Gallic style. Perhaps.

"Yes or no, André?"

Mornet stood up and reached for his kepi. Villiers stood as well, taking Mornet's action as terminating the conversation, but it was not.

"Please, Gerard. Walk with me for a few minutes. It's a beautiful day." Mornet took the older man's arm respectfully and guided him out the door. In a few moments, they were out on the Champs de Mars. It was a gorgeous summer day. The overcast skies from earlier in the day had burned off. The Eiffel Tower loomed in the distance. Paris at war. It wasn't so bad. Not today, anyway.

"Yes. I agree. I will let you interview Johann von Caboga. You, on the other hand, will discuss my proposition with your client and let me know immediately if she is interested in cooperating with us. If she does, a passport violation and deportation. If not, then the prosecution is continued."

"When can I see the prisoner, Caboga?"

"When will I know your answer?"

"Within a day after I meet him," Villiers said, stalling for time.

"Very well. You can see Caboga today if you want. Tomorrow. He is here in Paris. *La Santé.* The prison infirmary, however. I understand he may not be in good health. One leg, you know. Nice chap, I will say. Funny, even. They're not like the Germans. An aristocrat for sure. Wounded in the war with Russia right at the beginning."

"And you want this man in front of a firing squad?"

"No. Not really. But we're in a war, Gerard. We need to know things. We need to know who our friends are and who our enemies are. We know the Germans have even penetrated the *Deuxième Bureau* itself with double agents." The Deuxième Bureau was the French espionage and counterespionage service, controlling all French spying everywhere in its empire and across Europe and the Mediterranean.

"So it's the big fish you're after?"

"Exactly."

"Not my client or her fiancé?"

"No."

"Thank you, André. You have been very candid and, I might add, very professional. Your father would be proud of you."

After a few more minutes of pleasantries, Gerard Villiers parted company with Mornet and began making his way to La Santé, the prison for men, located in the Fourteenth

Arrondissement where Mornet had revealed the young von Caboga was confined. Villiers knew the prison well. It was a maximum-security facility used to hold prisoners sentenced to death before their executions, which were publicly performed by guillotine on the *Boulevard Arago* beside the walls of the prison.

Time was running out, Gerard Villiers thought as he hailed a cab. There was so much he could do, but much that he couldn't simply because he had no time. One thing he hadn't mentioned to Mornet had been an adjournment. He was annoyed with himself at this lapse. Could it be that he was fading? He wondered. He was sixty-four, after all. Gerard hated being old and that he was even thinking this about himself. His energy, so remarkable in a man his age, his friends thought, was diminished. He had money. Why did he keep doing this? Most men his age had quit the practice of law. Maybe they became judges where the workload was easy and the pay was, well, *pas mal*.

It was the thrill of a challenge. It still made his adrenaline rush. The whole thing. The stress of preparation. The battles in the courtroom. Matching wits. It made him feel alive. It made him feel ageless. When he was involved in a big case, he was the caged lion let loose. His whirlwind preparations were legend. *Let's hope not just legend*, Villiers thought. The taxi was nearing the entrance to La Santé. Villiers pulled out his billfold and paid the cabbie with a nice tip and then stepped out of the car.

Security was very tight at the prison. The exterior was posted with military police and that was the first check-and-search of many. Some of the guards at a particular checkpoint recognized him and passed him through. Others, the younger ones, did not and insisted on all formalities. Another half hour passed in discussions with the superintendent, who had received a phone call from Mornet, he confirmed, over where he would meet the prisoner, for how long, under what conditions, and so forth. It was all tedious and Gerard Villiers was growing impatient. At last, he was escorted to the prison infirmary and then to a medical conference room used by the prison doctors.

Sitting in a wheelchair next to a window, in a gray prison robe, was *Le Compte,* Johann von Caboga. His hair was long and stringy and he had a ragged, unkempt moustache and stubbly beard. He looked gaunt and pale to Villiers, a common appearance among prisoners here if they stayed for long. The food was terrible and the general conditions filthy.

"Greetings, *mein Herr,*" Villiers said.

"And to you, sir," Johann croaked. His voice was raspy, but audible. He was very alert and his rheumy eyes never left his guest.

"Did they tell you why I am here?"

"No. They simply said that there was a lawyer here to see me and they wheeled me in here."

"I see. Are you all right?"

"I wouldn't say so, monsieur ... what was the name?"

"I beg your pardon. Villiers. Gerard Villiers, Your Highness. Of course, I know your name."

"It seems so. Tell me, Monsieur Villiers, what can I do for you?"

Villiers told him of his representation of Maria and her upcoming trial for espionage. As he spoke, he noticed the manacle around Johann's right ankle. It was chained to the wheelchair. *Paranoia,* he thought, *but that's how prisons were.*

"So you've seen her? You represent her? Tell me about her. I want to know all about what has happened to her and how she is doing." Villiers was being diverted from his main train of thought. There was a purpose for his being there, after all. But he knew under the circumstances that he would get nowhere without first acceding to this poor man's request. He told him everything. More time, Villiers thought, but Johann von Caboga listened with rapt attention.

"What do you need to know, monsieur?"

"Let's start with the passports."

For the next hour, Johann calmly explained their predicament and their mistakes. If the *Ancona* hadn't been torpedoed, all would have been fine, but it had and it wasn't.

"There is one thing I must ask of you," Johann said as the interview concluded.

"What's that?"

"The maitre d'. Allegra. He has been a valuable friend to us. To my family. I can't reward him with this."

"He's an enemy spy to the people of France and Italy."

"Yes. I know. But he's a human being too. France and Italy have spies." Villiers thought of Mornet's words about the Deuxième Bureau. "I only ask this. If it is necessary to save Maria's life, then you must give him up. But otherwise, get him a warning to disappear before they get him."

Gerard thought about his instructions to Valerie a day earlier to contact the maître d' to get confirmation of the appendicitis and the fact that his client had indeed been a guest at the hotel. If Valerie had done her job as efficiently as she usually did, Allegra knew already that he would be a wanted man quite soon. He might already have dived underground.

"The only other name is the priest in Tunis. I would think him unlikely to be arrested by the French authorities there. I'd rather not, but what would you think, monsieur?" Johann began coughing and for a few moments, he struggled to stop. A bloody rag in his hand Villiers noticed that he dabbed at his mouth. *So that was it*, Villiers thought. *Tuberculosis*. He had seen it before. Too many times.

"I apologize, monsieur. I'm afraid there may be some

more interruptions like this. They say I am not eligible for transfer to a sanitarium just now. What can one do?"

This was a sorry situation, Villiers thought as he considered Johann's earlier question. Even *in extremis*, there was a certain casual but forlorn nobility to him that was so familiar among Austrian aristocracy. He had spent some time in Vienna years ago when he had been a guest lecturer at the Medical University of Vienna. He had attended many parties and balls and met quite a number of Austrian aristocrats. The invariable melancholy mixed with fatalistic humor and laconic remarks came back to him.

"I would think you're right, but here is what I will do. There's a good chance Signor Allegra is already aware that he should 'disappear,' as you say. I will not be a traitor to my country, but I will relate to him the circumstances of the situation and, if he should conclude that he should disappear, then I'm sure he will do so. That's the best I can do."

"Then I accept. Anything to save Maria's life. There is one more thing, though."

"Oh? What is that?"

"The American. Andy Bishop. Did anyone ever find out if he survived? We were never sure. Did you hear anything about him?"

Villiers recalled the interest that Mornet had expressed in the American. There were at least three people he now knew who were interested in the existence and whereabouts of this mysterious man.

"No. Do you know of any reason the French security service would be interested in your friend?"

"No. I don't. He's an American. A distant relative of another Austrian family. Their sons are good friends of mine. He came to visit as a tourist right before the war. We became such good friends, though. In such a short time, he was a better friend to me than I have ever had. It's that kind of a thing, monsieur. I was just wondering."

"I'm sorry I can't tell you. I had never heard of Andy

Bishop before a couple of days ago. I will try to find him. If he would corroborate your story—and Maria's—he could be a great help at the trial. But even if we find him, he might not be able to get here in time to testify. The trial is now only a few days away."

"Contact the von Windischgrätz family if you can. In Vienna. Otto and Elisabeth. I don't know how you could do it. But if you can contact them and ask about Andy Bishop, they will know."

Another day. Wednesday. Back at his office on the Boulevard Raspail, a telegram from Rome awaited him.

```
Hotel di San Floriano.
The documents you requested will
be delivered Thursday. And others
you may find helpful. A.
```

The message was short and to the point. Villiers reflected a moment. Mornet was not entirely wrong. The alacrity with which the response had arrived from Valerie's discreet inquiry suggested an "interested party." Someone who was very interested in the acquittal of Maria von Montfort. Allegra probably was a spy. But of course he was. That didn't mean his client was guilty, but she and her friends were not entirely innocent either. That's the way the tribunal would look at it, he knew.

Thursday, July 15. Villiers called at *St. Lazare* promptly at nine o'clock to see his client. After the usual, endless tedium of officious security checkpoints and formalities, he was eventually alone again with Maria an hour later. Every hour's waste infuriated him, but there was nothing to be done about it.

Villiers explained the situation carefully to Maria and she listened intently in silence. Her eyes welled with tears at his mention of Johann, but still she said nothing, listening to his entire report without a word. When he was finished, she wanted to hear all about Johann's condition and was clearly appalled at his description of his physical condition, the wheelchair, and the infirmary.

"So, what do you recommend? I don't know much of these things personally. I was in the hospital in Rome most of the time after war was declared. They told me these things. Andy and Johann did. What if they ask for details? I can't give it to them. They'll know I'm lying."

"They will want to know what you know. They can't ask for more than that. I can easily establish the truth of your appendicitis and the unusual situation in which all of you found yourselves. There are some things they want to confirm."

"Johann is still in prison. If I say what I learned from him, won't this hurt his case? My evidence will confirm that he was in contact with Austrian spies. That he procured illegal, forged passports. That the Roman Catholic Church facilitated our getting another set of false passports and money. Isn't that true? And then he will be convicted."

"I have been given assurances that the Republic of France is not going to prosecute you and Graf von Caboga, at least not much, if you cooperate and confirm the evidence they almost entirely have in their possession already, my dear. I must tell you, however, that is not my concern. My only concern is your acquittal and release to return to Austria."

"Yes. But you're a lawyer. Johann is my fiancé. He's in desperate circumstances. What assurance do we have that if I give them this information that he will be set free?"

"Assurances such as that are not written down, Maria," the old man said to her gently. "They are made between honorable men. The military prosecutor handling your case told me this himself."

"And you trust him?"

Villiers thought about it for a moment, but only a moment. "Yes."

"And Johann said that I should do this?"

Again. "Yes." He knew that would be what Johann would want him to say. Fly if you can.

"Then I leave it in your hands, Gerard. It seems everyone has thought this out far better than I can. You see all the pieces of it, don't you?"

"Yes, I think I do. Sometimes I'm wrong, my dear, but not often."

Back at his office, a package had indeed arrived from Italy. Greedily, Villiers leafed through it. Hotel bills. A notarized affidavit from the concierge of the Hotel di San Floriano confirming the incident of the appendicitis. The police had been notified when it happened.

Another affidavit from the Ospedale di Spirito Sanctus confirming Maria's confinement there until a few days before their departure from Italy. These would be helpful to a point, but there were still gaps.

Interest had been registered in the media. There was a post on his desk from an American magazine, *The New Republic*. *Le Monde* had a very small mention of it in the front section of the news. Only a paragraph or two, but still. *Espionage trial of an Austrian aristocrat ... Arrested in Tunisia ... Italian government said to be interested in the trial.* It was something. The American and British newspapers hadn't seemed to notice.

He opened the letter from the American magazine and glanced down to the bottom of the letter to see who it was from. David Bernstein. Paris editor. *The New Republic*. His card was enclosed. The letter was brief and requested an interview. "Very interested" in the story. Excellent.

"Valerie. Have a taxi bring this letter to a Mr. Bernstein at his office." As his secretary began to stir from her desk, Gerard scribbled out a reply, concluding that he would call at four o'clock that afternoon and hoped to find him in. He couldn't wait for Bernstein to come to him. There wasn't time. He would have to hope for the best. There was just time for lunch and "the Lion" walked out the door. He picked up a newspaper and headed to a nearby bistro.

It was a beautiful day again. The weather had cleared. He was waved to a table at *Le Coq d'Argent*. His favorite waiter brought him some cheese, bread, and his usual glass of wine. It was a good wine, actually. For the regular customers, the house kept a bottle of *Chateau Neuf de Pape* available—as Villiers knew. It was a little robust for some at this time of day, but Gerard Villiers loved it—as the restaurant knew. After so many years around the corner, there were no culinary secrets between Le Coq and Gerard Villiers.

The newspaper rarely made pleasant reading these days. The Germans still occupied large swaths of French territory and almost all of Belgium. Nothing seemed to be happening. *It was like a siege from the Middle Ages*, Gerard thought. The French and British were besieging the German castle, without much success. The British blockade and a land stalemate would eventually starve Germany into defeat, he thought, but it could take years.

The eastern front looked dire. Every day brought fresh news of defeat and retreat as the Central Powers advanced on virtually every front. The Serbians were barely still in the war. Even the Ottomans were advancing in Russian Armenia. *That's the worry*, Gerard thought. If Russia makes

Chip Wagar

peace, Germany and Austria will be able to crush Italy and perhaps even break through the French or British lines with millions more soldiers released from the Eastern Front. Who would collapse first? As he sampled the cheese, he began to think about what he would tell Mr. Bernstein that afternoon. It was a risky move to bring the press into this, he thought, but he had been taking calculated risks all his life.

23.

Return to Vienna

Andy slept fitfully on the night train to Vienna, unable to sleep through the intermittent stops it made in Innsbruck, Salzburg, and other small towns along the way. There was little to see during the night as the train made its way along, except in the stations, which were practically deserted. A little more than an hour from the capital, the sun rose and he could see the rolling hills and villages of Lower Austria passing by his window. He felt exhausted and even a little nauseous from the ordeal.

At the station in St. Pölten, the door to his compartment opened and a handsome man entered his compartment, asking politely if he could join him. It was Stefan Zweig.

"Andy?"

"Yes, how are you? What are you doing here?"

"I'm on my way back to Vienna. And you?"

"The same. Have you heard what happened to us?"

"No. The last we heard the three of you were leaving for America, but here you are! What happened?"

Andy told him about their trip to Italy, the sinking of the *Ancona*, his rescue and separation from Maria and Johann.

Stefan listened with growing wonder at each twist and turn of the story. Maria? In Africa? What will they do now?

A porter offered coffee and rolls. Thinking that if he could eat something, he might feel better, Andy bought a coffee and a croissant. Stefan declined with a wave of his hand. As the porter served the coffee and rolls, the conversation paused. Then, turned to what Zweig had been doing.

"I'm working on an antiwar play now that I call *Jeremiah*. They haven't arrested me yet," Stefan continued, seeming amused at the prospect, "but I don't know how much longer that will go on. I'm thinking of moving to Switzerland before the war gets much worse. It will get worse, of course."

"I don't know," said Andy. "The newspapers in Switzerland don't think it's going too well for the Entente. The Russians are retreating. The British seem to be taking quite a beating at Gallipoli. The Italians have been defeated badly along the Isonzo."

The porter announced that the train was fifteen minutes from the Vienna *Westbahnhof*. Stefan stubbed out his second cigarette, blowing the smoke toward the window.

Zweig agreed. "Who would have thought it? But how much longer can it last? It's been a year, now, hasn't it? And no end in sight. A whole generation being ground into powder. And for what?"

"Your country was attacked," Andy ventured, keeping up the conversation.

"Were we? A provocation it was, the assassination, no doubt. But it was a trap and we walked right into it. It's what they wanted us to do. The Serbs. The Russians. They wanted us to attack, don't you see?"

"What would you have done?"

"Well, we shouldn't have taken Bosnia in the first place. That's what got us crosswise with the Serbs and the Russians. We didn't need to do that. We brought more Slavs into the empire and Serbian Slavs at that."

"It's all been going on for hundreds of years. A province

here. A province there. It's the sport of kings and emperors. What do the people get? Blood and death and poverty. It was bad enough a hundred years ago when there were professional armies, a couple of big battles, a few barns, and houses burned in a war that lasted a few months. Look at it today. It's millions dead and lives ruined, vast areas laid waste, and a year of war already."

"If everyone thought like you do, the war would be over."

"Exactly, but people do think like I do. It's just that we're so docile. Our patience and capacity for suffering is monstrous. That's the mystery. The kaiser calls us to arms and voilá, off we go. Why? That's the question. You Americans fight for causes. Your civil war, for example. To end slavery. The revolution. We Europeans fight for provinces and prestige." Zweig shook his head in dismay.

Andy told Stefan about his new position with *The New Republic*. Zweig was visibly excited as Andy explained what his new assignment would be.

"Tell it all, then. You must tell them the whole story. Everything is not about emperors and territory. Tell your readers about the Vienna you know. How we really are. How we have ideas and hopes. Come and see us at the Café Central again. Everyone will want to hear your story and about Maria. Thursday night. All of us who are left will be there."

"I will," said Andy. "I'd like to quote some of you in my news stories."

"I'm not sure about that, Andy. There are the police, after all. It's not like before the war. The military controls everything nowadays. Maybe not direct quotes, but you can give your readers the idea. Would it make any difference?"

"No, I'd still like to come if they would have me." The train would be at the station in a few minutes.

"Excellent. Thursday evening, then. People start

wandering in around seven o'clock. You know how it is. Just come by. I'll be there. Get another perspective, let's say."

The train was slowing down, passing through the switching yard that foretold its final approach to the station. It was time to gather their things and get off.

"Auf Wiedersehen, Andy." They shook hands again.

Andy had telegraphed Otto and Elisabeth when he was in Switzerland that he would be arriving on Saturday, July 17. When the taxi deposited him at their house, his heart sank as he saw black bunting over the door. The sign of death in wartime Vienna. In an instant, the anticipation of seeing Otto and Elisabeth again was replaced with dread. Who was it?

Andy rang the doorbell and in a moment, it swung open. Otto smiled and embraced him wordlessly at the door. As they pulled apart, there were tears in his eyes. Elisabeth was also red-eyed as she came to him and embraced Andy as well.

"Thank God you are safe and have come back to us, Andy."

"Who is it?" Andy asked.

"Ernst. A few weeks ago. In Italy." Otto said quietly. "We had his funeral last week. He was so very fond of you, Andy, even though he was …" He couldn't finish the sentence. The remembrance of his lost son choked the words short.

"I know," Andy replied. "I'm so sorry. He had become like a brother to me."

Like the scythe in the hands of the mythical Grim Reaper, this was what happened every day in Vienna, Budapest … in every town and village of the empire. Like a plague, it made no distinction between high or low, rich or poor. Andy had never struck up the close personal bond with Ernst that he had with Rudi, but still, he felt an enormous sadness as they talked. As they sat down to tea in the salon, Otto told him the details that they knew of the engagement where Ernst had fallen. How proud they were of him. But he was lost. Forever. There was no escaping that.

Ernst had been the image of the young aristocratic heir who Andy had always imagined populated the halls of privilege and wealth of imperial Austria. Handsome in his gold braided uniform and plumed hat. Unfailingly correct. Conservative in his views, yet tolerant of other opinions. He had unquestioningly done his duty for crown and empire and laid down his life for it. The manner of his death, as an officer in the service of the Habsburg emperor, had been the fate of countless young aristocrats before him on the battlefields of France, Germany, Italy, and the Balkans over six centuries of Habsburg rule. Generations of Windischgrätzes had served and died for the monarchy when called. Ernst's name would now be added to the immortal list.

Rudi appeared from somewhere. "Hello, Andy," he exclaimed, embracing Andy with a wan smile. "I came home for the funeral. I'll be going back to the front in a few days. It's good to see you, Andy. I heard about the *Ancona*. Thank God you're all right."

"And you," said Andy. "Where have you been?"

"Galicia, mostly," Rudi said. "I'm a pilot now. I was allowed to fly home. We're operating deep in the Ukraine now. I'm flying with Julius Arigi's squadron. Have you heard of him?"

"No. Who is he?"

"He's our top ace against the Russians. A great flyer. He taught me to fly. I'm his wingman now."

"There's something else, Andy," said Elisabeth, interrupting. "It's about Maria von Montfort. We just received word that she's about to be put on trial. In Paris. For espionage."

"What?" Andy was speechless. Elisabeth told him what

she knew. There had been a telegram from Paris, routed through Switzerland. She gave it to him.

> Dear Andy. Just concluded an interview here with a lawyer representing two Austrians charged with spying. Your friends, Maria and Johann. Maria facing trial Monday next. Lawyer insists your testimony vital to defense and urgently requests you return to Paris. Please confirm arrival plans soonest. Your friend, David.

Maria and Johann had survived the *Ancona* disaster. Otto and Elisabeth had learned this from the emperor's chamberlain, Montenuovo. An Austrian agent in Rome had been in contact with them and had been making arrangements for their return, but apparently they had been discovered by French authorities in Tunis and arrested as spies. Then nothing. Apparently, they, or at least Maria had been transported to Paris for trial.

"A lawyer in Paris managed to make contact with us also," Elisabeth continued. "A Gerard Villiers. I don't know how he knew us. He sent us a telegram. He said they need you to be a witness at the trial, but it begins on Monday, July 19. I have his address."

"Monday?" Andy exclaimed. But it was Saturday. Two days? The family watched his reaction in silence. "My God, there's no time to lose. I must go."

Otto looked at Elisabeth and then back at Andy. "There's no way to get there in time, Andy. When we got this news yesterday, I checked the train timetables. I wish we could have gotten word to you. It's impossible."

Andy felt his heart sink. If only he had known. He could have easily gone from Italy to Paris with time to spare. Now this. A gloomy silence settled over the little group as the maid cleared the breakfast dishes from the table in the other room.

Then Andy thought of David Bernstein. He quickly explained to them his deal with *The New Republic* and Bernstein's position in Paris as his editor, a story that under other circumstances could have taken hours to tell. "I can cable him before I take the train and tell him to get word to this lawyer. Maybe they can delay the trial. He might be able to meet me at the station in Paris and get me there in time."

Nobody said anything at first. Was it hopeless? Then Rudi spoke.

"I have an idea. What if I could fly you to the border? If I could get permission to use my plane and if the weather holds up, I could get you to the border with Switzerland today in about four hours."

"But could you get permission in time? Wouldn't it have to be approved by someone? That could take hours, maybe days." Otto wondered.

"Mother ..." Rudi looked at Elisabeth. The palace. Everyone thought the same thing. A word from on high could make it possible.

"My plane is at the *Fliegeretappenpark* just outside Purkersdorf near the Baumgartner Forest. They would have to call there."

"Elisabeth, if Rudi could get him to the border, he might catch the express train that already left the Westbahnhof this morning. If he could catch the train there, at Lustenau, it might work."

Elisabeth considered the situation for just a moment. "I'll call the palace," Elisabeth said, "but there isn't much time. I may not be able to reach him. He knows about the situation. I spoke to him before, when you were caught in Italy, Andy. But I can't guarantee anything. Why don't all of you leave now for the airbase? If it works, you can go. If not ..." She rose from the table and left the room to go to the telephone.

Otto called for the car. Rudi bounded up the stairs to get his flight gear with Andy right behind. Andy pulled out a suit of clothes from his bag, some underwear and, oh yes, his passport. The suit was already wrinkled. but it would have to do. Otto found him a small leather bag, and in a matter of minutes, they all got into the car and raced for the airbase in Purkersdorf, just west of the city. It took a little more than a half hour to reach the airport, driving at top speed.

As the car pulled up to the aerodrome, they could see that an aircraft in Habsburg black and yellow had been pulled out of what looked to Andy like a large warehouse of planes. He could see other aircraft parked behind the building's huge sliding doors. A soldier saluted as the car pulled up.

"Hauptman Windischgrätz?" the soldier inquired. From the look on his face, he had received a call from the palace and was a little in awe of the entourage that got out of the car. "Your plane is ready. We have some gear for your passenger as well."

"Thank you," Rudi replied, saluting. It had worked! Andy was quickly fitted with flying gear while the sergeant went over the flight path on a map with Rudi. There was a small field near Lustenau where they could land. The sergeant would call ahead and advise them of their arrival. A *Luftfahrtruppen* officer would meet them there and drive Andy to the train station. It was eleven o'clock. The Vienna express train for Zurich should arrive at about six.

"I will wire Mr. Bernstein, Andy. Good luck. Come back to us safe and soon," said Otto.

"I don't know what to say. Wish me luck." They embraced a last time and with that, Andy and Rudi clambered into the Aviatik D.I. The sergeant started the engine, cranking the propeller. Rudi steered the plane out on the grassy field and gunned the engine. Andy had had no time to think of everything that could go wrong or how dangerous flying could be. He felt an immense thrill as the plane bounced into the air and rose up and up, over the fields, and toward the sun and the west.

The noise of the plane was deafening and it was cold. There was no way he could talk to Rudi who was sitting behind him, Andy realized, so for the next several hours he watched the breathtaking scenery pass below him. After about an hour, they passed over Salzburg with its fortress in the middle of the city, where Andy had first arrived in Austria.

The mountains had become almost frighteningly huge and the updrafts caused the plane to shudder violently at times, but the weather was perfect. A blue July sky cheered him as they passed over mountaintops that became higher and higher. Innsbruck passed below them after nearly another hour had passed and then Rudi made a turn to the northwest. Once again, row after towering row of mountain ranges passed beneath them until Andy caught sight of what seemed to be an enormous lake in the distance.

"*Bodensee*," Rudi shouted over the noise, pointing at the lake. "Almost there."

Slowly, Rudi guided the plane down after they passed a last range of enormous mountains that sloped down into a small plain where Andy could see a town that lay directly along a slowly curving river. It was Lustenau. There were numerous little squares between the edge of the mountains and the town with little farmhouses on many of them. Rudi turned the plane sharply north and began to descend rapidly. Andy realized that one particular field ahead of them must be where they would land and he braced himself inside the tiny cockpit for the impact, which came with a surprisingly soft bump. The plane bounced into the air nevertheless and then landed more heavily on the ground where it shook violently as it slowed to a stop.

Rudi gunned the engine to bring the plane up to what looked to be no more than a shack where some soldiers were watching them. They had chairs outside the tiny building and had evidently been playing cards. One of them waved as they approached, and then Rudi killed the engine. The silence assaulted Andy's ears. It was utterly quiet except for the voice of the approaching orderly.

"Hauptman Windischgrätz?"

"Yes, and my cousin, Andy Bishop."

"Welcome to *Flik* 37, sir," the soldier said, saluting smartly. Rudi returned the salute and began climbing out of the plane. Andy realized that he was very sore. He felt a cramp in his leg, but after a moment it passed and he was able to climb down to the ground.

"My God. That was amazing. I can't believe we're here so fast."

Rudi and the soldier smiled as if they had performed a magic trick.

"What time is it?" Rudi asked the soldier.

"It's about 3:30, sir," the soldier replied.

"We had quite a tailwind, Andy. We're here a little sooner than I thought."

"The car isn't here yet, sir. Would you and Herr Bishop like some tea?"

"Yes, indeed. Thank you very much."

In a few minutes, the table they had been using for cards was cleared and an admittedly crude kettle was brought from the shack with some odd cups. There were only three chairs, but the other soldiers simply sat on the ground, giving Rudi and Andy two of the chairs. The other soldier, another sergeant, took the last chair. It was Austria. Everyone knew their place.

The air was crisp and cool here, even in July, Andy noticed. The hot tea tasted delicious and, for a few minutes while they waited for the car, Andy was able to forget the mission he was on and enjoy the magnificent surroundings.

The mountains to the east were rocky and the sun shone brilliantly on them from the west.

"You're quite a pilot, Rudi."

"I do love it. I loved it the first time I did it." Rudi told him about his first flight in Galicia, including the strafing of some Russian artillery. "It didn't take long before my request to join the Luftfahrtruppen was approved. I think my mother had something to do with it. Julius trained me himself. I've been flying reconnaissance ever since."

"How are things in the east?"

"We've got the Ruskies on the run. They retreat, but we catch up and blast them. They retreat again and we catch them again. It's been like that for months now. Before I left on leave, they were saying we'd be in Moscow by Christmas, but I don't know. Christmas in Russia could be bad. Napoleon got to Moscow and it did no good, did it?"

Andy knew that Rudi was referring to the legendary disaster that befell Napoleon's *Grand Armée* in 1812 that began his downfall.

"We were hoping that we could envelop them with the Germans and destroy their army once and for all, but the Russians are too smart for that. They've retreated in good order, unfortunately. It's not over yet. They always stay just ahead of us. They've lost a lot of territory and a million men either dead or prisoners, but what's that to the tsar? As the weather gets colder, everyone thinks they'll dig in and make a stand."

The soldiers listened quietly, smoking their pipes, nodding in agreement. Then the sergeant spoke.

"A worthy enemy, no doubt. These Italians, though, that's another story. If we weren't fighting the Ruskies for our lives, we'd give these Wops a righteous whipping. Treacherous bastards, them." The contempt for the Italians felt by Austrian soldiers invariably contrasted with the dread mixed with grudging respect they had for the Russians.

Off in the distance, disturbing the pastoral quiet came

the sound of a motorcar. The little group looked off toward the town and saw a black Mercedes coming toward them.

"Time to get you to the train station."

It was just after four o'clock when the car pulled up at the shack. A military chauffeur saluted stiffly after alighting from the car. He picked up Andy's small bag and placed it in the car.

"Thank you, Rudi. Take care of yourself. Have a safe trip home. I hope I'll see you again soon."

"It's been a long time since we met in Salzburg, Andy. When I think of it every now and then, it seems like another life. Little did you know what you were getting into when you came to visit us last year. Little did any of us know. Good luck in Paris, Andy. Bring back Maria and Johann. God damn this war."

"Yes. God damn this war," Andy said. He shook the hands of the soldiers and then embraced his cousin. "God bless."

Andy made the train easily and arrived in Zurich early Sunday morning, exhausted as ever. A few hours later, he caught another express train for Paris. Two attractive French women joined him in his compartment. Sisters, perhaps. They eyed him appreciatively and seemed more impressed when he flashed his American passport at the border. They didn't speak English or German and, since Andy didn't speak French, attempts at conversation unfortunately amounted only to a few words and phrases. Andy arrived at the *Gare de l'Est* at four o'clock in the afternoon. David Bernstein was waiting for him on the platform.

"You missed the first deadline, Andy," David said with a smile as they shook hands.

"Let's hope I don't miss another one. Thanks for meeting me, David. Where are we going?"

"The lawyer, Villiers, is waiting for you. Come on."

They took a taxi to the address on *Rue Raspail* and arrived a little before five o'clock. The door was opened by a young Frenchwoman. David Bernstein introduced themselves to her in French. She showed them into a small conference room and left them there for a moment.

"Ah, Monsieur Bishop," Gerard Villiers said as he swept into the room extending his hand. *"Enchanté, monsieur. Vraiment, je suis ravie de faire votre connaissance."* He shook Andy's hand warmly.

"He said that he's delighted to make your acquaintance," David translated. *"Malheureusement, mon ami ne parle pas français. Seulement allemand et anglais,"* David continued, addressing the lawyer.

In German, Villiers continued, unfazed. "Herr Bishop, you have arrived in the nick of time. Unfortunately, time is something we lack in this case. Please, may we get you something? Some food? Perhaps some wine?"

Andy suddenly realized that he was very hungry and, guessing that the interview would take several hours, agreed that he would indeed like to eat something.

"Valerie!" Villiers shouted. The same young woman appeared again at the door. "Go to Le Coq d'Argent. Get my usual table. We will be along in a moment." Gerard turned to Andy amiably. "There's nothing like good food, good wine, and a bad girl, someone once said," Gerard continued.

"Said like a Frenchman," Andy smiled. Gerard seemed pleased that his little joke had been able to coax a smile from his guest.

"Yes, but it sounds better in the original French. Alas, we do not have much time. Let us begin." Villiers explained the dire predicament Maria faced, how the trial would be conducted, and Andy's critical role. He explained the conversation he had with André Mornet and the potential bargain that was pending. Then they left, walking the short distance to Le Coq d'Argent where they were obsequiously ushered to Villiers' table where Valerie was already seated.

"*Une bouteille de Chateau Mouton Rothschild, s'il vous plaît. Peut-être le 1909?*" After ordering the wine, there were interminable questions about the various critical facts of the case. Andy replied to them one by one.

The jovial demeanor that began their acquaintance was now gone. Villiers' face was a mask of intense concentration. At different points, he translated to Valerie who took notes. Questions resumed as food was ordered, came, was eaten, and went. The wine was exquisite and warmed Andy as the night went on, but also was making him a little drowsy. At last, over coffee, the inquisition ended.

"You will make a powerful witness, Herr Bishop. As an American, the court will be far more receptive to your evidence than anything else we have. There will be much activity before the trial begins. We will have to discuss the possibility of the … ah, arrangement with the prosecutor that may resolve the trial before it begins. In these things, you will have to trust me."

"Will I be able to speak with Maria?"

"Perhaps. Probably. But here is one thing you must remember. You should minimize your relationship with her in the courtroom. The more affectionate, the more the court will assume your testimony may be biased and untrustworthy. The facts are what they are, but there is no use giving the government more ammunition. Do you understand?"

As tired as Andy was, he found it difficult to get to sleep at David Bernstein's apartment. When morning came, he felt anxious and exhausted.

"Take one of my suits," David said when he saw Andy enter the kitchen in his crumpled suit from Vienna. "We're about the same size. You look awful."

"I feel awful."

"Have some coffee and toast."

"I can't eat anything. Maybe the coffee."

David regarded him over the kitchen table. "I'm going with you. I think there will be other reporters there. This has gotten a little publicity, thanks to M. Villiers."

"Really?"

"Oh yes. There's a fair amount of interest in it from the French press and, over the last couple of days, the London papers have perked up and asked for information. I wouldn't be surprised if there were quite a few people there. And us, of course."

"The New Republic?"

"Why not?"

This latest revelation did not ease Andy's mind at all. And yet, he could see the purpose behind it. The old lawyer was setting his traps.

"Come on, we'd better get going. Go into my closet. Pick out something that looks good and fits." Andy found a gray suit that seemed to fit pretty well and dressed quickly.

It was raining lightly when they stepped out into the street and hailed a taxi for the Palais de Justice. The gloomy sky further dampened Andy's mood as the taxi darted in and out of traffic until they arrived. Bernstein opened a large black umbrella and together they passed through the immense wrought-iron gate and up the stone stairs leading into the massive courthouse.

Inside, the air was cool. Dozens of lawyers, clients, police, clerks, and who knows who milled about inside or walked to and fro. A man, his head in his hands, dejected, sat on a stone bench staring at the floor. The low murmurs of voices and the sounds of heels clicking and clopping across the stone floor echoed within the atrium. From somewhere, Valerie appeared.

"*Suivez-moi, messieurs.*" A dimly lit corridor, up some stairs, down another long corridor, around a corner. Huge double doors within a suitably massive stone casement. Courtroom *Neuf.* As the doors swung open, Andy gasped inwardly at the imposing scene.

Heavy electric chandeliers suspended from a vaulted ceiling lit an enormous room. At the far wall was the judge's bench with the flags of France behind the dais and a huge gold emblem of the republic. Three empty thrones waited for the arrival of the judges. Two large, polished mahogany tables surrounded by leather chairs for the lawyers. Courtroom personnel sat at tables immediately in front of the raised dais, busy with papers of some kind. A gallery of pews filled the rest of the room. There were a number of people sitting in the pews. *Probably reporters*, thought Andy sourly, *since there were no friends or family of the accused who would be present.*

From a side door, Villiers and another man entered the chamber, talking animatedly and both carrying papers. They were dressed in black robes and wore some kind of round cap. Long, narrow white scarves or cravats flowed down from their necks.

Andy and David Bernstein eased into one of the pews, not knowing what else to do. Valerie nodded and proceeded to the front of the courtroom where she waited for Villiers to stop talking. He was trying to keep his voice low, but his excitement was getting the better of him, Andy observed. As the two men parted to opposite tables, Valerie approached and turned to look at Andy. Villiers followed her gaze and his eyes met Andy's. They were hard and angry. He nodded and put down his papers on the table. Another young man in a black robe was sitting at Villiers' table. Villiers bent over and spoke to him for a moment and then approached Andy.

"There have been some ... developments," Villiers began. His face was grim. Andy knew that the news must be bad. "The government has demanded that they be allowed to speak with you. There will be no deal without their having their way on this. I suppose they don't want to be surprised by your testimony, but something else is up. I can feel it. I don't like it."

The other lawyer had approached from behind Villiers and now spoke to Andy in English.

"Mr. Bishop. My name is André Mornet. I am the prosecutor assigned this case. I would like a word with you, if I might." Before Andy could reply, Villiers said something in French to which Mornet replied. David Bernstein leaned over and whispered in Andy's ear.

"He said to Villiers that his hands are tied in this."

"I will speak with you," Andy said, standing up. Mornet looked at Villiers and spoke to him again in French. David whispered again. "He says you must go with him, alone."

Villiers glared at Mornet, then back at Andy. In German: "Be careful what you say. Volunteer nothing." Andy nodded.

"Please. Will you come with me?" Mornet asked. Andy followed him across the courtroom and to another side door, opposite the one where he and Villiers had entered a few moments before. There was a corridor behind the door, then some stairs up to another corridor and then a room. As they entered the room, two men who had been seated at a small table stood up. One was in uniform, but the other was not.

"Good morning," said the one in uniform in English. He motioned for Andy to sit down. "I am Colonel Eduard LeBlanc. This is my colleague, Monsieur Henri Bellemont." The other man nodded, but said nothing. LeBlanc had a face pockmarked by acne, coal-black hair and a long thin nose that curled like a beak. His eyes were hard and piercing, in contrast to the ingratiating tone of his voice. The other man was plump and bald with a blank expression who fidgeted with his hat in his lap, nodding and saying nothing.

"What do you want with me?" Andy asked.

"We understand that you arrived yesterday. From Vienna. Is this true?"

"You know it's true."

The colonel smiled, but not in a friendly way. "Yes. We know. We know who you are. I'm sorry that we have to meet like this." His tone was not sincere. "I suppose you realize Miss Montfort is in serious trouble. And her fiancé, Monsieur von Caboga."

"Of course. That's why I'm here."

"Yes, of course, that's why you are here," the colonel repeated. He pulled out a pack of cigarettes and offered one to Andy. Andy declined and the colonel lit a cigarette and blew out a plume of smoke.

"When do you plan to return to Vienna?" the colonel asked. The pleasantries were over.

"I don't know. After the trial, I suppose. My editor is here."

"Ah yes, Monsieur Bernstein. Yes, indeed. You are a reporter, I understand."

"That's right."

"And you have been a reporter in Vienna for the past year, reporting on the war. You were aboard the *Ancona*. With the prisoners, yes?"

"Yes. You know I was."

"Yes. We know you were. We know all about it."

"You keep saying 'we.' Who are you, exactly, colonel?"

"I am with the Deuxième Bureau. Are you familiar with it?"

"Yes. Espionage, isn't it?"

"Counterespionage, to be exact. Your friends have been keeping company with some dangerous people."

"That's ridiculous. They're not spies."

"No? Well, that's for the court to decide."

"I repeat, Colonel, what is it you want with me?"

"Information."

"Take a seat in the courtroom. You'll hear what information I have." Andy felt himself starting to lose his temper. He had come to detest this arrogant man in a matter of a few minutes. It was all he could do to keep his composure.

"We're not interested in *that* information where you're concerned, monsieur. We're interested in what information you might be able to give us from Vienna."

Andy could hardly believe his ears. He played for time. You have contacts in Vienna? Family, yes, of course, but others too? Have you had conversations with the Ministry of War in Vienna? Not yet? But you will, surely. That sort of thing.

"What are you saying, exactly?"

"You're a reporter for an American magazine in Vienna. Surely it hasn't escaped your notice that we are at war with Austria-Hungary," he said sarcastically. "I would think it obvious what we want."

Andy looked at the fat, bald man. He continued to have no expression at all. Mornet avoided his gaze, saying nothing.

"Are you asking me to spy for you? In Vienna?"

"Spy? That's a harsh word, monsieur," the colonel continued. He smiled, but it was a malevolent smile. Andy noticed his teeth were yellow below a pencil-thin moustache. "Let's just say we would be interested in information, from time to time. As an American, you can pass freely between Vienna and Paris, as you have already done. As a reporter, you will be given access to important people in Vienna, no? The Austrians will not miss a chance to cultivate American public opinion. Or perhaps you have been doing this for them already? I have read some of your writing, Monsieur Bishop. Very friendly to the Central Powers. One might think you were in the Austrian secret service already. Are you?"

"Certainly not. I write what I see and hear. If it's favorable, then so be it."

"You should be grateful to the republic, monsieur. After all, we rescued you after two Austrian submarines tried to kill you."

"They weren't trying to kill me."

"All the same. We would be willing to pay for this, ah ... service."

"Forget it. I'm not a spy."

"You keep saying 'spy.'"

"That's what it is. What good would I be otherwise? As you say, you can read my articles. You can get all the information you want from them. That's not what you want, is it?"

"Not quite. No. But you seem to be forgetting something."

"What's that?"

"The guillotine that awaits Miss Montfort and her fiancé."

Andy froze. So that was it. It was blackmail. Pure and simple. Again, Andy played for time.

"The court will not convict her of spying. I'll see to that."

The colonel lit another cigarette and shrugged as he inhaled. "I wouldn't be too sure of that, Monsieur Bishop. We are in a war. Don't forget that. The court won't forget it. Let's just say the republic has an interest in this matter."

It was a threat. He was clearly intimating that the outcome of the trial was a foregone conclusion. *What did he know?* Andy wondered. *Was it really rigged? Or was this a bluff?* Villiers had seemed so confident last night. Perhaps he was a naïve old man.

"Of course, the government can dismiss this prosecution at any time," the colonel said, looking at Mornet. Again,

Mornet would not look at Andy. "She will be safe and sound and no one the wiser." Colonel LeBlanc smiled again as he blew another stream of smoke into the air. "You're an American. Nobody will suspect anything. Everything will be kept secret. As I said, we'll pay you well. It's a much better alternative than Miss Montfort taking her chances with the guillotine, wouldn't you say?"

Andy wanted to talk to Villiers in the worst way. "How long do I have to think about this?"

"Not long. About a minute. This is a one-time offer, Monsieur Bishop. If you walk out of this room without a favorable answer, well ..." He stubbed out the cigarette. "On the other hand, if you cooperate with us, we'll persuade Monsieur Mornet that he hasn't got a very good case at all. What do you say, Monsieur Bishop?"

A devil's bargain, Andy thought. *Lose Maria or become a spy for France against Austria. Yes or no.*

"What about Johann von Caboga?"

"Ah yes, I had forgotten about him. Is he important to you as well?"

"Important enough. Yes. What about him?"

The colonel looked at the fat man. He nodded.

"Very well. Here is what I can do. You can understand that we would need some—shall we say—security for our arrangement, yes? At least for a while. So Monsieur Caboga will have to remain here. As our guest, you could say. But I will persuade Monsieur Mornet here that there is no hurry to place him on trial. In time, of course, we would let him go."

Andy felt the heat rising in him, but once again, he quenched it. Yes or no? This time, it was not just Johann's fate in the balance. He had never asked Villiers the ultimate question, he realized. Would Maria go free after the trial? He knew what his answer would have been. He would not guarantee anything. Would do his best. There were no guarantees. A lawyer's response.

"You have no right to ask me to do this," Andy replied. "Evidently I have more faith in French justice than you do, monsieur. I don't believe you. I don't believe that this court is a sham. I don't believe that the verdict in this case is already decided. And I know my friends are innocent. You would have me betray my family and my friends and enter the service of a foreign power, which would violate American neutrality. Here is my answer. I will give my testimony and if this court should somehow convict Maria von Montfort of espionage, if I conclude that you have influenced this court in the slightest degree, if Maria von Montfort should be detained a moment longer in your prison after this trial, I will see that every word of this interview is published and expose this embarrassment to your government, to the people of the United States, and the world. Now, is there anything else?"

The two spies regarded Andy in stunned disbelief. André Mornet slowly shook his head from side to side and a wry smile crept across his face. Then Mornet spoke.

"No. There is nothing further. You may go, Monsieur Bishop." Andy rose from his chair, walked out the door, and couldn't remember whether to turn right or left, his head spinning. A bailiff sitting in a chair in the hallway recognized his predicament and pointed down the hallway to the left. Andy nodded and walked back to the courtroom.

As he entered the courtroom again alone, he saw Villiers spin around in his chair and look at him quizzically, but there she was. Maria. She was dressed in summer white, her black hair falling down to her shoulders. She was pale and thin, but as beautiful as ever. He covered the distance between them in an instant and held her once again in his arms, holding her tight. Quietly she cried and so did he.

There was a murmur from the reporters in the gallery. Had he done the right thing? Had he made the right decision? It all weighed down on him now.

"Monsieur Bishop ..." He heard the lawyer's voice and pulled back, looking into Maria's dark eyes awash and red with tears. "Monsieur Bishop? May I have a word?" Andy nodded.

"In a moment, monsieur." Then he turned to Maria again.

"Maria ..." He felt the lump in his throat as, in an instant, the thought of what she must have endured flashed through his mind. "I've come to get you. I'm going to get you out of here if it's the last thing I do."

"I don't know if you can," she replied in a shaky voice. "I'm so frightened. I don't know what is going to happen next. And Johann? Did you hear about him? He may die if he doesn't get out soon."

"I really must insist," Villiers said. "Every moment we lose could be fatal. Monsieur Bishop, please ..."

Andy squeezed her tight again. "Let me talk with him. I'll be right here. One way or another, I'll get you out of here." He tried to sound far more confident than he really was. Then he let her go and Villiers took him by the arm, hustling him out of the chamber and into the hall, leaving Emile behind.

"Now tell me. What did they ask you?" Villiers started.

"Nothing about the facts of the case." Andy related the gist of the conversation with LeBlanc as quickly as he could. Villiers' face once again transformed into a mask of intense concentration that became ever graver as Andy related more details until he was finished.

"You did the right thing, Andy. Leave this to me. This is a disgrace." Villiers hissed as he spoke the words *'eine Schande'* in German. With that, he whirled about and strode back into the courtroom.

Mornet had returned and was sitting at the table, playing

with his pen absentmindedly, waiting for the judges to enter the courtroom. Villiers approached him and stopped, towering over him. Mornet remained in his seat, looking up at him.

What followed was an animated conversation in French that, from the distance between them, neither Andy nor David could follow. Villiers was unleashing a tirade at Mornet when there was a loud thump. Three in a row. Then a door opened behind the dais and the three judges, robed in black, entered the room. Silently, they took their places beside their chairs. A robed bailiff shouted out something in French that Andy could not understand. It must have been a formal opening of the court, calling it into session. Everyone remained standing until the bailiff had finished and then everyone took their seats after the judges sat down. Villiers glared at Mornet one last time and then slowly ambled to his own chair and sat down.

The judge in the center of the three said something and then Mornet rose and began speaking. David Bernstein translated.

"May it please the court. After careful consideration of the evidence, the republic has concluded that it is not in possession of sufficient evidence to present its case of espionage against the prisoner at this time. Accordingly, the state moves the court for a postponement of the trial and the continued detention of the accused for further questioning."

Villiers now rose.

"May it please the court. The defendant has been imprisoned now for over a month, transported here from Tunis to stand trial. We have arranged for a witness to testify who is now in the courtroom. An American. He has come here from abroad at great cost and inconvenience. The republic has had ample time to assemble whatever evidence it may have while I myself was only appointed to this case a week ago to prepare her defense. Further, I have been given to understand that certain agents of the republic ..."

Mornet now interrupted.

"I must object to any further comments by Monsieur Villiers on the ground of state security and move the court to continue proceedings *in camera.*"

There was a pause and then the chief judge spoke.

"We will grant the government's motion to continue proceedings in camera, under the circumstances. Bailiff. Clear the courtroom."

With that, the bailiff stood up and ordered everyone to leave the courtroom and remain in the lobby with the exception of the prisoner and the lawyers. There was audible mumbling from the reporters and the others in the courtroom and then the gallery began to empty. Andy and David Bernstein stood, but before turning to go, Andy took one last look at Maria and she at him.

"Come on," David said. "We have to go." He took Andy's arm and guided him to the door as Andy continued looking at Maria, wondering if and when he would see her again. He knew that she was thinking the same thing. She was gripping the back of her chair, looking back at him as if memorizing his face and the moment, in case she never saw him again.

For nearly an hour, they waited. Andy paced the floor, sat down, and paced again. He wanted to smoke, but didn't dare leave the lobby area of the second floor outside the courtroom. A man approached him.

"Andy Bishop?"

"Yes, that's me."

"Richard Brown. *The Daily Telegraph.* I wonder if you could spare me a couple of minutes."

"It's a bit difficult right now."

"Yes, of course," but then he continued. "Are you acquainted with the prisoner?"

"You could say that. Yes."

"Do you know what the commotion in there was all about?"

"I really can't say anything at the moment."

"I see. Well, perhaps later, then. Here's my card. I would very much like to talk with you when you have a chance, Mr. Bishop."

Andy took his card and nodded. He watched the man return to his seat and speak with a couple of other reporters in a low voice. Then the door opened and Villiers came sweeping out of the room.

"It's over. The charges are dismissed. Maria is free. She will have to leave the country in three days, but she will be released later today."

"And Johann?"

"No. That is another case, Herr Bishop. He will have to remain behind. There will be a separate trial for him. That was never a possibility today. I'm sorry."

"I will talk to you later about him," Andy said. "But thank you for what you have done. Thank you very much."

"It was my pleasure," Villiers replied with a slight bow. "Now let us leave and get some lunch while they prepare Fraulein von Montfort for release this afternoon. Valerie! Le Coq d'Argent!"

24.

Farewell Paris

Villiers had told Andy that it would take some time to pass through the security at *St. Lazare* where Andy went to collect Maria later on the day of the trial. He had declined offers by the lawyer and David Bernstein to go with him to the prison. He wanted to be alone with her. There was so much to say—and so much more to do. As he waited in the visitors lobby, the minutes passed by slowly.

Johann's continued imprisonment at La Santé could not delay their return to Vienna. He had thought about it. Much as he wanted to stay to rescue him, Maria's three-day safe conduct made it impossible and she had been through too much to travel alone back to Vienna. The best he could do for Johann for now he had already done. He had paid Villiers a fat retainer at lunch to handle Johann's case, which Villiers had accepted with pleasure, promising to revisit Graf von Caboga the following day.

After what seemed like an hour, a door opened and Maria came into the room. She was wearing the same white dress—it was the only decent thing she had to wear. She ran to him and he took her in his arms. Tears again, but tears of happiness.

"Take me away from here, Andy. Not another minute in this place."

In few minutes, they were out on the street. It was late afternoon in Paris and the streets were full of traffic. Much more than in Vienna. Cars and horses clogged the street, but mainly cars. The July air was warm. Andy suggested that they get something to eat and, after a short cab ride, they were seated in a restaurant. A bottle of wine to settle the nerves. They talked. What had happened since the *Ancona* went down. Their lives had spun out of control, hadn't they? An early dinner was consumed and Maria seemed visibly to gain color and voice as the food and wine did their work.

"But what about Johann?"

"He's still in prison. Villiers will see him tomorrow. He'll tell him what has happened. I've paid Villiers well to represent him. I don't know what else we can do."

"What *you* can do, Andy. I have done nothing. You came to our rescue. You've done everything you could possibly do. We must see him, though. I can't leave without seeing him."

"I know. Let's see what we can do, but we only have three days. Villiers can probably get us in."

"Ask him, Andy. I'm afraid for him. Gerard told me he seemed very sick. In a wheelchair."

"I will."

"Where are we staying?"

"At David Bernstein's flat. Are you tired?"

"Yes, I'm feeling the wine and I would like to sleep in a real bed."

The next day, Maria and Andy went to Villiers' *bureau* and met the lawyer again. Yes, it would be possible for them to see him. It must be tomorrow because on the third day, they must leave. They would meet at Villiers' office tomorrow morning, and then to La Santé. There was just one thing, though. Villiers pulled his chair close to Maria and took her hands in his.

"You must be prepared, Maria. He is very ill. I don't know how to say this, but …"

"What are you telling me?"

Gerard Villiers stared at the floor for a moment. Then he raised his head and looked into Maria's eyes. He paused.

"Perhaps not, my dear. Perhaps not. Who can say? I just want you to be prepared for it when you see him."

"What is it?" Andy asked. "Why is he so sick?"

"Tuberculosis, I'm afraid," said Villiers. "So common these days. He is very sick. Did you not know this?"

"He was fine in Tunis," Maria said. Then she thought of the coughing. The bloody handkerchiefs. "He had a cough. He didn't seem to be very sick. Just a cough."

Villiers shook his head. "The conditions at La Santé are no better than where you were. Perhaps he has gotten worse. I have seen this before. Prisoners who seem well enough at first develop diseases and … well, you know. The despair. The poor medical care in the prisons. We must get him out soon, that's all we can do."

Johann was in the prison's hospital ward. Inside the ward, the only signs that it was in a prison were the bars on the windows and the male orderlies attending to a few dozen prisoners who were so sick that they could not get out of bed. They found him on a metal bed. He was so pale. Thin, bony arms and a gaunt face were the only parts of Johann's body not covered with a white sheet and thin blanket. A cross was nailed to the wall above the bed. There was no other adornment or sign of cheer in the room. Coughs and low voices from elsewhere could be heard.

"Oh, Johann," cried Maria as she rushed to the side of his bed. Johann held up his arms to keep her from him.

"Don't come near. You might catch it."

"I don't care."

"No! You mustn't!" But it did no good. Maria kissed his face, holding it in her hands. She sat down on the bed beside him.

"Andy …" Johann sighed. A rueful smile crossed his face. "Still on holiday, I see?"

Andy's heart sank as Johann made light of the moment. He was not going to make it. Andy knew it in a moment. He was dying. Dying in a bleak French prison. He forced a smile.

"That's right, Johann. Still on holiday."

"I heard what happened. It seems you've got me a pretty good lawyer, but I may not need him after all." He said it. He said what they were all thinking.

"Oh, Johann. Don't say that. Don't think that," Maria said, squeezing his hand. Then, turning to Villiers, "We have to get him out of here. Can you do that?"

Villiers, who had been sitting down in a chair at the foot of the bed replied. "I will try, my dear. That's all I can say. The court decides when it will hear the case. I will do my best to hurry it along, but …"

Johann was rolling his head from side to side on the pillow.

"Maria. I'm done for this time. There's not much time. Leave it to Villiers. Let's not talk about it right now. There's something I want to say to you before it's too late. To both of you. And you know what it is.

"Andy, take her away from all this. Take her to America. I'm sorry I won't make it. I did so much want to go, but …" Johann paused a moment to compose himself. His eyes watered. The strain of his emotions and his disease were exhausting him already. "I'm just so glad to see you one more time. We're all together again, after all this. You're free, Maria. Free of prison. And free of me. And, Andy ... you're alive too. I was so worried. Get away from here. Get away from this dying continent. Make a life for yourselves in America. There's nothing you can do for me now."

Even Villiers, the crusty old lawyer, had tears in his eyes now. Maria covered her mouth with a handkerchief to stifle the sobs. Andy stared at his friend, tears streaming down his cheek.

It was such a waste, Andy thought. *Such a waste.*

They talked for another hour. About themselves. Their times together and apart. They kept on as long as they could, each trying to make the other laugh or smile at some remembrance, until the time came to go. Andy would be back. He was taking Maria to Vienna first. But Andy would be back to get him. Soon. He must stay alive. There were doctors in Vienna who were famous for treatment of tuberculosis. Sanitaria in the Alps.

"You mustn't give up, my friend," said Andy. "You've been through worse than this. You didn't look so good in Kosice either, you know." Johann smiled. "This time you're awake to see it, that's all."

Johann smiled again. Behind the pale and gaunt skin and his shrunken body, for just a moment, Andy saw the flash of the fatalistic Austrian aristocrat. The sad, knowing smile, indulging you in your fantasy, disbelieving everything you say, but touched that you would take the trouble to say it. Andy bent over the bed and kissed him once on each cheek.

"You'll catch the disease, Andy, if you stay here much longer."

"What disease?"

"You're becoming an Austrian. That one." Johann's tired but smiling eyes blinked back at him.

"I'll be back for you. Don't go anywhere until I get back."

Johann chuckled. "I won't."

With that, it was time to go. Villiers bent down over the bed when he took his leave. As he kissed Johann on both cheeks, he said, almost in a whisper, his good-bye.

"Mein Herr."

Johann settled back in his bed, on his pillow and nodded. "I'll wait here. As long as I can."

The next day, Andy and Maria boarded the train for Switzerland at the Gare de l'Est. Leaving Johann behind was almost unbearable. It was a long and largely beautiful trip back to Vienna. The train passed through Burgundy, Franche-Comté, and then entered Switzerland. Beautiful snowcapped mountains in the midsummer weather as they quietly ate lunch in the dining car. There were no signs of the war here. Beautiful farms, hills, and forests. *There was no denying it, France was a beautiful country*, Andy thought.

"Are you still thinking of returning to America, Andy?"

"No. Not now. With my new job, I plan to stay in Vienna for a while longer. Probably until the war ends, whenever that will be."

Maria regarded him quietly for a moment over her plate. Her silverware in her hands. "So you will stay in Vienna?"

"Yes. For quite some time, perhaps."

She nodded and then continued eating.

They arrived in Vienna the evening of the second day. Countess von Montfort wept with joy upon seeing her daughter. Then they went to the Windischgrätz house. Another emotional scene. Wine and lamb for dinner served in the splendid dining room with crystal chandeliers lit by electricity that illuminated a bright and glittering scene amidst the darkened streets of the capital city, anxiously facing autumn and then winter and who knew what shortages might come. It had been a long time since that room had been a scene of cheer.

After the little party had ended, Otto and Andy had a brandy in the salon before retiring for the evening.

"Andy, you remember my telling you I had heard from my cousin about your ancestor, Matthias, and that she needed a little more time to confirm some things?"

"Yes, of course. Have you heard something?"

"Yes. I have. Sophie mentioned to me that on one of the family estates in Styria there is a collection of family Bibles and papers. This was the old family home until the time of Napoleon. While you were in Kocise, I went to Graz and visited another distant cousin, Friedrich, who is now the owner of this estate. He allowed me to read the Bibles and I took some notes. It was very curious. Matthias was born in Styria on the family estates there in 1728, the third of six children. All the other children's marriages and children were recorded in the Bible, but not Matthias's. All mention of him stopped and his name disappears without further details after the time we know he left for America in 1754.

"I thought this was very curious. At first, I thought perhaps because communication was so difficult in those times that the family had just lost track of him, but I began researching it in some of the other family papers from that time. Then I came across a letter from Matthias to one of his brothers after he had settled in America. He was describing his life there and asked about his family here, as you might expect. In the letter, he also asked about his wife's family."

"Why is that significant?" Andy asked.

"I copied the letter for you. Here it is."

Chip Wagar

> Philadelphia, June 16, 1756
>
> My dear brother,
>
> Thank you for your recent letter and the news of Father's death. Of course, I expected nothing from his inheritance. In spite of everything, I hope this letter finds all of my brothers and sisters in good health and well-being.
>
> Here, the Great War has spread to this continent from Europe. It seems strange that this peaceful land so far away from home has been drawn into a conflict that concerns it so little and yet that is the way it is. The friends I have made here have little knowledge or understanding of our country and, for us, this has been a wonderful fresh start.
>
> The colony of Pennsylvania, where I now live, is a state that was founded on the belief that every man should have the right to practice his own religion, without interference from the government. William Penn, a Quaker himself, established this principle here that should be a beacon to the world and which, as you can imagine, is a great comfort to Sarah and myself.

The letter went on with some references to their situation and obscure events that made little sense to Andy. And then the conclusion:

> In closing, my brother, I have a request from my dear wife that I will be grateful to you to fulfill. She wishes that her mother and father and the Kaufman family know that she is safe and happy and with child. God willing, we and our descendents will live in this happy land forever and know the Lord will protect us from the prejudices and spite of the

Old World from whence we came. God bless you all and keep you safe.

Sarah was a Kaufman. She was Jewish.

"Andy, in those days, Matthias would have been excommunicated for marrying outside the faith. We know nothing about this woman or her family or how it was that they met and married, but it's the obvious answer. He would have been shunned by the family in those days, during the reign of Kaiserin Maria Theresa. It makes sense. I suspect this is the reason he must have left for America, Andy. I could find no other reason why a son of this family would have left everything behind and gone so far away."

"But we're a Catholic family," Andy said as the implications of Otto's revelation began to sink in.

"Yes, of course we are. And by the fact that neither you nor your family have ever heard this before, it would be my guess that Matthias's wife might have converted to the Catholic faith or that, in any event, their children were raised as Catholics down to the present day. The whole affair may have been kept a secret. Who would have known better in America?"

"What about the woman's Jewish family?"

"The same would have happened to her. She would have been shunned by her family and her community. She would have been regarded as having died. Even more reason for them both to leave forever for a new life in America."

It could probably never be confirmed, but there it was. *It fit the pattern of immigration to America too,* Andy thought. They had settled in Pennsylvania, which, even in its colonial days, founded by Quakers, followed a policy of complete religious tolerance. Andy wondered what had become of the Kaufman family. Were they living in Graz or Vienna? Could he find them as his mother had found Otto and Elisabeth?

He thought about the old gypsy woman in Rome. *"You search for a dark secret. It is about your family. You will find the secret for which you search if you are patient. It will change your life."* Andy couldn't think why this discovery would change his life, but the old woman had been remarkable. How could she have known? He told Otto about the gypsy's prophecies.

"Who can say how these things are known to those people," Otto said after hearing the story. "They have a special gift, the Romani."

"She said I would return home, but never live there again. I assumed she meant my parent's home, but now I am wondering if she meant that I would never live in America again."

"Perhaps, after 160 years, God has brought you home again. Perhaps a circle has been completed. After all, you are one of us now. God has seen fit to call Ernst home, but perhaps he has given you to us in return. You are like a son to me, Andy. You must know that."

"I could never take Ernst's place, Uncle. But I love you and Elisabeth too. I feel at home here."

Otto took his hand in both of his own. "You will always be at home here."

25.

Denouement

Two days later, the telegram came. It was from Villiers. The cable had been written two days earlier, but with the delays of resending it from Switzerland, it had come remarkably quickly bearing its black news.

> ```
> Mr. Andy Bishop ...
> 
> I am dismayed to be the bearer of
> the worst news, but duty compels
> me to be the one to tell you that
> your beloved friend, Johann von
> Caboga, passed away the day after
> you left . . .
> ```

There was more, but Andy's heart was broken. Elisabeth hugged him as he wept, as she thought of her own recent loss. Then the dreadful task of telling Maria. The scene repeated again with the countess too. Then to the Caboga house and his mother. Like the deadly plague that had descended on the Imperial City since the war began, the death of one young man stung many households, one by one, as the news spread.

Andy went to France and retrieved his body after a complex, two-week series of diplomatic maneuvers. He was buried in the Zentralfriedhof in Vienna where, a year earlier, Andy had invited Maria to join him for a tour after Johann left for Sarajevo. He was given a military funeral with an honor guard. Hundreds came to the funeral mass and the cemetery. Andy watched as his mother, the countess, and then Maria, dressed in black mourning, took a silver shovel of dirt and splashed it on his coffin, a custom that was followed, one by one, by family and friends. Then they left him there.

Months went by and the war went on and on. The Italians continued to exhaust themselves, pounding themselves to death on the Alps and the Isonzo to no avail. In Russia, Warsaw fell on September 4. Another country entered the war. Bulgaria came in on the side of the Central Powers, however, and joined in an all-out attack on the remnants of Serbia. By December 1915, a year and a half after the assassination of the archduke, Serbia was utterly crushed at last. What was left of her army retreated into Albania and then was transported by the Italians to Greece.

Russian forces had retreated from the Carpathians deep into Ukrainian Russia and no longer posed any danger to the empire. The Russian fortress cities of Kovno, Novogeorgevisk, Brest-Litovsk, and Grodno surrendered with 325,000 Russian prisoners and 3,000 guns lost, Andy reported as September and October went by. By late October 1915, the weather was already becoming cold and rainy and, by November, the Austro-German offensive that had begun in May ground to a halt.

Andy had gotten his own apartment in Vienna. He could afford it. He found one on the Landstrasse, about midway between the Windischgrätz house and Maria's. December in Vienna was bleak with food shortages, frequent rationing of meat and animal fats, cooking oil, and, unbelievably, coffee. It wasn't starvation, but there were riots and strikes in Vienna, Budapest, and Prague.

A sullen mood had settled over the Viennese proletariat. Casualties abated, mercifully, due to the weather, and the Austrian victories that had knocked the hated Serbs out of the war. The bourgeois and gentry felt a certain guarded optimism, despite the deprivations and casualties. We weren't doing so badly after all, were we? Andy continued writing his essays and news stories to *The New Republic* punctually, every two weeks.

In December 1915, Andy and Maria met again at the Café Central. Andy was sitting at a table with Stefan Zweig when she walked in alone. She smiled when she saw him and came to the table. She was dressed plainly, but in any style of dress, her beauty still made Andy's heart skip a beat.

"Hello, Andy, Stefan. It's so nice to see you," she said, sitting down.

"Maria, what a surprise," said Zweig.

"Yes, it's so nice to see you, Maria," Andy said.

The three of them talked for quite some time, catching up on their news, Zweig's newest play, and Andy's plans to visit the Russian front in the spring. He would visit Rudi and report on the war from there, he told them. It didn't look as if the war would end any time soon. The conversation was awkward, at first, Andy thought. The presence of Stefan Zweig made any intimate conversation with Maria impossible, of course. Eventually though, perhaps sensing their need, Zweig excused himself to go to another table to talk with some other friends and they were alone.

"So, how have you been getting on?" Andy asked.

"Oh, it's another life now, isn't it? All my thoughts and

dreams are gone. I get by, day after day, wishing it would all be over. Like everyone else, I suppose."

"And then what?"

"I don't know, Andy. What will the world be like? I am against making plans anymore, Andy. Look what happened to us."

"Yes, I know. It's the same with me. I just write. Gather what news I can and write some more. I visit Otto and Elisabeth." Andy did not mention the letters he wrote to Katarina or the plans he had to visit her for New Year's Day. What was the point?

"Andy, I wonder if you would do me a favor."

"Of course. Name it."

"My mother received an invitation to a dinner party at the *Palais Esterhazy*. She would like to go and wants me to go as well. It's on Christmas Eve. Would you come? Would you be my escort? These days, all the young men are off at war and I hardly know who to ask ..."

"Of course, Maria. There's no need to explain. It would be my pleasure. Consider it done."

The Palais Esterhazy was on the *Wallnerstrasse*. The taxi driver knew it without mentioning the address. Countess von Montfort had been invited by one of the Esterhazy princesses with whom she'd gone to school in the last century. Her friend was from the ancient Hungarian noble family, former patrons of Haydn, and fabulously rich. There was no food shortage evident at the gathering.

A magnificent Christmas tree was decorated in the main salon, which was where Andy and Maria found themselves alone after a while—a blur of introductions and chatter completed. Splendid imperial uniforms, champagne, beautiful gowns, and sparkling jewelry filled the many rooms. August matrons swept by. Diplomats and aristocratic officers, on leave from the fighting, nodded and chatted as they smoked their cigars. The faint sound of an orchestra played in a ballroom nearby.

"It's beautiful," Maria said, looking at the tree.

"Yes. Very." Maria looked as stunning as the first time he had seen her in Salzburg. This time, however, she was dressed in a black gown and gloves. Perhaps it was for the Christmas season. Perhaps it was for the war. Or perhaps as an homage to Johann. It made no difference. The gown accented her black hair and dark eyes and contrasted with her white skin. As they had entered the residence, she had drawn immediate, appreciative looks from the many men standing and talking in the foyer, halls, and the salon. It had been a couple of weeks since they had met at the Café Central.

"What are your plans for the New Year?" Maria asked, sipping her glass of champagne.

"I'm not sure." He lied. Maria nodded.

"And you?"

"Normal life, I suppose. What can one do nowadays? What's normal living to you now, Andy?"

"There is no such thing in my life now. I left normal living when I came here."

"You have lived abnormally here. That's for sure." She laughed lightly.

"Maria, you remember what Johann said ..."

"Of course."

"I can't take you to America. Not now, Maria."

"There's no obligation on your part," she said coolly.

"You misjudge me. There was a time when it was my dream. You know that."

"Yes, I remember. We both dreamed it, didn't we?"

"Yes, but Johann didn't know that. And he knew you loved him in the end, not me. He didn't know what he was saying when we saw him in Paris."

"But he did. You're wrong about that, Andy."

"How?" Andy was shocked by this revelation. "Did you tell him?"

"No, but he knew just the same. He knew about us, Andy. It was Walther. He told him. Johann said this to me when we were in Tunis."

"Sit down," Andy said, motioning to some chairs in a corner. "Tell me what Johann said." Maria related her fateful conversation with Johann.

"And so, you see, that was his plan all along," Maria concluded. Andy leaned back in the chair, taken aback. Then she went on.

"And there I was. In Tunis. I didn't know if you were dead or alive. I didn't think I would ever see you again. And now, it's too late."

"What do you mean?"

"It's too late for us, Andy. I've thought about it many times in the weeks and months since then. I might as well tell you the truth. It doesn't matter now anyway. The truth is that I loved you both. I knew he couldn't live without me. You could. That's what I thought. I knew he needed me, even if he didn't know it himself. That's why I chose him. Do you see? If we had made it back to Vienna, who can say what might have happened. I might have become his wife anyway, even after what he said."

"But it didn't happen that way," Andy remarked, taking it all in.

"No. It didn't. It all fell apart. Everything. And now he's dead. I left you for another man, Andy. I know that. I can't expect you …"

"I don't look at it that way, Maria. I look at it that you left him for me. And then the war changed everything."

"Yes. That is the truth. I know that, but do you? Really?"

The little orchestra in the other room some distance away began to play. It was the "Künstlerleben," the same

An American in Vienna

waltz played at Luchow's in Salzburg when they had first met. The conversation and chatter seemed to rise as the lilting melody floated in the air through the rooms. Maria's head turned toward the music.

"Let's dance, shall we?" Andy stood up and Maria followed. Before long, Andy and Maria were waltzing together with dozens of other couples—young and old. Time seemed suspended. For this one evening, it was as if they had stepped back in time. Before the war. The old days. Andy realized that, in his lifetime, this was what they would be called. The "old days ... before the war." They were gone now. Gone forever.

Snowflakes fell outside the Palais Esterházy. The warm, yellow lights of the palace lit the dark streets below. Passersby that Christmas Eve, looking up at the windows, could just hear the faint sound of an orchestra playing a waltz as Maria von Montfort and Andy Bishop danced the night away. They made no plans that night.

Epilogue

Kaiser Franz Josef died little more than a year later, joining his murdered wife and suicidal son in the crypt of the Capuchin monks. He lies in his tomb there to this day, the eleventh and final Habsburg kaiser to be interred there. His multinational empire collapsed two years after his death of starvation, exhaustion, and the defeat of his ally, Kaiser Wilhelm of Germany, who had come to his rescue in 1914.

In the meantime, to the astonishment of the world, Austria-Hungary and her allies defeated and occupied Serbia, Montenegro, Russia, and Romania, one by one, and her troops stood on Italian soil as far south as the River Piave until the last days of the war in 1918. Not a single foreign soldier stood on the soil of the Austro-Hungarian Reich when the war ended—the only time in history that an empire has fallen in this way.

Gone from the map of Europe for the first time in more than six centuries by harsh treaties imposed by the victorious Entente, the Habsburg Empire was replaced by tiny, weak—but independent—successor states which, in less than two decades, had either become harsh, fascist dictatorships themselves or were overrun by neighboring, totalitarian Soviet or Nazi police states gone mad from the harsh settlements imposed on them after their defeats in the Great War.

It will always be a question of what "might have been" if a confused chauffeur in Sarajevo had not made a wrong turn on June 28, 1914, or whether the history of Europe might have been better or worse if Franz Ferdinand had become the kaiser of this unique amalgamation of peoples of different nationalities, religions, and histories, but it could hardly have been worse. It would take nearly a century after the assassination of this misunderstood Habsburg archduke—perhaps the most calamitous murder of all time—and the formation of a new multinational, multicultural European Union before Europe would ever regain its place in the world.

Copyright © 2010 by Chip Wagar. All Rights Reserved